Sophie King is a pseudonym for journalist Jane Bidder, who contributes regularly to national newspapers and women's magazines, including *Woman* and *The Times*. She also writes short stories for *Woman's Weekly* and *My Weekly*. She was runner-up in the Harry Bowling Award in 2002 and the winner of the Romantic Novelists' Association's Elizabeth Goudge Award in 2004. Sophie King grew up in Harrow and now lives in Buckinghamshire with her husband, three children and dog. They once went through four au pairs in one year and are still wondering how it went wrong. *The School Run* is her debut novel.

SOPHIE KING

The School Run

HODDER

First published in Great Britain in 2005 by Hodder and Stoughton
A division of Hodder Headline

A CIP catalogue record for this title is
available from the British Library

ISBN 0 340 83836 1

Typeset in Sabon MT by Palimpsest Book Production Limited,
Polmont, Stirlingshire

Printed and bound by Mackays of Chatham Ltd, Chatham, Kent

Hodder Headline's policy is to use papers that are natural, renewable
and recyclable products and made from wood grown in sustainable forests.
The logging and manufacturing processes are expected to conform to the
environmental regulations of the country of origin

Hodder and Stoughton Ltd
A division of Hodder Headline
338 Euston Road
London NW1 3BH

To my late mother Sally, who always knew I would. To my husband Bill, who always said I should. And to my wonderful children William, Lucy and Giles, whose antics nearly made sure I didn't! Also to my father Michael and sister Nancy.

This book is *not* dedicated to the speed camera at Hemel Hempstead which nabbed me when the lights suddenly went orange.

ACKNOWLEDGEMENTS

Special love and thanks to Betty Schwartz for getting me on the road; to my agent Phil Patterson of Marjacq Scripts for having faith in a learner driver; to my editor Sara Kinsella for her smooth gear changes and perceptive map reading; to the Romantic Novelists' Association for its advice, friendship and pitstops at the Trout; and to Dame Kitty Anderson for recognising a bookworm in a small, dyscalculate schoolgirl.

Finally, to all my friends for their encouragement, including Jane (and our Friday coffees), Maggie, Catherine and Anna.

Any similarity between the children in this book and my own, is entirely ~~intentional~~ unintentional.

MONDAY

1

*'This is Capital Radio and it's nearly seven a.m. on a
lovely bright summer morning . . .'*

'The *phone*! ForGod'ssakewillsomeonegetthe*phone*? Who's
taken it? Why doesn't anyone put the flipping thing back when
they've finished? Find it, Bruce – quickly. It might be Dad.
Great. It's stopped. Now look what you've done. Can you
hear me or am I just screaming at myself?

'OhforGod'ssake don'ttellmeyou'renotevenup? Do you know
what time it is? Jess, *out* of bed, now, or I'll take you to school
without you. Yes, I know that doesn't make sense, but you're
fuddling my brain. No, Bruce, I don't know where your school
trousers are. *Don't* say they're still in the tumble-dryer.
Doorbell! Get it, someone. No, Jess, you *can't* open the packet.
It's for Dad. Where do you want me to sign? Right. You
wouldn't like to drop the kids off on the way, would you? Just
joking. *Quick*. It's the phone again. Got it? Charlie? . . . Oh,
Pippa . . . No, that's fine. Just a bit frantic this end, that's all
. . . I see. Poor you. Maybe it's that virus. Half Bruce's class
has got it. Oh, and, Pippa? We might be a bit late. OK?'

*'We're coming up to eight a.m. and it's nearly time for
the news. This is Capital Radio, bringing you the latest—'*

Harriet switched off the radio, squeezed her pelvic floor up
to the third storey and crunched into fifth gear instead of

third. Charlie's gears were different from hers but it made sense to use his bigger car while he was away. The steering was heavier too and her hands were sweating (gosh, it was warm today) on the steering-wheel. There was also the smell of cheese and onion crisps, which she'd foolishly allowed them to eat last week, despite Charlie's No Food in the Car rule – she'd have to clean it before he got back. A quick squirt of Chanel should help.

Squeeze, squeeze. Only recently, when she'd sneezed, had she realised she'd got so . . . well, out of condition. The book she'd bought had suggested doing exercises in the car or when she was washing up. You pretended your inside was a lift, going up three storeys and then down, one by one. She always descended in a splodge.

I might as well slap an 'Out of Order' notice on myself, thought Harriet, grazing the kerb as she swung out into the main road. Bother. She'd only just had the rear tyres replaced last week even though they weren't that old. 'Wear and tear,' the garage chap had said, when she'd balked at the size of the bill. 'Volvo tyres don't come cheap.'

'But I only use it for school runs and the odd bit of shopping,' she had protested.

The mechanic had grimaced. 'School runs are the worst. All that stopping and starting. Wears the tyres out.'

And to think the government wanted more kids to walk to school, thought Harriet, wryly. Fine, if you live round the corner or have a chauffeur, like most of the cabinet, but it would take hours for Jess and Bruce to get to St Theresa's and, besides, she wouldn't consider them crossing these roads on their own even if Bruce was nearly thirteen. Anyway, the school run gave you time to talk to the kids and catch up with their news and gossip. Anything to divert them and deflect questions on when Daddy was coming home.

'Don't you have a spelling test today, Jess? . . . Jess, will you listen to me or shall I get your hearing checked again?'

'She's got her Discman on, Mrs Chapman. Shall I tell her you're trying to talk to her?'

Harriet squinted as the low sun momentarily blinded her, flicked her fringe out of her eyes (she really must book that cut before Charlie got back on Friday) and wondered, not for the first time, why her kids couldn't be as polite as Pippa's. 'Thank you, Beth. That would be very kind.'

'Jess, your mum's trying to talk to you.'

'Wha'?'

Harriet yanked down the sun visor, took a deep breath and a sharp corner at the same time. 'The word "what" had a T in it the last time I looked. Anyway, it's "sorry" or "pardon". I said, haven't you got a spelling test today?'

'Sort of.'

'Well, you've either got one or you haven't. Pass me the list.'

'That's dangerous, Mum,' said Bruce, sternly. 'You can't read and drive at the same time.'

Couldn't she? She could put on her lipstick – with the spare she kept in Charlie's glove compartment – do her pelvic-floor squeezes *and* drive simultaneously, although now that the new law had been passed she didn't like to answer her mobile. She'd only got three points on her licence, which was nothing compared with some of her friends, but they niggled. One of the mums at school had lost hers altogether after one too many ladies' lunches and it was costing her a fortune in taxis. Still, that's what they all were, weren't they? Unpaid taxis doing the school run and the husband-to-station run. *When* your husband happened to be at home.

Swiftly she glanced at the spelling list, then back at the road. 'Hyacinth,' she said. 'How do you spell that?' Someone, she noticed, had tied a fresh bunch of roses to the lamp-post at the corner of Acacia Road. There had been flowers there for over two years and they always made her shiver. So many people seemed to do that now, when their loved ones had accidents. Far more effective than those 'Speed Kills' signs but horribly macabre. Like having a coffin open at a funeral. She slowed down automatically, as she approached the new speed bumps.

'Hyacinth,' she repeated. 'Come on, Jess.'

Jess hesitated. 'H-I . . .'

'No, Jess, *no*. Don't you remember anything from last night? It's H-Y. Now, go on.'

'H-Y-I . . .'

Harriet gripped the steering-wheel. Spelling came naturally to her but Bruce was hopeless and Jess was worse. What was it with them? Or was she just particularly tetchy today? She certainly had an excuse for the latter. This week was the one that would decide the rest of her life – and the children's. No wonder she hadn't been able to eat any breakfast even though her stomach was rolling on empty. She hadn't even had the heart to flick on her customary coat of mascara, unlike some of the mums on the run who looked as though they'd popped in to the Clinique counter.

'Shall we try singing it?' piped up Beth. 'Mum sings our spellings with us. She says it makes them go down more easily. We do it to a really pretty tune called "In an English Country Garden".'

How typical of Pippa! She was so nice, even to her own kids under pressure. Harriet had been like Pippa before children. Now she was always snapping. And hating herself for it. 'OK,' she said, making a sharp left. Blast! Another traffic jam. 'Let's sing it, then. Come on everyone. H-Y-A—'

'That sounds awful,' giggled Jess.

True, but giggling wasn't going to help her daughter in the morning's spelling test. If she didn't improve, she'd be moved down. Mrs Wilson had already warned her about that at the last parents' meeting.

'Beth and Lucy's mum's not feeling well today,' piped up Jess.

'I know. Don't change the subject.'

'She had a row with Dad too,' said Beth, quietly.

'Beth, I *told* you not to say anything,' said Lucy, angrily.

Bruce snorted. 'All parents argue. You should hear Dad when he gets going. Talk about flying saucers!'

'Bruce is right, dear.' Oh, God, how much had he noticed? 'It's normal for parents to quarrel sometimes, just like children do. Don't worry about Mum – she's probably got that bug that's going round.'

She'd have to buy some more echinacea, Harriet reminded herself. A cold was all they needed at the beginning of the summer holidays next week. There was the sound of a quiet snuffle in the back. At the red traffic-lights Harriet turned round briefly and took Beth's small warm hand reassuringly. 'I'm sure it'll be fine, sweetie.'

Beth smiled bravely although tears were glistening in her eyes. Why, wondered Harriet, could she be so nice to other kids yet so foul to her own? But it was easier, wasn't it, to be nice to children who didn't really know you and who weren't likely to tell you to shut up or, as Bruce last week, to sod off?

'Open the window, Mum,' whined Bruce. 'I'm baking.'

'It will interfere with the air-conditioning.'

'But I'm hot and I've got Betty Swallocks.'

'Betty Swallocks? What on earth's that?'

'You just change the letters round, Mrs Chapman,' announced Lucy. 'It makes Sweaty Boll—'

'I get it,' said Harriet, quickly. 'Bruce, I don't want to hear that again. Especially not in front of your father when he returns.'

The lights changed and Harriet crunched into first, trying to work out her priorities for the day. She'd ring Pippa as soon as she got back, although maybe she'd still be in bed or at the doctor's if she'd managed to get an appointment (unlikely on a Monday morning). It would be good to talk to her and offload some of this awful tension that was making her feel sick and, if she was honest, causing her concentration to waver. Why, oh, why hadn't Charlie rung? For nearly a week, she'd been expecting him to confirm the arrangements for Friday.

She tried to think straight. Dubai was four hours ahead. He'd be in the office. Or lying on a beach. Or . . . Sometimes, she wished she didn't have an imagination. It was too easy to conjure up what might not be happening at all.

'Did Dad text you last night?' she asked, as she pulled up outside the school gates.

'No. And he *promised*,' pouted Jess, hauling her bag out of the back seat.

'Never mind, he'll probably ring tonight.' Harriet put out her hand to stop the bag scratching the Volvo's rear end. 'Mind the paintwork or Dad'll go mad. You shouldn't have so much in that, Jess – you'll hurt your back. Bruce, stop. You've forgotten your sports kit.'

He took it, wordlessly.

'"Thank you, Mum." That's a pleasure, Bruce,' she said tartly.

Defiantly, her son untucked his shirt so it hung fashionably out of his trousers, the way Harriet (and the teachers) hated it. It added to his generally unruly appearance, which included odd socks (what was it about footwear that divorced overnight in the linen cupboard?).

'Whatever, Mum. See you.'

''Bye,' she called, suddenly repentant. Before Children she'd never have been sharp like that. 'Have a nice day, all of you. And tuck your shirt *in*, Bruce.'

They'd gone. Only the two who didn't belong to her bothered to turn and wave. Almost immediately they were sucked into the tidal wave of schoolchildren making their way reluctantly to the school gates, weighed down by massive designer shoulder-bags that would undoubtedly destroy their posture for life.

Beth disappeared through the primary school entrance while the older ones, who went to the senior school next door, strode boldly along with the kind of confidence Harriet would have loved at that age. A tall girl, with a bouncy blonde pony-tail, wearing a prefect's badge but no uniform, swanned past, arm in arm with a youth carrying a trumpet case. He bent to kiss her as they passed and Harriet found herself unable to look away. The boy seemed impossibly young, with his smattering of acne, while the girl, wearing flawless makeup, could have passed for her early twenties. The look in her eyes said it all. First love. True passion. Which Harriet had never felt for Charlie.

Alongside her a car hooted, and the driver gesticulated, wanting to know if Harriet had finished with her space. She shook her head and fished around in her bag for her mobile. Quickly, she scrolled down for Charlie's number, which was too long to remember.

'Hello, this is Charlie. I'm not available at the moment but please leave a message and I'll come back to you shortly.'

'Charlie? It's me. The kids thought you were texting them last night and they're a bit disappointed. Do you think you could remember tonight? Ring me about Friday. I could pick you up at the airport. I want to talk before we get home, because of the children. 'Bye.'

Harriet hoped her voice had conveyed the right mixture of disapproval about not texting with a businesslike attitude to Friday. It seemed almost impossible that two months had passed since that terrible evening when the phone had beeped in the bedroom while Charlie was showering and she had automatically pressed the open-message button in case it was something urgent from the office.

'Thanks for last night.' That was all. Followed by a row of Xs. No name.

As she had stood there, staring with disbelief at the screen, he had come out, a towel wrapped round his waist. Unable to speak, she had merely handed him the phone.

He glanced at it disinterestedly. 'It's not what you think.' He looked at her straight in the eye, unblinking. 'She's just a girl in the office who's a bit friendly. I helped her with a file last night and we've had the odd drink but that's it.'

Harriet's voice came out as someone else's: 'Charlie, she sent you a row of kisses.'

He snorted. 'She's a kid. They all do that. Stop making a fuss, Harry. And haven't you got any more towels? This one's wet.'

'Sod the towel.'

'So you don't believe me?'

His eyes challenged her and she hesitated. Unlike her father, Charlie simply wasn't the type to be unfaithful. He was too straight, sometimes too abrupt. But totally honest. They both were. She could never understand how people lived their lives in any other way. 'Yes, I do believe you, but I think we need to talk.'

He turned round to slip on his pyjama bottoms and she suddenly realised, with a shock, that he didn't want her to see him naked. 'OK, if you want to talk, Harriet, we'll talk. I haven't been having an affair but if I had no one could blame me. You never show me any affection and it's as though I come in at the end of your day like an appendage. As for sex – well, forget it. It hardly ever happens.'

Her chest tightened. 'That's because you're tired and so am I. You don't know how much time the children take up. And I never ask you to do bedtime or get up in the night when they wake.'

'Harriet, I've got a *job* to do.'

She'd been scared then, really scared. 'Don't, Charlie, don't say any more.' She tried to put her arms round him but he pushed her away, then sat on the edge of the bed, looking up at her, his eyes hard and angry.'

'Can you honestly say, Harriet, that you never wonder if there's more to life than this?'

'More to life than our children? What else is there?'

He stood up when she tried to sit next to him. 'Exactly. That proves my point. Look, the office wants me to go to Dubai to handle the takeover. I was going to do it in several trips but I could stay there for the two months it'll take. Let's use it as thinking time. We'll tell the kids it's a business trip.'

'You've got it all sorted, haven't you?' Harriet's legs felt like water. She'd read about this happening. Seen it from a distance with other mothers at school. But no one had ever told her that it was like being run over or having your breath squeezed out of you while you felt violently sick. She glared at him. 'I suppose this admirer of yours from the office will be there too?'

He shook his head. 'No. And I told you. She meant nothing. She was just someone who showed me the kind of care and affection that you don't.'

'*Care and affection?* What are you? A kid yourself? Perhaps I should have a Baby On Board sticker on the car.'

'There's no need to be nasty.'

She could feel the heat of her anger rising up her neck in red blotches. 'But how could I have known something was wrong or that you were feeling neglected if you didn't tell me? You're a bastard, Charlie, do you know that? Go to Dubai for two bloody months. And take that time to think it over. Don't worry about us. The kids and I will look after ourselves. We always have done. And we don't need you.'

Briefly, he had looked frightened, as though he had understood suddenly what he was throwing away. Then his eyes narrowed. 'I'll spend tonight in the spare room.'

'Fine.'

When she'd woken that morning and remembered what she'd said about not needing him (he must know it wasn't true) she'd felt sick and chilled, but he had already gone, leaving her to tell the children that Daddy had rushed off on another business trip. Not even a note.

What had happened to the Charlie she once knew? When had this callous stranger slipped into his place?

Over the weeks, he had rung the children and texted them most nights. Occasionally he had spoken to her but mainly to discuss practical matters like finance and when the boiler blew. They spoke politely, as though the argument had never happened, and Harriet was scared to raise it in case she precipitated something worse. Part of her had yearned for a 'Sorry' phone call or a bouquet of flowers. Nothing. And now, this Friday, he was due to come home. Reckoning time at last. Part of her was so hurt she couldn't breathe, yet another part was desperate to see him. It might have helped, she thought, if she still felt that initial anger but, inexplicably, she could now only feel hurt. And disbelief.

She'd talked to only two people about this, Monica and Pippa. But neither could do what she really wanted, which was to glue life back to BTM (Before Text Message). If you were lucky, thought Harriet, you had a normal life but it wasn't until it stopped being normal that you began, with hindsight, to appreciate it. And then it was too late.

Someone in a turquoise Discovery hooted at her. An irate mother in sunglasses indicated that as Harriet's car was empty she could darned well move and let *her* deposit her own small, wriggly charges.

EV1 – personalised number-plates were *so* common – hooted again. Harriet flashed the woman a dirty look and moved off, noting with satisfaction in her rear-view mirror that the blonde was having great difficulty in squeezing her shiny turquoise bottom into the space Harriet had just vacated.

It was just as she approached the traffic-lights – green for once – that the mobile rang. Sugar! Where had she put it? Frantically, with her left hand, she scrabbled in her bag for her phone. It was like that party game she'd played when you felt a sock to guess the contents. She could detect her purse, keys, lipstick – everything but the small plastic rectangle she needed. The jingly tone rang mockingly. Someone hooted. Help – she'd drifted over to the centre of the road. Pull in. Where? Don't stop ringing. There's a space! She wrenched on the handbrake, tipped the contents of her handbag out on to the front seat and the ringing stopped. At that moment she saw the phone in the dashboard drinks container. Smirking.

DAD, it said on the screen.

Harriet hit the green button. 'Hello, this is Charlie . . .'

She flung the mobile on to the front seat and allowed hot tears of frustration to roll down her cheeks. She'd missed him. Again. But this time it felt like an omen.

2

> *'This is Capital Radio and it's nearly seven a.m. on a lovely bright summer morning. I'm Sarah Smith with an update on the traffic. Long queues are . . .'*

'Don't turn that off, Robin. It was the traffic report . . . Yes, I *do* need to listen. I've got to get your kids to school and then I'm seeing Bulmer at nine . . . True – one third of the kids *is* mine. I gave birth to him so I'm hardly likely to forget. But if Rachel hadn't suddenly decided to land your lot on us this week, it would have made my life a lot easier . . . All right, all right, it's not easy for them either. No, they can't go with Martine because there isn't a spare seat-belt while their Rover's in the garage. And don't put that in the dishwasher – I haven't unloaded yet . . . Yes, I *am* aware you've got another interview and I *would* have wished you luck if you'd given me time. Your suit's in the dry-cleaning bag. And remember to pick up the kids . . . No, I *can't.* I've got that video conference with the States. Remember? Dinner's in the freezer. Lasagne. Seven minutes on full power . . . No, *seven.* It's on the packet. And don't forget to put the girls' sports kit in the washing-machine . . . For crying out loud, Robin, if we can't cope during the term, what are we going to do next week when it's the holidays?'

> *'We're coming up to eight a.m. and it's nearly time for the news. This is Capital Radio . . .'*

'OK, everyone, strapped in?'

Evie, who'd been buffing her naturally almond-shaped nails while she waited, turned round to check. If she smiled brightly, they might just smile back. Reflective grimacing, just like reflective listening, thought Evie, wryly. It might be funny if it weren't for the circumstances. Trying to look happier than she felt, she surveyed the occupants of the back seat, which was satisfyingly upholstered in cream leather to her own exacting standards. Pity she couldn't impose her own specifications on the girls. The fourteen-year-old twins, Natalie and Leonora, stared back stonily while Jack beamed at her from his toddler seat. Thank God for Jack. Her heart melted at the sight of his sweet little face, which shone in contrast to those of his half-sisters.

'Are you allowed to wear makeup for school, Nattie?' asked Evie, frowning at the heavy black eye pencil round her stepdaughter's eyes. She hadn't looked like that at breakfast, she was sure. Not that Evie had eaten anything – too fattening – but she always made sure the children had their muesli and yoghurt. She sure as hell wasn't going to have their mother on the phone, demanding to know why she hadn't fed them properly during her absence.

Natalie smirked. 'Yes, I am. Just like you're allowed to wear the disgusting perfume. It's a non-uniform day today. And my name is Natalie. To you. Open the window, can you? Your smell makes me feel sick.'

Evie turned back so that the girl couldn't see her face. She didn't want another row, not when they were all trapped in the car for the next half an hour. Illogically, the bit about the name hurt more than the rudeness. Everyone called her Nattie – everyone who was her friend, that is. But Natalie had made it clear from the minute they had been introduced that Evie would never rise to that category. She was a fool to let it hurt still, but it did, and there was nothing she could do about it except carry on in this so-you-both-hate-me-but-I-don't-care

15

manner. Just as she had done as a child at school when the other kids had loathed her.

'Got your prep, Leonora?' she said, forcing her voice to sound even.

Her other step-daughter – older by twenty minutes – scowled, reminding her, with a nasty jolt, of Robin's face when she had left the house a few minutes ago. 'If you mean my home-work, yes. And, by the way, we need a quid each. We have to pay for non-uniform days.'

'Why?'

'It's for charity. Mum told you. It would have been on her list.'

Evie gritted her teeth. 'She didn't send one actually. I just got a barrage of commands over the phone. And next time please make sure both of you have made your beds before you leave the house. It's not fair to expect me to do every-thing. I made mine when I was your age.'

I made mine when I was your age.

Evie didn't need to look in the rear-view mirror to see the girls mimicking her. Sometimes it was best to ignore them and only get cross about the big things, as that step-parent guide suggested.

'Pick your battles,' the author had advised. 'You can't win every fight so ignore the things that don't matter and make a stand for the ones that do.'

The cover had declared the author to be a successful step-mother of five, but as a seasoned magazine journalist Evie could decode a publicity blurb. On closer reading, it tran-spired that the five step-kids were now grown-up and out of the author's way, which meant she could look back with rose-coloured contact lenses on what it had really been like. Evie couldn't wait for the two in the back to grow up and go as far away as possible, leaving her and Robin with the remote hope of some quality adult time with Jack. Even though the girls didn't live full-time with them, they were near enough to be with their father at weekends and holidays, and during term-time when Rachel was away. Their constantly morose and critical presence meant she couldn't enjoy the precious few moments she had with Jack after work. But if the girls weren't with them, Robin fretted. Either way, she couldn't win.

'Did Mum tell you we're going out on Friday night?'

'No, Leonora, she didn't. Where are you going?'

'Bar Med. It's a party.'

'But you have to be eighteen to get in there.'

'We've got fake IDs.'

'You've what? Where did you get them from?'

'The Internet. They cost ten quid. You just send off for them.'

Despite herself, Evie couldn't help feeling impressed.

'Show them you understand what it was like to be young,' the step-parent book had urged.

'I wouldn't mind a fake ID to say I'm eighteen,' she said lightly.

'In your dreams,' muttered Natalie. 'More like fifty.'

'I'm sorry you can't take a joke, Natalie. Well, you're not going to any club, fake ID or no fake ID. And that's my last word.'

No one, thought Evie, can say I don't try. Seething silently, she kicked off her black, stick-heeled designer shoes, slipped into her flat red loafers and checked that her Palm Pilot was in her Joseph bag. Right. She was ready to meet the day, arguments or no arguments. 'Off we go, then,' she said brightly, smiling at herself in the mirror to prove to the girls that she didn't care. Then she swung the Discovery, with its resident's permit sticker on the windscreen, into the street.

Think positive. That was the trick. So what if she was working and Robin was unemployed? Hundreds of other couples were in the same position – *Express Woman* had run a feature on it the other day under the headline 'WHY WOMEN ARE THE

BREADWINNERS WHILE DAD STAYS AT HOME'. Evie would have considered running something similar in the magazine if it hadn't been too close to the bone.

'Traffic's building up again near Wimbledon Common and Bo's mum has just rung in to warn of an accident on Balham high street. Thanks, Bo's mum, and do continue with your calls, everyone. If it's safe and legal, we'd like to hear from you.'

'For God's sake, turn that off,' groaned Natalie. 'It's so uncool. Can't we have Filth? Mum always lets us.'

Evie was tempted to retort that since Mum wasn't here it wasn't relevant. Bloody woman! Rachel was with her current lover, Chris, on a yacht in the Med. When she rang the girls, it was always when they were all having dinner and phone calls were normally forbidden. But, of course, Evie was overruled when Rachel was expected to ring and the resulting excited telephone conversation would neatly scupper the meal. At least when that happened Evie could get up and clear the table. But here, in the car, they were trapped.

'Sorry,' said Evie brightly. 'Out of Filth CDs at the moment. And do you mind not saying "God" in front of Jack.'

'Well, you say "Christ" enough,' retorted Natalie.

'You're right. Maybe I shouldn't.' Evie mentally patted herself on the back. Good one. Parents should occasionally admit when they're wrong – even step-parents. It showed kids they weren't the only ones. They'd just run a feature in the magazine on adult role models called 'Do What I Don't and Not What I Do'.

For a while they drove along in silence, punctuated by bleeps as the girls texted their friends (they seemed unable to amuse themselves unless they had a mobile in their hands) and Jack's occasional comments. 'Look! Dog!' he cooed, pointing to a car next to them at the lights, with a Border collie in the back.

'Clever boy,' said Natalie, and cuddled him.

Even the girls loved him. Two was such a sweet age, thought Evie wistfully. At times, she resented Robin for having that precious time with Jack at home – time that her own relentlessly busy schedule refused her. She yawned. That meeting last night – on a Sunday, for heaven's sake! – had gone on so late that it was still buzzing round her head. No wonder she found it hard to focus on the road. She wound down the window, bracing herself for the cool morning air that would wake her up, unlike the dull air-conditioning.

'Shut the window,' groaned Natalie.

'No, keep it open,' giggled Leonora.

'Bloody hell – who's farted?' asked Natalie admiringly.

'Pooh. He who smelt it dealt it!'

'Shut up.'

Evie frowned, trying not to breathe in as the stench invaded the car. 'Can't you put those phones down for a minute? Why do you need to text your friends when you're seeing them any second? And please don't say "shut up" in front of Jack.'

At the sound of his name, Jack leaned forward. 'Flowers!' he said, pointing to a bunch tied to a lamp-post at the corner of Acacia Road.

'Why did someone put them there?' asked Leonora.

'Because someone was killed at that spot, dumbo,' snapped Natalie. 'Just like Mum says we'll be killed one day if Evie doesn't stop driving so fast.'

'What?' Evie glanced furiously over her shoulder, and turned back just in time to stop as the car in front slowed. 'Say that again.'

'Nothing,' mumbled Natalie.

Evie could feel herself sweating underneath her cool, well-pressed Stella McCartney suit. 'Well, you can tell your mother that I *don't* drive fast. I drive very carefully. And if she's worried she'd better come and talk to me about it or drive you to school herself. Got it?'

For a few moments, there was silence in the back, punctuated by the odd titter from the girls, who had clearly enjoyed the effect they'd had on their step-mother. Evie promised herself a showdown with Robin over this one. Bloody cheek! How dare Rachel talk like that behind her back? Just because she didn't hang around in the traffic – you couldn't afford to when you were battling to make Registration – didn't mean she was unsafe. She knew when it was OK to take risks, just like that red Fiesta with the dog in the back was doing now, sailing through an amber light.

In fact, she prided herself on her skill with the school run, which was pure unadulterated chaos. You needed sharp instincts plus a finely tuned sense of distance to avoid car doors that opened in your path or idiots who forgot to indicate when pulling out from the school dropping-off bay and who would – if Evie hadn't reacted sharply – have been recuperating at the bodyshop by now.

'Badron, badron, badron,' chanted Jack.

'Not again,' moaned Leonora. 'That's getting on my nerves. Where's he picked it up?'

'Probably a child at nursery who's upsetting him,' said Natalie. 'Never mind, Jack. You tell this Ron kid that we'll sort him out for you.'

They loved Jack far more than they could ever like her, thought Evie, grimly. Thank heavens they were nearly at school. Now all she had to do was park. Good, a Volvo was about to move off. She honked to indicate she was in a rush. The driver – a skinny blonde in sunglasses – gave her a filthy look, put down a mobile phone and pulled out, only just missing her left wing mirror. Lethal. If that woman had had a *'How am I driving?'* notice in her back window, Evie would have reported her. She wasn't sure about Martine either, and wondered how Rachel could trust her to share a regular run.

'OK, out, everyone,' she instructed, and slid into the tight space, which was partially over a double yellow. 'Don't forget your PE stuff in the boot. And peel that chewing-gum off the seat.'

She shuddered. When she had been a child, her father's beaten-up Cortina, which he drove at weekends when he was not in the cab, had been festooned with garage freebies like Tiger Tails and always reeked of fags. That was why Evie kept an air-freshener in hers and a Gucci carrier-bag in which she deposited illicit sweet packets. When she'd first started doing the school run, she had forbidden eating in the car but the girls had complained to Robin and he had pointed out to Evie that he wanted them to feel at home when they were with him. Reluctantly she had given in but it didn't stop her feeling furious when they treated the Discovery with the disdain they normally reserved for her.

Natalie swung her long legs out of the back and stood up, tossing back her hair, then sauntered off without a goodbye.

'Bye-bye.' Jack flapped his chubby little fist.

Leonora looked back and leaned into the car to plant a kiss on his soft cheek. As she did so, she glanced guiltily at Evie. 'She didn't mean it.' Leonora was the softer of the two, if there was such a thing. 'She didn't mean to tell you Mum said you were a dangerous driver. And I don't think Mum meant it either.'

'Well, she shouldn't have said it.' To her horror, Evie felt her eyes prickle with tears. She looked away hastily, so that Leonora couldn't see, and watched the Fiesta squeeze past her, almost scraping the Discovery's side. 'That's what you call dangerous driving,' she said angrily. 'Not mine. Well, go on, then, aren't you going to be late?'

Leonora hesitated. 'Mrs Foster wants to see Mum. This morning. She was meant to come in last week but she didn't. Mrs Foster says that if she doesn't see her this morning, she's going to write to Dad and . . .'

Evie sighed. This wasn't the first time it had happened but Robin usually sorted out these problems. 'What have you been doing now?'

'Nothing. I just called this girl something I shouldn't because she said something nasty to me and then I hit her so she hit me and . . . Oh, God, Evie, I'm really in trouble this time. Please help me. I didn't dare tell Dad.'

Evie was torn between anger and pleasure that Leonora had chosen to confide in her. Despite herself, she also felt sorry for her. The anxiety on Leonora's face reminded her of the problems she'd had at school. Not that the girls would understand *that*.

She looked coldly at her step-daughter, who was waiting for an answer. 'I can't come in now. I'm on a double yellow.'

'Please, Evie. I'm really going to be in the shit if you don't.'

'Don't use words like that.' Evie glanced around to see if there were any traffic wardens. If she was quick, she could explain to Mrs Foster that Rachel would come in to sort this out when she got home.

'Stay there,' she instructed Jack. 'Don't move. I won't be a second.'

She didn't like leaving him but Jack was getting too heavy to carry and his dawdling would slow her down. 'Come on, then. Quick.'

They walked briskly past a child in a scruffy black blazer. 'But it's non-uniform day,' he was saying, into his mobile. 'Please bring in my jeans, Mum, or I'll be the only one like this.'

Poor boy, thought Evie. Kids hated being different – like many an adult. To her relief, Mrs Foster was in the staffroom. Evie explained the situation, awkwardly conscious that Leonora was near enough to hear. 'My step-daughter's mother is away at the moment but she'll come in as soon as she's back. I'd be really grateful if you could make allowances. Leonora has been through a difficult time recently.' She gave the woman a warm smile, the kind that said, 'I know your job's difficult but it's bloody hard work being a step-mother too.'

Mrs Foster nodded. 'Leave it to me, Mrs Brookes. I know what girls are like. I've got three of my own. Now, Leonora, why don't you show your mother – I mean step-mother – the way out?' She smiled again. 'This place is like a rabbit warren if you don't know it.'

Wordlessly, Leonora led the way, her face red with the embarrassment of having an external adult next to her while her classmates walked past.

'Don't worry,' whispered Evie.

'I'm not,' retorted Leonora.

Evie's heart sank and her new confidence evaporated. The brief intimacy had passed and she felt punctured. Why should it bother her that Leonora no longer needed her protection? But it did. How pathetic was that?

She put on her sunglasses (easier to observe the world than allow it to observe her) and walked briskly out of the school towards the car, checking the expensive watch that Robin shouldn't – in view of his redundancy – have bought her last Christmas. Blast. That Mrs Foster hiccup had made her late for Jack's nursery, and if the traffic was bad she'd be late for the meeting with Bulmer about circulation figures. Of all the appointments in her day, that was the one she couldn't be late for. Over the last three months, Gareth Bulmer had been unfairly critical of her circulation figures, which were improving at a time when magazines were grappling with pro- duction costs and readers who were defecting from the glossies to affordable weeklies. Evie had to be on the ball for this morning's meeting. She had to—

Christ! What was that noise? It sounded like the car alarm. Evie ran towards the Discovery, and saw, with a stab of fear, that the back seat was empty.

Calm down. Jack must have unstrapped himself again and would be playing in the front. She zapped the car door and turned the handle. Locked! She must have left it open so Jack had let himself out . . .

'Jack!' she screamed. She unlocked the door and looked under the seats in case he was hiding. Then she opened her mouth to scream again but nothing came out. Even worse, she felt wet between her legs; wet with fear because she must have (oh, God, no!) peed herself just as she had at school when things went wrong. Her legs paralysed, she looked wildly up and down the street. No one, apart from a few straggling mums, chatting outside their cars.

Jack had gone. *Jack had gone.*

Then the scream came, louder and shriller than any car alarm. So loud that Evie didn't know she was doing it until the other mothers turned and looked at her, eyes wide, mouths open.

'Jack! Jack! *Where are you?*'

3

*'This is Capital Radio and it's nearly seven a.m. on a
lovely bright summer morning. I'm Sarah Smith with an
update on the traffic . . .'*

Juliana, Juliana? God, I can almost reach out and touch your
face. No, don't go. I need to ask you something. Come back.
Please.

'Dad, wake up! It's seven o'clock. Your alarm's been going
for ages! I've put the washing-machine on and walked Mutley.
You said I could drive if we were ready on time. *Please?* Dad,
you're talking in your sleep again. Come on! I can't be late!
It's Monday, prefect duty. Look, I've brought you some coffee.
Careful, it's hot . . . Yes, I know it's nearly ten past seven.
That's what I've been trying to tell you. You're not a morning
person, are you, Dad? Remember how Mum used to say that?
. . . Yes, Dad, you *did* say I could drive. I've got the L-plates
out. I'm seventeen now, Dad. You've got to let me grow up
some time. Besides, I like driving Mum's car. It makes me feel
she's still here . . . I can? Thanks, Dad. I'll go slower today.
Promise.'

*'. . . coming up to eight twenty-five and first it's the
sports news. Arsenal's revving up for the big match
tonight and . . .'*

Nick froze with terror as Julie squeezed through a narrow

space outside school, her beautiful face gritted with determination. This place was getting more like the dodgems every day. It was a miracle no one had been killed.

'Look out! You nearly went into the side of that Discovery.'

'It wasn't my fault, Dad. She shouldn't have swung out like that.' Julie pouted.

Nick felt the familiar pang of loss. At seventeen, she was the spitting image of her mother at that age. Sometimes Nick could hardly believe he had met Juliana when she was barely out of school. He remembered it as if it was yesterday. Fresh and beautiful, she had been chosen as New Face of the Year by a teen magazine and he was the lucky photographer who had been commissioned to do the shoot. And even though he was nearly ten years older, it had been love – not just lust – at first sight.

'Easy does it. That's right. Straighten up now. *Straighten up, I said!* Oh, God!'

Nick covered his face with his hands, unable to look as Julie reversed clumsily into the space that, by some miracle, had just been vacated in the school-run scrabble. As he raised his head, he caught sight of himself in the wing mirror. He looked like a scared stranger – but, then, he often felt like that when he looked in the mirror. Sure, the basic bits were still there: the strong nose that Juliana had called handsome; the short, fashionable haircut that made him (if he said so himself) look younger than his forty-five years; the intentionally semi-shaved chin that made life easier in the morning rush and which Juliana had always loved to nuzzle; and the laughter lines round his eyes, which still felt hollow with grief. What right did he have to smile with Juliana's makeup still on the dressing-table?

'I know what I'm doing, Dad. See?'

An exultant Julie grinned at him, having successfully – if unevenly – reversed into the space. He couldn't help grinning back, with a wave of relief that they were still in one piece. His daughter's dark looks (inherited from the West Indian side of Juliana's family) were stunning, and her sparkly eyes under that cluster of black eyelashes challenged you not to sparkle back. Her lips were full, again just like her mother's, something she took pride in. Since her mother's death, all Julie had wanted was to emulate her. She even insisted on everyone calling her Julie, instead of her real name, Jani, because it was more like Juliana. And, even worse, she only wanted to do one thing in life: be a model like her mother. What would Juliana have said? What would she think about Julie driving? About her first boyfriend?

'So can I apply for my test?'

Nick turned up the radio. 'Hang on a minute, it's the sports report.'

Julie turned it down again. 'Dad, don't change the subject.'

Nick sighed. He had wanted to hear the bit about Arsenal. 'What does your driving instructor say?'

Julie pouted again. To Nick's expert eye, it looked well practised, probably in the mirror. 'He said I should wait a few weeks so I can have more lessons.'

Nick mentally blessed the driving instructor. 'Let's do that, then, shall we? In the meantime, we'll get in as much practice as we can.'

'But, Dad, it takes ages for tests to come through. Wouldn't it be better to book now?'

Nick knew he was on a losing wicket. Since Juliana had died, he had felt so full of guilt and remorse that it had been difficult to refuse their daughter anything – apart from the one thing that really mattered to her. 'We'll see.'

Julie grinned. They both knew that meant 'yes'. 'Pick me up at four, then? I can drive back.'

Nick glanced at a pretty mother, who was smiling at them. She'd been one of Juliana's acquaintances. Briefly, he smiled back, not wanting to start a conversation. It was always a mistake. The women meant kindly but their eyes shone with pity, which made Nick feel uncomfortable. 'There goes that poor man whose wife died.' Or 'How are you managing?' if he let them. He always tried to change the subject. He and Julie were managing just fine, and if they weren't, it wasn't anyone else's business. Just as it was no one else's business that last night's plates were still in the sink and the beds unmade. He had got Julie to school – or, rather, she had got him there – without any arguments about modelling careers, boys, not eating enough breakfast or any of the other issues that hid the real biggie, and that was all that mattered.

'Dad, why are you looking at that woman like that?'

'I'm not. She smiled at *me*.'

'Yeah, right.' Julie's voice was scornful and disapproving. She hated him looking or even talking to a woman. Nick understood this: what recently bereaved teenage girl would want a replacement mother? About six months ago, he had briefly dated another photographer, a woman of about the same age as Juliana who didn't have kids. Julie had sulked and only spoken when it was absolutely necessary. Consequently Nick had terminated the relationship and Julie had returned to normal. He hadn't liked to initiate a talk about it because he felt wretched at having upset his daughter.

'I'll pick you up at four,' he said, stumbling on to safer ground, 'unless the shoot overruns. I'll ring you if it does.'

'Shoot?' Juliana's beautiful eyes glistened with curiosity in her daughter's face. 'What are you doing today?'

He groaned. 'Lingerie. It's an advertorial for a new chain store. You should see the stuff. God knows how I'm going to make it look hot. I haven't seen the models yet, but if they're anything like the clothes I've had it.'

'You'll manage, Dad. You always do. Mind you, if you had me doing it, I could make it work.'

Nick cursed himself for walking into that one. 'Except you've got school. Now, off you go, young lady.'

Julie shrugged. 'Have it your way. See you later then. 'Bye, Mutley.' She gathered up her bag and the glossy magazine that had been delivered with the papers that morning, then buried her face in the dog's coat to kiss him as she always did when she left. 'Gosh, Mutley, you stink! We must bath him this weekend, Dad. And look at his hair all over the seat!'

It was true, he thought, but it didn't stop her kissing the dog once more before she left him. Mutley was her security, one of the constants that had remained to fill the huge gap Juliana had left. In a funny way, the dog was the same for him. That was why he often took him to photographic sessions, depending on how amenable the client was. A dog – especially one like Mutley – often put people at their ease and made them relax in front of the lens. A bit like the car radio, really. There were times when it performed wonders in filling awkward gaps in the conversation or changing the subject.

Nick pushed Mutley back to where he was meant to be sitting and watched his daughter walk off jauntily, falling in beside a tall, lanky boy whose body language – even from the back – suggested that he was smitten with Nick's little girl. He felt a surge of protectiveness. As he watched, a bulkier youth pushed into the one accompanying Julie, knocking them both. Julie's companion said something angrily to him and the bulky kid, whose solid shoulders bulged underneath his T-shirt, put his fingers up in an aggressive gesture that had existed even in Nick's day. These kids were so big, thought Nick, they could be mistaken for teachers. The school was getting rougher and he had wondered if he should have moved Julie to do her A levels somewhere else. But Juliana had picked this school – she had even been on the PTA committee. Taking Julie away was impossible without her mother's permission.

They seemed all right now, Julie and the boy. The big kid had gone. Nick glanced down to put the car into gear and saw his daughter's purse on the front seat. She'd need it. He leapt out of the door without looking and stood back, just in time, as a cyclist sped past, shouting at him – not without justification. He reproached himself and began to race down the pavement. 'Julie!' He waved to catch her attention. 'Darling, your purse!'

A group of mothers – whom he didn't recognise – stared at him coldly. Maybe he shouldn't have said 'darling' but he couldn't help it: his little girl had always been his darling, his princess. That was why he was keeping her out of the modelling world for as long as he could. It had destroyed his wife and he was damned if he would let it do the same to his daughter.

He ran on through the swathes of schoolchildren, who didn't trouble to stand back and let him through. So much for respect! He almost bumped into an older woman helping a little boy out of a turquoise Discovery. Nick's artistic eye caught the child's dark auburn curls. Nice-looking kid. 'Julie!'

To his relief, she turned round. For a minute, she looked at him as she might at a stranger, then recognition flashed into her eyes. 'Dad! What's up?'

He held out the purse, and took a good look at the boy next to her.

'Thanks, Dad. This is Jason.'

Nick almost held out his hand. 'Hi, Jason, nice to meet you.'

Jason gave what passed for a nod. What the hell does she see in this oik? wondered Nick. Moody face, greasy (waxed?) lock of hair across forehead and thin lips. He only hoped he didn't drive. That really spooked him: the realisation that if he didn't ensure Julie learned to drive safely, she would soon reach an age where other kids of her age would be driving *her*.

'See you tonight,' he said, feeling suddenly awkward.

'Sure.' Julie looked as embarrassed as he felt. Still, what kid wouldn't when a parent meets a boyfriend for the first time? He'd felt like Jason when he'd met Juliana's dad.

'Don't you think you're a bit old for her?'

'Some people might think so, sir, but I love her and I'm old enough to look after her properly in the way some wouldn't.'

Nick's honesty had won over the old man but the conversation still rang in his head. *I'm old enough to look after her properly.* It was exactly what he hadn't done, and now Juliana was dead.

He began to walk back briskly towards the car (walking helped when he had terrible thoughts like this) and the older woman he'd seen earlier – maybe a granny? – approached him, holding the auburn-haired child's hand.

'Excuse me, do you know who this little boy belongs to?'

He wondered if he'd heard her correctly. Hadn't he just seen her opening the Discovery parked down the road and helping him out?

'Er, no.' He looked down at the child. He wasn't mistaken. That hair was unforgettable. 'Is he lost?'

The woman nodded. She was short and plump with heavy lines creased into her forehead. Her lipstick was smudged and her rather old-fashioned, pale pink checked coat had milky-looking stains down the front. If she hadn't been part of the school-run remnant, Nick might have mistaken her for a bag-lady.

Nick got down on his knees so he was the same height as the little boy. 'Do you know where Mummy is?' he asked.

The little boy shook his head solemnly.

Nick tried again. 'What's your name?'

Suddenly, without warning, the child burst into noisy tears, which made everyone walking by stare at them. Hell! thought Nick. Any minute now I'll be accused of molesting a child.

'Where did you find him?' He stood up. The woman in the pink coat had disappeared. Shit. Now what was he going to do?

'Jack! *Jack!*' A young woman tore up to them and flung her arms round the child. One look at the little boy told Nick, to his relief, that this was indeed his mother. 'What the fuck are you doing with him?' she said, raising her tear-stained face.

'Nothing. I was trying to find out who he belonged to,' said Nick. 'Some woman – oldish – had him. She said he was lost and asked if I knew where his mother was. Then she just . . . disappeared.'

'Really?' She was scowling at him. 'Then how do you explain that I left him in the car only a few minutes ago? I've a good mind to call the police.'

This was ridiculous. 'Listen, if you want to do that, go ahead. I'm telling you the truth. I've got a kid at this school myself and I've just dropped her off.'

The mother's expression softened. 'OK, I'm sorry. But I was scared. I knew I shouldn't have left him in the car and I panicked.' She hesitated. 'Thanks for looking after him.'

'You need to be careful,' said Nick, firmly. 'That woman looked a bit odd. You get some weird types around here.'

Her eyes hardened again. Over-plucked eyebrows, observed Nick. They did nothing for her. 'I *am* careful, thanks very much. It's OK, Jack. Mummy's here.'

'I'll be off, then.' Nick wondered if now was the time to remind her that they knew each other slightly. He'd thought there was something familiar about her face and it was only when she'd been sounding off that he'd remembered. She was the editor of *Just For You* magazine, one of his clients. Maybe it was as well she hadn't recognised him. Rumour had it that you didn't want to get on the wrong side of Evie Brookes and now he could see why.

Right now, he hadn't time to worry about that. If he didn't get a move on, he'd be late for his session at the centre before the shoot at twelve. He'd been seeing Amber for the last three months at ten o'clock on Mondays. He wasn't sure if it had helped – and he hadn't told Julie about it – but the GP had encouraged him. He had tried initially to get Julie to see someone too. School had been good – a Mrs Greathead had contacted him to see if Julie would like to see one of the counsellors who visited school when children needed extra support, but Julie had adamantly refused. 'I don't want to talk to a stranger about Mum,' she had said. 'How could they understand when they never even met her?'

Nick had taken her point. But it was precisely because Amber hadn't known Juliana that he had hoped to find relief. Maybe someone with an objective point of view could put all this into context. So far, she hadn't done a lot to clear the terrible wrangling in his head but maybe he should go today. It might help him prepare for Friday.

Friday . . . It seemed impossible that Juliana had died two years ago. Nick hated anniversaries and all the superficiality that went with them. He rubbed his eyes, raw from lack of sleep. If you really loved someone, you missed them every day of the year, not just on one day.

Especially when you had helped to kill them.

4

MARTINE

> 'Long queues are already building up on the Marylebone
> bypass, causing severe congestion.'

*Dear Diary, what is Congestion? I must seek it in the dictionary or
my Roget's Thesaurus and engrave it in my vocab book like my
tutor said. My tutor, she also say to write this diary and listen to
the radio. Me, I always record in a diary every day even when I
am at home. I do not know if it is aiding my studies and the
radio speaks so quick. But I want to try hard and I think it is
arriving. Last night I dreamed a morsel in English. I was lying in
a proper bed – these English mattresses are so lumpy – with my
bolster instead of these pillows that Sally donates me. The shutters
at the window were open and Maman was calling me to get up.
'Come, it is breakfast,' she is saying. I smell the coffee – real coffee,
not this nasty little grains – and croissants that dissolve like
butter. And then I wake and find it is me who has to get the
children breakfast. The English bread, he is heavy, and the
marmalade, she is bitter. Now I am obliged to adorn Ellie and
Sam for school. When I was their age, I got my own selves up but
these enfants are spoilt. Sometimes I feel like leaving them in a
residue so they learn a lesson. But then I would be reprimanded.
Maybe if Simon and Sally were not so busy working, they would
understand. It is part of being a good boss, yes? Even if they are
famous. In the interim period, I must endeavour to perform my
optimum. You see how I try?*

'Capital Radio, da-da-dah!' sang Martine. 'It ees a nice tune, no, children?'

Ellie and Sam giggled, nudging each other and rolling all over the leather seats, kicking the back of Martine's.

'Da-da-dah!' imitated Ellie; then convulsed with laughter, the kind that sounded like the snorting sounds Martine sometimes heard from the spare room when Simon had come in from what Sally mysteriously called a 'late night', long after he'd finished at the studios.

'Stop that at once,' said Martine sharply. All this stress was making her desperate for a cigarette but she didn't dare – her employers would smell it in the car like last time. 'When you kick, you hurt my back. In addition, it is rude to laugh. Yes?'

'Wee,' sniggered Ellie.

'Wee-wee,' added Sam, between snorts. 'W-what do you think of my p-p-p-pronunciation, Marty?'

Scratching her head (why was her scalp so itchy?), Martine turned up the radio, determined not to lower herself to their level. She could have sworn that Sam pretended to stutter just to annoy her, and it made it even harder to understand him. The English spoke so fast and the words came out in a different order from her textbooks. Sometimes she felt as though she was the one sane person in this crazy country and that everyone was speaking a mad language that only they understood.

Martine blew her nose, trying to hide the tears that were coming back again. It was so difficult to be an au pair. The agency in France had said the host family would treat her like a member of their own family. If they went out for the day, they would take her too. She would be like a *cousine* but a *cousine* who helped look after the children and drove them to school.

In reality she was no better than a slave. Simon and Sally were friendly when they saw her but they were hardly there! There had been a housekeeper when Martine had arrived but she had left, and now Martine was expected to do the laundry too. She had complained to the agency but they had said it was in her contract to wash and iron children's *vêtements*. And, no, she would not get extra money for this chore – which, her mother had agreed in her last letter (it had smelt so poignantly of Maman's fragrance), was most unfair.

'Traffic building up on the Staines bypass and it's nearly twenty to nine . . .'

'Twenty to nine?' Ellie stopped giggling. 'Sheet, Marty, we're late.'

Again she and Sam collapsed into mirth. For once Martine understood the joke. When she had first arrived, Sally had asked her to put fresh linen on the beds. Afterwards she had announced proudly that she had 'changed the shits'. It wasn't until Sally explained the difference between sheets and something a little less fragrant that she had understood. *Vraiment*, only a language like this could encourage such ridiculous confusion. Even the radio was crazy. Why did it go on about traffic in some place called Staines when she was in Bal Ham?

Then there was the way people drove on the left while the rest of Europe was on the right. She kept having to remind herself about this, although luckily Sally wasn't aware of it. There were several things her employer didn't know about because she spent most of her time on television. At first, Martine had been impressed when the agency had told her she would be working for the famous couple who had their own show at teatime, interviewing celebrities, and ordinary people who had done something unusual, like that girl who had sold her virginity for such a low figure.

'You must watch the children all the time,' the agency had impressed on her. 'Simon and Sally Pargeter are very well known and they are naturally concerned for their children's safety.'

Now when Martine recalled this she couldn't help feeling that if anyone kidnapped those two children they would soon give them back when they discovered how much trouble they were.

'Nearly a quarter to nine now and . . .'

'Hurry up,' interrupted Ellie, tapping Martine's shoulder. 'We're going to be late for Registration.'

'Never molest the driver,' said Martine, horrified. 'I will tell your mother.'

'F-f-fine. G-g-go ahead,' challenged Sam. 'We'll t-t-tell her you're l-lying.'

Martine pulled up at the lights. A mother crossed, pushing a pram, and Martine's heart did a little jump. 'Out. Now.'

Both children stared at her. 'But we're not there yet,' said Ellie.

'I do not care.' Her eyes were still fixed on the mother, who had now reached the other side safely and was bending over her child. 'You can walk.'

'I'm sorry,' said Sam.

See? thought Martine. No stutter.

'Me too,' said Ellie.

A green Saab hooted from behind. Martine scratched her head and drove on. She couldn't leave them, even if she felt like doing so. After all, they were only children. Wicked children but children nevertheless.

'Can you help me with my French homework?' said Ellie, quietly, from the back. 'I've just remembered I should have done it for today.'

'Non. *Tu es un enfant terrible.*'

When she felt like this, it was hopeless trying to speak or think in English.

'Martine, I said I was sorry. I just want to know if you can help with my homework.'

'*Trop tard*.'

Sam glowered. 'I'll ring ChildLine. I know the number.'

'We'll do nipple cripples again,' hissed Ellie.

Martine winced. She knew what that involved: it was a ritual among English children to twist each other's chests, which had them screaming with pain and hysterical laughter in the back of the car. She had complained about this to Sally, who had said it was part of a 'natural exploration of their inner selves'. Martine knew the phrase word for word because she had copied it into her diary for use in class if the occasion arose.

'I do not care,' said Martine, unhappily. 'You are so cruel to me.'

'You're cruel to *us*,' said Ellie, indignantly, getting out.

'I'm ringing ChildLine right now on my mobile,' announced Sam. 'You'll be sorry when Dad finds out.'

'No shit, Sherlock,' added Ellie, sniggering.

Martine held back the tears until they had slammed the door. How much more of this could she take? Thank goodness it was Monday – one of her college days. It would take her mind off her misery and, with any luck, *he* would ring before she got to her class.

It made Martine feel better when she thought about the man with whom she had fallen in love. He was married but her own father had been married when he'd met her mother. Besides, their meeting had been down to Fate, she was certain. Sam had had a friend over to play one day and the father had arrived to pick him up. Martine had opened the door and invited him in. Never before had she been able to talk to a man *and* feel aroused by him.

When he rang the following day, she wasn't surprised. Not even when he told her that he didn't normally 'do this sort of thing'. So English, thought Martine, fondly. And although she insisted she didn't want to be responsible for breaking up his family, he announced one night that he and his wife were having a trial separation. 'I need to go away on business,' he had said, 'but when I'm back on the twelfth, I'll come for you.'

The twelfth! Friday! Just five days away! Martine felt warm inside. Her life was going to change. And she couldn't wait. If only her head didn't itch so much . . .

In the meantime she had to get some petrol. The black arrow on the dial showed the tank was nearly empty. Martine tried to remember what kind of petrol Simon had told her to get. In France it was green because that was better for the atmosphere, but was it the same in England? Indicating right, she turned left into the big garage on the corner and jumped as the car behind her hooted.

Martine crunched to a halt and examined the petrol pump. Red or green? What about black? Desperately she looked towards the shop, but the cashier's face was turned towards the customers who were paying.

'Get a move on, love,' yelled a youth from a car in the long queue behind.

'Which pump do I require?' called Martine.

'The one on the right, I should think, love.'

Right? Was that *droite* or *gauche*? She'd always had a blockage about that. Green or black?

'Come *on*, love!'

Maman! Martine yanked out the nozzle and plunged it in.

5

'This is Capital Radio and it's nearly seven a.m. on a lovely bright summer morning. I'm Sarah Smith and . . .'

Sod Capital Radio. Sod lovely summer days. And Sod Sarah Smith. Sod everything for being so bloody normal. I can't remember the last time I swore. 'Be positive,' said Derek, prodding me reluctantly with his short, stubby fingers. That's him to a T. Never panics unless it happens. Never panics unless he really cares about something. Like fishing or when the computer crashes or when Man U are down. But it's not him who's got something wrong. Fine. So I'll see the doctor and then we'll know whether to worry. I'll have to ring up for an appointment, which I won't get because it's Monday and everyone will have been ill over the weekend and got in before me. And if I do get an appointment, I'll have to ask Harriet to do the school run even though it's my turn. Even if I don't, I don't feel up to doing the run – I just want to go back to bed and wake up again without this horrible wave of panic that's stopping me thinking clearly. God, I'm scared. My mouth's gone dry and I don't feel hungry. I just want a cup of sweet tea. And yes, Derek, I *would* like sugar today.

'This is the news at eight a.m. The American schoolboy who is . . .'

'Lucy!' yelled Pippa, standing at the bottom of the stairs. 'Breakfast! You're going to be late for Harriet. Canyouhearme? Orhavelgottocomeupthestairstogetyou?'

No, *not* the phone. Who in their right mind could ring during the peak pre-school-run panic? 'Yes?' snapped Pippa into the receiver.

'It's me,' said Lucy, coolly. 'Just to say I'm coming down in a minute.'

'Are you ringing me on your mobile?' Pippa was incandescent with fury. 'Do you know how much it's costing? Come down here this instant.'

Reluctantly Lucy mooched downstairs, walking with exaggerated slowness, her school tie hanging loosely round her neck.

'Give me your phone. Now.'

Lucy glowered. 'Why?'

Pippa snatched it from her. 'Because it's for emergencies, like when I lose you in TopShop, not for ringing me in the house because you can't be bothered to answer or come downstairs.'

'If you don't give me my mobile back, I won't be able to call if I'm abducted from school,' said Lucy smoothly.

'Too bad. If you behave – *if*, mind – you can have it back at the end of the week. Now, hurry up and eat your breakfast. Harriet's going to be here in a minute.'

'I don't want to go with Harriet,' said Beth, looking up from the kitchen table where she was taking a last look at her spellings for today's test. 'Bruce is always trying to pinch me.'

'You encourage him because you fancy him,' said Lucy, triumphantly.

'Do not!'

'Do.'

'Be quiet, both of you!' Pippa's head was ringing. She didn't need this, not on top of *that* – and she'd just remembered she

41

had a deadline for Thursday. Her editor, Jean, had already extended it by a week and she didn't dare ask for longer. 'Just eat your breakfast and go to school so I can have some peace.'

'That's not very nice, Mum,' said Beth, reproachfully.

'I know. But neither are you two,' snapped Pippa. 'And look at this mess. I'm just an unpaid servant.'

'That's what mums do.'

'Well, not this one, not any more. From now on, service *isn't* going to be included!'

'Thanks.'

'And don't be cheeky, young lady. In our day, we didn't talk like that to our parents.'

'But this isn't your day any more, is it, Mum?'

'Stop right there. Harriet's outside. Get a move on, both of you. Don't you want to kiss me goodbye?'

They gave her a token peck and she watched them amble down the path. She waved to Harriet from the door, then closed it behind her. She sat at the kitchen table, still in the tartan pyjamas the girls had given her (via Derek) for Christmas, and tried to think clearly. It was eight o'clock and she couldn't remember the last time she had felt incapable of dressing herself – even during her pregnancies when lots of other mothers allowed themselves to relax. She had always been a get-up-and-doer.

Eight o'clock. The surgery might be open now. Trembling, she dialled the number. Engaged. She waited another minute. Still engaged. Damn it. She'd do ringback. Seconds later, it called.

'An appointment this morning?' The receptionist sounded amused. 'I'm afraid not, Mrs Hallet. We're very busy after the weekend and the last appointment has just gone. I can squeeze you in tomorrow if it's urgent.'

'It is,' said Pippa, grimly.

She wrote down the time, then went back to the table, cupping her cold hands round her mug of coffee, breathing in the aroma to calm herself. No, it was no good. She couldn't banish the nauseating fear that was taking over her mind. She reached for the phone and punched in Harriet's number. She'd get the message when she returned from school. 'It's me. I can't get a doctor's appointment until tomorrow and I wondered if you wanted to come over for coffee after the run.'

Pippa shivered. Harriet would put this mess into the context it deserved, although with Charlie coming back this week, Pippa should be helping Harriet. Maybe she shouldn't mention her own problem until she'd seen the doctor. She was always worrying about things that turned out to be nothing. Still, Harriet was her best friend, if you didn't count Gus: if she couldn't tell her, she couldn't tell anyone.

Sometimes Pippa wondered how she would cope without Harriet although, ironically, their worlds were so different that if it hadn't been for motherhood – one of life's biggest introductory agencies – they might never have met. On the surface they were so different. Harriet was a home-lover; her children were her life. Pippa, too, adored her children but her work as a translator was important as well. She had turned freelance when Beth was born because she hadn't wanted to be one of those working mothers who never saw their kids. She had built up a reputation as a reliable and accurate translator for publishers of cookery books and, more recently, school texts. The deadlines were tough, especially when the girls were at home in the holidays, but Pippa loved the escape that her work provided from the mundane routine of home life.

Yet she had a lot in common with Harriet. Neither had grown up in a conventional family: Harriet's father had left when she was a teenager, but Pippa's parents had been killed in a train crash and she had been brought up by a kindly uncle and aunt. She had been aware that she was different, the only child in her class not to have parents. Although no one had bullied her, she'd been terrified that girls who made friends with her only did so out of pity. She didn't want that

– she just wanted to be like everyone else, but it was difficult when you were constantly scared that something was going to go wrong again. As a teenager, she had been worried perpetually, about boyfriends, exams and getting into university (which she did, quite effortlessly).

It had been Harriet's determinedly positive outlook on life that had drawn Pippa to her when they'd met at the school gates nearly . . . what was it now? Heavens, seven years ago? Lucy was starting school and so was Harriet's Jess. Amazing to think they were now in their first year at big school! But it had been Bruce whom Pippa had first spotted when they were waiting in their parked cars for the gates to open, while she tried to reassure Lucy that school would be just as much fun – more, even – as being at home with Mummy.

'Look at that boy!' Lucy had said, wide-eyed with admiration as she pointed to the child clambering out of the back window of the car in front. He was too big to behave like that, observed Pippa, and as she watched, he turned, grinned and ran off down the street clutching something. The slim blonde woman in the driver's seat hopped out and raced after him, and Pippa remembered being impressed by her speed. Moments later they had returned, the woman talking calmly to the boy with a firm hand on his shoulder. As they passed Pippa's car, she gave a kids-will-be-kids smile. 'Naughty boy ran off with his sister's teddy. Honestly, one of these days, he's going to outrun me.' Her eyes travelled to the back of the car where Lucy was still sitting in her crisp, newly labelled school uniform. 'First day for you, is it? It's my daughter's too. Come and say hello. She's called Jess and she can't wait to join her big brother. School's brilliant, you know!'

It had been the beginning of a firm friendship. Harriet, who lived a few streets away in one of the more up-and-coming roads in the area, frequently pressed Pippa into leaving that 'wretched computer of yours' and joining her for a salad at lunchtime. The salad invariably turned into a glass of Chablis with mushroom quiche and the kind of womanly chat that Pippa hadn't had for a long time: the demands of her work had prevented her socialising with other local mums.

Occasionally they met each other's husbands either during the school run, if one of the men had a rare day at home, or over a casual supper. But by unspoken mutual agreement, both women preferred to meet without their husbands. Pippa had never warmed to Charlie, who had always seemed distant – with her and even his children. Unlike his wife, he was tersely impatient when Bruce misbehaved. 'Bruce, don't do that,' he had snapped one afternoon, when his son tore past him through the front door after Pippa had brought him home from school. 'Say thank you for the lift. Where are your manners?'

'It's all right,' Pippa had said. But she could see from his face (noble aquiline nose and bushy black eyebrows with the odd grey hair) that it wasn't. It was little things like this – and other incidents to which Harriet alluded casually – that had stopped her being totally surprised when Harriet had told her about the text message and Charlie's two-month stint in Dubai, which seemed highly convenient for him, if not for his wife. At times, she thought secretly that her friend would be better off without her handsome husband, who seemed so much more interested in his banking career than his family. But it was hard to cope without a husband nowadays, even given the high number of women who did. Derek might not be able to show his feelings as much as she'd like but at least he was there for her and the children. Life without him was unthinkable. But how would he manage if anything happened to her?

Pippa stood up, willing herself to stop. It wouldn't help to go down this road. Besides, she had to tidy up the chaos around her before Harriet got here. With a supreme effort (why was she constantly tired?), she began to clear away the mess that the girls had left in their wake. Harriet was always telling Pippa how well behaved they were in the car, and sometimes Pippa wondered if she was talking about the same children. Why was it that your own kids were always so much nicer when they were with other people?

Yet now they were gone she felt guilty at her lack of patience that morning. If she *was* ill, would they remember her as a mother who was always snapping and trying to meet deadlines?

As she ran upstairs to get dressed, she vowed she would be nicer to everyone – providing she had the chance. Quickly, she slipped into a pair of jeans and a T-shirt, then fastened on Gus's silver necklace. She had worn it all the time since he had given it to her on her twenty-first birthday at university. Sometimes Derek bought her (cheaper) necklaces and occasionally she wondered if he was testing to see if she would swap loyalties. But she couldn't do that, and if it annoyed him he never showed it.

'Hi! Anyone at home?'

Pippa dusted her face with powder, ran a brush through her hair (once blondish, now light brown) and flew downstairs. Harriet had wandered in, as she usually did in the summer, through the conservatory that was joined on to the kitchen. The sitting room was on the next floor where, in theory, Pippa and Derek could have some peace. In practice, there was never time for that.

Harriet was in the kitchen, leaning against the range. Pippa gave her a hug. 'You got my message?'

'What message?'

'I asked you round for coffee.'

'Actually, no. I thought I'd just pop in to see how you were. Better not be catching or we'll have a great start to the summer.'

Pippa tried to smile. 'I don't think it is. It's just a . . . well, a kind of funny feeling.' She stopped, wondering whether to go on. 'To be honest, Harriet, I . . . Oh, don't cry, Harry. It'll be all right.' Shocked, she led her friend to the checked sofa (a *Good Housekeeping* offer) next to the french windows and put her arm round her while Harriet sobbed into her shoulder.

'I'm sorry, Pippa, but I'm so scared. I don't know what Charlie's going to say when he comes back and I'm frightened. Suppose he wants us to split up? Suppose he *is* having an affair?'

Pippa tightened her grip. 'Then you'll have to be brave. It happens, sometimes, but you'll get through it and I'll help you.'

Harriet raised her tearstained face.

She was so pretty, thought Pippa. That bastard didn't deserve her.

'So you *do* think he's having an affair?'

'I didn't say that,' said Pippa, carefully. 'I just think you have to face the facts. Some woman sent him a text. He's been away for two months.'

'But he wanted time to think,' said Harriet. 'I can understand that.'

She doesn't want me to point out the obvious, thought Pippa. And she certainly couldn't burden Harriet with her own problem now. She stood up. 'How about that coffee? Look, I've even got some yummy *pains au chocolat* from the new bakery. Fancy one?'

'No, thanks.' Harriet looked as though she might be sick. 'I can't eat much at the moment. I never can when I'm all churned up. But I'd love a cup of tea – with sugar.'

'You never take sugar,' said Pippa.

'I need the sweetness.'

'I'm the same but I eat too. It's why we're different shapes.' Pippa looked down ruefully at her comfortable size-fourteen figure and across at Harriet's size ten. Harriet smiled through her tears. 'That's better,' said Pippa. 'Damn! That's my mobile.'

'You've changed the ring tone.'

'No, Lucy did. She also spent ten pounds on downloading a new one for herself.'

'She didn't!'

'Unfortunately, yes. I only found out yesterday and I went mad. Derek said it showed initiative. There, it's started again. I'd better get it. Here, have a look at the paper. I won't be a minute.'

Pippa ran upstairs with the mobile in her hand. She waited until she had reached the sitting room before she answered. She knew who it was, of course, from the screen.

'Hi, Gorgeous, how's it going?'

Pippa relaxed. Only Gus could make her feel truly at ease with herself. It wasn't just the way he always called her Gorgeous, even though she knew perfectly well she wasn't. It was that he had known her longer than Derek and, more importantly, he understood. He never told her to stop worrying like Derek did. He just accepted that that was the way she was.

'Not too brilliant.' Her voice cracked.

Instantly his voice was filled with concern. 'Why?'

She gave him a brief run-down. Funny, she didn't even feel embarrassed about the physical bit – not as embarrassed as she'd felt with her husband that morning. But she'd always been able to do that with Gus – and he with her – could come straight out with an intimate subject that most married women couldn't discuss with anyone other than their husbands. For his part, Gus told her details about his relationships with other women, which flattered her and – if she was honest – made her wonder what it would be like to be in their place.

'Really? What does the doctor say?'

'I can't get an appointment until tomorrow.'

'Well, for God's sake, go to a specialist not just some ordinary GP.'

'Mine's very good.'

'You do have health insurance, don't you?'

Pippa swallowed. Derek didn't believe in that kind of thing and, besides, money was always tight. There never seemed to be enough with two children and the supermarket bill and the council tax and all the other outgoings. Derek was also what her aunt called a 'careful' man. Some people, Gus included, translated that as mean.

'No. But my GP *is* good. Really. Don't worry.'

'Well, I will. Of course I will. You've got to ring me as soon as you come out of that place. Promise? Is Derek with you?'

'No. He had to go to work.'

'I see.' Gus's disapproval was almost tangible.

'But I've got a friend here.'

'I hope it's a woman. I don't want any competition.'

Pippa felt better. Gus and she always flirted like this but each knew it couldn't mean anything.

'Well, I'll be waiting for your call tomorrow,' he said. 'You can get me on the mobile.'

'Must go now. Harry's waiting.'

'I thought you said it was a woman.'

'It is. Harriet. You know. Talk tomorrow.'

'Can't wait.'

Pippa ran down the stairs, aware she'd left Harriet longer than she'd meant to. Her friend looked up from the paper. 'You really don't look well, you know. You're awfully flushed.'

Pippa turned her back to put on the kettle and hide the glow on her face that she always felt after speaking to Gus. He made her feel so good about herself; desirable – in a way that Derek never did. 'I'm fine,' she said evenly. 'Now, let's have that tea, shall we? I'm desperate.'

6

KITTY

'This is Capital Radio and . . .'

Let's see. First lesson with year nine. Great – that's Bruce, God help me. Must remember to maintain eye-contact when giving instructions – vital for hyperactive kids – and make sure he's not by the window again (too much distraction). Then science with Mrs Griffiths's class if she's still ill. Note: get Leonora and Natalie to wear labels indicating which is which. After the coffee break it's year ten. Oh, no, that means Kieran . . . Lunchbreak duty, followed by – if I survive – *Othello* with year thirteen. Note Two: take black trousers to change into after school for Big Date. Who am I kidding? Mark (that *was* his name, wasn't it?) really isn't my type – far too loud and flash. It's not that I'm being picky. It's more that I've seen too many Mr and Mrs Wrongs. School is full of them, and I'm talking parents *and* teachers. All I want is Mr Right. Someone who comes up to scratch in my marking book. Someone's who's ten out of ten and not seven or eight. Like Mandy says, I could do better. If I really tried.

'It's coming up to eight fifteen. The American schoolboy in Ohio, who has taken his classmates hostage, is thought to possess a gun.'

As the sound faded in and out, Kitty adjusted her headphones at the bus stop. There was something wrong with them, which was irritating as she enjoyed listening to the radio – even when there were scary incidents like the one concerning the gun-happy American kid. It passed the time when she was waiting for the bus and provided diplomatic immunity from the kids, who were fascinated by teachers outside school. It was as though her appearance beyond the classroom gave them *carte blanche* to tease her, like an animal in the zoo.

'Can I borrow your headphones, Miss?'

'I've got a pair just like those at home. My mum got them from LowPrice. Crap, aren't they?'

'Stop sucking up to the teacher, Kieran.'

Kitty pretended she couldn't hear them and tried to look as though she was concentrating on the road, which was packed with cars, vans and lorries but no buses.

Blast. It was late, which meant that unless the bus developed turbo wings, Kitty was going to be late for school. She'd been waiting for ages and although she normally liked to think of herself as a reasonably patient person, the kids were getting on her nerves.

'That's my teacher.'

'Fit, isn't she?'

'Got any biology for us, Miss?'

Kitty got out her mobile and pretended to study it for messages. The kids who were trying to get her attention were from St Theresa's, her school. St Theresa's was good teaching experience, but it came at a price. When Kitty had dreamed of being a teacher at her own quiet, home-counties school, she hadn't realised she'd need to develop such a thick skin. Some of these London kids were impossible and the teachers weren't much better. One was having an affair with the married mother of a child in year nine and another had been married to the head of science until he went off with a teacher from the primary school. The staffroom was a hotbed of sex, weak coffee and educational magazines they were all meant to be reading in preparation for the Ofsted visit later this week.

In fact, everyone had someone, except her.

'Here's the bus!'

''Bout time.'

'Got your biology book ready, Miss? We're doing reproduction today, remember? Mrs Griffiths is still ill, you know. So you'll be taking us, won't you?'

Looking straight ahead, she attempted to climb on board in a dignified manner, even though sharp elbows on either side were digging into her in the rush to get on.

'One at a time,' said the driver, loudly, raising his eyebrows at Kitty. She acknowledged him with a smile. It was always the same man. He had a rather nice smile and open face (a bit like Jonny Wilkinson's). And she couldn't help noticing that he always wore a crisp polo shirt, open at the neck, instead of uniform. Maybe that *was* uniform nowadays, or perhaps in this heat they were allowed to leave off their jackets. He spoke differently from the other bus drivers too. Kitty knew it was snobbish of her (and she wasn't usually a snob) to notice this, but still . . .

'Morning!' He barely glanced at her pass.

'Hi.' She gave him a quizzical look. 'You're late today.'

He ran his hands through his hair – short, but not too short. 'Tell me about it. This traffic drives you mad.' He glanced at the kids behind her. 'It's your lot that cause the trouble. All these cars taking everyone to school.'

How did he know they were 'her' lot? Did he think she was a mum or was it obvious that she was staff? Kitty didn't like to think she was such clear teacher material: it made her feel dull. 'I know. When I was at school we walked or got the bus.'

'Or you were packed off to board like me.'

'Really? How awful.'

'I had a great time, actually.' He raised his voice: 'Stop pushing, you lot out there, or I might not let you on.'

Embarrassed to be holding up the queue, Kitty moved down

without saying any more. Pity she was too late for a seat. Standing in the gangway, she cast meaningful looks at the kids, some of whom were in her classes. If they'd been brought up properly, they would have leaped up and offered her theirs. But no. Instead they seemed content to sit and chat.

'Fancy him, do you, Miss?' asked one boy, who was chewing gum without any idea of how to keep his mouth shut. 'Want me to give him your number?'

Ignore him.

She turned up the volume on her radio and moved down the aisle. Fantastic! There was a space at the back that she hadn't seen until now. She sat down gratefully, legs aching after standing in the queue for so long. It was good to put her bag down too – it was heavy after all that marking last night.

'Now for the rest of the news. A new survey shows that nearly eighty per cent of secondary-school children and almost forty per cent of primary-school children have been offered drugs at some point during their school career.'

Too loud. These headphones were a disaster. Kitty took them off and stuffed them into her bag, then wrote down the statistics she'd just heard on the back of her hand.

As an English project, she was currently doing drugs with year nine (no pun intended, as she'd told the class at the start of the lesson, to win their concentration) and the figures might come in useful. In some ways, she wasn't surprised by them. There were so many dangers now, like drugs and misuse of the Internet, that it was a wonder any of these kids grew up into normal human beings. It couldn't be easy for their parents either, although judging by some of those she taught, many weren't as tough as they should have been. When it was her turn (if?), she'd be different.

A boy in front hung over the back of his seat so that his cheeky freckled face was almost in hers. 'What we got for English, then, today, Miss?'

Eye-contact. Treat them as you would want them to treat you.

'You'll find out soon enough, Kieran.'

Kitty looked suspiciously at the big bruise on his forehead. Had someone hurt him? She'd been told at college to look out for signs of domestic violence. 'What have you done to your head?'

'Squash ball, Miss. My brother did it. You cut one in half and hold it against your head and it makes a mark. Cool, isn't it? Like a lovebite! Look, we've all got one. It's a craze. I could do one on you if you like, Miss.'

Serve you right, Kitty Hayling, for being so inquisitive, she told herself, trying not to smile. 'Well, I hope for your sake that it wears off. Now, why don't you get on with the homework that's on your knee?'

'Ooh, she's looking at your knees, Kieran. Maybe she fancies you.'

Sod it.

'Shut up, all of you. We're not at school yet so I'm not your teacher until the bus stops.'

'Losing your temper, are you, Miss? Can't do that or we'll ring ChildLine.'

'Listen, they've heard and they're ringing *you*, Miss. Isn't that your phone?'

Mandy always called at this time, mainly because she'd been up since four a.m. with Tom, Kitty's new soon-to-be godson.

'Hi, Mandy.'

'You don't sound very happy.'

'It's difficult to talk.'

'Don't worry, Miss. We won't listen. You just go ahead.'

'What's that noise, for heaven's sake?'

'I'm on the bus.'

'And the rabble is all around you?'

'Something like that.'

Mandy laughed. 'Remember what it was like when we were at school. You used to fancy the driver—'

'I did *not*.'

'Don't go getting amnesia on me, Kitty. Talking of which, how's the man front?'

'Er, OK.'

'Don't forget Alex is coming on Sunday with Cheryl.'

Kitty sighed. How could she forget? Quite why she should mind that her ex-boyfriend from her early twenties (nearly ten years ago, for heaven's sake) was coming to the christening because he was a good friend of Rod, Mandy's husband, she didn't know. She was over him, Kitty told herself sternly. But even so it would have been nice to have had someone to bring too so Alex didn't think, Poor Kitty, still no man, like everyone else.

'Are you seeing anyone at the moment?' asked Mandy, point-edly.

Kitty tried to talk quietly into the phone. 'Tonight. Maybe.'

'Ooh, what's happening tonight, Miss?'

'Can we come too?'

'They sound awful,' said Mandy, happily. 'Worse than we were.'

'They are, believe me.'

'The trouble with you is that you're too picky.'

Kitty sighed. They'd been through this so many times that it wasn't worth arguing, especially with a busload of kids breathing down her neck. 'I'm not.'

'Yes, you are. If you really tried, you could find yourself someone nice. Why don't you bring this date from tonight to the christening?'

'No, to the second question, and as far as the first allegation goes, I *have* tried.'

'Tried what, Miss? Pot? It's legal now, you know.'

'No, it's not.' Kitty put down the phone for a minute. 'The government has relaxed the penalties but it's still against the law.'

'What does that mean, Miss?'

'Mandy, I can't talk now – it's hopeless.'

'I knew you'd say that. Good luck for tonight and don't forget he's welcome on Sunday if he measures up to your strict standards. But if he doesn't, don't worry. It will be lovely to see you, and Rod says the same.'

Rod, Mandy's husband, was not only perfect for her but he was also rolling in money *and* nice. They'd met at university when Kitty, who was at a different one, was still wondering why none of the men she met matched up to the ones that Mandy so effortlessly found. Then, when Kitty had been visiting Mandy, Rod had introduced her to his friend Alex. For six months she had been madly in love until he had left for his third year in France. Stupidly, she had thought they could make it last but somehow it had fizzled out – on his side anyway. He hadn't met anyone else, he assured her, he just felt they were too young to be tied down. Through Mandy, she now knew that, after ten years of playing the field, Alex was well and truly tied down with a fiancée whom he was marrying next year. It was Kitty who was still footloose and fancy-free.

After she had made the final arrangements for Sunday Kitty put down the phone thoughtfully. It would be so much better to go to the christening with a date instead of being on her own and getting landed with all the ancient uncles and aunts. But she could hardly find herself a date in a week – not for something like a christening, which was for couples who were firmly embedded, all puns intended. 'A week,' she muttered to herself. 'Could I do it in a week?'

'What could you do in a week, Miss?'

Cripes, she must be getting really ancient if she'd started talking to herself. 'Mark all your homework,' she said quickly. 'You have finished it, haven't you?'

That did it! A sea of guilty faces looked away.

'Well,' said Kitty crisply, 'you'd better get on with it fast, on the bus – just like we used to.'

She grinned at them and they all grinned back. That was the great thing about kids. They helped you keep your sense of humour.

'Hey, Miss, is that your phone again?'

'Kitty, it's me! Just had a thought – don't know why it didn't occur to me before. Actually, I do. Tom's knocked the brain cells out of me, bless him. Anyway, what was I saying? Oh, yes. Rod's got a friend called Duncan who's just moved into a flat near you. He's really dishy, works in finance and isn't married. Shall I give him your number?'

'No, thanks!' Kitty could have screamed with exasperation. 'Stop trying to match-make, Mandy. It makes me feel so inadequate. Sometimes I think all that breastfeeding has made you go ga-ga.'

'Breastfeeding, Miss? Are you pregnant?'

'Look, I've got to go. This lot need their facts of life sorting out – breastfeeding comes *after* pregnancy, Kieran – and I've got a job to do.'

'And I haven't?'

Mandy sounded tearful. Perhaps that's why she was being so pushy: all those hormones playing up. 'You've got the most important job in the world, Mandy. Now, give Tom a big kiss from me and I'll see you on Sunday.'

'With the boyfriend. I bet you a weekend at Champneys that you could find one.'

'Now I know you're mad. Who can afford Champneys?'

'Rod – he'll treat us, but you've got to accept the bet first.'

Kitty shook her head. Maybe Mandy had post-natal depression – she was so up and down. 'OK, if it makes you happy. Now I must dash. I should have been at school ages ago.'

As she spoke, Kitty was already walking down the bus, so she could be first off. As soon as the doors swung open, she

flew down the stairs and wove her way through the parents
and children parked at the kerb. If she was lucky, she'd get
to the staffroom just in time for the morning meeting.

'Morning, Kitty!'

'Morning, Frank.'

It still seemed inappropriate to call the deputy headmaster
by his first name. It hadn't been that long since Kitty had
been at school when teachers weren't human enough to have
first names. It was the same with the staffroom, which stank
of BO and weak coffee. In her day (and still today, thank
goodness), this hallowed room had been out of bounds to
the pupils but she could remember giggling outside with her
friends, imagining the mysteries within. Even now, she had
this crazy feeling that she wasn't entitled to be in the
staffroom. Now she looked around it and wondered if all
staffrooms were the same. This one was disappointing, con-
sidering the mystique it doubtless held for the children outside. It was a smallish room with metal-framed chairs around
the walls and a couple of sofas that had seen better days.
Kitty never sat on them because if she did, she found herself squashed up to other teachers whom she didn't really
know. She would have headed for one of the three armchairs
but they had always been taken by wiser staff members who
came in early to beat the crush. Usually she stood by the
coffee machine and nibbled one of the plain biscuits that
were provided.

'Catching up on breakfast?'

Kitty nodded guiltily. ''Fraid so, Frank.'

He shook his head disapprovingly. 'My wife always makes
me start the day with a good bowl of bran flakes. Gives you
energy and, believe me, you need plenty with that lot outside.'
His eyes swept over her and Kitty wished she'd worn a longer
skirt. 'Still, I expect you're learning about that, aren't you?
How's your first year been with us?'

Hastily, Kitty swallowed her mouthful. 'I've enjoyed it,

thanks, Mr . . . Frank.' Oh, God, should she have said that? Were teachers meant to enjoy their job?

'Glad to hear it. You seem to be settling down all right with the children – at least, we haven't had any bad reports about you.'

Kitty wasn't sure if that was a joke or not. 'Good,' she said hesitantly, and sipped her coffee. 'Actually, Frank, there was something I wanted to ask you about. I'm doing a project with my year-nines on drugs and I've been quite worried by some of the things they don't know about. They don't realise, for example, that cannabis is illegal. I don't know if you're aware but a recent report says nearly forty per cent of primary-school children have been offered drugs in the playground and nearly eighty per cent in secondary schools.'

Frank raised his eyebrows. 'Really? That's interesting.'

'I thought we could have some outside speakers in to give a talk,' she went on.

'Maybe next spring: we need some speakers then, although more for careers talks, really. Our timetable is already full for next term and I don't need to remind you that we're in our last week, thank the good Lord. Going anywhere nice for the summer?'

'I'm not sure. But, Frank, don't you think it's important to get a speaker in fast? I mean, drugs are a big issue and the sooner we can get the message across to the younger ones, the less likely they are to continue the habits of their older siblings.'

'Kitty, dear.' Frank patted her shoulder. 'I admire your enthusiasm and I hope it will last, but there are enough posters around the school for the kids to get the message, and we have to hope that their parents do their bit in this direction. At the moment, to be honest, we're all far more worried about the Ofsted visit. It was meant to have been last month but the inspector was ill and now, heaven help us, it's on Thursday. The last week of term! Couldn't be worse. Are you ready?'

'Well, I've prepared my lessons for this week, as usual.'

'I'm sure you have. But would you know what to do if the little devils in your class ask awkward questions, which they love to do whenever we have visitors – especially official ones?'

'What kind of questions?'

'Dear me, Kitty! Embarrassing questions designed to make young teachers like you feel inadequate. Just be on your guard, that's all. We didn't get a very good Ofsted report last time and we need to improve. Otherwise we might be in trouble. All right?'

7

NICK

'Now we're moving on to our doc spot where our very own Dr Jim offers alternative health advice.'

'Change channels, Nick, darling,' said a girl who was walking past him in just a pair of pants. 'That station's really boring – my granny listens to it.'

Good for her, thought Nick, looking the other way as he adjusted the lighting in the studio. In some ways, it had been fortuitous that Amber had postponed today's session until tomorrow. She'd sounded a bit put out when he'd said he couldn't do tomorrow. Tough. Besides, today's cancellation had given him longer to walk Mutley and prepare for the shoot.

'No, love,' he called. 'Can you stand where I first put you? Over there. That's right. Tilt your chin to the right – a bit more. Lovely. Now I want you to close your eyes and open them, thinking of something you'd *really* like to do.'

The other girls, waiting at the side in their dressing-gowns, tittered, unlike the model in front of the camera: she looked as though she'd rather be naked than wearing the tarty pink bra and pants set that Nick's assistant had had to cajole her into. 'They're hideous,' she said. 'Can't I wear something else?'

'Sorry, love. This is the kit,' Nick had said. 'But your amazing looks are going to make everyone want to buy them.'

He hoped it was true. As a fashion photographer, it was his job to make everything look so tempting that the readers

(who were as diverse as the magazines and advertising cata-
logues that he worked for) instantly lusted for them.
Advertising paid best, but the clothes were usually awful. He
preferred magazine shoots because they were more prestigious
and used more interesting merchandise. The only one he didn't
like working for was *Just For You*, which had a ghastly deputy
editor who insisted on going to every shoot and picking holes
in everything.

Still, when Julie went to university, he'd need to do more
advertising if only to pay her fees and accommodation.
University! Nick's heart always sank at the prospect of his
little girl going away but he knew it was the right thing for
her – and that Juliana would have wanted it. She'd have been
so proud of their daughter, who had turned out to be quite
a linguist. She would also, thought Nick, wryly, have been
able to help him steer Julie through her penultimate year at
school. The A-level system was so complex nowadays: you
could take and retake modules to get a better grade rather
than having to perform well in one batch of exams at the end
of the sixth form. Julie had already retaken one of her French
papers although the results wouldn't be published until August.

Pity, thought Nick, that he couldn't retake Life. He'd have
done it all so differently. 'Great.' He was studying the Polaroid
with his assistant. 'Lovely, love.'

Nick always called his models 'love'. It saved him having
to remember their names and, because he used it with all of
them, it stopped them getting crushes on him. When Juliana
had died, Nick couldn't imagine ever again being close to
anyone but, as the months went by, he could almost hear
Juliana telling him to go ahead. 'I don't want you to be lonely,'
she would croon into his ear. But it might just be his own
voice, reminding him that he couldn't remain a monk for ever,
whatever Julie thought.

'Right, love, just tilt your chin back to its original position.
Lovely. Over there. Look at the dog – behind me. Fantastic.

Open your mouth as though you're going to talk to him. Great. No, Mutley – *no!*'

Nick broke off to restrain his dog, who had decided to join the model.

'He's so sweet,' she said, kneeling down to stroke him.

'He's OK when he's doing what he's meant to,' said Nick. 'Back, Mutley. Sit, stay. Can you tilt your chin, love, and push your hips in the other direction? Talk if you want. What's your name again?'

'Juliana.'

Nick's hand wobbled.

'Sorry?'

The model pouted. 'Sofia.'

He felt his hands sweat on the camera as he took some more shots. God, he must be going mad if he was hearing things like that. Perhaps he ought to see Amber tomorrow after all. 'Right, love, just keep talking. What's your favourite animal?' He carried on, asking the inane questions that would achieve his original purpose of getting her to look as he wanted. Even so, it took a good four hours to wrap it all up, by which time the girls were complaining of hunger and he was pretty knackered himself.

'Fancy a late lunchtime drink?' asked one of the girls, as she brushed past him, flashing smooth brown skin under her dressing-gown.

Nick poured water into Mutley's bowl. 'No, thanks. I've got to do the school run.'

'The school run?' squealed one of the others. 'How old are your kids?'

'I've got just the one. She's seventeen and, actually, she drives *me*.'

'So cute,' said a tall blonde girl, who was bending down to stroke Mutley. 'Does she drive your wife too? I used to practise with my mum.'

Nick looked away. 'My wife is . . . She isn't exactly here any more.'

A flash of pity crossed the blonde's face. 'I'm sorry.'

'Thank you,' said Nick, quietly. He waited until they had all left, then got out his mobile. Four missed calls but none from Julie. He always checked in case she needed him. Then he punched in the number of the centre. 'Can I leave a message for Amber? It's Nick. No, just Nick. She rearranged my session from today to tomorrow but I said I couldn't make it. If it's not too late I'd like to come after all. Is that all right?'

BETTY

'Towards Kingston temporary traffic-lights are causing more problems. Dangerous Dan has just rung in about an accident outside Harrow. Betty from Balham has also called to warn drivers of the new speed bumps along the high street.'

Funny to hear my own name on the radio again – fourth time in a month. 'Betty of Balham' has a certain ring. 'Dangerous Dan' shows people don't care any more. You can see that from my window – hardly anyone's bothering with the thirty m.p.h. limit. Cars packed with mums and dads and kids, all trying to get to school or work on time. Don't care who they hurt to get there.

My flowers on the lamp-post look nice. Roses, this week. They smell absolutely heavenly.

Terry used to buy me flowers. 'Here you are, Mum,' he'd say, when he came back on Saturday evenings after his little job at Tesco. 'Got these for you.'

Then he'd give me a hug before he went out. Tall boy, Terry. Always did look older than he was. Still does. I'm the one who's aged.

The new house helps, even though everyone thought I was mad. 'What do you want to do that for?' asked my sister. 'Fancy moving to—'

'Don't say it,' I said sharply. 'I don't want you saying it.'

There are days when I can talk about what happened and days when I can't.

Terry and I, we listen to the radio while I cook breakfast. Great one for general knowledge is my Terry, like his father. Always talking about the Tories and the greenhouse effect and that kind of stuff.

Not all kids get a cooked breakfast. Bet that poor kid in the car this morning doesn't. How could his mother have left him? Sitting duck, he was. Did you read about the lorry that went into the Mini with a four-year-old in it at a petrol station? Killed the kid outright. I've got the newspaper write-up here, propped up against the cereal box. I eat corn flakes every morning, like Terry. I still keep the plastic figures they give away and put them in his room, lined up on the windowsill. Just like when he was little.

I was tempted. It would have been lovely to take that kid home and make him a nice boiled egg with soldiers. Just for ten minutes. But I didn't, did I? I took him to that nice-looking man and asked if he knew who the child belonged to. After I got home, I saw the mum turning up from my window. (Good view, just like the agent said.) I was glad she was upset. Teach her a lesson.

Then I phoned up the radio and told them everything. Well, almost. About how the traffic was building up again on Balham high street and how it was really quite warm for the time of year. And the girl at the other end, who seems to like me, passed my message on.

They haven't played it yet. But Dangerous Dan hasn't had a look-in either.

Maybe tomorrow. We'll see, won't we, Terry, love?

MONDAY P.M.

*'. . . and we're coming up to the four o'clock news. But
first an update on the traffic. Betty from Balham reports
that it's surprisingly quiet this afternoon . . .'*

'Who p-p-put the wrong p-p-petrol in the car? Who p-p-put
diesel in?'

'Shut up, Sam. You keep going on about it.'

'W-w-well she did! That's w-why we're in D-Dad's spare car.
The other h-had to be drained. D-Dad sounded mad on the
mobile.'

'Hurry up, Fartine. We're going to miss my favourite
programme.'

'Why c-can't we have a TV in the car like Hugo? Then we
c-could watch Mum and Dad. Go on, Fartine. Ask them.'

'When's Dad coming home, Mum? He still hasn't texted. It's
been ages.'

'And I had a horrid day – it was all your fault. You forgot
it was no-uniform day, Mum. I rang but you just had the
answerphone on. Where were you?'

'What do you mean your teacher forgot to give you the
spelling test? After all my hard work! I've a good mind to com-
plain. And don't drink that fizzy muck in the back, Bruce. You'll
spill it like you did last week. We'll need to clean this car before
Dad gets back.'

'For God's sake, Julie, there's a speed camera right there. You
can still get points as a learner, you know.'

'Mum would have picked you up, girls, but she needed a bit
of a lie-down. She'll be there when you get back. Don't worry.
I'm sure it's this virus doing the rounds. It comes and goes
like flu. Let's hope you don't get it too.'

*　　*　　*

'Where the shit is Dad? Evie said he was picking up, didn't she?'

'Ring him on the mobile.'

'I have, stupid. Stop crying, he'll be here soon with Jack.'

'Everyone else has gone.'

'I know.'

'Look. No, over there. That weird woman opposite is looking through her curtains at us again.'

'Fuck! Hang on, someone's picked up. Jack? Jack, get Dad can you? No, darling, Nattie will talk to you later. Oh, for God's sake, talk to him, Nattie. He won't hand over otherwise.'

'Jack? Yes, I love you too. Yes, naughty Badron. Can you get Dad now? All right, you can say goodbye to Lennie first.'

"Bye, Jack. Dad? Thank God for that. Aren't you meant to be picking us up from school?'

'No, Mark, that's fine. I totally understand. Yes, I'm sure meetings like this are unavoidable. Another time? Let's just see, shall we?'

TUESDAY

8

'It's eight forty-nine a.m. A new survey out today claims families spend more on travel costs than food or entertainment. Meanwhile, debate continues over the university top-up fees . . .'

'Squeeze,' Harriet told herself. 'Hold for six. Down again *slowly*.'

'This is *so* boring, Mum,' said Bruce, leaning forward to twiddle the radio knob. 'Can't we have Radio One?'

'Leave it alone – you're distracting me,' said Harriet sharply. 'I'll do it.' Momentarily taking her eyes off the road, she adjusted the tuning. It was the noise that got to her. The cacophony from the kids arguing and their music. Wasn't there a law that said noise in an office shouldn't exceed eighty-five decibels? She wouldn't mind betting the level at home was more than that.

Since Bruce had joined a band at school, he'd not only got louder but he'd also become an overnight expert on what music was cool and what wasn't. Still, at least his trumpet gave him something to do in the evening other than annoy his sister. Harriet had even managed to impress him the other week by letting slip that in her younger days (pre-Charlie, of course), she'd been to a Sex Pistols concert. Now she was more into Classic FM. How sad was that? She'd even wanted to hear more on the news about travel costs. As a family, they spent a fortune on petrol. Charlie's flights, of course, were paid for by the company. Which meant there had been nothing to stop him coming home during the last two months if he'd wanted to.

'Best not to, I think,' he had said, during the first week, when Harriet, still stunned by the speed with which the text kisses had changed their lives, had made yet another phone call to his hotel in Dubai. 'We both need time to think. Don't we?'

She had been taken aback by his coolness – he must have thought this all through before. 'Don't you miss the kids?' she asked.

It was her trump card, even though she hated to admit it. Charlie adored them – though he found Bruce hard work – and she knew he had to be missing them, even if he was happy to leave her. They needed him too. I might be old-fashioned, she told herself, but kids need two parents. Charlie can't just walk off like this. He can't.

It had been Pippa who had suggested counselling. 'You need to talk it through,' she had said, during one of their lunches soon after Charlie went. 'See it from all the different angles.'

'I'm sorry. It must be boring for you to have me sounding off all the time.'

'Don't be daft. But I know you too well – and I don't really know Charlie – so I can't be objective. Frankly, I think he's behaved appallingly but maybe there's a reason for it.'

'You mean me?'

'Will you get off your guilt trip?' Pippa had shaken her head in mock horror. 'Only a prat would blame his wife for not showing enough affection when he hardly went over the top himself in that department. No, you need to think why he's doing it. Middle-age crisis . . .' Pippa's voice tailed off.

'An affair, you mean,' said Harriet quietly.

Pippa had shrugged. 'Well, you've got to admit it's possible. Even if he says not. A counsellor might help you work out what you'd do if it turned out that way. Go to Dr Bitland. She'll refer you.'

Harriet had made an appointment and, without giving details (something inside her shied away from that), was referred to the counselling centre.

'There's a waiting list, I'm afraid,' Dr Bitland had warned her. 'In the meantime, I could write you a prescription. Something that might make you feel a little less stressed.'

She had taken the tablets for a day or so, then put them in the back of the cupboard. Anti-depressants had rarely had a good press and now she could see why. The small yellow tablets had made her feel as though she wasn't there at all – and that scared her, especially when she was driving.

As luck would have it, she received a phone call from the counselling centre two weeks after Charlie had gone. There had been a cancellation. Would she like to come for an assessment and, after that, a course of five sessions? Monica, a calm, quiet woman in her late fifties, wearing lavender Jaeger, was refreshingly normal and not too dissimilar from how Harriet saw herself in fifteen years' time. Nor did she seem surprised by what Harriet told her, which made her feel as though this ghastly mess could be resolved. From then on, Tuesday mornings at nine o'clock – straight after the school run – were circled in red in her diary. Today was the last session and, depending on what happened on Friday, she might or might not need another course.

It all seemed so far removed from the giggling threesome in the back. Would Jess, Beth and Lucy ever have to go through what she was enduring? Would Bruce, who was quiet for a change, listening to his Walkman, ever behave as his father had? Harriet fervently hoped not. The girls were still happily into miniature ponies, whose hair constantly needed plaiting or blow drying. She had been the same – even then she had dreamed of a family. And now it was about to collapse around her.

'Shall we practise those spellings again?' she asked half-heartedly. 'Just in case your teacher remembers today.'

'She won't. It's Tuesday. We don't have spellings on Tuesday.'

How nice to be able to say 'I don't have spellings on Tuesday', or 'I don't wait in on Tuesday for international calls that never come', or 'I don't need to go to a counsellor on Tuesday'. Harriet blinked back the tears. There were times when she would do anything to go back down the years and swap places with the girls laughing in the back seat.

The trouble was, Harriet reflected, you only really knew you had been all right when you weren't all right any more. Then you looked back and wondered why you hadn't enjoyed being happy.

Once upon a time she might have been able to share that thought with Charlie. But not now. She couldn't even confide in her mother, who lived miles away and would have been devastated if she'd suspected her daughter's marriage was shaky, after her own divorce.

'Mum?'

Jess's voice rose above the radio.

'Mmm?'

'What's masterbation?'

Harriet stiffened. 'Why?'

'Because that's what Bruce has written in his homework diary.'

'Give it to me, bitch.'

'Bruce, don't you *dare* use words like that!'

'Well, she shouldn't read my stuff.'

'Anyway,' said Lucy, clearly, 'you've spelt it wrong, Bruce. It has a *u* and not an *e*. Isn't that right, Mrs Chapman?'

'*Mum!*' Bruce's voice was indignant. 'Mum, Jess is nipple-crippling me. Stop her!'

Harriet forced herself to keep her eyes on the road. 'What do you mean – nipple-crippling?'

'It's when someone twists the bits on your chest,' said Beth. 'It teaches boys a lesson. Some girls do it at school.'

'Well, we're not doing it in *this* car. Jess, stop it immediately or I'll tell Dad when he gets back. Now, be quiet, everyone. I want five minutes' peace without *anyone* talking. OK?'

'You're so embarrassing, Mum,' said Jess, reproachfully.

'It's a perk of the job,' replied Harriet, smartly. 'Just wait until you're a mum. Embarrassing your kids is one of the few pleasures you get.' She smiled at them in the mirror. 'That's a joke, by the way.'

'Sorry about Mum, everyone,' said Bruce. 'She's being really weird this week.'

NICK

> '*Meanwhile, debate continues over the university top-up fees, and in America, the schoolboy holding his classmates hostage shows no sign of giving himself up.*'

'I think it's awful, making us pay to go to university,' said Julie, her eyes flashing in that dangerously sensual way that Nick remembered so clearly in her mother.

'Yes.' He checked the clock. Late again. They should have reached the roundabout by now. 'Keep your eyes on the road or you'll never get there.'

'That's not funny, Dad.'

'Sorry. That's right. Keep looking in the mirror. Watch the Volvo that doesn't know where it's going.'

'Roses. Look.' Julie pointed to the lamp-post on the left. 'Last week, they were freesias. Now they're roses. How romantic. Someone must have loved that person very much.'

He couldn't work her out. Sometimes he couldn't even mention death without his daughter's eyes filling with tears, and at others she seemed to wallow in it by pointing out things like those bloody roses.

Amber had suggested that she was confused. It was one of the few sensible things she had said during their sessions. The rest of it was, frankly, the kind of amateur psychobabble that he could have got from a self-help book. So, why did he keep going? Part of him felt he owed it to Julie and to Juliana. Amber was a qualified psychotherapist. Maybe it was his fault she wasn't helping him. He really would try to listen to her today and see if any of her stuff made sense. Nine o'clock, his appointment was. Straight after the school run.

'Doing anything nice today, Dad?' asked Julie, as she reversed swiftly into a space.

Yes, I'm seeing a counsellor. 'Just work. Not so fast. Watch that Mini. OK, sharp left now. *Stop*.'

Julie leaned across to open his door and check how close she was to the kerb. Not close enough, thought Nick. With any luck, she'd fail, even though she'd passed the theory with ease last month.

'Hi.' It took Nick a few seconds to translate the grunt. Jason was standing next to him – too close: those pimples were sharply in focus. Julie's eyes sparkled. 'Hi, Jason. How are you doing?'

'What do you *see* in him?' Nick wanted to ask. But he couldn't. He didn't need a counsellor to tell him that that was the worst thing a dad could come out with.

'Don't worry about picking me up, Dad. Jason's going to give me a lift home.'

Nick's mouth went dry. Julie knew perfectly well she wasn't allowed to be driven by other teenagers. It was a rule he had instituted when all her friends had started.

'Actually, I'll be passing, love – and, besides, we were going shopping. Remember?'

Julie gave him a challenging look from under her eyelashes. 'Shopping! Well, that's an offer I can't turn down. Maybe tomorrow, then, Jason.'

Off they walked. Not quite hand in hand but close enough. Nick breathed a sigh of relief. He had got out of that one but he'd have to have another word with his daughter. He was damned if that boy was driving her anywhere.

9

Harriet would have liked to have turned down the radio in the waiting room, even though it was on low. It was usually tuned to Radio 2 to put people at ease, along with the cold-water and coffee machines, the pile of magazines (surprisingly more up-to-date than those at the doctor's surgery) and the posters on the wall. One showed a woman with her head in her hands, slumped over the kitchen table. *'Battered but daren't say anything?'* Another had a cartoon of a surprised baby in a thought bubble coming out of a woman's head. *'Pregnant?'*

No chance of that, thought Harriet, wryly. When she had first started coming here, she had sat on the edge of the brown-upholstered chair, terrified in case someone she knew came in. Now she felt almost relaxed. There was so much she wanted to tell Monica. How stupid she felt about booking an appointment for highlights this week, followed by a manicure, because she still, after all he'd done, wanted to look good for Charlie – show him what he'd been missing and how she could get on without him. But also how much she yearned for him to put his arms round her and say it had all been a mistake. If only his phone calls had given her some indication of how he felt. But, on the whole, they were to the point. Sometimes warm and sometimes cool. So confusing. Such a mess.

'You don't happen to have change for a pound, do you?'

She looked up at the tall, broad-shouldered man in the brown suede jacket who was examining the coffee machine. Harriet felt a twinge of panic. He was familiar and she'd been so careful not to let anyone, apart from Pippa, know she was coming here.

Seeing a counsellor was tantamount to admitting you couldn't cope, and she didn't want the whole world knowing that.

She looked down at the magazine. 'Afraid not. I used my last coin in the car park.'

'Never mind. I'll have water instead. Sorry to bother you.'

He was nervous, she realised – picking up one magazine and then another.

'Does it work for you?'

'Sorry?'

'The counselling.' He grinned shyly. 'Does it help?'

She was reluctant to be drawn into such intimacy with a near stranger. 'Depends who you get, I think. My . . . er . . . counsellor has helped me.'

'Mine hasn't. I've been seeing her for three whole months but she doesn't say anything. Just listens to me spouting.'

'That's what they're meant to do. But then Monica . . . my counsellor will ask a question and it helps me formulate thoughts in my head that had been there all along although I hadn't registered them.'

The man was nodding. 'I can understand that. But Amber – she's mine – repeats everything I tell her like a parrot. And then – can you believe this? – last week, she said, "I want to give you something – a gift." Well, I thought that was a bit odd but then she said, "Imagine I'm wrapping up all your thoughts and giving them back to you. Then I want you to open them up and examine them as though you're seeing them for the first time."'

Harriet was taken aback. 'That's weird.'

'Pure psychobabble.' The man took a gulp of water, then looked at her again. 'Listen, this is probably very incorrect of me and all that . . . but don't I know you from somewhere?'

'I was wondering the same thing,' admitted Harriet.

'You're not a model, are you?'

For a chat-up line, that had to be the worst. Disappointed, she looked down at her magazine. 'No.'

'Sorry – it's just that I'm a photographer. I tend to notice things – and not see the things I should sometimes. But I know I've seen you somewhere.' His face cleared. 'At school. St Theresa's. I drop my daughter off every morning – well, she drops me off. Do you have a child there?'

'Two. One is in year seven and the other in year nine.' She leaned forward. 'Look, I'm not being funny but I'd rather you didn't tell anyone you've seen me here.'

He looked appalled. 'Wouldn't dream of it. I'd be grateful if you did the same.'

'Of course.' She smiled awkwardly. 'Your daughter drops you off, you say. Is she learning to drive?'

He smiled ruefully. He was a very attractive man, thought Harriet, surprising herself. She had never, during her fourteen-year marriage to Charlie, looked at anyone else. But she felt unusually drawn to this nice man with the understanding greeny-blue eyes: he seemed so interested in what she had to say.

'I'm trying to keep her a learner as long as possible. But since her mother died it's one of the few things that has made Julie happy.'

So that was why he was here – bereavement counselling. The look on his face showed he could see she had made the connection. Something inside her made her want to put him at ease. 'My husband's left me. Well, not exactly "left me" but gone away for two months so we can think things over.' Even as she spoke, she was horrified with herself for being so open.

'That's not very fair on you – or the kids. Can't he make up his mind?'

That was exactly what Harriet had been asking herself since Charlie had left. She smiled faintly. 'Apparently not. He says there isn't anyone else.'

'And you believe him?'

Harriet nodded emphatically. 'Yes. That's the one thing I'm

sure about. Charlie wouldn't lie to me. He's not that kind of man.'

'Harriet?' Monica put her head round the door, smiling. 'Would you like to come in now?'

She stood up quickly, knocking over her bag as she did so. Everything spilled out, diary, purse, tampons – oh, God. And now he was helping her stuff it all back in. How embarrassing!

'Thanks,' she said, feeling hot. ''Bye.'

As she followed Monica up the stairs, she tried to remember everything she'd been storing up in her head about Charlie to tell Monica so she could make some sense out of the nightmare. But something was niggling at her. Something she had just said to the man in the waiting room. *He's not that kind of man.*

How often had she said that to herself – and to Monica – and believed it? But now, after her declaration to a complete stranger, whose expression had clearly stated he wasn't convinced, she wondered if it was true.

'Sit down, Harriet.' Monica indicated the chair opposite hers.

Harriet sank into it gratefully. Over the weeks, she'd found Monica could see things that Pippa couldn't – the advantage, she supposed, of talking to a stranger who could afford objectivity.

Monica smiled encouragingly. She was wearing her usual Jaeger suit with the matching scarf. Harriet wondered wistfully if her life was as well co-ordinated as her outfit. 'So, Harriet, how have you been since I last saw you?'

Harriet felt disappointed. Had Monica forgotten that this was *the* week? She took a deep breath. 'Uncertain. Charlie gets back on Friday and I'm terrified.'

Monica nodded calmly. 'And what exactly are you terrified of?'

Harriet ran her hands through her hair. 'Everything. I'm worried he won't want me. I'm worried that the kids will be difficult and annoy him. And I'm worried in case this woman actually does mean something to him.'

Monica leaned forward and Harriet could see the top of her black bra peeping above her blouse. Had she been through this kind of thing with her husband? 'You sound, Harriet, as though you're expecting him to make all the decisions. You have a choice too, you know.'

Harriet closed her eyes. 'But that's just it – I don't! If he says this woman means something to him, I can't stop him going. And if he says he wants to stay, I have to pretend life is normal for the sake of the children.'

'Not necessarily,' Monica replied. 'If Charlie says it's over between you, you have a choice about whether to fall into a deep depression or get on with it. And if he wants to continue with the marriage, you still have a choice.'

'No, I don't. I watched my mother's pain as she put up with my father's affairs and I vowed I wouldn't do the same. Then, when Dad finally went, it felt so different and wrong because home wasn't the same without him.' Harriet's eyes filled with tears. 'I don't want to put my children through that agony. And I can see now why Mummy put up with Daddy's affairs. She was frightened of being on her own – just as I am.'

Monica handed her a tissue and waited. 'Let's go back. Tell me again what you said about your marriage when you first came here. No, don't look like that. I haven't forgotten. I want to remind you.'

Harriet swallowed. It was so hard, so painful. 'Well, our marriage hasn't been great for the past three or four years but it hasn't been terrible either.' Suddenly she thought of the fierce love etched on that sixth-former's face yesterday. 'We never had what you'd call a grand passion,' she said, flushing, 'but we were both in our late twenties and settling down seemed more important. He wasn't married – single men were becoming rarer – and we were both ready to have babies. In

Charlie, I saw someone loyal and steady whom I could rely on. Ironic, isn't it?'

'And what were the first few years like?'

'Comfortable,' said Harriet wistfully. 'It was nice making a home together and doing grown-up things like choosing carpets. I was thrilled when I became pregnant with Bruce just before our first anniversary and couldn't wait to give up work. I was an assistant in a public-relations company and I hated the artificiality. All I'd ever wanted was a family. Jess arrived a year later and we felt almost smug at having one of each. It all seemed so easy.'

'Until when?'

'Until Charlie's job began to take him away more.'

'And the sex?'

Harriet wriggled in her seat. 'It sort of tailed off.'

'Did he mind?'

Harriet felt defensive. 'He didn't say so. Just being together with the children seemed enough – until that text.'

'What does that tell you?'

'That he should have told me earlier how he felt?'

Monica nodded. 'Yes, but what else? Let me give you a clue. Have you gone to pieces since he left?'

'Not exactly, but it hasn't been easy.'

'It never is. What about the children?'

'They've been all right – but only because they thought he was coming back.'

'Children also suffer if their parents stay together for their sake, Harriet. They pick up on vibes, and later, when they're older and realise how unhappy their parents were, they blame themselves for "keeping them together".'

Harriet was silent. She remembered how she'd wished her parents had split up earlier to save her mother the continued pain.

'Let me ask you another question. What kind of practical things have you learned since Charlie went?'

'Well, I've sorted out the bills. I've changed most of them to direct debit, which is much easier.'

'Anything else?'

'It's not been as lonely, somehow, as I thought it would be. When the kids have gone to bed, it's rather nice to be able to sit down with a book and a snack on my knee instead of having to cook a proper dinner for Charlie and listen to his day, even though he never bothers to ask about mine.'

Monica smiled. 'You see? You've just told yourself something you hadn't realised. If you did find yourself on your own, you'd manage better than you think.'

'But I don't want him to go.' Harriet's eyes filled with tears again. 'We've been together too long. I always thought we'd get old together.'

Monica stopped smiling. 'Longevity, Harriet, is no reason for continuing a marriage. You're not going to get a long-service award for hanging on to a relationship that's past its sell-by date. Don't get me wrong, I'm not telling you to leave him or ask him to go. You have to make up your own mind on that. I'm simply pointing out the options.'

She glanced at the clock that stood on the table between them. This always happened, thought Harriet, frantically. They'd reached a crucial point just as their session was ending. 'I've got this horrible feeling that even if he says he wants to go, I'm going to beg him to stay,' she said softly.

'I can understand that. But supposing he did and then he agreed to stay, how would you feel?'

'That he stayed because of the children and not because he loved me.'

'I can understand that too. Harriet, I'm sorry but our time is up. You know, don't you, that this is our last session? I hope you feel it's been helpful.'

No, Harriet wanted to yell. No, I want you to come with me and hold my hand when Charlie gets back. 'Yes, thank you.'

'If you want another series of sessions, you'll have to ask Dr Bitland to refer you again.' Monica handed over a sheet of paper. 'In the meantime, I wonder if you'd mind filling in this survey. It's entirely confidential but it will help us work out whether you found the counselling useful and how we can improve it in any way.'

Harriet took it wordlessly. Somehow it had reduced all Monica's wise words to a mundane commercial level. How could you ascertain how successful or helpful a counsellor had been until you had put your experience into action?

She thanked Monica again (should she have brought her a present?) and went down the stairs into the street, hoping, as she always did, that no one would see her. If by some bad luck they did, they would perhaps assume that she was a volunteer for the counselling service rather than a client. Women like her were usually on the other side of the table, weren't they?

Harriet's stomach rumbled but she still didn't feel able to eat. The prospect of Charlie returning and all the decisions and choices she could and couldn't make were tying her stomach in knots. She didn't want to go home either. When the children were there, the noise drove her mad, but the silence when they were at school was worse. It made her think and she'd done enough of that already this morning.

She'd go to the gym. If she hurried, she'd just make the yoga class she sometimes went to with Pippa. Harriet nipped back to the car to collect her leotard from the boot and jogged across the road to Fit For Life, the gym that had opened the previous year. There was another a little further down the high street, but Harriet preferred this one. It was lighter and brighter but, most importantly, all the instructors had a positive outlook. Harriet always came away feeling better about herself.

She flashed her membership card at the girl on the desk, then changed swiftly and made her way to the yoga class, which was held in an airy room with mirrors down one side.

Jill, the instructor, who was wearing a pink T-shirt with

Fun, Fearless, Female printed on it, smiled at her. 'Come on in, we've only just started.'

Harriet found a space towards the back. She had been to enough classes to know what to do, and the easy pattern her body fell into helped her mind to relax. The music was soft and calming. If she closed her eyes, she could pretend that Charlie wasn't coming back this week, that life would go on in the normal way. Normal? Harriet felt a shock go through her. Yes, in a strange way, life *had* become normal during Charlie's absence. Did that mean she *could* cope without him?

'Raise your right hand and stretch gently to the right,' said Jill, through her microphone. Harriet followed the girl in front. Perhaps she should get a mike to use on the kids. It might make them listen to her. She smiled: that was better. Then she caught sight of herself in the mirror: her face looked taut and her breasts non-existent. She stopped smiling. Was that why Charlie had gone off her – because he didn't find her attractive any more? After breastfeeding Jess her breasts had gone down two sizes, but there was nothing she could do about that, except wear balcony bras. Implants seemed too scary – and artificial.

She looked at the other women in the class. They all appeared serene and, worse, were full-chested. Was the woman who had sent the text well endowed? Or did Charlie find her more intellectually stimulating than a wife who was at home all day with the kids?

The thought bothered her through the rest of the class and she came away without that lovely feeling of well-being. Something else worried her too. When she'd looked in the mirror and seen her taut face, she'd been reminded of her mother. Would she turn into her if Charlie left?

Harriet got back into the car and fished out her mobile. She rang her mother at least once a week, but with the panic of Charlie coming back, she hadn't spoken to her for several days. 'Mum, it's me. Hi. How are you?'

'Fine, darling. And how about you?'

Her mother sounded bright but she might be putting it on. Harriet knew she found it hard to be on her own and wished she didn't live so far away. She, and sometimes Charlie, took the children to see her at least four times a year but Sussex was a good two-and-a-half-hour drive from here, depending on traffic.

'Fine. I've just been to the gym and now I've got to tackle Waitrose.'

'Isn't Charlie coming back this week?'

'Yes. On Friday.' Harriet tried to think of something neutral to say. She hadn't told her mother about their problems and didn't want to burden her with them – she was in her late sixties, after all. Besides, her mother had always liked Charlie and it would be hard to admit that things weren't right.

'It will be lovely for you, darling, to have him back.'

'Yes. Yes, it will. What have you been doing this week?'

'Oh, quite a lot. We had our weekly walk yesterday, and on Friday we've got the church dinner. Some nice people have moved into the village over the last few months, which makes things like the dinner more interesting. The garden is looking beautiful too. I wish you could see it.'

'I will. The children finish school this week and I was thinking of coming down shortly afterwards.'

'How about Sunday? Or do you think Charlie will want a weekend at home after being away?'

The keenness in her voice made Harriet feel worse. Her mother was lonely: she needed them. On the other hand Sunday was too soon for Charlie, who would want to collapse on a chair in the garden, especially if this weather continued. The thought of piling the kids into a hot car and trying to stop them arguing on a long journey would be exactly what he didn't need. Well, he'd just have to cope, wouldn't he?

'Sunday would be lovely, Mum. Can't wait to see you. Lots of love.'

10

Nick watched Harriet leave the waiting room with her counsellor. He didn't want her to go: she had been so easy to talk to, and Amber was on a completely different wavelength from him.

'Nick,' said Amber, walking in briskly. 'I'm ready to see you now.'

He followed her into their usual room and sat down reluctantly.

'Sorry I had to cancel yesterday,' she said.

He waved his hand, dismissively.

'Now, how have we been doing?'

'We'? How patronising was that?

Amber looked down at the notes on her expansive lap; the lower half of her body was shrouded in a shapeless black cheesecloth skirt. 'Last week we ended when you were telling me that your daughter disapproved of your girlfriend.' She put down her pen and looked at him almost coquettishly. 'How important is it to you, Nick, to have female company?'

God, this was embarrassing. 'Well, I'm not some sex maniac, if that's what you think.'

Her face remained impassive.

'And for over a year I wasn't ready for another relationship. But now I'm aware that I miss certain things. Not just the physical bit but the warm feeling that comes from talking to someone who knows what you're going to say before you say it. Yet I can't hurt Julie. I feel guilty enough as it is.'

'Guilty?' Amber frowned. 'In the last session you also said that, in your view, you had helped to kill your wife.' She glanced at her notes. 'You hadn't "physically killed her" but your "attitude precipitated her death".'

God, thought Nick, appalled. Had she written all that down? Would it – could it? – ever be used against him?

'Well, in a way, I did.'

'Why do you think that?'

Nick sighed. 'I've told you. Juliana took a break from modelling after our daughter was born. Said she was sick of it. Then she decided she wanted to go back. By then she'd been out of it for over six years. She was older and none of the agencies wanted to take her on. Then a new one said they'd consider her if she lost some weight. I told her that was stupid, that she was slim without being skinny, but she kept going on and on about it.'

Nick stopped. He put his hands over his eyes to shut out Amber so that he could pretend the world didn't exist. Even now, he couldn't believe he had been so crass, so thoughtless.

'And what happened then?'

Amber's voice had a quiet authority he hadn't heard before. Nick lifted his head. 'One evening, when she kept insisting she was too fat to go back to work, I snapped. I said – oh, God – "If you feel that way, do something about it instead of wearing us all down."'

He rubbed his eyes, staring at Amber pleadingly, willing her face to soften. 'She'd got on my nerves. Awful, isn't it? But when someone talks about nothing else all the time, it finishes you off and, I don't know, I was tired with work and tired when I got back.'

'And then?'

What was this? Bloody *Desert Island Discs*? 'Then she stopped eating.' He'd been crazy to hope that Amber would understand. No one could. 'Well, anything that had calories. She lived on apples. Then pineapples because she'd read they broke down the fat she didn't have. Not bananas. And not one ounce of flour or butter or pasta or anything else.

'She got so thin it was painful.' Nick swallowed the lump that was blocking his throat, threatening to stop him breathing. 'She was tired all the time but wouldn't see the doctor. I'd make appointments for her but she refused to go. Then I'd find her in the kitchen in the middle of the night, cramming food into her mouth so it dribbled down her chin. After that I'd hear her retching in the loo. The bulimic stage lasted only three months. Then she stopped eating. Well, anything of substance.' His voice wobbled. 'She lost three stone in six months.'

'So that's why you think you killed her?' Amber's voice was flat. Like a weather report

Nick stared at her. 'I put the idea into her head. And now I'm terrified in case Julie finds out exactly how her mother died and stops eating too.'

'What do you mean, "how she died"? What happened?'

Nick tried to talk but the words wouldn't come out. Amber spoke again: 'Why does it scare you that Julie might find out?'

Nick stood up, almost knocking over his chair. 'Because she didn't know her mother had anorexia – I said she died of cancer because I was scared Julie would stop eating. Look, Amber, I'm sorry but this isn't working. You don't understand and you're driving me crazy with your rubbish about giving me gifts and saying, "Why?" all the time. Juliana is dead and it's my fault. And nothing you can sodding say is going to help me accept that.'

He strode to the door and turned. Amber looked shocked and, for a second, he was pleased. 'Don't you want to finish your session?' she asked, almost like a child with the Alice band that was too young for her middle-aged, frown-dented forehead.

'What does it look like? Frankly, Amber, as a counsellor you're hopeless. In fact, I'd say you were in the wrong job.'

He slammed the door and walked down the stairs, out into the daylight and back to normality. Had he been too hard on her? Maybe. But it was true: she *had* been hopeless in that she had made him feel worse about this whole bloody mess instead of helping him reach his own conclusions, as counselling was meant to do.

For a few minutes, Nick walked up and down the high street, trying to regain his composure. All around him, there were normal people. A woman with a pushchair and a waist so wide it wobbled under her shapeless skirt, but who, judging from the way she was smiling at her child, didn't seem worried about her appearance. A young couple, arms entwined, who almost walked into him. A scruffy woman in a pink coat, who handed him a leaflet that he folded and put into his pocket. If he had had more patience with Juliana, if he had taken the time to make her feel better about herself, he might have been walking down this street with her now.

It was only the realisation that his parking ticket would soon expire that made him return to the car. Miserably, he fumbled in his jacket pocket for his car keys. His hands felt the phone, bigger and bulkier than his own, which he must have put it into his pocket when he was helping Harriet with her bag. He could turn it on to see if he could find her home number, but that seemed like an invasion of privacy. Slowly he put it back into his pocket. With any luck, he'd see her tomorrow on the school run and be able to give it back.

11

EVIE

*'. . . and the siege in Ohio continues. It's eight forty a.m.
According to a new survey, families spend more on travel
costs than on food or entertainment. The average adult
forks out sixty pounds a week on petrol or public transport . . .'*

Interesting. Evie made a note on her Palm Pilot as she revved
the engine on the Pargeters' immaculately swept gravel drive,
which boasted two ostentatious and unnecessary lamp-posts
by the stone steps that led up to the front door.

'Where Does Your Money Really Go?' might make a good
feature. Her readers would consider sixty quid a lot of money
but, frankly, she was surprised it wasn't more. She and Robin
spent more than that on drink each week. The radio was
always good at sparking feature ideas. And for taking her
mind off the problems in the back.

'Come *on*,' she said, drumming her freshly manicured fingers
on the steering-wheel. She was tempted to hoot. Martine was
always late getting the kids ready when it was Evie's turn to
pick up Sam and Ellie. Bloody cheek, especially when Simon
and Sally were, no doubt, sleeping off yesterday afternoon's
performance, blissfully oblivious to the chaos below. School
runs could only work when everyone stuck to their schedule
and was in the right place at the right time. And if Simon and
Sally couldn't cope with that, they should learn to.

Where *were* they? Impatiently, she turned up the radio.

Evie's own life was so busy, especially when the girls were with her, that she hated wasting even a minute when she could be doing something else.

'According to a report by the Association of Building Societies, over eighty per cent of women say they are happier after divorce or separation compared with fifty-three per cent of men. The Association interviewed nearly two thousand men and women all over the country.'

Another good idea, mused Evie, opening the Palm Pilot again. In her experience, women were usually better at making changes in their lives and coping with them. Definitely a feature. Just as there was another about men who couldn't find things in the house. She'd almost been late this morning because Robin couldn't unearth a clean shirt. Even though he had all day to find it himself, he still needed her help. Ridiculous! Some men needed a map to get to the linen cupboard – just as Martine clearly needed a stopwatch to get the kids out of the house.

Right, that was it. She was going to get out of the car and see where the hell they were!

'Here they come,' said Leonora.

If there was one thing that stirred the twins out of their early-morning lethargy, it was picking up Sam and Ellie: they might spot one of their famous parents. Leonora, Evie knew, nursed secret hopes of being a television presenter herself on one of the inarticulate teen programmes that dominated early-evening television. Sally had fuelled her hopes when she had airily promised to find her a work-experience placement when she was older.

'I am so regretting,' said Martine, bustling out behind the children. 'Ellie she will not get up. Your music, Sam, where it is?'

'B-b-bugger. It's in the m-m-music room.'

Evie raised her recently waxed eyebrows, both at the swear word and the existence of a music room. Poor kid. His stutter was getting worse, despite the treatment he was having. 'Run and get it, then,' she said, firmly but kindly, 'or we're going to hit all the traffic. Come on, Ellie, in you hop. Strop yourself in next to Jack – I mean "strap".'

A Freudian slip if ever there was one, she thought, as she waited for them to get in, then crunched down the drive and waited again, this time for the huge black electronic gates to open. Sod Martine. She'd forgotten to press the release button. This time she *was* going to hoot.

'You'll wake up Mummy,' said Ellie. 'We're not meant to make a noise in the morning.'

'Then your au pair ought to remember to do the gate,' retorted Evie, hand on horn.

At last! Evie swung the Discovery through, just missing the right-hand gate, which seemed out of synch with the left. Natalie whistled. Evie ignored her. She had enough to worry about without another battle with her step-daughters. For a start, she was still livid with Robin. How could he have forgotten to pick up the kids last night?

'Anything could have happened to them,' she had raved, when she'd got back from a late-night meeting and discovered what had happened. 'What's got into you, Robin? It's not as though you've got much else to do.'

OK. She shouldn't have said that. Not when redundancy was the new impotency. But it had just come out of her big mouth and now it was too late to suck it back.

Slowly Robin opened the bottle of Chardonnay. 'Actually, I had an interview. Remember?'

She hadn't. 'How did it go?'

'They're going to let me know.'

They were always going to let him know. And when they did, he would spend weeks applying for more jobs that would eventually let him know. In that knowledge, they had spent last night as far apart from each other as their double bed would allow. Usually, at some point, Robin would reach out for her and clasp her to him. Last night he hadn't bothered.

Even in our sleep we're growing apart, thought Evie, wistfully. Despite its sadness, the phrase had a good ring to it. Maybe a coverline. But first she had the conference with Bulmer to get through – the one that should have happened yesterday but which he had cancelled at the last minute. Evie knew why. He was trying to unnerve her. Well, let him. He might be the publisher but he couldn't scare her with his ABC figures. *Just For You* was all over the place. It screamed its presence at the top of the stands in Smith's. It was an intelligent, interesting glossy, and it was her baby. She'd show him.

'F-f-fuck.'

Evie turned, eyes flashing. 'Sam, I won't have that word in this car. Jack will pick it up.'

'Fuck, Fuck,' chanted Jack. Leonora giggled.

'What's wrong?' asked Natalie.

'D-d-did anyone pick up the v-v-violin when Martine got it out of the music room?'

'No,' said Evie, 'because we're not your servants. As it was, we had to wait while you got your music.' She shouldn't speak to him like that, as she would to her own, in case he told his parents. But, really, that boy was impossible.

'In that c-c-case,' said Sam, cheerfully, 'I m-m-must have left it on the drive. C-c-can we go back?'

'No,' snapped Evie. 'We can't. I am not your father's chauffeur. I have an important meeting to get to and I haven't got time to chase up things you are old enough to be responsible for yourself.'

'That's *so* rude, Evie,' said Leonora, disapprovingly.

'Tough. I'm sorry, Sam, but you'll just have to explain to your music teacher that you left your violin behind. Maybe it will teach you to be more organised.'

'You m-m-mean, teach M-M-Martine.'

Evie felt a flicker of sympathy for the young woman. It couldn't be easy coping with those two – they'd be a challenge for the most experienced mother. 'Don't blame your au pair.

She's doing her best.' She glanced into the rear-view mirror. Sam was looking at his shoes, downcast. 'I don't mean to sound harsh,' she said, more gently, 'but you need to learn to take responsibility for yourself. You all do. It's part of being grown-up.'

'But you're always saying we're *not* grown-up yet,' retorted Natalie.

'You are when it suits you, young lady. You keep telling me you're grown-up enough to sit for hours on the computer without me checking what you're up to. And you think you're grown-up enough to go to that party on Friday even though it's in a bar.'

'Well, I am.'

'Your father and I disagree.'

'I'll ask Mum.'

'Do. *If* she rings.'

She shouldn't have said that. Rachel hadn't called that week, and every time the phone rang one of the girls had rushed to it, hoping it was their mother.

They drove on in silence. 'I'm sure your mother will ring tonight,' said Evie, as a conciliatory gesture.

'Shut up,' said Leonora tersely.

'Don't be so rude.'

'Then don't be rude about Mum not ringing.'

'I wasn't.'

But she had been, thought Evie, miserably. She had descended to their level while a good step-mother would have seen it from their point of view and made allowances for a pair of teenage kids who were not just going through the usual hormonal angst but also had to cope with their mother flitting from one man to the next.

She pulled over. 'Hop out here, everyone. Quickly – I'm blocking someone in. 'Bye. Have a good day. And, girls?'

The twins glared at her from the pavement.

'What?' said Natalie sullenly.

Evie swallowed hard. 'I'm sorry.'

'You will be,' said Leonora, tucking her arm into her sister's. 'Come on, Nattie. Let's go to school. At least people are nice there.'

Evie dropped off Jack at nursery and made her way to work, feeling wretched. She hadn't meant to be bitchy about Rachel but the girls were impossible.

Bulmer, of course, was already waiting for her in the meeting room. It was furnished, according to minimalist taste, with just a pale beech table and eight chairs at the sides with a ninth at the top that he was sitting in. Janine was with him (how did she do it, considering she had kids too?), leafing through some papers.

'Ah, Evie.' Bulmer glanced at his watch, although Evie knew she was five minutes early. It wasn't her fault if Janine and he chose to get there even earlier. Janine looked immaculate in a crisp white shirt that made her look both feminine and professional. Bulmer, on the other hand, was displaying his usual poor taste: today, his shirt was dark plum with a yellow spotted tie. His waist bulged out of his expensive suit and his hair – what was left of it – was either greasy or over-waxed. Evie often wondered how old he was. Forty, maybe, forty-five. But she had to admit he was good at his job. Bulmer had a reputation for getting the most out of magazines – and for being ruthless in achieving his aims. Evie knew at least two editors who had been told to clear their desks at an hour's notice. Well, she wasn't going to be another.

She settled herself in the chair opposite Janine, then poured a glass of sparkling water from the bottle on the table and got out her notes. At conference, she and Janine discussed the features they hoped to put into the next issue. They worked eight weeks in advance, like most magazines, which meant it was tricky to be both time-sensitive and up-to-date.

'I thought we could do something on the new report that says over eighty per cent of women are happier after divorce or separation compared with fifty-two per cent of men,' said Evie.

'Actually, Evie, it's fifty-three per cent,' said Janine, smoothly. 'We were discussing that while we waited for you.'

'Yes.' Bulmer narrowed his eyes – Evie couldn't help wondering how any woman could bear to go to bed with that mass of blubber. He had nothing – absolutely *nothing* – going for him, apart from his salary.

'By the time we come out, the tabloids will have done it to death,' Bulmer went on. 'It would be much cleverer to pursue Janine's idea of turning it round and seeing what the children feel. Are *they* happier after their parents' divorce?'

'We could interview five families, representing different socio-economic groups,' said Janine.

Evie listened while she outlined the feature idea. She had to admit it was a good one. Blast. She should have considered the timing herself but that row with the kids in the car had blunted her thinking.

'Right,' said Bulmer, tapping his pen impatiently on the table. 'What else have you got for me?'

'Something on why women are so disorganised and why men can't find things,' said Evie.

Janine laughed brittly. 'Had a bad morning, Evie?'

Bulmer frowned. 'Rather sexist, isn't it?'

'Not really.' Evie tried to marshal her thoughts but they wouldn't get into line. 'Some men need a map to get to the linen cupboard.' She paused, waiting for a laugh. None came.

'I'm the organised one in our house,' said Bulmer. 'What else have you got?'

Evie ran through her ideas, followed by Janine. Bulmer picked up on some, played with them and tossed them out. After an hour or so, the editors from Practicals, Cookery and Health came in. Finally, when it was well past lunchtime, they had completed the flatplan for the October issue.

'Right, everyone.' Bulmer looked round the table. 'Thanks

for your input. I'll be e-mailing you all shortly to confirm what we've agreed. Evie, can you stay behind for a bit?'

Great. She was starving *and* desperate for the loo – had been for the last hour. She hoped he wasn't going to ask her for lunch to go over ideas for the Special – the name given to specialised editions of the magazine that ran alongside the regular monthly ones. The next – focusing on family issues – was due out in January. Evie hadn't yet pulled her thoughts together on it.

He waited until the room was empty. 'Thank you for your time, Evie.'

A chill flitted through her. Bulmer was at his most dangerous when he was polite. Again, he narrowed his eyes. Just like Shere Khan, thought Evie. Jack adored *Jungle Book* which they were reading together, in picture book format, at bedtime.

'I have to say, Evie, that I wasn't impressed by your ideas today, or the ones you came up with last month or the month before that. Circulation figures are continuing to drop, and if we don't do something about it all our futures will be at stake.'

'But—' began Evie.

'Please let me finish.' Bulmer was drumming his stubby fingers on the table alongside the ring he had made with his glass of water. 'I want a proposal from you by Friday on how to turn this magazine round. If it doesn't sing, your head is on the block. Right?'

Evie nodded numbly. OK, so she hadn't been performing in the way she used to before Jack – and before she'd met Robin. But that was because she had other things in her life now. Not that she could tell Bulmer that.

Her head on the block?

Evie shivered as she gathered up her papers.

Two of them unemployed was too unbearable to think about.

12

'Top-up fees now look as though . . .'

Bernard Havers, acting head of St Theresa's senior school, looked annoyed. 'Would someone please turn off the television? We haven't finished yet. Now, does anyone have any more questions about the Ofsted visit?'

He glanced round the staffroom, his forehead creased with anxiety. He looked a wreck, thought Kitty, and it wasn't surprising. Until today's staff meeting (postponed from yesterday), she hadn't known how many problems the school had and she wondered if the parents were aware of the situation. Bernard had informed them that a group of sixteen-year-olds had been caught smoking cannabis in the playground. They had received a warning but if it happened again they would be suspended. In the meantime no one was to mention this to anyone outside the staffroom in case the school's already doubtful reputation was damaged.

Kitty put up her hand. 'Yes?' said Bernard. She could see he was struggling to remember her name even though she had been there for nearly a year. Staff didn't last long at St Theresa's, which was why Bernard was currently 'acting' head. The actual head was currently recovering from a nervous breakdown, reputed to have been caused by pressure of paperwork and pupil behaviour.

'I just wondered,' said Kitty, nervously, feeling the eyes of all her colleagues on her, 'why St Theresa's doesn't have a policy of excluding pupils immediately when they've taken drugs.'

There was a murmur, with some people nodding and others shaking their heads. 'Since you are relatively new, Miss Hayling, you may not know that this is an issue we have discussed several times. However, the governors feel that in a mixed area such as this, children should be given a second chance to mend their ways. Any more questions?'

Kitty would have liked to ask if this was a matter they should keep from the Ofsted inspector on Thursday but suspected it was. Like most of the other teachers, she couldn't help feeling apprehensive about the visit.

'Well done,' said Judy Foster, as they made their way out of the staffroom to their respective classrooms. 'I've been fighting for instant expulsion for ages. I've got three girls of my own and there's zero tolerance in our house.'

Kitty liked Judy Foster, who seemed to embody everything she had hoped to be: a good teacher with a balanced family life.

'How did your date go last night?'

Kitty had forgotten she had told Judy – and she wouldn't have if Judy hadn't seen her changing in the ladies' after school before she had received the call from Mark saying it was off.

'He blew out,' she said airily. 'Made up some excuse about a meeting.'

Judy's eyes looked sympathetic. 'He *might* have had a meeting.'

'Somehow I don't think so. Anyway, I'm not bothered. He wasn't my type.'

'Why don't you go on one of these dating evenings that are advertised everywhere?' said Judy, as they walked down the corridor.

'I'm not that desperate.'

'I don't mean speed-dating. I'm talking about those upmarket dinner parties for professionals. I think Vivienne Price – you know her, she teaches IT – is going to one tomorrow. I heard her talking about it. Do you want me to ask her?'

'No, thanks,' said Kitty hastily. 'I've got loads of marking to do and, really, I don't want to meet a stranger.'

'All men are strangers until you get to know them. Sometimes they become strangers after you marry them.'

Kitty looked at her carefully. 'Really?'

'Not that you need to worry about that at the moment. But give the idea some thought – occasionally we all need a helping hand.'

'I will,' promised Kitty. 'Thanks.' She popped into the loo to get away.

Why, she thought, as she rinsed her hands in the basin (no soap again) couldn't she find anyone nice? She looked at herself in the mirror. A reasonably pretty – if ordinary – girl stared back, with shoulder-length curly hair, a splash of freckles, and brown eyes. She smiled. That was better. She looked more approachable now.

Mandy's call yesterday had reminded her of how far adrift her life plan had gone. When they'd been at school, she and Mandy had had their lives mapped out. Mandy was going to be a scientist and Kitty was going to teach before they had families. They were going to have done both before they were thirty so they would have plenty of time after the children had left home to do other things like exploring the Himalayas.

Mandy had stuck to her life plan although she'd had Tom a week before her thirtieth birthday, which was later than she'd hoped. As for Kitty, she'd managed the teaching bit but there was no prospect of a boyfriend, let alone a husband, she thought. She'd been out with a few boys at university but had failed to find anyone who matched up to Alex. Although she wouldn't admit it to Mandy, that was one reason why she had taken the plunge and moved to London this year. It would surely, she reasoned, broaden her scope for a social life. But, so far, it had been a dismal failure. She hardly knew any of her neighbours in the block where she rented her flat, and if she'd hoped for a social life via St Theresa's she was disappointed.

'There might still be Mark,' she told herself. He had sounded genuinely regretful about cancelling their date. She'd met him last week at a party held by a university friend. He was a financial adviser, which hadn't struck a chord, but perhaps Mandy was right about her being too picky. *If* he rang again.

As for their 'bet', it was ridiculous. A serious boyfriend in a week indeed! How crazy was that?

Kitty glanced at her watch. She'd better hurry or she'd be late for her next lesson.

'Bruce, I told you before. I don't want you sitting by the window. Come here. That's right. The front row.' Kitty waited while Bruce stood up sulkily and carried his books to the table she had indicated. 'Now you can get on with the essay that everyone else is writing.'

'What's the title again, Miss? I've forgotten it.'

Kitty took a deep breath. In the short time she'd known Bruce, she'd discovered that she got further with him if he was on her side. 'It's on the board, Bruce – "What I'm Looking Forward to This Week". I've given you all some ideas. Maybe it's somewhere you're going at the weekend, or perhaps it's a favourite television programme. I don't care what it is, as long as you're interested in it.'

Bruce fixed her with the glazed look he frequently adopted. 'You don't mind what I write about?'

Kitty felt a qualm. 'As long as it isn't rude.'

The rest of the class tittered and Bruce went pink. Instantly Kitty realised she'd said the wrong thing and made him feel uncomfortable. 'Just write something you feel passionate about, Bruce,' she said gently. 'I'm sure it will be great. You're good at writing stories.'

'I am?' He went pink again.

'Well, what I've seen of your work has been good.'

It wasn't strictly true, thought Kitty, as she watched Bruce bent over his work, his pen flying across the page, but the flattery seemed to have worked. In fact, the whole class appeared engrossed. Maybe she'd hit lucky. Kitty smiled to herself. That was the joy of teaching. When it went right, there was nothing better than seeing a child's face light up with the knowledge that he or she had done something well.

She was still glowing after lunch when she bumped into Vivienne in the staffroom. 'Judy says you're interested in coming to the dinner event tomorrow night.'

Kitty did a double-take. 'That's not what I said.'

'Oh.' Vivienne's face fell and she poured herself an anaemic cup of tea. 'What a shame. I was dreading going on my own, and when Judy mentioned it I felt so much better at the thought of someone coming with me. It's not one of those awful dating agencies, you know. It's Meet a Professional. You pay thirty pounds and you sit at a different table for each course and talk to as many people as you like. There's no obligation but you never know – you might just meet someone nice . . .' Her voice tailed off.

'What is it about this week?' asked Kitty. 'Everyone seems to want to pair me off.'

'Don't you want that?'

Kitty wanted to say that she definitely didn't want to end up like Vivienne, who was on the wrong side of thirty-eight, hadn't heard of electrolysis and hadn't found a passion apart from IT. But instead she heard herself say, 'OK, then. What time does it start?'

'Eight o'clock. Thanks, Kitty. It's really nice of you. It could be fun.'

13

MARTINE

> '*And now for a lighter piece of news. Today is National Impotence Day and we've got Dr Michael Shaw with the latest advances.*'

Dear Diary,
It is good not to do the school run today. It permits me time to do the ironing and vacuum and make the beds and clean the windows as Sally instructs me. I can also listen to the radio to improve my English.

Martine scratched her head and frowned as she put down her pen. She switched on the iron.

> '*Impotence is a malaise of the modern world and a consequence of the stress we live in.*'

Malaise? That she could understand, but it didn't explain what 'impotence' was. Where was her dictionary? She usually left it here by the phone. Maybe it was in the car.

She put the door on the latch and went outside. She would be glad when the bigger car came back from its service. The smaller one that Sally and Simon had found for her wasn't big enough for all the children with their things and they got so squashed. Martine opened the door and shook her head at the sight of all the rubbish and school books she should have reminded them to take in. Everything was here, apart from her dictionary.

'Oy, love. I need to get in.'

She looked up at the huge lorry on the other side of the gates. Sally and Simon had said something about plants being delivered for the sunhouse next to the pool. The driver grinned down at her and Martine, glad to see a pleasant face for a change, smiled back. 'Please wait. I let you in.' She ran to the security panel just inside the front door and punched in the numbers. Slowly the gates swung open and the lorry drove across the gravel. Only then did Martine see what was lying in front of it.

'Stop, wait!' She ran in front of the lorry, waving her hand.

'Look out, love,' roared the driver.

There was a hollow crunch.

'Oh, no,' whispered Martine, and fell to her knees.

The lorry driver had leapt out and was running towards her. 'What's up?'

Martine surveyed the fragments of wood and leather rue-fully. 'The violin,' she said mournfully. 'It is departed.'

'Bloody hell, you had me worried there for a minute,' said the driver.

Martine scratched her head. 'You have a dictionary, yes?'

He looked at her strangely. 'Not on me.'

'Then, please, do you know the meaning of this word. Now, what was it again? "Impotence." What does it mean?'

The man eyed her doubtfully. Tiny beads of sweat glistened on his forehead. A real man, thought Martine. 'You having me on, love?'

And then they heard it. A loud, high-pitched noise that set the dogs off and hurt her ears. A window opened above them and Martine looked up.

'For pity's sake, do something,' yelled a familiar voice. 'Can't you hear the smoke alarm?'

'Sheet,' said Martine, going pale. 'The iron. I have failed to turn it off.'

The lorry driver was still gawping. 'Is that who I think it

is?' he asked, and ran after Martine into the kitchen. Clouds of black smoke were coming from the iron. Hastily, she threw the extinguisher blanket over it, like last time. There was a smell of burning but no flames, thank God.

Suddenly she was conscious of the driver behind her, not quite touching her but nearer than the situation demanded.

'Bloody hell, you were lucky, girl. By the way, that woman upstairs – isn't she on the telly?'

Martine nodded, trying not to scratch her head in front of this nice man, who seemed so interested in her. But the more she thought about not scratching, the more she needed to.

'Well, I'll be damned. Any road, where do you want these plants?'

'I show you. This way, please.' She smiled over her shoulder. 'Your name, what is it?'

'Barry, love. Like it says on the front of my lorry.'

She looked across the drive and saw 'BARRY' in big letters stuck to the windscreen.

'That is good, yes,' she said. 'Me, I write things down too so I don't forget them.'

'Well, remember my name, won't you, love?'

Martine led the way, sensing that his eyes were focused on her neat rear, which she swung provocatively as she walked, just as her mother had taught her. It was a good feeling, she told herself. She might already have a man but it was nice to be admired. Besides, Barry might be able to explain what this 'impotence' was. Maybe she could put it in her essay to impress her tutor.

'Something wrong with your head, love?'

Martine flushed. 'I am apologising.'

Barry grinned. 'No need to do that. Couldn't help noticing you've been scratching away since I got here. Got a dose of headlice, have you?'

Martine frowned. 'Dose?'

'It's not the dose that's the problem – it's the lice. Little creatures. In your hair. My sister's kids have them all the time. You get them when you're near kids.'

Martine could feel her fingers creeping closer to her head. She had no idea what Barry was talking about but he had mentioned hair and the word was enough to make her head feel on fire again. 'Your sister? She has a baby?'

'Only if you count her old man! Nah, her kids are six, eight and ten-going-on-sixteen. Blimey, you have got it bad, haven't you, love?' Barry was looking at her kindly and she felt warm inside. 'Go and see the chemist, love. Tell them you've got an itch.'

Itch! She could understand that. Chemist, too. Martine did not trust English pharmacists but maybe it was better than going to the doctor. The last time she had gone for her pill prescription, the doctor had not been *sympathique* about her history.

'Thank you,' she said.

'Any time,' said Barry. 'Now, where's this pool, then?'

It took her all morning to sort out Barry and the pool. The poor man was so thirsty and he enjoyed talking as well. It was so nice to chat to someone who was genuinely interested in what she had to say about her work and her employers.

By the time she had finished and Barry had gone, promising to return tomorrow with the second load, it was almost time to collect the children. Where had the day gone? Martine stubbed out one of Simon's cigarettes and tried to think. First, before she picked up Sam and Ellie, she had to go to the supermarket. It was not her job to do the shopping but Sally had been most insistent.

So, too, was Simon – but, so far, she had managed to hold him off. She had her principles, after all.

She did not like English shops, thought Martine, pushing the trolley through the swing door. There was not enough choice and the assistants were too proud.

'Excuse me, madam, would you like to try this?'

Martine smiled at the man in the crisp white coat who was offering her a small glass. How nice! Perhaps she had been too hard on British shopkeepers. She had not realised they gave out free drinks.

'You don't like it, madam?' asked the man.

Martine struggled to be polite. 'It is very *sec* and in France this drink she has more body.'

'Perhaps you would like to try this one, then.'

Martine knocked it back, as her mother had taught her. 'Very good. I prefer this.'

Feeling much happier, she tried to follow Sally's complicated shopping list and slipped some chocolate cake into the trolley for Barry tomorrow. It was hard to pack it all into the boot so a lot had to go on the back seat.

'You're late,' said Sam, accusingly, when she got to school.

'I had to go shopping.'

Ellie tried to get in. 'There isn't room. Where are we going to sit?'

'Where you like.'

'You s-s-smell funny.'

'Don't be rude, Sam.'

'You do. You smell like Daddy does sometimes. Have you been drinking?'

'Ellie, you are a rude girl. Get in now. I am going to drive. If you do not get in, we will be late for television. And then you will not see your parents.'

Martine smiled at herself in the rear-view mirror. She glanced at the children, who were dwarfed by tins, bottles and packets. It had been a nicer afternoon than she had anticipated. Maybe she should go shopping more often.

Even better, when they had returned and she had unpacked all the shopping, made the beds (no time earlier) and run the vacuum-cleaner round the house, she discovered a letter addressed to her that Sally must have slipped under her door. Martine frowned. She had checked the post that morning and there had been nothing. The envelope was loosely sealed – had Sally opened it?

She locked her door and lay on the bed. Maman's familiar writing immediately wafted her away from this horrible place to the old shuttered house in Vérazy, where her mother had also been brought up and her mother's mother.

My precious daughter,

I hope you are well and that your employers are not giving you so much work now. The children sound horrible but I have heard that the English abuse their children with artificial drinks and television. They have only themselves to blame.

I have some good news for you. Madame Devally has moved back to Paris so she cannot cause any more trouble for you. There is still no news of Monsieur although it is rumoured he is still in Calais. People are not talking so much now and those who are say Madame Devally deserved it because she was not a good wife to her husband. Since you left, they are more sympathetic to you and say you were just a young girl.

Do not feel too sad, Martine. There will be other babies. You did what was right, I am sure of that.

Your affectionate Maman.

Martine tore the letter into tiny pieces. She would have liked to keep it but she did not dare: those awful children might find it. Her eyes filled with tears as she flushed the bits down the lavatory. She had not wanted an abortion but her mother had persuaded her it was the only thing to do and, besides, Monsieur Devally had not wanted to know. But that did not stop her thinking of the baby, who would have been nearly a year old now.

She blew her nose. Maman was right. There would be other babies, maybe with her new friend. But, she promised herself, when she did have a child, she would make sure it behaved far better than those children downstairs.

14

'And now the daily service . . .'

Pippa pressed the off switch on the car radio. She wasn't exactly irreligious but she wasn't a firm believer either. Christmas and Easter, that was what church had meant to her since she had left home. Her uncle and aunt had attended services, of course, and when she'd been younger she had gone with them. But as she'd got older, it made less sense. A caring God wouldn't have taken away her parents. A caring God wouldn't have let a lump grow in her breast.

'It might not be what you think it is,' Derek had said again last night, when she had had a good cry in bed.

'But how do you know it *isn't*? You always think everything will be all right.'

He had put down his trade magazine and rubbed his eyes. 'And you always think the worst.'

'Supposing I'm right this time,' she had persisted, edging away from him. 'Supposing I'm ill. And die. You'll have to look after the kids. Have you thought about that?'

'We'll face it if and when it comes. No point in panicking until we know. You've got to stop worrying about everything, Pippa, or you'll make yourself really ill. Right now, the thing that will make you feel better is a good night's sleep.'

To her surprise, she had slept. Deeply. When she woke this morning, her first thought had been that she still had the lump. The second was that she had an appointment with the doctor, who should be able to tell her if it was something to worry about. Pippa had read enough about breasts in women's magazines over the years to know that a lump with a slightly jagged edge was one to be feared. But a smooth-edged one was usually all right. Or was it the other way round? Why couldn't she think straight?

'Live the day as if 'twere thy last,' sang the radio. Weird. She was sure she'd pressed the off button. Besides, she hardly ever had Radio 4 on – the kids never let her. Derek must have changed it over when he'd taken the car for his squash game last night. Pippa switched to Radio 2 but the hymn line resonated in her mind. *Live the day as if 'twere thy last.* Suddenly the hideous waste of a life hit her: she hadn't done half of the things she'd intended to do. Surfing in Australia. A walking tour in Italy. Translating something interesting instead of cookery books. Making wild, passionate love. And not, she realised with a pang of something that hovered between regret and excitement, necessarily with her husband.

'And now for that unforgettable golden oldie by the Hollies . . .'

Pippa drew a sharp breath as the radio broke into song. That particular tune always reminded her of Gus and the discos they had been to in the seventies. That amazing line about needing air to breathe still had the capacity to knock the breath out of her own body.

Just thinking of Gus made her feel better – it always had, ever since they had met at university and discovered, to their mutual surprise, that they had something in common. Like Pippa, Gus was practically parentless. His elderly father had died a few months earlier and his mother had already remarried and was living in France. Pippa's friends had been surprised by and envious of her new acquaintance. Gus was stunning to look at, with his dark chestnut hair, lopsided grin and chocolate-rich accent.

Occasionally, Pippa fantasised about a romantic friendship but – apart from one near-miss – it never happened, even after university. They had fallen out only once and that had been about Derek. 'He's boring,' Gus had decreed, after she had introduced them. 'I think you could find someone far more interesting. Besides, you're too beautiful for him.'

Pippa had flushed and waited for Gus to go on. He hadn't. The following summer, desperate to create the family she had never had, she married Derek.

The song was reverberating round the car, coursing through her blood.

Now she pushed the off button. It was too painful. She had wasted her life – no, that wasn't fair. The children could never be called a waste and she did love Derek. But was she *in love* with him? Had she – what an awful thought – ever been in love with him, experienced a passion that now, with the lump, might be lost to her?

Pippa's temples began to throb. If only life could be as it was last week. She'd give anything to be doing a routine task – even the school run. It felt weird to drive past the girls' school and not stop. Even their rubbish in the car made her feel as though they should be there. Pippa glanced at the sweet papers stuffed into the side pockets. There was an empty crisps packet on the floor and Lucy's maths exercise book, with the tattered purple cover, lay on the back seat. Maybe she should drop it off at school on the way back.

She took a sharp left, swung into the surgery car park, stopped the car and made her way into the waiting room. Last year Dr Bitland's practice had moved from a decrepit grey building to a modern purpose-built red-brick block, with Venetian blinds, green carpets and a water machine.

Unfortunately the only thing that hadn't changed was the receptionist, who was scarily sharp for someone in her early twenties. Pippa had always disliked her: when you rang for an appointment, she always acted as though she was doing you a huge favour. Pippa was also acutely aware that she had blotted her copybook a few weeks ago in forgetting to cancel an appointment for one of the girls who had had a seemingly bad sore throat that had cleared up on its own.

'I've got an appointment at ten,' she said.

The girl barely looked up from the paperwork in front of her. 'Dr Bitland is running late, I'm afraid. You may have a bit of a wait.'

Inwardly groaning, Pippa made her way to one of the few remaining grey- and black-flecked chairs. The surgery was packed, but perhaps some of the other patients were for Dr Bitland's partners or the nurse. Listlessly, she picked up an old copy of *Good Housekeeping*, wishing, too late, that she'd remembered to bring a book or, even better, some work. The magazine looked familiar: she'd read it before or maybe it was even part of a bundle of old magazines she had delivered to the surgery as penance for having forgotten Beth's appointment.

She discarded the magazine in favour of another, and tried to read it, but all the fears she'd been been trying to block out ever since she had found the lump in the shower flooded back. Would Dr Bitland lance it then and there, as had happened with a case history she'd read in *Woman*? You could tell from the fluid if it was malignant or not. Or would she send her straight for a mammogram and, if so, how long would it take?

'Mrs Hallet?'

Pippa stood up as Dr Bitland came out into the waiting room, holding her file. Sweating with apprehension, she followed her down the corridor to her room. The doctor settled herself in front of her screen and indicated that Pippa should take a seat. 'Now, what can I do for you?'

'I've got a lump.' Tears were swelling into her eyes. 'I felt it in the shower yesterday but I couldn't get an appointment until today. It's here, just under my armpit.'

Dr Bitland's voice was cool and calm. 'Can you slip off your T-shirt?'

Awkwardly, Pippa did as she was told. She could feel the lump aching slightly. That was a good sign, she knew. Malignant lumps didn't normally ache. 'Left a bit,' she said.

'Yes, I can feel it.' Dr Bitland focused her eyes on the wall behind while her fingers gently kneaded the lump. Pippa wanted to talk but Dr Bitland's concentration stopped her. 'Slip your top back on.'

She turned her back to Pippa and typed laboriously, one-fingered. 'I'd like it checked out. Under the new NHS guidelines, patients who present with symptoms like this are seen within a fortnight.'

Pippa's pulse raced. 'But it's nothing serious, is it? I thought it was just a cyst. It's a bit painful – more of an ache than a pain. I thought that was all right.'

Dr Bitland addressed the wall behind her. 'We always like to have lumps checked out. The consultant might suggest a mammogram. Are you covered privately?'

Pippa shook her head.

'That doesn't matter. You'll get a phone call in a day or so from the hospital and the results will either come here or the doctor will tell you directly.'

Pippa stood up unsteadily, willing herself not to cry or she'd never be able to walk back through the waiting room. 'Can't it be any sooner than a fortnight?'

'Not unless you want to pay. Even then the waiting list might not be any shorter. A fortnight isn't long, although in these cases I appreciate that the sooner you're seen the better.'

Pippa didn't want to hear any more. Why couldn't they teach doctors to be human and show some sympathy?

'Try not to worry too much,' added Dr Bitland, as Pippa moved towards the door. 'You say it's the first time you've felt it and that's good, because it means we've caught it early.'

Caught what? And suppose the lump had been there all the

time and Pippa just hadn't felt it? She didn't examine herself as regularly as she should, partly because she was always busy. In fact, she'd only noticed it by chance because she'd shaved herself instead of her usual wax. That meant the lump might have been there for months . . .

Somehow she made her way back to the car. Trembling, she switched on her mobile. No point in ringing Derek: he never had his on unless it was a lunchbreak. Besides, it wasn't him she wanted to speak to.

'Gus? It's me.'

That was how they always announced themselves to each other and they always knew who it was, despite Gus's entourage of admirers.

'Pippa! I've been so worried. How did it go?'

He'd been waiting for her call. Had Derek?

'She wants me to have it checked out.'

'Good. Much better than ignoring it.' Gus's voice was wonderfully reassuring and in control, as though he wouldn't let anything happen to her. 'Just as well I'm in town. What are you doing for lunch tomorrow?'

'Sorry. Hang on a moment, can you?' She leaned back against the headrest, forced herself to swallow the sob in her throat and blew her nose.

'Are you OK, Pip?'

'Sort of.'

'Can you see me tomorrow?'

Pippa thought of the Thursday deadline on the manuscript that was lying, unfinished, on her desk. 'That would be lovely.'

'Right. I'll be at your place by twelve thirty. Get yourself dressed up and we'll go somewhere special. All right, Gorgeous?'

'Are you sure? Aren't you busy?'

'Pippa.' Gus's voice sounded deeper and more serious than it had for a long time. 'Nothing is more important than this.'

She drove back, feeling slightly better. She ought to ring Harriet too, but maybe she'd wait a couple of days. Her friend had been in such a state over Charlie, damn him, that Pippa felt she couldn't put any more on her. As for Derek, well, she'd tell him when he got back. He'd have to take her seriously now.

Pippa felt her eyes fill again. A mammogram! The doctor hadn't dismissed it as an ordinary cyst that could be ignored. What would happen to the girls? How long might she have? Who would plant the geraniums that were still bumping around in the boot from Sunday's trip to the garden centre? *Why the heck was she worrying about geraniums?*

The car in front stopped at a zebra crossing and, for a ghastly minute, Pippa couldn't remember where the brake was. She applied it just in time. The driver in front remained at a standstill as the man who was crossing came up to his window, obviously asking for directions. On another day the delay would have irritated her. Yet now, as she sat there with the traffic building up behind her, the interruption seemed meaningless. Nothing was important any more. Only life. Which she had taken for granted until now.

Finally she pulled up outside the house, almost too tired to get out. She should have mentioned it to the doctor – the over-whelming exhaustion she'd been feeling for weeks, if not months.

She stumbled up the steps and fumbled in her bag for the key with its 'I Love Mum' tag, which the girls had given her on Mothering Sunday. She shut the door behind her, then made her way to the bottom of the stairs, where the carpet was wearing thin, and put her head into her hands. 'I don't want to have a lump,' she howled, hot tears streaming down her face. 'It's not fair.'

Finally, when she'd stopped sobbing and blown her nose on the last square of lavatory paper in the downstairs loo, she picked up the phone and punched in Harriet's number.

'Harriet and Charlie aren't in at the moment. Please leave a message and we'll ring you back.'

Pippa slammed down the receiver. At least she was seeing Gus tomorrow. He'd understand.

15

BETTY

No Betty of Balham today. It's my throat again. Too sore to talk. It's always been my weak spot since it happened.

The parents seem to be behaving themselves this morning. That wicked woman in the green-blue Discovery didn't leave her little boy alone like she did yesterday. Still drive too fast, of course. All of them. Had a letter from the council about that today.

Dear Mrs Holmes,

Thank you for your letter dated 26 June. Your suggestion of a second speed camera is currently being considered. You are, however, aware that there is already one camera on the stretch of road you refer to.

We were sorry to hear of your experience but assure you that road safety is important to us too.

And so on.

Waffle, like Terry says. Utter waffle. One of his favourite phrases.

The trick is to keep myself busy, like Terry tells me. The leaflets take up a lot of my time but they're worth it even if they just stop one person speeding. Had them typed out and copied at the shop on the corner. They know me so well they ought to give me a discount.

GO SLOW!

That's the headline, as the girl called it.

CALLING ALL PARENTS! PLEASE GO SLOW ON THE SCHOOL
RUN OR YOU COULD HIT A CHILD.
ONE DAY THAT CHILD MIGHT BE YOURS.

That's all. If you put too much, they don't bother reading it. Today I'm handing them out by the library. Tomorrow it's Boots. Terry prefers the library, don't you, duck? All right, all right, I'm nearly ready now. You too? Off we go, then.

HARRIET

Harriet had only just put the key into the lock when she heard the phone ringing in the hall. Charlie! It had to be.

She dumped her bag on the doorstep, flew in and grabbed the receiver just before it cut into answerphone.

The sound of her friend's voice was acutely disappointing.

'Pippa! Hang on a minute. I've just got back from the super-market and my bag's outside. One sec . . . Right, I'm back.'

'I've got a lump.' Pippa's voice was flat. 'In my breast. The right one. I found it in the shower on Monday morning.'

What?

'Why didn't you tell me before?'

'I didn't want to bother you, but I've been ringing you all day. The answerphone's been on.'

'I'm sorry. I had an appointment. Then I went to the gym and did some shopping.' Harriet felt awful – she sounded so self-centred. She'd done nothing but think of herself this week. But a lump! Cancer! It put everything else – including Charlie – into perspective.

'Have you been to the doctor?'

'She's sending me to a consultant.'

'When?'

Pippa laughed hoarsely. 'Within a fortnight, apparently. It's going to be the longest fortnight of my life.'

Harriet tried to think rationally. 'A lump doesn't have to be . . . well, you know what.'

'But it could be.'

'Yes. But even if it is, there are so many things that can be done nowadays. My mother's friend had a double mastectomy five years ago and she's fine now.'

'But I don't want to lose my breast.'

God, she'd said the wrong thing. 'Pippa, don't even start thinking about that yet. It hasn't happened.'

'Thanks. That's what Derek says. He's not even worried.'

'I'm sure he is. And so am I, but I'm trying to put it into perspective for you. Now, forget about the kids. I'll pick them up. Make yourself a cup of sweet tea and go and lie down for a bit.'

'I can't. I've got a deadline.'

'Sod the deadline. Tell your editor you're ill.'

'If I do she won't give me any more work.' Pippa made a funny noise at the other end of the phone. 'Then again, maybe I won't be around for more work.'

Harriet glanced at her watch. If she had more time, she'd go over there right now and put her arms round her friend. But if she did she'd be late for the children. 'Let's have lunch tomorrow. Or we could go to yoga – we haven't been together for ages.'

'I can't. I'm seeing Gus.'

Harriet had never met Gus but she had heard about him. 'Good for you. Well, call me afterwards and we'll do something on Thursday.'

'That's my deadline day.'

'Look, I'll see you tonight when I drop the kids off. Are you sure you're all right on your own?'

'Fine.'

Harriet was reluctant to put down the phone. 'Try not to assume the worst.'

'OK.'

Pippa wasn't reassured, thought Harriet, rushing back to the car to unload her shopping before she dashed out to collect the kids. And frankly, if she were in her shoes, she wouldn't be either.

KITTY

My dad's in a place called Dewbi and he's been there for ages. At first he used to ring us but now he dusn't do it as much. He's coming home this Friday and I'm really looking forward to it. I think he went away becos I am sumtimes nawty but I'm going to be good now. I want to be good becos I don't want him to go away again. My mum sumtimes cries becos he's not here. I've seen her. She puts her head on the kitchen table and cries into her arms so we can't here her. But we do. Sumtimes she is very happy and larfs a lot espeshully when she is talking to her friend Pippa. When dad gets home, I hope she'll larf even more.

Kitty had got back earlier than usual, thanks to a lift from Judy Foster, and put down the exercise book on the desk in her living room, which doubled as her bedroom. Poor kid. Guiltily she thought of all the times she'd been impatient with Bruce. If she'd known about the family situation she'd have been more understanding. Why hadn't his mother told the school that something was wrong? On the other hand maybe nothing *was*. Lots of fathers worked away from home, and just because Bruce's mother had a good cry every now and then it didn't necessarily mean the family was breaking up.

Kitty had a bit of a weep occasionally and it made her feel better. She looked round her room, which wasn't hers at all but belonged to her landlady. It really was a dump, with the eighties flowered wallpaper and purple carpet. Next term she'd find somewhere nicer; maybe she'd even have saved enough for a deposit. 'It would be nice to have someone to talk to in the evenings,' she said aloud. Things *must* be bad if she'd started talking to herself. Was she really so lonely?

Maybe she should have taken up Mandy's offer of Rod's friend. Kitty reached for her mobile. Should she or not?

She'd get to the end of this batch of essays, then decide.

TUESDAY P.M.

'Nice to have your old dad picking you up, then?'

'It's OK. Hugo's dad does it *every* day when he's home.'

'*I* like it, Dad. Evie hates us eating in her car.'

'Yeah. It's really boring.'

'Still, Dad, your car's in a bit of a mess, isn't it?'

'OK, we'll clear it out.'

'Five quid.'

'Three.'

'Shit, Dad, we've left Sam and Ellie behind!'

'What? No one told *me* we had to bring them back.'

'That's right, sing it. Like this. H-Y-A-C-I-N-T-H.' Well done, Jess. Maybe singing *is* the way to crack it!'

'I thought we were going shopping. You just said that, didn't you, so Jason couldn't drive me back? You've got to let me grow up some time, Dad . . . Knightsbridge? Now you're talking, Dad. Thanks. You're the best. And I promise. Just a couple of shops and then I'll do my homework.'

'Ig-ig-ignoranus, Marty. That's w-w-what you are. Ha, ha. *Aynus, aynus, aynus . . .*'

Very well thought-out, Bruce, and nicely structured. 9/10.

WEDNESDAY

16

*'Wake up to Wogan, dah-dah-dah . . . The American
school siege is now in its third day . . .'*

Harriet didn't usually have this programme on but one of the
children (Bruce?) must have been fiddling with the radio. At
least the pleasantly mindless banter seemed to be keeping them
quiet in the back, giving her time to squeeze her pelvic-floor
muscles *and* think about Pippa.

A lump was one of the top five fears in any woman's list
– God, what must Pippa be feeling? Clearly Derek wasn't any
help.

No, that wasn't fair. He just couldn't show his feelings. Yet
Harriet had always thought she and Charlie were open with
each other and had been taken aback when he had said he
felt neglected. But that wasn't keeping his emotions to himself: it was just plain childish. She shivered, wishing she'd
brought her cardigan. It seemed cooler today.

'Mrs Chapman, can you test me on my geography, please?'
called Beth. 'Mummy didn't have time last night.'

Harriet took a sharp left; it was her new short-cut to beat
the traffic that was building up at the temporary lights ahead.
'Darling, as I've said before, please call me Harriet. I'll do my
best but it's a bit difficult to test you and drive at the same
time.'

'You wrapped up Susie's birthday present last week while
you were driving,' pointed out Jess.

'Yes, but she shouldn't have.' Bruce was full of righteous indignation. 'You're meant to have both hands on the wheel.'

'I was at traffic-lights for most of the time,' said Harriet. 'Tell you what, Beth, why don't you ask me the questions and then you can tell me if the answers are right? You could pretend to be the teacher.'

'She'd like that,' said Lucy. 'She's bossy enough.'

'Shut up.'

Poor girls, thought Harriet. She didn't know how much they knew about Pippa but she was pretty sure there'd be some tension at home. 'Right, let's have question number one.'

Beth coughed importantly. 'What does CAP stand for?'

'This isn't biology, is it?' enquired Harriet, doubtfully.

'No, geography.'

'CAP? Gosh, I'm not sure.'

'Common Agricultural Policy,' announced Beth, with relish. 'It's something that the EU introduced to make sure that farmers have a decent standard of living; that there's a good balance of food in Europe and that everyone can afford food at a reasonable price.'

'Beth, you *are* clever. Bruce, did you know that?'

'Yes. No. I don't care anyway. Look! No, idiot, over there! It's my art teacher and he's smoking!'

Harriet smiled at the indignation in the back. There had been so many anti-smoking talks at school that they were all deeply against it. She wondered briefly what they would say if they met her father. She hadn't seen him for nearly two years but last time they'd met he was still getting through at least forty a day.

'He shouldn't smoke! He also teaches us PSHE and everyone knows smoking's bad for you.'

The young were so unforgivingly moral, thought Harriet. 'What about the next question, Beth?'

'Give five examples of farming.'

'Er, poultry, dairy, arable . . . I can't think of any more. Sorry.'

'Reindeer and diversification,' sang out Beth. 'Diversification is when the farmers. . . .'

Harriet tried to listen but her thoughts kept returning to her father. Since the divorce, she hadn't seen much of him and the children had only ever visited him three or four times. She had blamed him for that – he never suggested they came up to Yorkshire – but her fears about Charlie were now making her wonder if she should have made more effort with her father. If she and Charlie split up, would the children still bother to visit or take their own children to see him?

Harriet sighed. Divorce had so many long-term effects, right down the generations. Was Monica right about children being more resilient than she thought? She'd been devastated at sixteen (only four years older than Bruce) when her own parents had split up. But they had been vitriolic towards each other and her mother had actively discouraged her from seeing her father. No wonder they weren't close now.

In contrast, the children seemed to have accepted Charlie's absence. Then again, they would. He often went away on business – if not for two months at a time. Would they be happy to see their father only at weekends? Would she be happy to sleep and sort out the day-to-day domestic crises on her own? She'd coped during the last two months. But she would feel a huge gap. She and Charlie had been together too long for her to start again.

'Look!' said Bruce. His voice, cutting into her thoughts, made her swerve.

'Don't point like that,' she said sharply. 'It's distracting for the driver. You almost hit me.'

'Yes, but look! Too late. You've missed it.'

'What?'

'A big photograph,' said Jess, looking behind them. 'Above those roses.'

'It was a boy,' added Lucy, full of importance at having seen it too. 'Do you think he's missing?'

Harriet wondered whether to tell the children the truth, if only to make them cross the road more carefully. Despite what she was always telling them, she'd seen Bruce and Jess fly across without checking. That was the trouble with taking them everywhere by car. They weren't street-wise, as she'd been at their age.

'People put flowers by the road when someone's been hurt,' she said. 'Maybe that boy was run over there.'

'Do you think he was killed?' whispered Beth.

'Possibly,' said Harriet. 'That's why you need to look carefully when you cross the road.'

'Stop going on.' Bruce sounded impatient. 'Mum, drop me here. Now! No, not by those girls! God, you're so embarrassing.'

Jess giggled. 'He fancies that one on the right – the one with the earring in her nose, don't you, Bruce?'

'Shut up.'

'Don't hit me.'

'I didn't. Cry-baby.'

'Calm down,' said Harriet. There was no point in reading the Riot Act – not just before they went into school. It would only upset her *and* Bruce, even though he hid his feelings. Far better to praise him when he did something right. The first time she'd read that in an American magazine, brought home by Charlie after a trip, she'd dismissed it as rubbish. But when she put it into practice, she found that praising him and ignoring some of the bad things worked better than Charlie yelling at him.

Bruce didn't bother to say goodbye. She watched him, in her wing mirror, walking past the girls and flushing when one turned to say something. He was only young, but already the opposite sex was playing a part in his imagination. Long may that last. The thought of a teenage bed-hopping Bruce was too much to contemplate.

'Got everything, girls?' she said, getting out and going

through the boot to check they hadn't left anything behind. Lucy's violin, Jess's shoulder-bag – so heavy she could barely lift it – Beth's hockey stick. ''Bye. Your mum's picking up tonight, remember.'

'Excuse me.'

Harriet turned round to see the broad-shouldered man from the waiting room yesterday. He was parked alongside her in a red Fiesta with an L-plate on the front, but there was no sign of the daughter he had mentioned.

He was holding something out to her. 'Hi. It's me. Nick. From yesterday. Remember?'

She nodded, embarrassed.

'This must have fallen out when your bag fell open. Sorry – I must have picked it up by mistake.'

'My phone!'

The man patted his top pocket, grinning ruefully. 'Couldn't live without mine.'

The back of his car was packed with camera stuff – tripods and big black boxes. 'Well, I expect you need it in your job,' Harriet said.

'Yes. Actually, I was wondering . . .'

On Nick's behalf Harriet made an apologetic sign at the van behind. The driver was hooting.

'I'd better move on,' he said. 'See you, then.'

She got back into the car, deflated. He was nice – at least, he seemed nice. God, Harriet. Just because your husband might or might not be leaving you, doesn't mean you have to start noticing every bloke who smiles at you.

She turned on the mobile and pressed the unlock key. She'd been looking for it all over the house, ever since yesterday, wondering if Charlie had phoned again. When she'd rung it from the landline, in the hope of locating it, she had connected with its answerphone. MESSAGE, it now said. Message! The kids had taught her how to text soon after Charlie had gone to Dubai. It was part of a campaign that was being run in schools nationwide, sponsored by the parents of that poor girl who had been murdered. 'Teach Ur Mum 2 Text', it had been called, and Jess had taken it seriously. As a result, Harriet could just about send a message to the children – and receive one.

'Bck early. Thursday. Flight arrives 11.10. Will get taxi. M.'

Shaking, she scrolled down to reply: 'Will meet u at airport. Luv H.'

It was only after she'd sent it that she realised he hadn't said 'love' in his text or even dropped in one tiny X.

Harriet drove home as fast as she dared. Thursday! Tomorrow. And still so much to get done. Her hair for a start – thank goodness she'd got her appointment this afternoon for her highlights. And the house – she'd have a good tidy-up. Charlie hated mess. Oh, God, the bathroom cabinet! Bruce had accidentally brought it down off the wall. His story was that he had just opened the door and it fell off. Jess had said he was clambering on top of it. Harriet had been intending to get someone in to Rawl-plug it back but, with so little time, she'd have to do it herself.

She pulled up outside the house and headed straight for the garage to find Charlie's drill. It wasn't there, although nearly every other piece of DIY equipment was present. She'd have to go next door to borrow one.

Her neighbour, a kindly man in his late sixties, took ages to find his. 'Must be here somewhere. Ah, yes, thought so.' He produced it with a grin. 'Under the stairs. Never use it myself. Goodness, Charlie's lucky to have a handy wife – and a pretty one.'

'Thanks. Sorry I can't stay but I've got to dash.'

Her neighbour had nodded understandingly. 'I know. You young, always rushing around. My daughter's the same. Hardly see her.'

Harriet took the drill and escaped. She wasn't going to get into another guilt trip about her father. He had left her mother and had only himself to blame. She was going to concentrate on getting the house ready for Charlie.

Standing on a chair, she tried to remember how her husband did it. First she needed to drill a hole into which to push the Rawl-plug. Then she had to lift the cabinet (just possible if she balanced one side on the basin) and twist in the screw. Simple.

She plugged in the drill and pressed the button. Nothing. She pressed again. Still nothing.

How was she ever going to cope if she couldn't even do something as simple as turning on the drill? And now the bloody doorbell was ringing.

'What?' she yelled out of the window.

Her elderly neighbour was standing below. 'I'm afraid I've given you the wrong drill, dear. That one doesn't work. It's why it was under the stairs.' He waved another at her triumphantly. 'You need this one. It's a real corker. My daughter gave it to me for Christmas. Shall I come up? The door's open.'

Thank heavens! 'Yes, please.'

He brought it up to her. 'Can I do it for you?'

'Actually, if you don't mind, I'll do it myself.'

Harriet plugged in the drill, held it against the mark she'd made on the wall and pressed the button. There was a loud roaring noise and red plaster dust flew everywhere. She wasn't hopeless. It had been the drill, not her.

'You're not going to lift that cabinet on to the wall on your own, are you, dear? If you don't mind me saying so, that really is a two-man job.'

Harriet eyed it. 'Sure you don't mind?'

Her neighbour smiled. 'My dear, it's a pleasure to be needed.'

After that, she had to make him a cup of tea, cut a slice of home-made Victoria sponge and listen to his warblings about the daughter in France who always had him over in the summer. Eventually, she explained about her hair appointment and made it to the salon just in time.

After the drill scene, it was a relief to sit still for a while. Highlights always took ages but she had booked a manicure as well.

'Going somewhere special, then?' asked the girl, as she buffed Harriet's nails while another girl wrapped her hair in foil.

'Not really. I just felt my nails needed doing.' Harriet hesitated. 'My husband's coming back tomorrow after a business trip.'

'Ah, that's sweet. You want to look nice for him, then.'

'I suppose so.'

For a ridiculous second, Harriet felt like a bride on her wedding day. No, that was stupid. She and Charlie had had all that. Now they had to face some hard home truths. The hair was just a form of self-protection: she wanted to look good – or at least as good as any other woman Charlie might have come across.

'That's lovely,' she told the girl, when she'd finished blow-drying it.

'Glad you like it. Do you want some spray to keep it in place?'

'Just a bit. Actually, I must dash or I'm going to be late for the children.' She pressed a pound into the girl's hand. 'Thanks very much.' She should have given her more but she'd run out of cash. If she was quick, she could nip to the bank before Pippa brought the children back. But first she needed the chemist. While she had been flicking through a magazine at the hairdresser's, she'd spotted an advert for a tampon-like device that strengthened the pelvic floor. Worth trying, especially if Charlie was coming home.

Harriet blushed as she scanned the shelves. 'Excuse me, I'm trying to find something called Aqualift,' she said shyly, to one of the assistants.

'Over there, on the pregnancy-products aisle,' said the girl, loudly.

Harriet looked round, worried that someone she knew

might be about. Pregnancy products? That hadn't been there when she was expecting. Still, here it was – and there was a shelf full of Aqualifts, indicating a needy market. Harriet examined the pretty blue box curiously. It looked like one of Jess's Polly Pocket toys from when she was younger but inside there was a white plastic cone. According to the instructions, you added small metal weights to it to strengthen your inside.

Harriet paid at the counter, then headed to the bank. The queue, as usual, was horrendous but she couldn't remember her pin number which had changed last week. That ruled out the hole in the wall. Why were there only ever two cashiers? To pass the time, she read most of the leaflets on the stand. *Saving Up for a Baby. Saving Up for Your Wedding Day.* There should be *Saving Up For Your Divorce or Uncertain Future*, she thought. Now, that would be really useful.

Finally, it was her turn. Harriet pushed across her credit card. 'A hundred pounds please. In tens.'

'I just need to check your balance,' said the girl.

Harriet sighed. She came here every week and the bank knew perfectly well they were good customers. Charlie earned an extremely respectable salary, although during his absence he had suggested she had a separate housekeeping account to make it 'easier'. He would, he promised, pay part of his salary into it. Harriet had been surprised but with the upheaval surrounding his departure, it hadn't seemed significant. Since then, though, she'd noticed that the staff's attitude to her at the bank had been less friendly; almost as if she was a less important customer now that she had a separate account from her high-earning husband.

'I'm afraid we can't give you the money,' said the girl, pushing a piece of paper towards her. 'You're already overdrawn and extra money will take you above the agreed overdraft.'

'But I can't be. My husband was paying in some money this week.'

'I'm sorry. If you would like to see the manager, you can join the queue over there.'

Mortified by how much the people behind her could hear (why didn't banks have a private room any more for this kind of thing?), Harriet took the piece of paper, screwed it up and walked out. Why hadn't Charlie paid in the money? A cold shudder went through her as she realised that this was what it would be like if she was on her own: she would be worrying constantly about her outgoings. She hadn't been used to this – and it wasn't fair. She would tell Charlie so. Enough was enough.

17

EVIE

> *'There have been unconfirmed reports of gunfire at the school in Ohio where a schoolboy is holding his classmates hostage . . .'*

Why was the news always so depressing? Evie slid a CD into the slot. Ella Fitzgerald's rich, throw-it-at-me-and-I'll-survive voice always gave her strength, even on a day like this when she was stuck behind a stupid L-driver who was meandering all over the road. There should be a law banning them from driving in rush-hour.

Thank God Martine had been able to take the kids to school that morning. This was the third time in as many months that the bloody Discovery had refused to start, which meant she'd had to take Robin's old Saab to the office. She hated not driving an automatic – damn, she'd stalled again. She disliked his choice of radio station and she couldn't believe the mess this car was in.

God, she was in a bad mood – as Robin had pointed out that morning. But he'd been in a filthy one too. Evie had written features on how redundancy affected marriages but, like all the other gritty issues in life, you never knew what they were really like until you'd experienced them yourself. She didn't need one of the glib consultants they used on *Just For You* magazine to tell her that Robin's lack of self-esteem had spread to below the sheets. On top of that, with the way things were going, they might not be able to afford Jack's fees at the pre-prep in two years. As it was, Robin felt it was unfair: the girls were at state school for financial reasons, and he thought Jack should follow suit.

'Don't think about it,' she told herself firmly. She'd sort it out, as she always did. It wasn't for nothing that she'd been up all night, working out a fierce campaign to get her career back on track. She'd got some cracking ideas, if she said so herself. All she had to do now was sway Bulmer at the all-important meeting on Friday morning.

But first she needed to stop off at Boots to get another pair of tights. At the last lot of lights, she'd noticed a snag in the pair she was wearing. Evie checked the mirror, to ensure that there weren't any traffic wardens on the loose, then parked on a double yellow and leaped out of the car, straight into a passer-by who loomed up out of nowhere.

'Ouch!'

Evie looked in dismay at the old woman. She seemed familiar – a former cleaning lady? A neighbour?

'Look where you're going,' grumbled the woman, rubbing her shoulder.

'I'm really sorry,' said Evie.

'Well, you can make up for it by taking one of these.' She handed Evie a leaflet.

Evie, who always accepted leaflets – journalistic curiosity – scanned it.

CALLING ALL PARENTS!

'Do you have a personal interest in this?' she asked.

The woman snorted.

She wasn't as old as Evie had first thought but the lines on her face were deep. Grubby nails too, Evie noted, with distaste.

'My son got run over two years ago. Sixteen, he was. Driver didn't stop.

'I'm so sorry.' Evie re-read the leaflet. 'Actually, I might be able to help you. I edit a magazine and we're doing a piece on campaigners.'

'Yer what?'

'We're writing a story about people like yourself who are trying to get other people interested in their personal causes,' said Evie, patiently. 'Do you think I could take your number and contact you? Then I could tell you about it when we both have more time.'

'I'm not on the phone. Can't afford it.'

'Oh. Well, do you want to tell me where you live?'

The woman glared at her suspiciously. 'Not really.'

'I see. Well, maybe I could send my features editor down here later on to talk to you. Would that be all right? It might help you in your cause – stop people driving so fast.'

'I don't know. Maybe. I'll think about it.'

'Fine.' Annoyed, Evie walked into the shop to buy her tights. Sometimes women like that didn't know what was good for them. Fancy going to all that trouble to print those leaflets, then turning down the kind of publicity for which advertisers paid a fortune.

It wasn't until she had paid for the tights that she remembered the car! She'd left it on a double yellow but her conversation with the woman had made her forget about it.

'Keep the change!' she called to the astounded till girl, and ran out of the shop. She reached the car just as the traffic warden was writing the ticket. 'I'm sorry,' she panted. 'I had to buy something urgently. Some cough medicine. For my son.'

As she spoke, she dropped the Boots bag and the packet of tights fell out on to the pavement. They both looked at it and Evie felt like a criminal.

'I've started writing so I can't stop even if your son *is* poorly,' said the traffic warden, her voice laden with sarcasm. 'You're causing an obstruction, which can be dangerous.'

'I'm sorry,' said Evie. As she climbed into the car, she saw the leaflet woman throwing her a reproachful look.

She felt wretched all the way to the office, and the thought of that poor sixteen-year-old haunted her. She was so lucky to have Jack – and Robin. From now on, she'd be more grateful. She'd also give Dad a ring that night: they hadn't had a good natter since last week. His mind was sharper than hers, at times, and he still drove, part-time, but she was conscious that this year he'd be sixty. No spring chicken any more. Besides, he liked talking to her about her work and Evie always felt bad that she never had enough time for him. But, right now, she needed to focus on work.

She pulled into the car park, stopped and leaned over for her files. She'd go through the ideas with Janine – if she was in. The girl had got herself pregnant again, which was highly inconvenient. When you were aiming for the top (and she was pretty sure Janine was), you could only have two kids, max.

As Evie picked up the files, a piece of paper fluttered off the back seat to join the rest of the rubbish on the floor. She picked it up and stuffed it into the side pocket, next to an A4 file. Something on the front caught her attention. It was the name of a loan company. She opened it and skimmed the piece of paper inside. No address or even a phone number. Just a list of figures and a demand at the bottom to pay . . . How much? Her eyes widened. How could he possibly owe all this? She knew, of course, about the second mortgage but this was impossible! It was so far beyond their reach that it was almost laughable.

There had to be a mistake. Quickly, she punched in Home on the phone. 'Hi. This is Evie and Robin . . .' Then his mobile. He answered immediately, as if he was expecting a call. It was clear from his voice that he wasn't expecting *her*.

Evie felt a cold shiver pass through her. 'Robin,' she said tightly. 'We need to talk.'

18

NICK

Nick couldn't help singing along with Elton. To Julie's chagrin, he loved accompanying all the golden oldies on the radio with the volume up and the windows down. 'When you're my age and taking your kids to school, you'll do the same,' he'd say to her. 'Aren't you impressed I know the words?'

'Kind of,' she'd say, grinning. 'You haven't got a bad voice, you know, Dad. At least, not for someone your age.'

It was great when they larked around like that. The journey to school – as long as her driving wasn't too terrifying – provided him with a great opportunity to talk to her. And, according to every parenting article he had read, it was vital to keep communication channels open with your teenager.

Now, even though Juliana wasn't in the car, he still loved singing along to Elton. He could see Juliana dancing there in front of him, through the windscreen, in a scarlet, backless dress that was too tight after their daughter had been born . . .

Christ, he'd been stupid. Why hadn't he stopped her trying to get back into modelling? She'd been out of it too long – and she could have done something else. Set up her own model agency like other ex-models. Anything. But she had been determined. Just as she'd been determined to be the perfect mum.

Now, as he parked the car at the magazine offices near Waterloo Bridge, he mentally kicked himself, just as he did every day of his life. He should have told her she couldn't do everything. But he had been so keen to help that he had done the very thing he shouldn't. He'd even gone on a diet with her.

'Hi, Nick. The models are getting changed inside.'

Janine was getting out of her car. She was four, five months pregnant, thought Nick, with a practised eye, but that hadn't blunted her ambition. Like Juliana, she wanted to get to the top and have a family. Why not? Some people did it, like her editor, Evie.

Nick walked up to the offices with Janine, shouldering his heavy camera and carrying his light meter. Niall, his assistant, should be here soon. 'How are you feeling?' he asked, out of politeness.

'Fine,' said Janine, promptly. 'Now, about the shoot. I want it to look fresh for autumn. Maybe a blue background. And what do you think about . . .'

Nick listened to her ideas, which she had obviously thought through beforehand. Janine was clearly one of those women who didn't do pregnancy patter. It was as though she was trying to say, 'OK, I'm pregnant but that isn't going to affect my output.' God, it must be hard to be a woman in a competitive world. Briefly he thought of Harriet. Pretty woman. Sad eyes. Nicely streaked blonde hair that might be soft to touch. Did she have a job? He didn't think so.

He and Janine got into the lift together. A woman wearing a crisp mint linen suit was already inside it. 'Janine. Good. I want a word about the shoot before I start my meeting.'

She looked at Nick briefly, without interest, then back at Janine. Great. She hadn't recognised him. Even though he had only been trying to help when she'd lost her kid, Evie had succeeded in making him feel as though he'd been in the wrong. He'd had enough of an emotional roller-coaster this morning, thinking about Juliana, and then that row with Julie about her being out late last night. He needed peace now to concentrate on the job.

They got out at the ninth floor, Evie still instructing Janine, who looked as though she didn't appreciate it. 'Don't I know you from somewhere?' she said to Nick.

Nick hesitated.

'Nick did our last cover,' interrupted Janine. 'The one Bulmer liked so much. Remember?'

Evie's face cleared. 'That's right. Well, make sure this one is just as good.'

'Something's bitten her this morning,' murmured Janine, as Evie marched off. 'Probably worried about the meeting on Friday.'

'What's that about?' asked Nick, hoisting the camera on to his other shoulder.

Janine smiled smugly. 'Can't say, I'm afraid. But I'm hoping it'll be good news.'

Tough cookie, thought Nick. That was where women like Janine were different from Juliana. They might share ambition but Juliana had had heart. Julie, too. She was kind and loving but stubborn. And it was up to him to make sure she didn't go down the same road as her mother, which was why he couldn't allow her to go out tomorrow night. Only one night out during the week – that was the rule. And he didn't really feel happy about that.

Thinking about his daughter and that boy had distracted him. It was with a supreme effort that he pulled himself back to perform under Janine's beady eye.

'Right? So we're clear on the background colour, Nick?'

'I still think you should go for something warmer. It's the Christmas issue. Readers want to feel cosy.'

'I'm well aware of what readers want, thank you very much.'

'No.' Evie had come into the room without either of them noticing. Now she spoke quietly but firmly: 'Let's listen to him. What do you suggest, Nick?'

'Red, as I said at the beginning. Not a harsh red, a warm one.'

'It won't work, Evie.'

'I'm not sure.' Evie was silent. Both Janine and Nick knew better than to interrupt. 'We'll do two and compare them.'

Janine was astounded. 'But that'll push us over budget.'

'Not if Nick's careful.' She looked at him and smiled dangerously. Nick felt his skin prickle. 'Do you think you can do it?'

He thought of the university fees coming up and the prospect of more work at *Just For You*. 'I reckon so.'

It had, he thought, stopping the car at the off-licence next to Boots on his way home, been a close shave. No doubt about it. He had annoyed Janine by pushing for his own idea but he was certain (well, 99 per cent) that it would work. The magazine world was stiff with enemies and he only hoped Evie, who had seemed interested in his ideas, was going to hang around. If she moved on, he would have to answer to Janine.

'Have a leaflet, sir.' A woman with greasy hair in an elastic band pushed a poorly printed piece of paper at him.

He glanced at it, unseeing.

GO SLOW!

Hadn't he had one of these before? If these do-gooders had his problems, they might realise how lucky they were. If he was quick, there was just time to nip into Tesco and get some supper for tonight. On the other hand, maybe they'd just have a takeaway as a treat. It might not be very nutritious but there were times when every parent had to recognise their limits. He'd spend the afternoon developing the negatives from yesterday and drop them off with the client on his way to school. Picking up Julie was a relief, not a chore – even with her driving. Sometimes, he thought, if he didn't have his daughter to talk to, he'd go mad.

If he wasn't heading that way already.

19

   'Screech, crash, screech . . .'

What kind of music was that? thought Kitty disgustedly, and tuned to another station.

'What yer listening to, Miss?'

'Let's hear it, then!'

'What kind of music do you like, Miss?'

Standing in the bus queue with the kids squawking, Kitty pretended not to hear them through the headphones. It would be different when she got to school where it was her job to listen to them and to coax out all the potential that, she was certain, lay dormant under those brash exteriors. But at eight twenty a.m., she was still Kitty Hayling, with a life of her own outside St Theresa's.

The bus was on time this morning, Kitty observed, as she let the hordes surge on ahead of her. It was easier that way – she wouldn't get bumped so much, even if it did mean she had to stand.

She nodded at the bus driver, who said something she couldn't hear. Kitty removed her earpiece. 'Sorry?'

'I said, I don't know how you cope with that lot.'

'How did you know I was a teacher?'

'Because your bag is always full of exercise books and because the kids have told me. Little terrors, aren't they?'

'They're not so bad.' What did he mean, the kids had told him? Had he asked them or just heard them calling her

'Miss'? She was about to move on when her eye fell on a book that was lying at the front of the bus, near to the wheel. He saw her expression. 'Even bus drivers can read classics, you know.'

'It wasn't that . . . I mean, well, to be honest, I never seem to have got round to Trollope.'

He raised his eyebrows. 'You ought to some time, if you're a teacher. This one's a great piece of work, even if the title's a bit misleading.'

'Right.' Kitty nodded. 'Well, I'd better move on and let you get started.'

She shouldn't jump to conclusions, she told herself, standing in the aisle, balancing her schoolbag on her shoulder and trying to read the morning paper at the same time. That had always been her downfall. She was too quick to dismiss people or, worse, accept them into her heart, then realise they were wrong for her. Look at poor Bruce. That essay showed talent: he was writing from the heart even if the spelling was atrocious. But maybe there was a reason for that. She'd already made a note to check whether he had been tested for dyslexia. If not, she'd have to raise it with his mother after sports day on Thursday. Sports day! More to cope with – and great timing: smack after the Ofsted inspection. Kitty lurched forward with the bus. As she did so, she caught sight of a car moving alongside with two kids in it, waving enthusiastically. Lucy! Such a sweet girl. Kitty waved back more cheerfully than she felt. It might only be Wednesday but already she couldn't wait for the week to be over – especially tonight. Professional dating! What on earth had she let herself in for?

PIPPA

'And now we're coming up to the eleven o'clock news. The American boy who has been holding his school-mates at knifepoint in Ohio has been captured. However, *it is thought that there are at least two casualities, one serious.'*

Pippa leaned forward to switch off the radio (who needed news like that?), wishing that she had brought some flat shoes to drive in and changed into these ridiculous heels later. That was the trouble when you spent your life in flat shoes: when you wore a pair of heels you couldn't walk, let alone drive. But today she had wanted to dress up. 'You look nice,' Derek had said, before he left for the office.

She had felt awkward and stupidly guilty. 'Thanks.'

He took a second look at her pale blue dress which Pippa had kept quiet about: even Monsoon sale bargains were an expensive outlay in Derek's book. Until now she hadn't had an opportunity to wear it.

'I didn't know you were going out.'

'I told you last night. I'm having lunch with Gus and some of the others.'

'The others' was a loose term referring to the group of friends that she and Gus had hung around with at university. In fact, Pippa hadn't seen any of them for ages but in the past, when she and Gus had met up for lunch, she had been uncomfortably aware that Derek might read something into the situation that wasn't there so she had often included 'the others' when she referred to her occasional outings. It wasn't a deceit, she told herself. It was simply to avoid any misunderstandings.

'Have a good time.' He brushed her cheek. 'And don't worry.'

'Why not?' Pippa glowered at him. 'Why shouldn't I worry when for all you and I know, I might have—'

'Sssh. The children are coming down. See you, then. Enjoy yourself.'

'Enjoy yourself? Why, where are you going, Mum?'

Pippa put on her apron to preserve her dress and plonked a plate of wholemeal toast in front of Beth. 'Out for lunch.'

'With Harriet?'

'What is this? Some kind of interrogation? No, with another friend.'

Beth looked hurt and Pippa instantly felt repentant. 'What have you got on at school today?'

'My geography test. Remember? You were going to test me last night.'

She'd meant to but somehow it had been forgotten in the usual chaos of getting them to bed, cooking Derek's supper and the hundred and one other things that had had to be crammed into the evening. 'Beth, I'm sorry. Do you want me to do it now?'

'There isn't time. Isn't that Harriet's car outside?'

How could *anyone* be early for the school run? Pippa dashed into the hall to yell up the stairs, 'Lucy, come *on*. You haven't had breakfast yet and Harriet's here.'

To her shame, she'd had to send her daughter off with a banana and a Pop-Tart to eat in the car. After that, she'd managed to do a bit of work, send an e-mail to her editor to ask for her deadline to be extended by a day, then get into the car to meet Gus. He had phoned earlier to ask if she could make her own way to Soho since an important meeting had held him up.

Le Poiret was one of those expensive restaurants with a deceptively understated exterior in black and red. As soon as she went in, she could tell from the waiters and stiff tablecloths that this was the kind of place to which she and Derek would never go. On their last wedding anniversary they had gone to the new Italian round the corner that Harriet had recommended, and Derek had spent all evening ogling the prices. It was so nice, thought Pippa, as the waiter took her jacket, to have a treat.

Gus was already waiting for her at a table near the window and her heart leaped. 'Hi, Gorgeous!' He stood up to kiss her cheek. Then she tried to sit down but he was then kissing the other and their faces bumped. Embarrassing – but thrilling too.

Gus's eyes swept approvingly over the blue dress. 'You look amazing.' He pulled out her chair (something else Derek rarely remembered). 'Sit down and have a glass of bubbly.'

She eyed the expensive bottle in its silver wrapping. 'Celebrating, are we?'

He reached across the table for her hand and grasped it firmly. Pippa felt a knot of fear form in her stomach. If Gus was trying this hard, he was worried too. 'Only way to do it, darling. Now come on, Pip, what's this all about? Tell me everything, from the beginning.'

He listened attentively until she had finished.

'But why hadn't Derek spotted it earlier?'

'*Derek* spot it?'

Gus took her hand again. 'Doesn't he touch you? I once had a girlfriend who put me in charge of her monthly breast checks.' He grinned. 'In fact, they became far more regular than that.'

Pippa looked away.

'Sorry, that was crass of me. But, seriously, I can't understand why he didn't notice.'

She took a gulp of champagne. 'Because we're not always that close . . .'

'Are you kidding?'

'I don't mean we've stopped. It's just that . . . Oh, I don't know. We're always tired, and when you have children it's different.'

Gus sighed. 'That old excuse. Well, if I was married to you, it wouldn't matter how many kids we had. I'd be "close" to you, as you so sweetly put it, all the time.'

Pippa took another large sip to quell her nerves: the conversation was getting deeper than their usual light flirtation. 'It's difficult for him at work right now. And he has to go through an appraisal this Friday – everyone has to, no matter how long they've worked for the company. I've been helping him fill in this ridiculously complex form, stating what he contributes to the company in his view and where he feels he's going.' She stopped, aware that she was twittering on.

'Work's tough nowadays. How's your business going?'

She loved the way he called it her business instead of her 'freelance work', as Derek referred to it. 'Busy. I should be working now.'

'Everyone needs time off to chill.' Gus topped up her glass and handed her the menu. 'Take a look, Pip, and then we can talk properly.'

She scanned it quickly, settling on salmon and salad. 'Just what I'm having,' said Gus. 'Now, seriously, back to Derek. He's probably telling you not to worry because he's scared himself. It's the kind of thing men do.'

'Would you?'

He looked at her, his eyes locking with hers. 'No. I'd tell you outright that I was scared stiff for you. But, then, I'm not like many other men.' His eyes took on a dreamy look. 'I sometimes feel I go through life thinking completely different things from other people.'

'So do I!' exclaimed Pippa. 'Derek never sees things the way I do. He just doesn't understand why I worry. Neither does Harriet.'

'The friend you were with the other day when I rang?'

Pippa nodded. 'She's lovely, but she's not like me. No one is.'

'Except me.' Gus was challenging her with his eyes.

'Like you,' said Pippa softly.

They both looked at each other without saying anything. Then, as Pippa was beginning to feel really heady with the champagne (she hardly ever drank in the middle of the day and even a few sips did this to her), their food arrived.

'*Bon appétit*,' said Gus.

Pippa smiled weakly.

'Know what you've got to do?'

'What?

'Live a bit. None of us, even those without lumps, know what life has in store. And as long as we don't hurt too many people it's up to us to make the most of what it has to offer.'

Pippa ate a mouthful of salmon, then put down her knife and fork. 'Gus, at university . . . do you ever wish – do you ever wonder what it would have been like if we had been, well, more than friends?'

There. She had said it.

Gus dotted his mouth with his napkin, his eyes fixed on hers. 'Every now and then. But we did come near to it once, didn't we?'

She was glad – and flattered – that he'd remembered. She would never forget that hot Sunday afternoon when they had been sitting on her bed, listening to James Taylor. She had been exhausted, having worked on an essay until the early hours of the morning and, more from familiarity than anything else, had laid her head on his shoulder. The window of her room had been open, allowing the breeze to waft through.

'Isn't this perfect?' she had murmured.

His lips had come down on hers, totally – and wonderfully – unexpectedly. They were softer than she had imagined and she had done a lot of imagining. Within seconds, she found herself below him, her body arched up towards him, begging, pleading. She was going to melt. Evaporate. Die.

Then he had rolled away. 'I'm not going to make love to you, Pip. You know that, don't you?'

She hadn't, but she had nodded dumbly. Then, overcome with shame and disappointment, she had got up from the bed and run to the bathroom at the end of the corridor. Her face, she saw in the mirror, was puce – she always went red when she was upset, scared or nervous. Now she was all three. Frantically, she had splashed water on it to cool it down. When she returned to her room, wondering if he had gone, she saw, to her relief and embarrassment, that he had put on another record and was sitting in the tattered easy-chair in the corner.

He looked up with his usual friendly smile as though nothing had happened. 'What do you think of this album? Not as good as the other, is it?'

They had never again referred to that moment. Now, as they sat in the restaurant, Pippa wanted to ask why he hadn't made love to her when neither had been attached and they had obviously felt something for each other. Was it because, as Derek had unkindly insinuated over the years, Gus was gay? She had been certain he wasn't but Derek's comment had made her uncomfortable. Had he backed off because he just didn't fancy her? Or – and this was the best of the three options – was it because he hadn't wanted to ruin their friendship?

'Gus?'

'Another . . . Sorry!'

They had spoken at the same time, and laughed.

'You first,' he said.

No!

'You.'

'I was going to ask if you wanted another drink.'

Pippa covered her glass with her hand, wishing she'd painted her nails. 'I daren't. I feel quite light-headed already, actually, and I'm doing the school run. I shouldn't really have had any-thing.'

Gus grinned. 'Plenty of time for that to get soaked up, especially if we have one of those delicious puddings over there.'

Pippa looked at them longingly. 'I'd better not.'

'Why not?' Gus touched her hand briefly. 'I've told you before, Pippa, you're gorgeous. Men don't like skinny women. They want girls they can get hold of.'

Pippa felt her resolve melting and allowed the waiter to cut her a piece of pavlova with a peach slice on top.

'Same for me, please,' said Gus. 'Now, what were you going to say to me?'

'When?'

'Just now, when we spoke at the same time.'

Pippa flushed. 'I can't remember.'

'Liar!' He grinned again.

'Honestly.'

He raised his eyebrows. 'Have it your way. At least you can, on one condition.'

Pippa forced herself to put down her fork, leaving half of the pavlova to prove she had some resistance to temptation. 'What's that?'

'You come home with me and have some decent coffee.' He lowered his voice. 'The food in this place is divine but the coffee's undrinkable. Besides, I want to show you some new curtains I've just bought.'

'OK, but I can't be too long. I've got to leave by three at the latest. It would be earlier but the girls have got netball tonight.'

'Netball.' Gus beckoned the waiter over. 'I like a girl who plays netball. Did you?'

'I did, actually. I was a goal shooter.'

'You ought to play again.'

'I should.' Who was she kidding? She'd never play netball again if this lump was malignant.

'Darling, don't cry. Here, have this.' He handed her the starched pink napkin. 'It's going to be all right. I can feel it in my bones.' He was pushing his chair round the table so that he was next to her, his arm round her. Pippa leaned against him. It was comforting. Warm. Sexy.

She blew her nose on the napkin, hoping no one was looking. 'It's just the uncertainty. That's what's so awful.'

'I can understand that. Come on. Let's get out of this place and go back for that coffee.'

Gus's car – a smooth silver Cadillac – was in the car park

near hers. He brought it round and somehow she got in, tee-tering on the unfamiliar high heels.

'Just lie back and close your eyes,' said Gus, and slipped in a CD. 'You'll love this.'

The dulcet tones of James Taylor's new album resonated through the car from the speakers at the back. Had that been intentional, wondered Pippa, as she allowed herself to drift off, or merely coincidence?

By the time she woke up they were almost there. Gus lived in a tall, beautiful white Georgian house in a part of Battersea that was on the up. No garden, but Gus had bought pots – of clipped yew, geraniums, fuchsias – and placed them at front and back, with variegated ivy by the shiny black front door.

He pulled up and ran round to open the car door for her. Unused to such gallantry, Pippa got out awkwardly. He touched her shoulder and they walked to the door where he keyed in his security number. The door opened automatically. 'Come on in. I'll get the coffee on. The guest bathroom is on the first floor if you want to freshen up.'

He always thought of everything, mused Pippa, as she made her way up the elegant mahogany staircase to the loo. She could have stayed here for a fortnight: it had everything any woman could want, from big fluffy towels to Molton Brown soap and hand cream. She thought of the single bathroom at home, with the scraps of soap that were too paltry to use but not small enough to throw away, and the bath mat that was always wet because no one, apart from her, ever put it on a radiator to dry.

She brushed her hair in the mirror and reapplied her lip-stick. That was better. She felt less light-headed from the champagne and as for the lump, she would shut it out of her mind and enjoy this time (their last?) with Gus.

Carefully, she picked her way across the beautiful black and white tiled hall, with its chandelier, into the kitchen.

'You must smell this,' instructed Gus, getting down a tin

of coffee from the Shaker cupboard. He prised open the lid and Pippa inhaled the rich scent appreciatively. 'A friend of mine gets it from Kenya. Fantastic stuff. You won't taste anything better in London.'

It was impossible not to be infected by his enthusiasm. She could smell something else, too – something delicious coming from the gleaming stainless-steel cooker. Gus bent down to open a door and lifted a lid. 'I've got some friends coming round tonight so I made this earlier. Pity you can't stay.'

Pippa wished she could. The prospect of dinner with Gus, laughing and feeling irresponsible like she used to, was so much more inviting than tea with the children squabbling, then keeping Derek's dinner hot when his train was late.

'The kitchen looks beautiful,' she said. 'You've had this done since we were here last.'

She and Derek had come for supper about three years ago. It hadn't been a success. Derek had been silent while she and Gus had fallen over themselves with laughter, stupid jokes and do-you-remembers. Derek, who had been seated next to one of Gus's girlfriends, had appeared almost rude in his refusal to join in and she had told him so in the car on the way home. 'They're not my kind of people,' he had said sullenly.

Pippa had been furious. 'Well, I make an effort with your friends and colleagues. How about that boring office party I had to go to last year?'

Since then Gus hadn't invited them back together. As if by unspoken mutual consent, he and Pippa met up for lunch when Derek was at the office.

'I'd forgotten. You haven't been here for ages. I've had lots done since then. Bring your drink. I'll show you.'

She followed him along the corridor into another room with stained floorboards and an expensive-looking rug. 'What do you think?'

Pippa gazed with awe at the Regency striped curtains. Very smart and very male. The furniture was beautiful too, including a walnut bookcase filled with leather-bound volumes in order of size. Gus had inherited an antiques business from an uncle. It had become so big that he had recently had to take on more staff, which freed him to travel round the country and abroad to source more stock. He was his own boss, like Pippa. Another reason why he understood her.

She took down one of the books from the shelf and flicked through it. It was old with that wonderful dusty smell that took you back to days when lumps probably weren't recognised early enough. 'This is lovely.'

Gus laid a hand briefly on her shoulder. 'Still translating cookery books?'

She grimaced. 'And school stuff. What I really want to get into is literary translations or maybe even children's fiction.' That idea had occurred to her just this week when she'd been reading to Beth and wondering if she would still be around next year.

'That reminds me. Come upstairs. I must show you what I found when I was clearing out the attic.' She followed him, feeling awkward as he led her into a vast bedroom she hadn't seen before.

It had to be his. There was an enormous four-poster bed with tapestry hangings. An ottoman stood at the foot with a freshly pressed shirt lying on it. Fleetingly, Pippa wondered who did his ironing. There was a mahogany side table by the bed and next to it a bow-fronted chest of drawers with a pile of yellowing Arthur Ransomes.

'Remember *Swallows and Amazons*?'

Pippa leafed through the pages, tracing the illustrations with a finger. 'I loved all of them. When I was a child, I dreamed of sailing away.'

'Me too.'

He sat on the side of the bed, the book in his hand. 'Look at this picture. How could they make fires so easily?'

'And run off with pirates.' Pippa sat next to him. It seemed so natural. 'But I always wondered how their parents managed to let them do it. I'm scared if my children are out of my sight for one minute.' She tried to swallow the huge lump that came from nowhere into her throat. 'God knows what they're going to do if I die.'

'It's OK.' Gus's arm was round her shoulders again but this time he was massaging her.

Pippa laid her head on his shoulder. 'Oh, Gus, I'm so scared.'

Without warning, she felt his lips on hers. They were soft, as they had been all those years ago, but more demanding now. Meaningful. Determined. Grown-up.

Slowly, looking her straight in the eyes, he took off his shirt. His chest was broader than Derek's. It had been so long since she had seen another man's body that somehow she had imagined them all to be the same shape.

He held her to him, his right hand slipping down the back of her dress as he unzipped it deftly. Somehow (later, she couldn't remember how) he helped her out of her dress. Too late, she remembered she hadn't worn a bra because the straps showed. Scarcely believing what he was doing, she watched as he stroked her breasts, then bent his head and sucked her nipples. She shuddered with pleasure.

'God, you're beautiful, Pippa.'

He was on top of her before she knew it. Her body arched towards him. Wanting him. Before it was too late.

He was looking down on her. 'Pip, there's something I ought to—'

'No,' she whispered. 'No. Please.' She pulled him to her, determined, this time, not to let him get away. He seemed to hesitate. 'Yes. Please. Oh, God.'

He was in her. The waves inside built up as though she was going to explode. Then, suddenly, she had a picture of Derek. Derek, with whom she had done this a month ago – or was it two? The same thing but different. Less exciting, but comforting

– more comforting than it was with this stranger, who seemed nothing like Gus. This man who was heaving himself up and down inside her, gripping her buttocks so hard that it hurt.

What was she doing? This wasn't make-believe or the harmless flirtation they had carried on for so long. This was real. The kind of real that got you into trouble. Too late. He was there already.

She rolled away, tears running down her face.

'Pip.' He spoke between gasps. 'I'm sorry. I didn't mean to hurt you.'

She buried her face in the pillow. 'You didn't, Gus. I've hurt myself. I'm sorry. I'm just not me any more.'

He nodded. Gus had always known how she felt. But they had crossed the line. And now it would never be the same again.

'Gus, there's something I need to ask you,' she said.

He knelt beside her and put his arms round her. 'The question you were going to ask in the restaurant?'

She moved away. 'Yes.'

'Go on.'

'At university, that day when we were on my bed and you kissed me, why didn't you make love to me?'

Gus stood up and wrapped a towel round his waist. 'I didn't want to ruin our friendship. We have something special, Pippa, something that doesn't happen often between a man and a woman. I was scared that sex would spoil it.' He knelt down again, cupping her chin in his hands. 'Tell me it hasn't now. I couldn't bear to lose you as a friend.'

She shook her head. 'It's still the same,' she lied. 'But why did you change your mind? Why make love to me now when I'm married with children?'

He covered his face with his hands. 'In case I lose you, Pip. I'm sure the lump will be all right, but if it isn't, wouldn't we have regretted not doing this? Besides, you looked so fragile and scared. I wanted to comfort you.'

She held the sheet to her breasts and kissed the top of his head. 'I needed the comfort too. But now I feel so guilty. I do love Derek, and the children mean the world to me. But they don't understand me the way you do. And sometimes it's all so hard at home – all work and no fun.'

'Ssh, don't cry. I'm here, Pip – I'm always here for you.'

'But how can we look at each other in the same way?'

His face showed his distress. 'We have to, Pip. I can't imagine not having you as a friend.'

'Nor me you,' she whispered.

'The shower's through there. Shall I leave you for a few minutes?'

The water made her feel better, cleaner, but by the time she had slipped back into her dress she felt racked with guilt again. The phone rang in her bag and she answered it unwillingly.

'Pippa!' It was Derek's voice. He sounded relieved. 'I've been trying to get hold of you for ages.'

'Sorry. I had it on silent.'

'The hospital rang. They've had a cancellation. The consultant can see you tomorrow at ten a.m. I'll come with you.'

'Right. Thanks.' Her voice belonged to someone else. 'Listen, Derek, can you ring and confirm it for me? I'm with the others at the moment. We're just about to, er, leave the restaurant. It's difficult.'

'Don't worry. It'll be all right.'

Pippa felt sick: the sound of his voice made her feel as though he was in the room and knew what had just taken place. She switched the phone to off, wishing she could do the same to the last half-hour.

Gus was standing in the doorway. 'Derek?'

'Yes. Don't panic.' She felt sick again. 'He doesn't suspect anything. It's the hospital. They can see me tomorrow.'

'I'll come with you.'

'Derek will.'

He nodded awkwardly. 'You won't want coffee now.'

She smiled weakly. 'No.'

He pulled her towards him and pushed his hand inside her dress, stroking her shoulder slowly and rhythmically as she sobbed.

Afterwards, when he'd given her a glass of water from his American fridge ('It will clear your head') and kissed her goodbye chastely on the cheek, she got into the taxi (thoughtfully ordered by Gus to take her back to her own car), feeling both terribly guilty and, inexplicably, better. She'd been terrified about the hospital appointment, but now she felt strangely calm.

If only she felt the same about Gus.

20

MARTINE

> *'Time's coming up to eight thirty. There have been uncon-firmed reports of gunfire in the American school in Ohio where a boy is holding his classmates hostage.'*

Dear Diary,
I am writing this while I am waiting for the twins to arrive in the car. They are late again but I cannot be cross because they have a step-mother who does not get them up in time. Poor Nattie, she tells me all about it.

'Ah, there you are,' said Martine, wearily, as the twins and their little brother climbed into the back of the car.

'Sorry – Evie left before us and she hadn't made our packed lunches,' said Natalie, matter-of-factly, as she fastened Jack's seat-belt.

Martine softened as the little boy sat still and beamed at her in a way Sam never had. Poor girls! It must be terrible having a step-mother, especially one like Evie who looked so hard when she frowned. When Martine became a mother, she would not frown like that. She would be happy and her children would be happy too. 'You have food now, yes?'

'Yes, thanks, Martine.'

That was the other twin. What was her name? Leonora?

'Martine, do you think you could ask Sally if she's had time to sort out that work experience at the studio she promised to look into?'

Martine frowned. 'Work experience? You want to work for

that woman? I do not think that is a good idea.'

'W-w-why not?' demanded Sam. 'D-don't be so rude about m-my mother.'

'We'll tell her you said that,' chipped in Ellie.

Martine shrugged.

'I'll ask her for you,' said Ellie.

'Thanks. Er, Martine, did you know you just signalled right and went left?'

'Nattie, shush.'

'Well, she did.'

Martine pretended not to hear them. If the English drove on the correct side of the road, this would not be a problem. Besides, look at that car in front, the one with the L sign. She was driving very badly indeed.

'The traffics!' sighed Martine to herself. 'Terrible!' And it was so inconvenient having to take these children as well as Ellie and Sam. If she did not hurry, she would be late for her class.

'Stop here, Marty. No, *here*.'

'Ellie, do not be so bossy.'

'I'm not, but you were going to miss it again. You always park too far up.'

'Thanks for the lift, Martine,' said Natalie, smiling.

'You will remember to ask Sally for us, won't you, about the job?' added Leonora.

'*Absolument. Au revoir.*'

There was, Martine thought, glancing at the clock, just enough time to go to the chemist, as Barry had suggested. However, the pharmacy in the supermarket did not open until nine o'clock and she had to wait until the pharmacist arrived. She would be late.

'My hair, it itches.' She scratched her head to prove the point, and the man in the white coat stepped back. 'My friend, he say you can help. You can give me some medicine, please?'

'I'll just put on these and have a look.'

Why did he need rubber gloves? She was not sick!

'Thought so. Are you in close contact with children?'

Martine nodded. 'I am au pair. And I have a baby of my own.'

It didn't feel like a lie. It just came out as if it was true.

'Well, you won't have got it from the baby but headlice – that's what you've got – are easy to catch from older children. The good news is that you can get rid of them easily if you use a special shampoo. I would recommend this one.'

'Lice? What are these?'

'Little black creatures that live in the hair.'

'But they are alive? *Non! Non!*'

'Please do not distress yourself. It really is more common than you might realise and it has nothing to do with personal hygiene. On the contrary, lice prefer clean hair.'

Martine did not understand everything he was saying but she could just about work out what the children had done to her. Lice! They had given her nasty black creatures in her hair and she would see that Madame Pargeter knew about it. She would ring the agency too. Ugh! She would go home now and wash her hair in Sally's shower, even if it meant being late for class.

By the time she reached her language school, Martine's scalp was less itchy. Whatever was in the shampoo had calmed it down, thank goodness. The pharmacist had told her to tell the children's mother so that the family could be treated too. Martine was in two minds about this; perhaps Sally should suffer so that she understood what Martine had gone through.

'*Bonjour, chérie,*' said Véronique, making room for her. 'How are you?'

Martine would have liked to tell her about the lice but something warned her that Véronique might not want to sit next to her. 'I am glad to be here, away from my terrible family,' she whispered. That was why she loved her class; it was such a relief to find other girls who were homesick.

'Now, class, I want you to turn to page one hundred and thirty-two. We're doing verbs today.'

'Ugh!' murmured Véronique. 'I detest verbs.'

'Me too.' Martine's hand wandered to her head, which was itching again. No, she mustn't. She tried to concentrate on the text in front of her. 'This exercise is impossible,' she said, under her breath, to Véronique.

Bleep, bleep.

Martine reached for her bag under the desk. Carefully, she slid her phone under a book so she could open the text message without the tutor seeing.

'Bck early on Thursday. C U then.'

That was it. No time or place. Martine felt warmth flood through her. He was coming home, and even though the details were scant, her beau, as her mother called him, would find her.

'You look pale,' muttered Véronique. 'Are you all right?'

'My family work me so hard. Now I have to be their cleaning lady too. And last night, Simon, he came back drunk again. They had a big row and I cannot sleep.'

Véronique whistled. 'You should tell the newspaper. You could make some money. They love gossip like that.'

'Really?' Martine hesitated. 'But that would not be kind.'

Veronique pouted. '*Chérie*, they are not kind to you. As the English say, teet for tat. *Tu comprends?*'

BETTY

I don't feel like the radio today.

I think it's because Terry's face is on the lamp-post, in black and white, smiling at me. 'I'm fine, Mum,' he's saying. 'Honest.' Luckily he's in a plastic folder from that nice office shop down the road so he won't get wet when it rains.

They tried to wrap him in plastic afterwards but I soon ripped that off. 'He needs his duvet,' I told the ambulance man. 'He'll get cold without it. How would you like it if someone put you in a polythene bag?'

He didn't have an answer for that so we tucked him up in his red and blue duvet, the one with the Simpsons on it, and then he was all right.

I had other babies before Terry. But they came too soon. Terry was only five pounds two ounces but I fed him until he grew. He got so tall that once someone in the supermarket thought he was my husband! We still laugh about that, don't we, duck?

The kids in the playground opposite are laughing. That's why I moved here – to keep an eye on them. Never enough teachers on duty.

Hang on. Who's that man over there? The one in the suit, talking to the girls on the other side of the fence. I'll just get my binoculars. That's better. The girls look identical. Twins, maybe. I'd have liked twins. Sometimes I wondered if one of the early babies might have been twins.

That odd bloke is trying to put his hand through the wire fence. What does he think he's doing? Now he's going and the girls are waving at him. Perhaps they know him but that doesn't mean it's all right. Sixty per cent – or is it fifty-five? – of victims know their attackers. It was on the radio.

He's getting on a bus now. Funny. You'd think a man in a suit like that would have a car. I'm good at observing things like that. 'Spot on,' Terry says, when we watch detective films on telly and I always get the one who did it.

Should I ring the school? They didn't like it last time. Better to stand here and watch, in case he comes back. Like Terry's always telling me, you can't be too careful nowadays.

WEDNESDAY P.M.

'Evie? It's us. Didn't you say Dad was picking up? He's not here again.'

'Sorry I'm a bit late. I had a lunch. No, Beth, my breath doesn't smell of wine. It's water. Very expensive water, actually. Bruce, do you mind not kicking my seat, dear? You're hurting my back. And *please* keep your head inside the car or I might cut it off by accident when the window goes up. Hang on, Jess. Don't get out until I've stopped. Just sit there for a minute, girls, can you? I need to tell Harriet something about tomorrow.'

'Why is that woman screaming in the car, Mum? Look over there. The blonde woman in that old Saab. Yes, Beth, it *is* a Saab. Didn't you know that? She's got her mouth open. Listen, you can hear her if you turn the radio down.'

'Please refrain from playing football in the car, Sam. Or I tell your mother when she emerges from the screen. And do not talk to me in those words.'

'I c-c-can't help swearing, Farty Marty. Maybe I've got Tourette's syndrome. Like that f-f-footballer. You know. The one who won't give interviews to the paper because he can't help saying r-r-rude things. Hugo swears and his n-nanny doesn't mind.'

I can't take any more. Not the kids, not Robin and not Bulmer. I feel like screaming and why not? No one can hear me in the car, particularly if I turn up the radio.

That's better. I've got it out now. Maybe I ought to do that more often. Perhaps it could be a feature. 'How to Destress on the School Run'. Not bad. At least, it would be if I didn't have this crap with Robin to sort out. He sounded really odd when I asked him about those figures. A mistake, he said. The bank had got it wrong. He said he'd explain later, but why isn't he answering the phone? Well, he'd better have some answers when I get home.

'Why can't I go out tomorrow, Dad? I never have any homework on Thursday nights. Mum would let me, I know she would.'

'Betty from Balham has just rung to remind everyone about the new speed restriction along the Wimbledon road. Thanks for reminding us, Betty. Like you say, we can't drive too safely.'

21

WEDNESDAY NIGHT

KITTY

'Will you be mine tonight, tonight . . .'

If she tried really hard to block out the music, which reminded her of a cheap hotel lobby, she could just about pretend to be at a private party. Kitty had to admit that the room, in a London club, looked pretty with its clusters of small tables and bright red cloths, each with a matching carnation in the middle. The food was delicious – that asparagus starter had melted in her mouth. She looked quite nice too, if the mirror in the ladies' was anything to go by; she was glad she'd worn her longish green skirt instead of a dress, which would have been too formal. All in all, the evening would have been quite bearable – if it hadn't been for the company.

'So, tell me, Kitty, as a teacher, what do you think of the new A-level system?'

She groaned inwardly. Anthony was exactly the kind of man she had known would come to an event like this. Not only was he an accountant (boring) but he also had an urgent need for whatever it was that men put on their hair nowadays to get rid of the grey or make it grow – preferably over that shiny bald patch at the front. He had already mentioned at least three times that he was in his thirties, but Kitty suspected he was much older. He also had an unnerving habit of repeating her name in every sentence.

'It has its good and bad points,' she began. 'It's good that the workload is spread out so it doesn't all rest on the final exams. But there's a lot of pressure with the coursework.'

'I agree, Kitty. My sister, who has two children, says that . . .'

But the view of Anthony's sister who, Kitty had already been informed, lived in Cirencester and had five children ranging from two to seventeen, remained unexpressed: much to Kitty's relief, a loud bell rang, indicating that the men had to move one table to the right. As he got up, Anthony pushed a business card in front of her. 'Please give me a ring, Kitty,' he said. 'I mean it. I'd really like to see you again.'

Vivienne, who was across the table, gave her a sympathetic look. Even she thought he was a sad case – and she was desperate. Kitty felt even worse. She should never have come and for two pins she'd just get up and go – but no, too late, here came the next.

'Hi, my name's Keith.' He extended a bony hand. 'How do you do?'

If there was one thing she loathed more than anything else, thought Kitty, it was a limp handshake.

'I'm in electronics,' he added, tucking his napkin into his purple shirt (top two buttons open, no tie). 'What do you do?'

Kitty smiled brightly, checked that Vivienne was listening and leaned forward confidentially. 'Actually, I'm an actress.'

Keith looked startled. 'Gosh, really? I've never met an actress before. What are you in?'

'Oh, nothing big. I do mainly voiceovers. For cat food, that sort of thing.'

'Ah.' Keith looked disappointed. 'Not *EastEnders*, then. That's my favourite. I once had a mate who did the electrics for the set . . .'

By the time they'd reached pudding (or 'afters', as Kitty's next companion, John, described it), she'd had enough. 'Sorry,

I've got to go,' she said, as the coffee arrived. 'Still got some marking to do before tomorrow.'

'Marking?' John looked taken back. 'But I thought you said you were a riding instructor.'

'I am. But there's theory involved too, you know.' She glanced across at Vivienne, who was happily involved in deep conversation with an older man called Justin. 'Sorry, Viv, I've really got to make a move. Do you want to come with me?'

Vivienne looked crestfallen. 'Can't you wait until we've had coffee?'

'Please, allow me to get you a taxi home,' said Justin.

Vivienne flushed. 'If you're sure.'

Kitty didn't need further reassurance. 'See you, John. 'Bye, Vivienne. See you tomorrow at – er – the stables.'

Vivienne gave her a peculiar look. 'What?'

'Must dash.'

Kitty grabbed her coat and walked briskly down the street towards the tube station. It was dusk but there were so many people around that she felt quite safe. Even on the tube she felt secure – more secure than she had felt at that awful dinner. In some ways, though, she was glad she'd gone. If the only men available were the Anthonys and Johns of this world, she'd rather be alone. Maybe she'd be one of those women who didn't find the right man until they were much older. That wasn't what she'd had in mind but it was better than second best.

Her flat was only a short walk from the tube. Kitty opened the door and felt pleased to be home even though, just a few months ago, home had been with her parents in Reading. Perhaps if she hadn't taken the easy route after university and moved back with her parents to avoid paying expensive rent, she'd have found someone sooner.

Kitty took off her shoes, sank down on the sofa and pressed the play button on her answerphone. 'Kitty? It's Mark. Look, I'm really sorry about Monday. I wondered if we could reschedule.'

Reschedule? What kind of man used that word outside the office? She pressed delete.

'Hi, er, Kitty. My name's Duncan. I'm a friend of Rod and Mandy's. I live in London, not far from you, actually, and I wondered if you'd like to meet up on Friday for a drink . . .'

Delete.

Forget that stupid bet, thought Kitty, as she sat down on the sofa with the marking that she really did have to finish before tomorrow. She wasn't going to find a proper boyfriend by Sunday. And, what was more, she was beginning not to care if she didn't find one this year. Champneys would just have to wait.

THURSDAY

22

'It's coming up to eight but first the weather. Cool to start off with, followed by scattered showers and light winds . . .'

Harriet knocked again on Pippa's door. She was late – which was a sin on the school run when every minute counted. Last year, a mother had actually missed the school coach for a trip to France and taken her son to Calais to catch up with it.

She knocked again. Odd. Pippa usually had the girls ready and waiting, Lucy's plaits neatly tied and Beth with her music case. But today the upstairs curtains were still drawn. Dear God, don't let her be ill, not really ill. Harriet didn't usually pray but since Pippa had told her about the lump, she had made more than one angry plea to whoever was up there.

'Knock again,' demanded Bruce, who had dashed out of the car, leaving the door open on the roadside.

'I am. And shut that door, quickly, before something goes into it. Bruce, go *on*.'

'I'll do it,' called Jess.

'Honestly, Bruce, you're impossible,' muttered Harriet, and knocked a fourth time.

'Sorry.' The door opened to reveal Derek in his dressing-gown. 'We're running a bit late this morning. Bad night, I'm afraid.'

Derek was never home at this time. He worked in the City,

173

which meant a six thirty start from home. Something must have happened.

'Everything all right?' asked Harriet, cautiously. Beth had just appeared behind her father, and she didn't want to ask too much in front of her.

Derek nodded tersely. His skin looked grey with worry and he hadn't shaved. 'The hospital rang. There's been a cancellation so Pippa's seeing the consultant today.'

'She might be a bit late for sports day,' announced Beth, importantly, 'but she'll do her best to be there.'

Sports day! With all the panic about Charlie coming back early, she'd forgotten. His plane landed at eleven o'clock. Would she have enough time to get to school by two thirty – and had the children got their sports kit? She tried to remember. She was pretty certain Bruce's was still in the dirty linen bin. But did any of it matter when Pippa might have something seriously wrong with her?

'If Mummy's late,' she said to Beth, 'you can do the three-legged race with me. That's if they still have it. Sports day is meant to be non-competitive nowadays, isn't it? All team work!'

She laughed, trying to make Derek smile. Anything to make life normal again.

'Probably.' Derek nodded uncertainly. 'Now, come on, girls, you'd better get going. Had something to eat, have you?'

'No,' said Lucy, coming down the stairs. 'We usually have toast but you didn't make any.'

Derek looked puzzled. 'Do you? Didn't I?' He glanced at Harriet ruefully. 'Pippa's still asleep. She didn't get much rest last night and I didn't want to wake her.'

'Don't worry,' said Harriet briskly, relieved to be presented with a situation she could sort out. 'There's a packet of cereal bars in the car for emergencies. They can have one of those and get a drink at school.'

'Cereal bars!' Lucy's eyes lit up. 'Mummy never lets us have those. Yummy!'

'Well, don't tell her or she might be cross with me,' joked Harriet, desperate to lighten the tension. 'That reminds me. I usually make a cake for sports day.'

'You can't this year,' said Beth. 'We all got a note – didn't Bruce and Jess give it to you? No one's allowed to bring home-made cakes any more in case someone gets food-poisoning. They have to be proper ones, from shops.'

'How ridiculous! Right, then, off we go. Into the car, everyone.'

She waited until the girls had heaved their sports bags into the boot and climbed into the back with Jess. Bruce, as usual, had hogged the front passenger seat, to which he insisted he was entitled as he was the eldest. She touched Derek's arm. 'I hope it goes all right. What time's the appointment?'

'Ten o'clock.' He glanced up the stairs. 'I'd better wake her soon.'

'Tell Pippa I'll ring when I'm back from the airport – Charlie's coming home a day early.'

'I will.'

'I'm sure everything will be all right,' she added lamely.

'Yes.' Derek stood at the top of the steps, his hands in his dressing-gown pockets. He looked like a small boy. 'I hope so.'

The traffic was appalling on the way to the airport, and by the time Harriet had found a parking space at Arrivals, she was running ten minutes late – and she'd wanted to get there cool and unflustered. She flicked open the mirror on the sun-visor and checked her foundation, hastily dabbed on a bit more (dripping some on the upholstery), then touched up her mascara.

She got out of the car and headed inside the airport. There were so many people at the barrier that it was hard to see if Charlie had already come through. Harriet scanned the crowd: mothers with babies, young women with briefcases, a frail old man, a couple (newlyweds?) who were almost joined at the hip, oblivious of the world around them. And then, in the middle of them all, Charlie.

She almost didn't recognise him. He seemed taller (impossible) and thinner (suited him). The beard was gone and his jacket was new. Harriet felt a pang. Since they'd been married he'd never bought a jacket without her before. And how was it possible that she had almost not recognised her own husband? He'd only been gone two months.

'Harriet!' He walked towards her, a calm professional.

For a second, Harriet thought he was going to shake her hand. Then he bent down and his lips brushed her cheek. She felt a stab of panic. Was that all, after such a long absence? 'How was the flight?' she asked.

'Fine, thank you.' His eyes swept over her. 'You look brown. Has the weather been good?'

Why were they talking about the *weather*?

'I've been gardening. Everything's growing so much at the moment.' She glanced down at his luggage on the trolley. 'I'm parked on the second level. Sorry I couldn't get any nearer.'

A flash of annoyance crossed his face. 'Never mind.'

They walked in silence towards the car park. He hadn't commented on her hair, which looked nice, even if she said it herself, Harriet thought. So did her nails, although she was beginning to feel that the spray-on tan, which the hair salon had persuaded her to have, seemed tacky. Why had she lied that she was brown from the garden? Why not just tell him she'd spent all day at the salon, beautifying herself because she wanted him to feel he'd missed her?

She helped him lift the suitcase into the boot, then handed him the keys. Charlie hated being driven: he needed to be in control. He looked at the car critically. 'Bit grubby, isn't it? And is that a rip on the seat?'

She'd spent ages vacuuming it that morning but she hadn't noticed that. 'It was easier to use this car when you were away because it's got a bigger boot for the children's clobber.'

Charlie's lips tightened. 'It's too good for the school run.'
He started the car and drove out of the airport towards the
main road. 'Everything been all right?'

She took a deep breath. If he wanted to talk banalities, she'd
go along with it. 'Well, quite a lot has happened. Jess did reasonably well in her exams.'

'And Bruce?'

'Not too bad,' she lied.

Charlie's mouth tightened again.

'Pippa's not very well,' she continued. 'She's had a bit of a
scare – a lump scare – and she's seeing the consultant today.'

'I'm sorry.'

His detached tone prickled. Why couldn't he show more
concern? He knew how close she and Pippa were.

'It's sports day this afternoon. The children were hoping
you'd be able to come.'

'I'm shattered, Harriet. I've just had a long flight.'

'But I promised them.'

'You shouldn't have. I ought to go into the office, anyway.'

'Charlie, you've been away for two months! The kids have
missed you. I've missed you. Don't you think you owe it to
them – to us – to go to sports day?'

He looked at her coolly. As though she had spoken out of
turn. 'All right, Harriet. If it means that much, I will. But I
need to make some work calls first. You must understand
that.'

Harriet willed herself not to rise to the bait. Charlie was always
implying that because she didn't work, she didn't understand the
pressures of the real world. What *he* didn't understand, she
told herself, was the pressure of bringing up children to become
decent human beings. 'Fair enough,' she said, trying to sound
steady. 'But we also have to think about ourselves. We need
to talk, Charlie, before you start ringing the office.'

'Talk?'

'Yes.' Harriet was surprised at her own bravery. 'We need to talk about us.'

He sighed. 'Harriet. I'm very tired. Maybe we do need to talk but not now.'

They were almost silent during the journey home. By the time they got back, Harriet had worked herself up into such a nervous state that she now wished she hadn't mentioned talking. It was much safer to concentrate on unpacking his case and asking him what he wanted for lunch. 'Nothing, thanks. I ate on the plane.'

'Cup of tea, then?'

'Thanks.'

He's talking to me as though I'm a stranger, she thought, as she tried to busy herself with making a pot while her stomach rolled on emptiness and panic. She'd not been able to handle more than a cup of tea for breakfast, and although she felt hungry now she couldn't eat anything. Not with the uncertainty.

She handed him tea in his Dad mug (from last Father's Day) as he sat in his usual chair by the fireplace. 'By the way, I went to the bank yesterday and they wouldn't let me take any money out. It was really embarrassing. They said your money hadn't been paid in.'

'I know. We had an e-mail about it. It's going to be a bit late this month, thanks to some new accounting system, but it should be there by now.'

'You could have told me.'

'I wasn't here.'

'Yes, but—'

'You've moved the sofa.'

'I thought it looked better there.'

He frowned. 'I preferred it where it was. And what happened to the cabinet in the bathroom? There are marks on the wall around it.'

'It fell off but I put it back.'

'Well, you didn't do a very good job. I'll have to paint the wall this weekend.'

This was crazy. She had to know the score or she'd go mad. 'Charlie.'

'Yes?'

Harriet's right leg began to shake. She tried to stop it but it refused to listen. 'Do you . . . what . . .' She took a deep breath. 'Do you want to stay with us?'

He nodded slowly. 'Yes.'

The relief almost drowned her. Thank God for the children's sake, if not her own. 'Then why did you go?'

His voice was even and businesslike. 'I thought it would help us to have a break.'

'And did it help you? Because it was bloody hard work for me. The kids always wanting to know when you were coming back. Me having to cope with the day-to-day problems and emergencies like the boiler.'

'I'm sorry, but it was also important for my job.' He put down his cup. 'It would have been nice if you had come out to see me. We need time together, more time for ourselves, away from the children.'

Harriet was almost speechless. 'The whole point was to give you thinking time away from me! And, anyway, who would have looked after the children?'

'Your mother.'

'But they're too young – I can't leave them.'

He smiled, in the way he always did when he was about to win a point. 'You always put the children first, don't you?'

I can't win, she thought. I just can't win. Harriet looked at the man sitting across the table from her. Did she want to spend more time with him? 'And what about that woman?'

'Which woman?'

Harriet's voice shook. 'You know perfectly well.'

'I've told you. She meant nothing.'

Harriet closed her eyes. Suddenly she was aware of Charlie's hand on her shoulder. 'I want to try again, Harry, but you've got to do your bit too.'

'I don't know how much more I can do,' she said miserably.

'Just try to think of my needs as well as the children's and your own,' said Charlie, briskly. 'I work very hard for you all, you know. I deserve a bit more consideration.'

No. She wouldn't say anything. Not now. He was tired from the trip and he'd say things he might not mean and then he might leave again. She didn't want that: she didn't want her children to go through what she had when her father had gone. They were too young. Maybe in a few years, if life became absolutely unbearable, but not now. As Pippa had said the other day, children needed both parents, even in this day and age.

Charlie stood up. 'Come on, then. If we're going to go, we might as well get on with it.'

'Go?'

'Sports day. I thought you said the children were expecting us. Get a grip, Harriet. I'm the one who's had a long flight, not you.'

She jumped up. 'Give me two minutes. I've just got to get Bruce's sports kit out of the tumble-dryer.'

Charlie frowned. 'Shouldn't he have it with him?'

'We were running late this morning,' said Harriet tersely. 'It's not easy, you know.'

Charlie snorted. 'If you had my kind of job, Harriet, you'd appreciate being at home. I wish I had more time for myself.'

Here we go again. How could she have forgotten the 'You don't know how lucky you are' and the 'If you had a proper job . . .'? But this time, instead of feeling inadequate and stupid, she heard a small, insistent voice inside her head. Monica's. A voice that told her she had a choice: that she didn't have to put up with this any more. If – and this was the big one – she decided not to.

23

'It's coming up to eight but first the weather. Cool to start off with, followed by scattered showers and light winds . . .'

Eight o'clock? It couldn't be! She shouldn't have taken that sleeping tablet . . . Evie stretched out her hand to the left side of the bed. Empty. Cold. Where *was* he? She'd known, with some terrible premonition, when the girls had rung last night to say Robin had forgotten – again – to pick them up, that this time something was wrong. Seriously wrong.

She shouldn't have phoned him about the money. She should have waited until she got home when she could look at him, eyeball to eyeball. But when she'd arrived, the house had been empty. At first she had assumed Robin had taken the girls somewhere after school. But then there had been the message on the answerphone from Sally, saying they'd had a panicky call from Leonora because no one had picked them up. Martine had been out so Sally had had to send the chauffeur. Evie had had to make up some story about Robin being called to an interview.

Staggering to the bathroom (the tablet was still making her feel unsteady), she almost collided with Natalie coming out.

'Where's Dad? Hasn't he come back yet?'

Evie was too woozy to lie convincingly. 'No.'

The girl frowned at her. 'Then where is he?'

'I don't know.'

Leonora smirked from her bedroom door. 'Maybe he's left you. Have you checked his passport?'

Evie felt like hitting her but stopped herself. Her own father would have belted her for saying half the things these girls did. But you couldn't do that kind of thing nowadays, especially when it wasn't your kid.

'Maybe he's gone to find Mum,' added Natalie.

'No. She's still with Chris. She texted me today,' her sister put in.

'You didn't tell me.'

'Well, maybe she cares more for me than she does for you.'

'*Shut up!*' Evie couldn't take any more. 'Shut up, both of you. Let's try to pull together for a change, shall we? You're always saying I don't treat you like grown-ups. Well, now I will. Your father has gone and I don't know why. And, if you really want to know, I think he's in some kind of trouble because he's been borrowing money and not paying it back. There! Satisfied?'

The horrified look on the girls' faces told her what she already knew: she'd gone too far. 'It's probably all right,' she added. 'He'll ring tonight.'

Tears glistened in Natalie's eyes and Evie felt a jolt of compassion. 'It's OK, Nattie,' she said, and tried to draw the girl towards her.

'Don't touch me! You're not my mother! Get away!'

Natalie ran out of the room and Leonora followed.

'Come back,' called Evie. 'We're going to be late for school.'

'Don't care!'

Jack began to cry. He hadn't woken up either. How on earth was she going to get them all out in time? Damn you, Robin, damn you.

'Badron, badron.'

'It's all right, sweetheart. We've all overslept but it's time to get up now.'

She lifted him out of bed and gave him a cuddle, her head whirling. Why had Robin taken so much money? Was it to pay for those new clothes he'd bought the girls, even when she'd told him there wasn't enough in the account that month? Or to pay for the drink he was consuming in vaster quantities since the last 'We'll let you know' letter? But that didn't explain why he'd needed to borrow quite so much money from a loan company so shady it didn't even have a contact number on its headed paper.

Evie helped Jack get dressed, then sat him at the table with his toast and rang Robin's mobile again. Still nothing. Not even an automated message. She couldn't take this – not when she still needed to prepare for her meeting with Bulmer. There was something else too. Something the girls had said just now that had rung alarm bells.

Have you checked his passport?

But there was no need to. He wouldn't have gone that far. He couldn't have. She went upstairs. The girls were still in their rooms. 'Come on, you two! And remember your games kit. It's sports day. Look at the state of your bedrooms! I left your sports stuff out last night and now I can't even see the carpet – let alone your clothes. And you left the phone on the floor again. Now, go downstairs and have some toast. It's on the table getting cold.'

Quickly, she ran back into her bedroom. She shut the door behind her and opened the top drawer of the large mahogany chest of drawers she and Robin had bought when they had had money to spend in antique shops. Slowly, she took out the file marked PASSPORTS.

Hands shaking, she opened each one slowly, including the girls'. Robin had insisted on keeping them as he didn't trust Rachel not to whisk his daughters out of the country. Natalie's picture had been taken when she was eight and hadn't learned to frown. Leonora smiled back at her in a way she never normally did. Jack beamed brightly. Evie looked glamorous, if she said it herself.

And Robin's wasn't there.

*   *   *

Evie drove herself to the office, the implications of her discovery reeling in her head. Face facts. Her father had taught her that as a child, and over the years she had found that some of his advice was sound.

Robin's passport has gone. He owes money. He hasn't rung.

Evie's hands sweated on the steering-wheel. Robin had left her. He'd left Jack, too, and his girls, in a way that was totally uncharacteristic. Unless – her chest fluttered – someone had made him do something stupid. Should she call the police?

Hoot, hoot.

Evie made an apologetic gesture to the car behind, which was pointing out vociferously that the lights had turned green. God, she needed to get back on track – and fast – before she got to the office. She took a sharp left and pulled into a side turning. She'd never been one for women friends and, until now, hadn't needed anyone apart from Robin. But when the crunch came there was one person she could rely on for advice. 'Dad? It's Evie.'

'You on that mobile again? The reception's awful. Hang on a minute.' She could hear him coughing in the background. 'That's better. How are you, love?'

'Still got that cough?'

'It's nothing. Just the usual.'

'You ought to stop smoking, Dad.'

'Evie, it's nine o'clock in the morning and you're on your way to the office. You haven't rung for a chat. What's up?'

Evie closed her eyes and told him everything.

'And you say this is all out of character?' he asked, when she had finished.

'Yes,' said Evie, sharply. 'If you knew him a bit better, you'd realise that.'

It was a mean shot and she knew it. Over the last four years Benjamin had tried to get over his aversion to Robin, but even Evie had to admit that any father might have had his reservations. When she'd met her future husband (at a work drinks do to which his accountancy firm had been invited), he had tweaked her normally elusive heartstrings by telling her about his adored twin daughters whom he'd been bringing up alone since Rachel, his wife, had walked out on them a year ago when they were only nine. Now she'd come back to reclaim them and, feeling that girls should be with their mother, he had agreed reluctantly provided he could see them at week-ends.

But looking after the girls for a year, single-handed, had meant giving up his job (he hadn't wanted to employ a stranger to care for them after school, after all they'd gone through). After the twins had gone back to Rachel, it had taken him months to find another and even this, he confided to Evie, after their third glass of Chablis, wasn't particularly secure. How true that had turned out to be . . .

By the time he took her home Evie – to her surprise – was hooked. Robin hadn't been her usual type. Usually she dated seriously career-minded men without kids. And until now, it had suited her to be unmarried: as a journalist she had inter-viewed celebrities across the Pond without having to consider anyone else.

Not that anyone before Robin had offered her commitment – which had confirmed Evie's deep-down belief that no one would want her. She might seem confident with her beautiful clothes and impeccable makeup but she was still plump little Jewish Evie with the home-made uniform, whose father drove a cab when all the other girls' dads had proper cars. The one who lived in a flat instead of a house, and was teased by her classmates because she was the only one who didn't eat pork.

It was this that had upset Benjamin. It didn't matter to him that Robin and Evie had got married on the quiet, or that Robin was made redundant. What did matter was that he wasn't Jewish and that Jack hadn't been circumcised.

'Don't get shirty with me, young lady. Let me think. Now, just because he's taken his passport doesn't mean he's done a bunk. He might have taken it for security, for validating documents.'

She hadn't thought of that.

'And I suppose it's possible he *might* have had an accident but if he had you'd have heard something by now – or you will soon.'

'Thanks.'

'Just trying to cover every eventuality, Evie. If I were you I'd sit tight for a bit and wait for him to make contact. He won't want to upset those girls of his either.'

'I'd like to think he's concerned about his wife too.'

'I'm sure he is. Now, look, you concentrate on the kids – and that includes the girls. They're tricky at that age – I should know after going through it with you. They might not be your own but they need someone to look after them even if they don't thank you for it. In the meantime, put Robin out of your mind and go to the office. Give it everything you've got – you can only focus on one thing at a time. Afterwards, give me another ring or come round and we'll work out what to do if you still haven't heard from him.'

'Thanks, Dad.'

'That's OK. If you're coming this way, bring me some more fags, will you? I'm running out.'

'Dad, you've *got* to give up. It'll kill you one day. Remember what Mum used to say.'

'Your mother would have a great deal more to say if she was around now. I know you think I keep going on about it, Evie, but it would break your poor mother's heart if she knew you'd married outside.'

Evie had to clench her fingernails into her palms to stop herself screaming. 'Give it a break, Dad. I can't be doing with that stuff now. See you later.'

She drove on, glancing at all the other drivers and passers-by in case one was Robin. He had to be out there. Somewhere.

* * *

Half an hour later, when she walked into her office, she knew immediately that something was up. The Australian receptionist gave her a reserved smile instead of her usual cheery hello and a couple of people who would normally have stopped to chat, scuttled past her.

'Ah, Evie, there you are. Rich has flown in from the States earlier than we'd thought and we're bringing forward tomorrow's meeting to today. That all right with you?'

It was a trick, thought Evie, willing her face to remain calm and composed. Bulmer had done this on purpose to catch her out, hoping she'd be unprepared. Well, he was wrong: she had already done her homework like the good schoolgirl she had always been. Her ideas were right there, in her slim black leather briefcase.

'That's fine, Gareth.' She enjoyed the discomfiture on his face. 'When do you want to start?'

'Now, if that's all right with you – unless you want to freshen up first?'

Evie needed the loo, but if Bulmer wanted to speak now, she'd give him now. 'In your office?'

'No. Rich is waiting in the boardroom along with the rest of the board.'

The board? Evie frowned. What were they doing at an editorial meeting? More alarm bells rang as she followed Bulmer down the corridor past another secretary, who failed to meet her eye. Her chest fluttered with apprehension.

Rich, the small squat American who owned the company, stood up and shook her hand. 'Good to see you again, Evie. Please, take a seat.'

Numbly, she did as he said, unzipped her briefcase and placed a neat folder of ideas in front of her. Around the table were faces Evie saw once or twice a year on formal occasions. Most were money men and women; a couple were former editors of other publications who had been brought in for their expertise.

Evie braced herself. 'Bulmer – I mean, Gareth asked me to draw up a plan to restructure the magazine,' she began.

Rich leaned forward. He was wearing a brace on his teeth. 'I'm afraid we won't be needing those, Evie.'

She glared back. 'Why not?'

'There's no easy way to say this, Evie, but we've decided to let you go.'

'Why?' she repeated. 'You can't just do that! I've built up this magazine. I've increased the circulation by ten per cent.'

'But it's not enough, is it, Evie?'

Rich leaned forward, his brace twinkling. 'We need more. We need an editor who is on the same level as our readers. Someone younger, more in touch.'

They were replacing her with Janine!

'Your deputy is the natural successor. Let's just say that her age and her maternal instincts are perfectly in step with our readers' profile and she has offered to shorten her maternity leave so she can maximise this opportunity. I'm sorry, Evie, you'll have the usual severance package, but I'd like you to clear your desk by four p.m. HR is aware of the situation and will be in touch. Oh, and remember to hand in the car keys by Friday, at the latest, won't you?'

Evie walked back to her office. One of the secretaries shot her a sympathetic look. They had all known before her. That was the way things worked in this place. You gave it your life and they took it away without a second's thought. She'd seen other women like her who had given their all to a magazine only to be dismissed at a managing editor's whim. Until this year, she had thought she was immune but now she knew better.

She also knew something else. For the first time, she understood exactly how Robin must have felt when he lost his job. It couldn't have helped that she, Evie, had such an amazing job. Well, it was gone now. She was in the same boat as him, except that she was here and he wasn't.

Swiftly, she cleared her desk, sweeping the contents into the bags her secretary silently handed her. 'I'm so sorry,' whispered the girl.

Evie nodded. 'Thanks.' Out. Just walk out now, head high, towards the car park. Shaking, she got into the Discovery. She needed to breathe properly and work it out. She'd lost her job, but she'd got a fairly decent handshake so she'd make do for a bit. But Robin was still gone. What had Dad said? Sit tight and wait – but, in the meantime, look after those children.

Evie turned on the engine. Last year she had missed sports day because of a meeting and the year before. If she didn't have a job now, she could at least be a decent step-mother and get there on time today. After that, well, she'd ring her father. He'd think of something. She'd always thought of herself as independent, but at times like this everyone needed someone.

24

'One fifth of teenagers between sixteen and eighteen now have a sexually transmitted disease, according to a new report out today . . .'

'Third gear, not fifth – I said *third*!'

'You're making me nervous, Dad, stop it.'

'I can't afford another gearbox, Julie. You're ruining it.'

'Well, if you let me practise more, it would be all right.'

She had been like this since she had got up this morning. To be fair, he'd been tetchy too. They always were on anniversaries, birthdays and at Christmas. Nothing was the same without Juliana. Two years tomorrow. Was that possible? Sometimes it seemed like ten, at others, like last week.

Lately, Amber had suggested counselling for Julie – just as school had done – but she wouldn't hear of it. 'I'm not talking to a stranger, Dad. Anyway, I've got my friends.'

Nick only wished they didn't include the spotty Jason, who refused to meet his eyes. He'd been there every day this week when he'd dropped off Julie, waiting to scoop her up. He made Nick's skin crawl. How far had they gone? How far would Julie let him go? He had tried to discuss safe sex but every time he broached the subject she said, 'Stop it, Dad. I *know* about that kind of thing.'

He only hoped she knew more about the pill and condoms than she did about the Highway Code. 'No, move into the *inside* lane. That's better. Now check your mirror. Good.'

If he'd hoped to restore the peace, he had failed. Julie's beautiful face was scowling, her lip curled in precisely the same way that her mother's had.

Silence. Unbearable silence. It was worse than the arguments.

'What have you got on at school today?' asked Nick, aware that it was a desperate question from a parent who needed to make a gesture of peace.

'Nothing much.' Julie's eyes were fixed firmly ahead. 'English and geography in the morning. Helping out with sports day in the afternoon.'

'Sports day!' Grateful for something he could relate to, Nick pressed on: 'Don't you do it yourself?'

Julie gave him a withering look. 'Dad, I'm too old! I help the younger ones – it's part of my Sports Leaders' Certificate. I told you.'

Of course. Too old for sports day. Too old to tell him how she was really feeling, two years after her mother's death. And too young for a serious boyfriend – at least, in his view. Nick's heart lurched. He'd give anything to go back to the days when he and Juliana had gone together to Julie's sports day. They'd hold hands at the side of the track. She'd lean her head on his shoulder and he'd kiss her neck. Once they almost missed Julie cross the finishing line. Julie, with her plaits and the smile that said nothing would ever go wrong in her life.

Nick rubbed his eyes. He had to go forward and blank out memories like that or he'd go mad.

'They might need some more dads for the fathers' race, if you're up to it.' Now her eyes twinkled mischievously.

Maybe I'm forgiven, thought Nick. 'But if you're too old to take part, then surely I'm too old to run,' he said.

'Nope. There aren't enough dads around today, according to Mrs Hedges. They've all buggered off so we could do with a few more runners.'

Nick hated hearing her swear but decided to ignore it in case she gave him the cold treatment again.

'What are you doing today, then, Dad?'

He groaned. 'Developing the prints from a catalogue shoot and taking them to the client.'

'Nothing else?'

'If you knew the client, you'd know that was enough,' said Nick lightly. Why was she always so suspicious? Amber had said it was natural insecurity after a bereavement, but when he'd asked how to deal with it, she had merely said it would take time.

'Cool car,' said Julie, as they pulled up alongside a yellow Beetle. 'I'd like one like that when I've passed my test.'

'We'll see.' He gritted his teeth. 'Aren't you going to find a proper parking space instead of holding up the entire road?'

'I'll hop out here.' Julie turned off the engine, oblivious to the hooting from the parallel car, which clearly didn't relish the prospect of being sandwiched in. 'I won't be back until late tonight. I'm going out.'

'I forgot.' Nick's stomach churned. 'Who are you going with?'

'Friends. Someone's birthday party. Stop fussing, Dad. I'll call you.'

So it was all right for her but not for him. The car they were blocking in hooted again. This was no place for an argument. Julie had timed it well.

'See you, Dad,' she said, and leaped out.

'Hang on!' Nick had leaned out of the window to yell after her, but Julie was already in a crowd of kids. And next to her, his arm slung casually around her shoulders, was Jason.

Just as he was about to move off, she turned round and mouthed something. He wound down the window. 'What?'

'Don't forget sports day. You know. The fathers' race.'

She laughed and Jason was laughing too. Bloody cheek. 'You're on,' muttered Nick. Amber had said it was important to maintain communication with Julie at all cost. Besides, he hadn't liked the way that boy had laughed. Fathers' race? No sweat. He'd show him.

MARTINE

> *'One fifth of teenagers between sixteen and eighteen now*
> *have a sexually transmitted disease . . .'*

'D-d-do you know what that is, Marty? S-s-sexually transmitted? Shall I look it up in the d-d-dictionary for you?' Sam erupted into loud giggles, rolling around on the back seat with Ellie.

Martine frowned into the rear-view mirror and noticed, as she did so, that the mother with the pram whom she'd seen earlier in the week was crossing the road. She strained to get a better view but the woman disappeared. 'Stop immediately. I will inform your mother.'

'Inform!' Sam snorted with mirth. 'I shall inf-f-form your mother. And I will inform her of your b-b-boyfriend.'

Martine almost stalled the car. 'My boyfriend?'

'Yes!' Ellie joined in. 'We know who he is, Marty. We've looked at your phone.'

Martine's hands shook on the steering-wheel. 'You had no right. You are bad children. You should respect my piratecy.'

'D-don't you mean p-privacy? Or shall we look that up in the d-d-dictionary too. Ellie, get it out.'

'No. It is you who will get out. Now.'

'But we're not there yet. And my head's still itching.'

'We are nearly there. I do not care about your head. I will not have you in the car a moment more. Take your bags. Now! I will return and tell your parents. They will not come to sports day to punish you.'

'They've got to. They're opening it.'

'Go! Now!'

She got out and opened the doors. 'And there are your bags.'

'But we've got to cross the road on our own! Mum doesn't like that.'

'Nor would she like the way you talk to me. It does not display respect. I go now.'

Martine was still shaking when she got home. Boyfriend, they had said. What did they know? It was insurmountable. Sally and Simon deserved to be punished for bringing up such terrible *enfants*. She would start in Sally's dressing room. This dress would pay for the time that Sam called her a b-b-bitch. And this suit, for the time that Ellie had put pepper in her chocolate drink. The pair of matching shoes could go in too. And that would be just the beginning.

The alarm button on the inside of the kitchen door bleeped – someone needed to be let in on the other side of the electronic gates. She flicked on the screen that would show her who it was.

Barry's handsome rugged face peered down from the cab of his lorry. 'Garden Services here to deliver some more plants and do the pool.'

'I am opening the gates immediately.'

'That you, love? How are you doing?'

She smiled bravely. 'Not very bad.'

Martine checked her reflection in the mirror and walked outside, feeling a delicious flutter of anticipation. Barry was parking the lorry carefully, sending up waves of gravel as he did so. Then he swung out his legs. If it were not for her special friend, thought Martine admiringly, she might be tempted.

'Can you remind me where the pool is, love? My mate normally does it but I've got to sort it today.'

'Over here.' She tripped along, in front, glad she had worn the short pink skirt she had bought in Paris. She looked back over her shoulder, coquettishly. 'You want me to bring you a drink?'

'That would be great, if you haven't got too much to do.'

She sighed. 'Ah, I always have too much to do. I never stop. My employers, they expect a lot.'

'Do they now?' He frowned and tiny beads of sweat broke out on his forehead. Martine liked a man who sweated. 'Well, you ought to tell them where to get off.'

'Get off?'

'Tell them to stuff their job, if it's too much. A nice girl like you could easily get something else.'

He squatted down by the pool, unravelling the tube that sent chemicals into the water to purify it. 'I might go this week,' confided Martine. 'My friend might come and get me.'

'Boyfriend?' Barry looked disappointed.

'A girlfriend,' she lied.

His face relaxed. 'Well, let me know before you do. Listen, love, I haven't got the right chemicals here. I'm going to have to come back this afternoon. You going to be around to let me in?'

'I am sorry, no. I have my class and then I am accompanying the rest of the family to sports day.'

'Well, I can't make it tomorrow. Tell you what, give me the security code to the gates and I'll let myself in. OK?'

Martine hesitated. Simon and Sally had always told her not to give it to anyone. But Barry only needed to get to the pool, not the house. He was a nice man and, besides, Simon and Sally would want the pool to be clean for their party tomorrow night.

'I write it down for you. Here. But you must promise not to give it to anyone else.'

Barry put it in his back pocket. 'Course I won't, love. Sports day, is it?' His eyes travelled admiringly down her legs. 'Going to run, are you?'

Martine gave him a challenging look from beneath her lashes. 'Perhaps.'

'Well, I hope you win, love. Good luck.'

She returned to the house, feeling better. Barry had helped her feel good about herself and – more important – her man would be home soon. And then, maybe, she could have another baby. It would not be the same but Martine knew she would be happy only when she felt another child moving inside her. Providing it wasn't anything like Sam or Ellie. But she'd make sure of that . . .

25

'And now for our selection of golden oldies, specially chosen by Gordon from Guildford . . .'

Derek switched off the radio as they pulled into the car park. Pippa shivered. She had always hated hospitals. She blamed this on the sense of desolation she had experienced, and could still remember, when her aunt had explained her parents wouldn't be coming home. She didn't know if they had been taken to a hospital after the accident; in fact, she didn't know many of the details as she had been too young to ask or be told. Now it seemed morbid to delve into the past. She hated the hospital smell too. She wrinkled her nose. It was a bit like a disinfected railway carriage whose windows hadn't been opened for weeks.

'Don't worry,' said Derek, when he came back with the car-park ticket (how could hospitals charge when you *had* to go in?). If he said that once more, she would scream, she thought as they walked towards the main entrance. She glanced up at his face, and a picture shot into her head of Gus sucking her nipples. With a supreme effort she blanked it out.

She gave her name at Reception and was told to wait in a lobby just off the corridor. 'Surely these people don't all have lumps,' whispered Derek. 'There are too many.'

'Mrs Goodall, Miss Peters, Mrs Hallet,' trilled a nurse. Pippa stood up unsteadily and gripped Derek's arm. 'This way, please.'

None of the others had anyone with them, observed Pippa, and she would have preferred to be alone, without Derek's kind face to remind her of what she had done to him.

The nurse led them down one corridor, then another, until they found themselves in a small lobby with oatmeal-flecked easy-chairs. The three women sat down and smiled nervously at each other.

'Mrs Hallet?' said another nurse, with a clipboard. 'This way, please.'

Pippa was back within ten minutes.

'What did he say?' asked Derek, jumping up.

'She.' Pippa blew her nose. 'She wants me to have a mammogram. I have to wait here until I'm called.'

'But it's all right?'

'I don't know.' She didn't mean to snap. They sat, pretending to read magazines for nearly half an hour.

'Mrs Hallet? We're ready for you now.'

Derek stiffened. 'Can I come too?'

'I'm afraid you'll have to wait here. Your wife won't be long.'

Pippa forced herself to give him a reassuring smile. How did the nurse know he was her husband and not a lover, like Gus?

The nurse was walking briskly ahead, her calves wobbling below her uniform. She drew back the grey curtains in front of a cubicle. 'Just take off your clothes, dear, down to your undies, then put the blue overall on. Call if you need help.'

Pippa sat in the cubicle to wait. She could hear someone else being escorted down the corridor to the cubicle next to hers, with the same patter about removing clothes. It was hot. Clammy. Pippa loosened her overall. Why were hospitals always so warm if the NHS was short of money?

Ten minutes later the nurse still hadn't returned. If she didn't get some air, she'd faint. She opened the curtains and peered out. The woman in the cubicle next to her was doing the same.

'Are you here for a mammogram?' Pippa asked shyly.

The woman – who looked older than her – nodded. 'You too?'

'Yes.'

'Your first?'

They might have been talking about babies, thought Pippa, ruefully. 'Yes,' she said.

'This is my fourth. The first two were routine but then I had a lump three years ago. Now another one's come up.'

Pippa swallowed. 'The first was all right?'

'No. But they didn't have to take the whole breast off. Now I wish they had because I might not be here with this one. I'm going for a radical if there's any doubt. Safer that way.'

'But shouldn't they know what's best? I mean, why didn't they do a radical mastectomy to begin with?'

The woman shrugged. She was well built with a rosy, healthy shine on her face; she certainly didn't look ill. 'It depends who you get. Some seem to have their own views.'

'Mrs Hallet.' The nurse came out of a door and bustled towards her. 'Sorry to keep you waiting. Would you like to come through now?'

The woman crossed her fingers. 'Good luck.'

'Thanks.' Heart thumping, Pippa followed the nurse into a small room with a large machine in the centre. It looked like a piece of naval equipment from the Imperial War Museum to which she'd recently taken the girls. Music was coming from a radio in the corner. Bach, guessed Pippa.

Another woman, in a white coat this time, smiled at her welcomingly. 'I'm Christine, the radiologist. Ever had a mammogram before? Well, it's quite simple, just a bit uncomfortable.' She spoke with the kind of no-nonsense attitude that discouraged potential panickers. 'I want you to slip off your robe and stand with your chin on this ledge. That's right.

Now I'm going to lift your breast up like this – sorry, my hands are cold – and gently bring down a glass plate so we can take an X-ray. Like this. All right?'

Pippa watched, horrified, as Christine picked up her breast and laid it on the slab below. As the glass plate came down, it squashed it out of recognition, so it resembled a hamburger in a glass roll. Horrible and grotesque and not part of her.

'Lovely, Pippa.' She was using her first name – presumably to put her at her ease – and talking as though they knew each other. 'Can you stand a little closer to the machine? Marvellous. Now lift your right breast up and put it flat on the plate. Perfect. This might feel a little uncomfortable but it shouldn't hurt.'

Pippa watched the glass plate coming down again; this was happening to someone else, not her. It was too much to cope with, the mammogram *and* Gus in one week. How could she have broken the trust between her and Derek? If he found out, it would be the end of their marriage.

Oh, God, what would the girls say? They would despise her with the self-righteousness of youth that cannot accept infidelity in adults. She could lose her family because of a stupid idea that she had somehow 'missed out' by not having had a relationship with Gus.

'Lovely. Now I want you to stand at a right angle. Perfect. Don't move.'

Christine went out of the room to press the switch.

'Right, Pippa, that's all. You can go back to the cubicle and get dressed now. The doctor will see you shortly.'

Pippa sat in the cubicle, shivering with apprehension. Through the curtains, she watched a door opening opposite as the woman to whom she had been talking earlier came out. Tears were streaming down her face and a nurse had an arm round her shoulder. 'It's all right, dear. Try not to worry.'

Pippa felt sick.

'Mrs Hallet?' The consultant she'd seen earlier was at her

curtain. 'Hello, again.' Dr Lightstone glanced down at her files. 'Would you like to come in now? Do you have anyone with you?'

'My husband,' said Pippa, quietly.

'Would you like him with you?'

'No.' She glanced behind her to check that Derek wasn't listening. She'd go through this alone: after Gus, she deserved the punishment. Derek needed to be protected.

'Please, sit down.'

Dr Lightstone glanced at her notes. 'I see you've had your mammogram. We'd also like to do what we call a "fine needle aspiration" which means drawing fluid out of the lump. If the results seem suspicious – or inconclusive – we will take it out under general anaesthetic.'

'When? When can you do the fine needle stuff?'

Dr Lightstone stood up. 'Right now. The pathologist will be able to give us the results this morning.' She smiled kindly. 'Better to get it over and done with, don't you think?'

26

KITTY

'Now, for all you kids who can't wait for the end of term, here's one for you. It's a classic – ask your parents. Yes, it's "Skool's Out For Summer".'

Kitty yanked off her headphones as she jumped on to the bus just before the doors closed. 'Gosh, thanks.'

The driver (he really *did* look like Jonny Wilkinson) grinned. 'That's OK. I'd have waited for you anyway – saw you running when I turned the corner.'

Kitty tried to catch her breath, vowing to get fitter in the holidays. There was so little chance to exercise when you were standing up in a classroom all day. 'I really appreciate it,' she said, hanging on to the rail as the bus juddered down the road.

'Got this for you.' He handed her a book.

Shouldn't he be keeping his eyes on the road? She glanced at the cover of the Trollope novel they had talked about. 'Great. I was going to get a copy but I haven't had time.'

'I've finished it,' he said. 'Saves you buying it. I know how skint you teachers are – I was one for a couple of years.'

'Really? Why did you give it up?'

'The paperwork got too much and all those Ofsted inspections. Besides, I wasn't a born teacher, not like some of them. I just fell into it after my degree because I didn't know what else to do.'

'And you prefer driving buses?'

'It's a no-brainer. I work half the day and spend the other half doing what I like. Bit of fishing, reading and chilling out. Reckon I might as well make the most of it while I haven't got any commitments.'

'Aren't you bored?

He lowered his voice. 'Well, to be honest, I'm also writing a novel but I don't tell many people in case it doesn't get published. I reckoned if I didn't do it now I'd get caught up eventually by the responsibilities of the family business my father's been trying to persuade me into.' He grinned. 'I didn't fancy the stationery world – at least, not yet – so I'm giving myself a belated gap year.'

Kitty wanted to know what the novel was about but people on the bus were staring at them. He seemed refreshingly unaware of this.

'Well, thanks for the book. I'll give it back when I've finished it but it might be next term now.'

'No rush. The name's Clive, by the way.'

'Er, Kitty.'

'Nice name.' Clive pulled into the next stop and glanced into his mirror. 'Move down the bus, you lot. Give the lady some space.'

Colouring, Kitty elbowed her way through a dense mass of children, all talking at full volume. Her head was ringing and her throat was sore after having to project her voice yesterday at a particularly unruly English class.

'Want a mint, Miss?' asked a ginger-haired boy, sitting nearby. Kitty would have liked his seat, but she didn't fancy the off-white sweet that sat in his grubby palm.

'No, thanks.'

'Sure?'

'Shove off, Callum! She said she doesn't want one.' An older boy – gosh, they came big nowadays – stood up and put his face too close to hers for comfort. He stared at her challengingly with hard black eyes, and for the first time in her teaching career Kitty felt threatened. She moved backwards, treading on someone's toe.

'Ouch, Miss! That hurt.'

'Sorry.'

The boy moved closer, smiling. 'How about a fag instead, Miss?' He took out a cigarette and struck a match.

'You're not allowed to smoke in here,' said Kitty, firmly.

The boy smirked. 'Is that right, Miss? Sure you don't want one? They're home-made, you know. I can sell you some if you like it.'

Kitty glanced back at Clive, whom she couldn't see through the crowd of kids. 'Someone's smoking down here,' she called.

'Bitch,' muttered the boy, and stubbed out the cigarette on the floor.

'*What's that?*'

Clive's roar took Kitty by surprise. 'Who's smoking?'

The bus ground to a halt and some of the kids moved sideways as Clive got out of his seat and strode down the aisle. He took the boy by his jacket. 'You, out! You should know better than to smoke that stuff in front of the younger ones.'

That stuff, wondered Kitty. She had never taken drugs but, come to think of it, that sweet smell was familiar from her uni days.

'Out,' Clive repeated, pushing the boy down the exit steps.

He almost stumbled, then picked himself up. His hard dark eyes stared up at Kitty through the open door. 'You'll be sorry, Miss,' he shouted. 'You'll see.'

Kitty shivered.

'All right?' asked Clive, gently.

'I think so.' She dropped her voice. 'Was he smoking what I think he was?'

'Smelt like it.'

'I'd better tell someone.'

Clive sighed. 'Well, be careful. Some of these kids are big – and they can hurt.'

When Kitty arrived, she went to see the headmaster but his office was empty. Nor was he in the staffroom, which was stiff with panic at the impending Ofsted visit. She couldn't even find the deputy.

'You look worried,' said Judy. 'Don't panic. Everyone gets so worked up about these things.'

'It's not the Ofsted visit,' said Kitty. 'It's something else.'

She told her about the bus incident and Judy frowned. 'That's bad. There is a bit of a drug problem in the senior school but any school that says it doesn't have one is lying. If I were you, I'd wait until tomorrow when things will have calmed down after the Ofsted visit. Then you can see the head. And don't worry about that boy. They all like to look tough but they're not that bad underneath. We haven't reached the stage they have in America, thank goodness. Or Russia, God help them.'

Kitty tried to get on with her day but it was difficult especially as she'd been asked to take an extra class – biology – since the usual teacher was ill and she'd done it as an A level. No one knew when their particular class was going to be joined by an inspector. Just as she was about to start biology with year sevens, a tall, rather good-looking man with a moustache appeared at the door, nodded at her and took a seat at the back. Just her luck!

The children had been told to expect a visitor but to behave normally. The trouble was, thought Kitty ruefully, 'normal' usually meant rowdy, especially with the sex-education module they were doing.

Holding the chalk as steadily as her shaking hands would permit, Kitty drew a diagram on the blackboard, hoping it was accurate and trying to forget that there was an Ofsted inspector at the back of the classroom. She pointed to it. 'Now, who can tell me how an egg is fertilised?'

'I know! I know.'

She turned round to face a sea of hands and eager faces. 'Yes, Lucy?'

Lucy was one of her favourites, even though Kitty knew she shouldn't have any. The girl was always so keen to please that she was any teacher's delight. 'The sperm swims up and hits the egg and it makes a baby,' she said.

'Please, Miss.' Adam, in the row behind, was straining as though he was going to burst out of his seat. 'My dad says it's like cricket. You think of the sperm as the cricket ball and the egg as a wicket. When the ball hits the stumps, it's all over.'

Kitty's lips twitched and she couldn't help looking at the Ofsted inspector at the back. He was grinning broadly. Kitty didn't normally like moustaches but she had to admit that his was rather attractive. 'That's not strictly accurate, Adam, but if it helps you to remember how reproduction takes place, that's fine with me,' she said. 'By the way, what do you think of England's chance with the West Indies this weekend?'

'Walkover, Miss. My dad says we're going to thrash them.'

Kitty smiled. If there was one thing she did know about, it was cricket – from her brothers. 'Now, moving on, who can tell me how long it takes for a baby to grow in its mother's womb?'

Silence.

She began to sweat. 'Come on, someone, I know you only did this last week with Mrs Griffiths. Can't any of you remember?'

'Two years and nine months, Miss,' called a boy from the back. Everyone giggled.

'Try again,' said Kitty. 'Do you think it's less than that, Joe?'

The boy she had targeted shifted awkwardly in his seat, making a noncommittal noise.

'Is that a yes-grunt or a no-grunt?' asked Kitty.

'Yes, Miss,' he said reluctantly.

'Would you care to remember what you've learned, then, Joe?' She indicated the poster on the wall beside her. 'There's a clue here to remind you.'

Joe ignored the poster. 'It's nine months, Miss.'

The boys around him began to push each other. 'How do you know, Joe? Got someone into trouble, have you?'

'That's quite enough,' Kitty said firmly. 'Now, turn to page ninety-three of your workbooks, everyone.'

To her relief, the rest of the class went relatively smoothly. However, as the children filed out, the boys' shirts hanging out of their trousers, it was difficult to tell what the Ofsted inspector had thought. Apart from the cricket analogy, he hadn't shown much expression.

''Scuse me, Miss, can you tell me something?'

Kitty looked up to see Lucy standing beside her, twiddling her hair nervously. 'Yes, Lucy?'

'If a woman has a lump in her – in her breast, does it mean she's going to die?' Lucy's eyes were wide with anxiety.

Kitty felt cold. 'Not at all, Lucy. Women get lumps in their bodies for all kinds of reasons. Why do you ask?'

Lucy looked down at the ground. 'Cos my mother has a lump in her breast and I'm scared she's going to die.'

'Come here and sit down next to me. Look, I'm sure it will be all right but perhaps I can have a word with your mum to tell her you're worried.'

'No, you can't do that.' Lucy looked scared. 'She's in hospital and Dad says we mustn't do anything to upset her. That's why she might be late for sports day. I've got a note in my bag about it that I should have given you. Sorry.'

'Don't worry.' Kitty wanted to give her a reassuring cuddle, but you had to be so careful nowadays: you couldn't even put a plaster on a child's knee without going through all sorts of protocol first. 'I'm sure everything will be fine.'

'Thank you, Miss.' Lucy looked less troubled as she walked

out of the classroom, but Kitty felt bad. What right had she to say it would be all right when it might not be?

'That wasn't easy.'

She'd forgotten the Ofsted inspector. 'I shouldn't have said it would be all right. If it's not, she won't trust me.'

The inspector said nothing and Kitty realised, too late, that she had just shot herself in the foot. Now his report would criticise her abilities as a teacher and leader.

'You did your best.'

He said it so quietly that Kitty almost didn't hear him. He had a kind face, she thought. Maybe she should tell him about the drugs on the bus. On the other hand, if she did that the head might be livid with her for not telling him first. 'Actually . . .' she began. But he was on his way out of the room.

Thoughtfully, she put away her books. Good-looking he might be but it wasn't his face that she couldn't get out of her head. It was Lucy's, creased with worry. Cancer! What must it be like to lose your mother at her age?

BETTY

'Desperate Dan has just called to say there are hold-ups in Greenwich due to a burst water-pipe.'

They didn't put me through today. Their loss, not mine. If they don't want a traffic update, they'll find out the hard way. 'Sides, I've got other worries, like those kids this morning. Crossing the road on their own, they were, with those heavy bags. Any decent person would have run out and helped them.

Didn't get much thanks for it, mind you. Rude little bastards. That's what Terry says about some of the kids at his school. Tell him off about his language, I do. Reckon he picked it up from that job at Tesco.

They had big bags because it's sports day today. That's what the girl told me. I might go along. Terry likes sport, don't you, duck? And I've got a few leaflets left over that I could hand out to the parents.

Sam and Ellie, they were called.

'You shouldn't talk to strangers, love,' I said to them. Their parents should have told them, like I told Terry when he was little. Never go up to a car that stops and asks you the way. The driver might drag you in and do awful things.

Terry and I have got some more pictures to put in the new album, haven't we, duck? When Terry was small, I was so busy looking after him I didn't have time to do that kind of thing. Now we've found all the old photos and we're getting them sorted.

Here's Terry on his first bike. He soon got the hang of it without the stabilisers. A natural, Harold used to say. And there he is on his first day at school in his green uniform. Always neat, my boy. And here he is with me at his cousin's wedding – only fifteen but all the girls had their eyes on him.

'I'm not interested, Mum,' he said, when I told him to ask one of them for a dance. 'I'd rather be here with you.'

What mum could ask for more? Of course, Harold had gone by then so he felt he had to protect me. Just like he does now. Don't you, love?

PIPPA

Pippa came out of the consulting room and made her way to the corridor where Derek was waiting. Even though that needle had hurt, more than she'd expected, she felt calm – almost peaceful, as though another woman was inside her body. Quiet, soothing music was coming from behind the reception desk. A ruse by the NHS to calm the patients, perhaps.

'Derek, I'm here.'

She watched him jump up expectantly. 'You were so long! What did they say?' He studied her face. 'It's all right, isn't it? I told you it would be.'

Pippa led him back to the chair and sat down beside him. She wanted to kiss his cheek but it seemed hypocritical. Instead, she threaded her arm through his, then withdrew it: the contact of her skin on his made her feel guilty.

She took a deep breath, aware that what she was going to say would take their lives into another stage. 'They weren't sure about the lump. They did a mammogram and also drew out fluid with a needle.'

Derek sucked in his breath.

Pippa forced herself to take his hand. 'I had to wait half an hour for the results – that's why I was so long – but they were what they call inconclusive. So they're going to take it out tomorrow, just to be certain. It means I've got to stay in overnight.'

His face crumpled like Beth's when she was upset. 'When? Today?'

'No, Friday. Just as well, as I didn't want to miss sports day this afternoon.'

'But you seem so calm.'

'I know. Weird, isn't it? Maybe it's the relief of knowing what's happened.'

'But you don't know.'

'Not really, but I do know they're doing something about it. Anything's better than waiting like I had to at the beginning of the week.'

He put his arm round her and she tried not to flinch. 'But is it cancer?'

'I've told you, Derek, I don't know. We'll have to wait. Come on. I don't want to talk about it any more until I know the result.' She patted his hand. 'I'm coming round to your way of thinking. There isn't much point in worrying until you know what there is to worry about.'

His eyes were moist. 'But now I *am* worried, Pippa.'

An image of Gus peeling off his shirt shot into her head. Go *away*. 'Well, don't. I need you to be calm. Please, Derek,

I want to get out of this place. You know how hospitals freak me out. If we get going we'll be in time for Beth's race.'

They walked across the car park and Pippa switched on her mobile in case the girls had called. 'Hang on, I've got a message.'

'Pippa? It's Jean. I know you said you required a longer deadline but we've brought production schedules forward and I need to see what you've done so far. Can you e-mail me what you've got. It's urgent now. Thanks.'

Pippa groaned.

'What?' said Derek.

'It's my editor. I should have handed in some work by now and I'm running late because of all this.'

'Just tell her you're ill.'

'I can't. She won't give me any more work.'

Derek laid a hand on hers. Don't, she wanted to scream. Don't love me like this – I don't deserve it. 'Pippa, love, you might not be able to work for a while. It's only fair to come clean.'

Would he want her to come clean with him? 'Maybe you're right.'

She picked up the mobile again and punched in the numbers. Good, it was the answerphone so she wouldn't have to listen to the woman's reaction. 'Jean, it's Pippa. I'm afraid I can't send you that work yet. I need to tell you something . . .'

27

HARRIET

> '*And that was the Beach Boys, everyone, just to show your kids that we too, were young once . . .*'

The music was so infectious, invoking so many memories, that Harriet couldn't help humming to it as it blasted out of the Tannoy. If she tried really hard she could almost pretend they were a normal family. Charlie was chatting to other parents over bowls of strawberries (painstakingly hulled by the eager PTA committee from which she had resigned last year) and keeping an eye on the races to see how his children were doing.

How many other couples were putting on an act like this? She glanced around at the groups of animated men and women, who were talking about Ofsted placings, childcare and school-run traffic. She thought she could see Simon and Sally Pargeter talking to the head but didn't want to stare. Still, when a high-profile couple like them chose to put their kids into the state system, it showed their faith in the school.

'Look at the groupie mums,' said a blonde woman, with very fine, overplucked eyebrows.

'Groupie mums?' asked Harriet.

The other smiled wryly. 'It's what I call the mums who are always cheering their kids on from the sidelines. You know, the kind who go to every match. They're in their element on sports day, yelling at their kids to win. They've been deprived, of course, by this team rule that prevents individual glory but it doesn't stop them yelling. Even their poor husbands have to perform!'

Harriet and her acquaintance watched a straggly group of fathers, ranging from the youngish to the middle-aged and portly, running to the finishing line. Only one – who wasn't that young – seemed to do it with ease.

'But he doesn't have a pelvic floor to worry about,' muttered Harriet.

'Ha, that's good! I like that. Pretty fit, isn't he?'

'Yes.' Unconsciously Harriet turned her head to check that Charlie hadn't heard – he'd only misinterpret it. 'Yes, he is. Gosh, I know him.'

'You do?'

Harriet watched as a tall beautiful girl with olive skin and black hair ran up and threw her arms round him.

'That's a young wife,' observed her companion, putting on her sunglasses.

'I believe she's his daughter.'

'Really? Come to think of it, I recognise him too. Isn't he a photographer?'

'Yes.' Harriet noticed that the woman was shivering. 'Are you all right? You look cold.'

'I'm fine.' She pulled her jacket round her. 'Actually, I'm not. I've had a shock today – two, in fact.' She looked up at Harriet, who was a little taller than her. 'Sorry, I don't know why I'm telling you this. We don't even know each other.'

'Sometimes,' said Harriet slowly, 'it helps to tell people we don't know.'

'Yes, well, I'm not usually that kind of person. Thanks anyway but I've got to go. 'Bye.'

Harriet watched her stride off across the grass, heels sinking into the turf, calling to a pair of girls who looked very similar (twins?) and a small boy. Together they climbed into a turquoise Discovery parked outside the gates. So that was who she was! Funny how you knew the cars better than the owners on a school run. She seemed more vulnerable outside her car, when you remembered her aggressive driving style.

Harriet was just about to go up and claim Charlie, who was talking animatedly to a pair of mothers in high heels (yummy mummies, as she and Pippa laughingly called them), when she felt a light touch on her shoulder.

'Excuse me. Bruce's mum, isn't it?'

Harriet turned to see a pretty auburn-haired girl with a serious but kind face. 'I'm Kitty Hayling. I take Bruce for English.'

'He's mentioned you. You're fairly new, aren't you?'

The girl nodded. 'I hope you don't mind me mentioning this but I'm a bit worried about Bruce.'

Harriet sighed. Every single one of Bruce's teachers had told her they were 'a bit worried'. 'He's not playing up again, is he? I know he can be lively but I really don't know what to do about it. I've taken him to the doctor and the health visitor but they say he's not hyperactive, just challenging.'

'One of my brothers was the same. Boys can keep you on their toes, can't they?'

Harriet was mollified that she seemed to understand.

'Bruce is actually very talented,' continued Kitty. 'I've been impressed by some of his essays and stories, which have shown real creative flair.'

'Really?' Harriet wondered briefly if they were discussing the same child.

'Yes, but you must have noticed his spelling is a little odd.'

Harriet groaned. 'His sister's is the same. It drives me mad.'

'Have you considered dyslexia?'

'But they don't get the letters the wrong way round. They just find it hard to spell.'

'That can still be a form of dyslexia. If you don't mind, I'd like Bruce to be seen by our special-needs co-ordinator. Maybe his sister could be seen as well if she has spelling problems, and it would make Bruce feel better too.'

'I can see you understand a thing or two about sibling rivalry.'

Kitty smiled. 'Like I said, I have brothers. Actually, there's one other thing.' She hesitated. 'In Bruce's last essay, he said he was really looking forward to his dad coming home.'

A chill passed through Harriet. 'That's right. My husband has been in Dubai for a couple of months.'

'Look, I know it's none of my business but he seemed a bit worried about your husband coming back as well as pleased. If there are any big changes at home, it's always helpful to know about them.'

How dare this girl interfere? Harriet thought. 'There are no big changes,' she said coolly. 'My husband has been working away, that's all.'

'Of course. Well, I hope you didn't mind me mentioning it. We just need to know if anything's upsetting the children, that's all. It helps us do our jobs better.'

Harriet didn't trust herself to say anything. If she opened her mouth, she would either tell this young teacher where to go or throw herself on her shoulder for comfort.

'Nice to meet you,' said Kitty. 'Enjoy the afternoon.'

Harriet watched her walk off. She was prickling with discomfort. Then, across the track, she spotted Pippa. She ran – faster than she would have done in any mothers' race. 'Pippa! How did it go?'

Her friend reached for her hand. 'Let's go and get a cup of tea shall we? I'll tell you on the way.'

MARTINE

'Now for the past tense. Decline the verb "to be". We'll do it together. I am, you are, he is . . .'

Martine shifted uncomfortably on the hard park bench and switched off the cassette. She was fed up with learning English. It was a stupid language, full of mistakes, just like the English themselves.

She reached into her bag and pulled out her diary. 'It is not fair,' she wrote. 'I am looking forward to sports day, which is a big English tradition. And now I cannot arrive. Sally say it is for parents, not au pairs unless the parents cannot attend. She say I stay at home and prepare tea.'

Slowly, she tucked her diary into her bag and walked across the road past the shops towards 'home'. 'Home.' She ran the word round her mouth. It still felt wrong, as though the sound should mean something else. The Pargeters' house was too big and colourless to be a real home, with its wooden floors and glass tables. Martine liked colours, the kind of colours she was looking at now in the shop window. That baby's bright pink cardigan was so adorable with its balloon embroidery. Last week there had been a perfect white dress with smocking that would have been just the right size now for her baby.

'Can I help you?' asked the woman behind the till; she was folding tissue paper.

Martine hadn't realised she had gone in. '*Oui. Non.* I am looking for my niece but I will return.'

Shaking, she left the shop and walked fast towards the Pargeters' house. The further she got away from her daughter (she was sure it would have been a girl), both in distance and time, the harder it felt. Sometimes Martine wondered if her mother – who was usually so right about everything – had been correct about the termination. Would a baby really have destroyed her life as Maman had insisted?

She walked even faster. Strange! The gates to the house were already open. Perhaps Barry was about to drive out. Briskly, Martine strode up the drive to the square outside the kitchen. As she did so, she could hear the alarm ringing.

'*Merde*, the kitchen door, she is open!'

As she stood there, a police car tore up behind her and screeched to a halt on the gravel. A man and a woman in uniform stepped out.

'Anyone hurt?' said the woman.

'I do not think so,' said Martine, shaking. 'But the kitchen door, she is open.'

'I'll check it out,' said the man.

Martine got out her phone. 'I must call my employers. No, the signal is off. They are still at sports day.'

The policeman came back, a grim expression on his face. 'Break-in, all right. Better call for back-up in case anyone's still there. You get into our car, Miss, if you don't mind. We'll need a statement from you down at the station.'

'Statement?' Martine tried to stop her knees jerking but they appeared to have a mind of their own. She sank on to the gravel, which dug into her bare legs. 'But I am not doing anything wrong. Besides, I need to wait. I have a friend who may be calling.'

'Sorry, but it's the law. French, are you? Speak enough English to understand? Did you see anyone suspicious this morning? No? Well, let's get down to the station and see if you can remember anything.'

THURSDAY EVENING

'You were fantastic, Beth. Your team did really well, didn't it, Derek?'

'We'd have come first if it hadn't been for that slow-coach Janet.'

'Never mind. I couldn't run at her age either. Now, listen, girls, I've got to go into hospital tomorrow for a small operation but I'll be out the next day. Nothing to worry about. Dad will be here to look after you.'

'Why have you got to be away for the night?'

'That's what the hospital says.'

'But we want you here.'

'I know. But you've got to be big girls. Daddy will get you

a video if you like and you can have fish and chips for supper.'

'Just one night?'

'That's right. I'll be back before you know it.'

'D-D-Dad, how do the gears work?'

'Like this. See? First, then second, then third.'

'Is it easy to drive?'

'It is when you know how to.'

'Then w-w-why does Martine k-k-keep trying to drive on the right?'

'I didn't know that.'

'You ought to ask her, Dad. She's got a b-boyfriend too. And she keeps talking to him on the phone when she's meant to be driving us.'

'Really? I'll have to talk to Mummy about that.'

'Why didn't Mum come back with us?'

'She had to go on to the studio.'

'Is it nice being famous, Dad?'

'Sometimes. Sometimes not.'

'I want to be f-f-famous too. But when I have k-k-kids I'm not having an au pair. Not like F-F-Farty Marty.'

'Farty Marty gave us nits, Dad. And we've given them to Hugo.'

'Are you sure?'

'Y-y-yes. She has this special sh-sh-shampoo. I've s-s-seen it.'

'That's why our heads have been itching, Dad.'

'I didn't know that.'

'Yes, you did, we told you. And she smelt of sherry when she picked us up this week.'

'Sherry? Are you sure?'

'Yes, Dad.'

'Right. We'll soon see about *that*.'

'Thanks, Dad.'

* * *

'Was it nice having me there for sports day?'

'Yeah.'

'You don't seem very sure.'

'Of course he's sure, Charlie. He's tired, that's all.'

'I liked it, Dad. Did you see my race too?'

'I saw all of them, Jess. Clever girl. But I don't know why you have to run in teams.'

'It's so no one feels left out.'

'But that's life, isn't it?'

'Yes. I suppose you're right.'

'Cor, Dad, I was really impressed. First in the fathers' race. I've never known you do that before.'

'Thanks. I was quite pleased myself. Maybe I'll take up jogging again.'

'Did the client like the pictures?'

'Amazingly, yes. It's incredible what you can do with tarty lingerie if you've got the right models.'

'Pretty, were they?'

'They looked good in the shots.'

'You haven't forgotten I'm going out tonight, have you?'

'Just don't be late.'

'What are you doing?'

'I need to nip back to the studio to check on some prints. Then I'll head home. Who did you say you were going out with again?'

'Just some friends, Dad. Stop fussing. Take a chill pill.'

'*What* kind of pill?'

'A chill pill, Dad. Stop looking like that. They're not drugs or proper pills. It's a state of mind. Got it?'

'I thought you'd be running, Nattie.'

'*Natalie*, Evie. My name's Natalie. We didn't have to run this year, if we didn't want to. It's a new rule. We ran last year if you remember, but you missed it.'

'I was working, but I got here today on time.'

'Yeah, a year too late. And isn't Dad back yet? He knew it was sports day. I told him.'

'I'm not sure where he is, to be honest. I'm sorry.'

'It's not like you to be sorry.'

'No, you're right, Natalie. It's not. I'm not really feeling like me at the moment.'

'What does that mean when it's at home?'

'Nothing. Do you want a takeaway tonight? For a treat?'

'What's there to have a treat about?'

'Nothing, really, but sometimes it's nice to have a treat even when there's no reason.'

'You're weird, Evie, you really are. When's Dad coming home?'

'And Mum?'

'Mum, Dad.'

'Good boy, Jack. Good boy. Don't do that to the car, Natalie. It's got to go back to the office on Friday and they won't like it if you've marked the seat.'

'Why has it got to go back?'

'I'll tell you later. Strap in now, everyone.'

'Hi, this is Mark. Look, I'm really sorry about cancelling on Monday but I wondered if you were free for dinner on Friday night. Eight o'clock? I could pick you up at your place . . .'

Delete.

'Hello? Kitty? This is Duncan. I rang the other evening but maybe you didn't get the message. My answerphone is always going wrong. Actually, it isn't. I just said that because I'm feeling embarrassed. I don't normally leave messages on strange girls' phones but I'd really like to meet you. How about Friday?'

Save.

'Betty of Balham has just rung in to warn drivers of congestion around Acacia Road. Apparently it's due to a local school sports day so drive carefully, everyone.'

28

THURSDAY NIGHT

NICK

'Lines are still open for tonight's phone-in on missing persons. If you've got a question or need some help, we'd like to hear from you . . .'

Nick switched off the radio, which he always left on in the hall when he was out, partly to deter burglars and partly to keep Mutley company. He felt stiff as he walked – more fool him to have run in the fathers' race at his age. Also – if he was truthful – he had to admit that he'd tried particularly hard when he had realised Harriet was watching. How crazy was that?

'Hi,' he called. 'I'm back.'

He slung his workbag on to the glass table by the door and wandered into the large, airy kitchen-cum-sitting-room that Juliana had designed before she was ill.

'Julie?'

Juliana's beautiful face looked down at him from the wall. At times he felt like taking it down. That and all the other black and white photographs that hung around the house. But something always stopped him.

'Julie?'

Where is my daughter? Why don't you know where she is? That was what she'd be saying if she was here. God, it was hard being on your own, thought Nick, climbing upstairs to the third floor where Julie had her room. Like every other room in the house, it was full of photographs of her mother. Juliana laughing. Juliana blowing a kiss. They were all there, in the same position that Julie had arranged them when her mother had died. All present and correct, except for Julie herself.

It was only nine thirty. She'd be home soon. Nick went back to the kitchen and the huge American fridge that Juliana had insisted on. The same fridge that he had found her inside, in the middle of the night, stuffing food into her mouth, then throwing it up in the downstairs lavatory so Julie couldn't hear. He wasn't hungry but he'd have a glass of Chardonnay.

By eleven, he was frantic. Julie had to be back by ten on a school night, she knew that. Why didn't she answer her mobile? Should he call the police? Was she out with that boy? Oh, God, what could he do?

Nick was tempted to call Juliana's mother. She lived in Newcastle and often visited in the holidays. But what was the point of worrying her when there was nothing she could do?

At nearly eleven twenty, just when Nick had decided he would call the police, Mutley barked and he heard a key in the lock. Thank God! He felt sick with relief.

'What the hell do you think you're playing at?' he demanded.

Julie, cheeks glowing, bounced in. 'Sorry, Dad. I couldn't get back until now. Hang on a minute.' She turned round on the doorstep and waved at a car. Someone called, 'Night, Julie,' as they drove off. A girl's voice.

'Who was that?'

'Jason. And some other friends. Can I have some of that?'

'No, you can't. You smell as though you've had a few already. Who was driving?'

She flopped down on the sofa and began to play with the TV remote control. 'Jason, if you must know.'

Nick felt hot. Did men get menopausal too, or was it just parent paranoia? 'I told you, Julie, you're not to be driven by other teenagers. It's a rule. I won't have it.'

She rolled her eyes as she flicked through the channels. 'Oh, give over, Dad. Anyway, if you really want to know, he wasn't driving. I was.'

'You were *driving*? That's illegal.'

'No, it's not. We found some L-plates. Well, at the front, anyway. And I needed the practice. It's not as though you give me enough. Now, please, I'm trying to watch *Big Brother*.'

Nick grabbed the remote. 'How long has Jason been driving?'

'Dad, give that *back*!'

'Not until you tell me how long that boy has been driving.'

She rolled her eyes.

Nick could smell her breath from where he was standing. How many drinks had she had?

'A whole year. That's how long. Now, will you stop panicking? And give that *back*!' She snatched the remote from him.

'Then it *is* illegal,' said Nick. 'You have to have driven for three years before you can supervise a learner.'

'How interesting.'

'Julie.' He sat down next to her on the sofa. 'Look at me. You were lucky not be stopped by the police. Where did you go?'

'Some bloke in Jason's maths set. Jason needed to drop something off. Then we went to a bar. Chill out, Dad. It's no big deal. I'm eighteen in six months and then I can do what I like. Mum was only my age when she met you.'

Her trump card. Juliana. Tomorrow. Two years. He ought to make allowances. 'Let's go to bed.' He suddenly felt weary. 'I'll just walk Mutley.'

'Let me kiss him before you go.' Julie stumbled off the sofa and buried her face in the dog's neck.

'How many drinks did you have tonight, as a matter of interest?'

'Three Bacardi and Cokes.' She got up and turned up the

television volume. 'And before you ask, it was after I finished driving. Jason drove afterwards and he hadn't had anything. Satisfied?'

'I'm not happy about it,' he said quietly. 'It's not a good week, I know, but it's hard for me too.'

Her eyes softened. 'I'm sorry, Dad.' She leaned towards him and kissed his cheek softly, like her mother had at the beginning. 'I just want to see the end of this. If I'm not here when you get back, I'll have gone to bed.' She was looking at the screen again.

Maybe, thought Nick, the driving and the drink and the television were her way of getting through tomorrow. Perhaps Amber was right: he should respect the way she was dealing with her loss. Everyone coped differently with bereavement.

He bent down to kiss her. She smelt of cigarettes. Only a few years ago, he thought sadly, it had been baby lotion. 'Night, Julie. Sleep well.'

FRIDAY

29

EVIE

'It's Friday and nearly the weekend, folks! And it looks like it could be a scorcher . . .'

Scorcher? It was ice cold in here. No one had spoken for nearly ten minutes. Evie had been wrapped up in the radio item on missing persons she'd caught at the end, last night. The advice line had recommended finding the missing person's favourite place. But Robin's was home.

'Excited about the end of term?' she asked, trying to make an effort for the girls. 'You won't have much work today, will you? In our day, we just played games and did quizzes.'

'We want to know when Dad's coming back,' said Leonora, sullenly.

Evie swallowed, suddenly desperate for a cigarette – five years after having given up. 'I'm sure he'll ring soon.'

'Have you got a bottle for Mrs Hedges?' demanded Natalie.

'No, should I?'

'Mum always does at the end of term. She *is* our year tutor.'

'Damn.'

'Damn, damn,' chanted Jack.

'Don't swear, Evie,' said Natalie primly. 'It's bad for Jack.'

Gritting her teeth, she pulled into a garage. She'd buy Mrs Hedges a box of chocolates even if it made them late for school. She'd be damned – yes, damned – if anyone was going to accuse her of being a bad step-mother. 'You might have neglected your responsibilities, Robin,' she muttered to herself, as she strode across the forecourt, 'but I haven't.'

After she'd dropped off the girls at school, she'd go on to see her father. He might have different values from her, but when it came to the crunch, blood was blood.

'So, you've finally made time to come and see your old dad, have you?'

Evie cleared a pile of yellowing newspapers off the torn leather chair and sat down, hoping it was clean. 'Don't start talking like that, Dad. It's only been a fortnight.'

'Nearly three weeks.'

'All right, I'm sorry. But you know what it's been like.'

He patted her arm, lit another cigarette and leaned back into his chair. The flat reeked of tobacco, and in the background Helen Shapiro crooned softly from a record player Evie remembered from her childhood. A nasty smell of cabbage hung in the air; she ought to have brought him something decent for lunch, she thought.

'Any news of Robin?'

She shook her head. 'I'm going to have to report him missing soon.'

'I still think you should sit tight. If that boy's got something up his sleeve, he's not going to thank you for scuppering it.'

'Then why hasn't he rung to say he's all right?'

'Maybe he's tried.' Her dad eyed her mobile distrustfully. 'Those things aren't that reliable, you know, especially if he's ringing from abroad.'

'Don't.'

Evie felt so nervous that she began to inhale her father's fumes. She could do with a puff but she'd given up when she'd met Robin because he couldn't stand smoking. She ought to tell Dad she'd been sacked but she couldn't, not yet: he'd be so disappointed.

'How are you doing anyway?' Her eyes swept round the room. Benjamin lived in the top floor of a block of mansion flats in Hackney. In Victorian times it would have been a prestigious house, looking out over Clapton Square and surrounded by other four- and five-storey buildings. Now it was divided into several apartments, with high ceilings and spacious dimensions that froze the occupants in winter. She'd offered to install central heating but Benjamin had been adamant that his two-bar electric fire was enough.

He'd always been stubborn, even when Mum was alive. When Evie moaned about it, Robin would laugh and say that was where she'd got her determination from. He admired Benjamin, even though the feeling had never been reciprocated. People had to earn Benjamin Cohen's approval and it didn't happen overnight.

'How'm I doing? All right, I suppose.' Benjamin sniffed. He could look after himself well enough, Evie knew. She had offered him a place in their home, but he had turned her down. His brain was as sharp as ever. All those newspapers she had just moved were open at the financial pages. After he'd gone part-time as a cabbie, he had decided to do what he called a bit of dabbling. Evie hadn't taken much notice of it until Robin, after one of his increasingly long discussions with his father-in-law, had told her that Benjamin was doing 'rather nicely' with his portfolio.

'He wouldn't know one if it hit him,' Evie had said disbelievingly.

'You'd be surprised,' Robin had said. 'He's given me a few tips that have paid off.'

Pity her father didn't use the extra cash to do something about this place, thought Evie. She couldn't even have a cup of coffee because she knew the chipped mug would have a grimy ring round the inside.

'Coffee?'

'No, thanks.'

'My stuff not posh enough for you?'

This was so typical of her father. He'd start a conversation, as he had at the beginning, then veer on to normal things that didn't matter. 'No,' she said. 'I can't eat or drink anything until I know Robin's OK.'

'Know your trouble, girl?' He leaned towards her and she could see the white hairs inside his nose. 'You want everything straight away but life's not like that – there are no definites. If you keep on working for something, though, it usually falls into place. Mind you, when your chap does get back, he'll have me to answer to. I told him when you got married that if he ever laid a finger on you or hurt you mentally I'd make sure he paid.'

Robin hadn't told her that.

'He wouldn't hurt me, Dad, not like that. He's a good man and it can't be easy, not having a job.' She took a deep breath. She'd come clean after all. 'Actually, Dad, he's not the only one who's out of work.' Briefly, she told him what had happened at the meeting yesterday.

Benjamin's face remained impassive. 'That's business for you. Bastards, but they're the kind of people you're dealing with. You'll just have to get out there and find something else.'

'I will, but not until Robin gets back. Concentrate on one thing at a time – that's what you've always told me. Well, now I'm going to put my own career on the back-burner for a bit while I look to my family. Sorry, Dad. I know you've always wanted me to be a career woman but sometimes other things have to take priority.'

He looked at her admiringly, which wasn't what Evie had expected. 'You're so like your mother.'

'I am?'

'Quietly stubborn. In other words, bloody-minded. Well, maybe you're right. Meanwhile, let's have a look at those letters and figures you found in Robin's car.'

She handed them over and watched, desperately wanting her father to say it was all right, wishing he wasn't frowning as he turned the pages. 'Look at the letter underneath, Dad.'

'I'm reading it.'

She waited. Even now, she couldn't believe what was written there. She'd been shocked enough when she'd found it last night, in the same wodge of papers hidden in the car. And this morning, when she'd reread it, it hadn't been any better.

The letter was from the firm of solicitors that Robin's old firm had used.

Dear Mr Brookes,
   WITHOUT PREJUDICE
   Following our letter of 23 June, we are writing to inform you that unless you pay back the sum of £25,000 that you borrowed from your former employers, we will place the matter in the hands of the police.

Benjamin was shuffling the papers, reading and rereading them like a bad hand of cards. 'Twenty-five grand. That's what the letter says.'

Evie nodded.

'But he's borrowed a lot more from these loan sharks.'

'I know. Twenty-five thousand would be bad enough – we haven't got that kind of money to pay back. But the rest . . . Dad, I don't know what we're going to do.'

Benjamin lowered his glasses. 'Do you think he's being black-mailed?'

'I hadn't thought of that. But why?'

'I'm not sure – but it might explain why he had to borrow so much, to keep someone quiet. Is your pay-off enough to borrow against so you can settle his debts?'

'Not really. Besides, we need it to live on in case Robin doesn't come back.'

Benjamin's blue eyes glistened. 'You think he's done a bunk, don't you? Poor Evie.'

It wasn't what she wanted to hear. She wanted him to wave that magic wand, that bloody Tiger Tail, and make it all right. Everything she had built up over the years felt as though it was tumbling down around her. She wasn't the tough Evie of

Just For You any more. She might not even be Robin's wife for all she knew – although surely he wouldn't have done anything stupid, would he? She was short, fat Evie in the wrong school uniform in a class where everyone hated her.

Suddenly she felt a rough old cardigan against her face and the smell of rum mixed with tobacco. Benjamin's leathery face was pressed against hers and his arms were round her elegant Karen Millen jacket. 'It's all right, Evie. Leave it to your old dad. He'll think of something.'

She had a good cry then. She couldn't help it. And when she'd finished blowing her nose on the disgustingly cheap paper in Benjamin's bathroom (which needed a good clean too), she felt a bit better.

'How about that coffee, then, girl?'

'All right. I'll make it.'

He followed her out to the kitchen, watching her, bemused, as she gave the cups a good scrub (as good as she could in the absence of washing-up liquid) then put in the powder.

'Evie?'

She paused in the search for a clean teaspoon in the cutlery drawer, which contained breadcrumbs. She'd come back when she was feeling better and give this place a good going-over. At least she had time now. 'Yes?'

'Be a bit softer on those girls. You can be a bit tough sometimes. Like your old dad. Remember that.'

'I will.' She blew her nose again. 'There is one other thing. It sounds crazy and at best it's a long shot. But Jack keeps talking about someone or something called Bad Ron. We thought it was a kid at his nursery but it's just occurred to me that maybe Robin had mentioned his name on the phone or something and Jack picked it up. You know what kids are like.'

Benjamin shrugged. 'I don't know, Evie. You could be right, I suppose. I'll look into it. Now, have your coffee and try to calm down a bit. Put a slug of whisky in it. That's right. You'll soon feel better. You'll see.'

30

'Now for the four o'clock news with the World Service.'

Harriet woke with a start. Four o'clock! She must have set the radio alarm wrong. She didn't need to get up for another three hours, although the birds were singing so loudly that she doubted she'd fall asleep again. Irritated, she reached out for the radio and turned it off.

Lately she had often woken early; Monica had said it was typical of someone under stress but that didn't help her get back to sleep.

Harriet turned her pillow over but couldn't get rid of the thoughts that were whirling around in her head. Last night she had felt too awkward to undress in front of Charlie. Instead she had changed into her nightdress in the bathroom, then slipped, almost shyly, into bed next to him.

His back was to her. Slowly, she reached out for him. He turned over and moved her hand to his waist. 'Sorry, Harriet, I don't feel ready yet.'

She had felt both relieved and rejected. But at least his arm was round her and it felt comforting to have him next to her after so long.

Now as she tossed and turned, she became aware that Charlie was restless too. He seemed to be saying something in his sleep but she couldn't catch it.

'Charlie?' she said softly.

He rolled towards her and pressed himself into her body.

She was shocked, yet excited at how hard he felt. She arched her back – the effect was electric. He was urgent, desperate, demanding in a way she had never known. 'Turn over,' he instructed her.

She did as she was told. Part of her felt thrilled, excited. The other part was frightened. This wasn't Charlie. A stranger was pumping into her as though she was a prostitute. Oh, God, was that what he had been doing in Dubai? He groaned as her mind and body closed down with the horrible numbness of knowledge. She rolled away from him and took his face in her hands, forcing him to look at her.

His surprised expression, which asked 'Harriet, is that *you*?' said it all.

He fell asleep again almost immediately, but she lay there, tears streaming down her face. She had no proof apart from the way his body had behaved – but did she need any more?

Quietly, she slipped out of bed and went to the wardrobe. She put her hand into his suit pocket and withdrew his mobile phone. Then, without turning on any lights, she went down the corridor to the bathroom and locked the door.

Charlie's mobile was different from hers. She wanted to find the call register that would tell her who had phoned him and whom he had phoned. She scrolled through the options. Where was it? Well, at least she knew how to find the last call: you just pressed the green button twice and it came up with the number.

Ring, ring.

Harriet froze. She had pressed their own land line. My God! The phone was on his side of the bed. She switched off the mobile and ran back down the dark corridor, bumping into a wall and bruising her arm.

'Yes?' Charlie had the light on and receiver in his hand. 'Can you believe it? Who on earth would ring at this time of the morning?'

Harriet stood in her nightdress, the mobile behind her back. 'I don't know.'

'Well, we'll soon find out.'

He dialled 1471. 'That's my mobile number.' He stared at her, his eyes travelling down to the hand behind her back. 'Have you got my mobile there, Harriet?'

'It rang' – she was shaking – 'and woke me so I answered it.'

'You're lying.' He sat up in bed. 'You've been trying to find out who I've been ringing, haven't you? You don't trust me.'

'Ssh, you'll wake the children.'

He switched off the bedside light. 'Fine, if you want to play it that way. I'm going to sleep now and we'll talk about it in the morning.'

Harriet lay stiff on the bed, unable to move, as hot tears ran down her face. He was furious with her. Did that mean he had been seeing someone else or that he hadn't? She shouldn't have done anything. Now she might really have destroyed her marriage and it would be her fault.

When she woke again, it was to find he had got up before her. It was still early so, hastily, she showered and did her face. She wanted to look good for him; she wanted him to desire her as he had last night. Maybe she'd got it all wrong. Maybe there wasn't anyone, in which case she needed to make up.

He'd already made tea and was in the sitting room, staring into space. He looked at her, unsmiling.

'Morning.'

'Morning.'

His eyes went to the television. 'This is new.'

'The old one broke.'

'Couldn't you have got it mended?'

'It wasn't worth it.'

His lips tightened. 'I see.'

Wasn't he going to ask about the mobile, Harriet wondered, as she poured herself a cup of tea and went to wake the children for school. He had been unfair about the television. Of course things had changed over the last two months. There was a new toaster too. The people next door had put up a taller fence without consulting her.

She'd changed.

And so had Charlie.

'I'll take the children to school today,' he said, coming down the stairs in a shirt she hadn't seen before.

'They'll like that,' she said, and kissed his cheek. 'Can you pick up Lucy and Beth on the way? It's my turn to do the run.'

He moved away. 'As long as they're ready. I need to get into the office.'

Harriet began to make the packed lunches. 'You're not having the morning off, then?'

'How can I? I've been away for two months. I need to get back. If you worked in the real world, Harriet, you'd understand that.'

She waved them off in the car, hoping Bruce wouldn't do anything daft. After they'd gone, she looked at the toast crumbs on the table and the jam that had been dropped on the flagstone floor. It seemed strange to be at home on a sunny Friday morning, the last day of term, when she was normally doing the run.

The phone rang. Maybe it was Pippa. She should have rung to wish her luck for the op. She hoped with all her heart it would be all right: Pippa seemed too calm. Did she know something that the rest of them didn't? 'Hello?'

'It's me.' Charlie sounded cold even on the phone. 'I've left some files behind and I haven't got my keys on me. Are you going to be in?'

'Yes.'

'See you in ten minutes, then.'

She'd make him a proper breakfast, thought Harriet, with a flash. He'd only had a slice of toast. That was it! He liked a proper English breakfast – bacon and egg with mushrooms

– and it might get them off to a better start. Maybe she could even explain her fears about that stupid mobile.

Breakfast had been ready for nearly half an hour when she heard the key turn in the lock.

'Hi.' He touched her cheek and cast an eye over the plate she was putting on the table. 'Bacon? Sorry, Harriet, I can't manage it. I grabbed a croissant on the way back from the run. Besides, I can't stomach that sort of food in the morning any more. Too used to light hotel breakfasts, I suppose.'

Harriet bit back the hurt. 'Children get off all right?'

'Yes. Of course.'

'They would have liked you taking them.'

'What's that meant to mean?'

'Nothing. Just that it's a treat for them.'

'Don't start that again, Harriet. It's not my fault I had to be away.'

'I didn't say it was. I just said that it was nice for them that you took them to school. Don't be like that.'

'Like what?'

'Distant and cold.'

'That's what you are to me.'

'I'm not – but you've got to realise that it's strange for me too, not having you here and now having you here.'

'Well, you don't have to worry about that any more. I'm off to the office now I've got my files.'

Harriet felt cold. 'When will you be back?'

'I don't know. I'll call.' He gave her a hard look. 'From my mobile.'

Harriet's legs shook. Now was the time to explain but she couldn't do it. She didn't want any more arguments. She just wanted life back to normal. But, she asked herself, after he'd driven off and she started to tidy the children's bedrooms, was that possible after everything that had happened?

31

KITTY

'And here's a request from all the kids at Putney High who are leaving school today for ever!'

Kitty turned down the volume – next term she'd have head-phones that worked – and got on to the bus. 'You're right,' she said lightly to the driver.

'That's what I like to hear,' said Clive. He really did have a nice smile, she thought. 'What am I right about this time?'

'*Can You Forgive Her?*,' said Kitty, feeling almost coquettish at the prospect of eight wonderful weeks ahead. 'It's really good.'

He nodded, pleased. 'Glad to be of service.'

Kitty looked around her furtively. 'Actually, there is just one other thing . . .' After she'd explained what she needed – Clive didn't seem as surprised as she'd imagined – she moved on down the bus to where there was actually a free seat. She fumbled in her bag and took out the paperback Clive had lent her. It was well thumbed, with the odd stain on some pages – just the kind of book she enjoyed because it showed its owner had read it over a sandwich, unable to put it down. Kitty had added a few marks' from her meal-for-one last night, of her own. Shocking, that she'd never delved into Trollope before, con-sidering how long she'd been reading, but he was quite a find.

'Chatting up the bus driver, Miss?' Kieran's face loomed in front of her. He was leaning over the seat as he chewed his gum.

'No, Kieran. Actually, I like someone called Anthony.'

'Is he one of the teachers at school, Miss?'

'No, but he would have been a good one.'

'How old is he, Miss?' said a small girl opposite.

'Absolutely ancient,' said Kitty, settling into her book. 'So old that he's dead.'

Kieran's jaw dropped. 'You having me on?'

Kitty smiled. She could put up with the banter on the last day of term when everyone – including teachers – was allowed to slip into holiday mood. She had some educational quizzes in her bag and some games; if she could get the children to finish on a feel-good note, they'd be keen to start again next term.

'No, Kieran, I'm not having you on. Now, how about doing your homework or reading your magazine while I have a bit of time to myself with my book?'

She glanced at the cover of the publication he was holding, which featured a blonde with a voluminous chest. 'Isn't that thing a bit adult for you, Kieran?'

He grinned. 'We had Reading For Pleasure for homework last night so I'm just doing mine now, like you said.' He winked at her. 'Want a look?'

BETTY

'Sunny Sue has called in to warn drivers to look out for cyclists. She says drivers ignore cycle lanes. What do you think? We'd like to hear from you.'

That's it! Why didn't I think of that before? Thanks, Sunny Sue. You might be new to this – I haven't heard your name before – but welcome on board! As soon as we heard you, Terry reminded me about his old bike in the garage.

Down I go, over the road and up to the school gates. I can get really close this way. Terry and I can see their faces quite clearly, can't we, duck?

Cripes, that car was close. I'd feel safer on the pavement

but there are too many children. Isn't that a friend of yours over there, Terry? He doesn't seem to recognise us. No, don't talk to him. Concentrate on finding that woman. You'd recognise her, wouldn't you, love? She was near enough. Me too. You'd left your homework behind, remember? I came running out with it behind you. Tossed up in the air, you were, like one of those balsa wood planes you used to put together. I saw everything, right up to when she drove off. Everything except the number-plate. But I'd recognise her. Oh, yes. Like I keep saying to your auntie, it's why I bought the house on this very road so I could look at the drivers, day in, day out, and wait for her to turn up again.

This one? No. Wrong hair, but I suppose she might have had it dyed. Heavens, the wind's a bit strong today – it's almost blowing me off.

Hang on. That's the car. *And* the driver. Same nose. Same eyes. Same hair.

Stop! Stop!

PIPPA

'Where'er you walk, green trees shall fan your shade . . .'

Handel, thought Pippa, hazily. She was sure it was Handel, playing somewhere. They used to sing that at school on Founders Day because Handel had had a link with the building before it became a school.

'I want you to count from ten backwards.'

The anaesthetist was bending over her, and she could see her mouth moving through the mask. There was the pungent smell of disinfectant and everything seemed white. The sheet, the mask hovering above her, the strange stiff gown they had put her in . . .

'All right, Pippa?' Derek's hand tightened on hers.

'Ten . . .'

Gus's bedroom. Gus kissing her. Gus in her head. Gus in her body.

'Nine . . .'
Guilt. Lump. Derek.
'Eight . . .'
The girls. Cyst. Malignant.
'Seven . . .'
Nothing.

MARTINE
  *'So, Claire, how would you suggest that Susie changes
  her life?'*

Dear Diary,
*I usually listen to this programme to help my English. I would
like Claire to give me some advice but I do not know how to
approach her on the radio.*
  *Simon and Sally have told me I have to go. They are very, very
cross that I gave Barry the code to the gates. I tell them he is a
nice man. They do not know he broke into the house. When he
gets back to work, he will be able to defend himselves. Anyway,
nothing was stolen, apart from some money in Simon's bedroom
and some tapes. The police, they say the burglars were disturbed.
They could have hurt me if I had seen them. What is that,
compared to tapes?*
  *Sally and Simon say I must go for other reasons too. But they are
not fair. The children say I was drunk when I picked them up
the other day. I say I was not. It was a very bad apéritif that the
supermarket gave me as a present when I went shopping.*
  *They say it is not right to drive and drink. But I did not
exceed the limit. Then they blame me for a magazine that Sam
buys. It is not suitable, they say. I tell them it is not my fault. He
asked for comic money so I gave him. I am not his nanny, no?*
  *So on Saturday I depart. But it is good because my man, he has
telephoned. He has been delayed but he will be here very soon.*
  *Véronique, she says it is time to ring the paper. She says a lot of
people watch Sally and Simon. Even little things, like Simon's pink*

*underwear, would be of interest. So I called the paper and spoke to
a nice girl who is going to meet me tonight and take me out to
dinner. That is kind, yes? It will help to pass the time until my
man can come.*

NICK

'So, Claire, how would you . . .'

'My God, look out for that bike!'

Nick grabbed the steering-wheel and threw himself across
Julie as he did so. The car stopped a fraction away from the
woman's front tyre. He leaped out. 'What the hell do you
think you're doing? You could have been killed!'

The woman, in a dirty pink coat and headscarf, got off the
bike and ran up to Julie's side of the car. 'Murderess!
Murderess!' She beat her fist on the car window and Nick
saw his daughter's scared face. 'You killed my son! Now
you're going to pay for it!'

Nick took her arm. She tried to shake him off but he was
too strong for her. Dimly, he was aware that several people
were watching. 'What are you talking about?'

Tears were streaming down the woman's face. She was mad,
thought Nick. She had that wild look in her eyes, the same
look he had seen in Juliana's when things were bad. 'She killed
my son.' She was howling now, like an animal in distress.
'Two years ago. Knocked him down, she did, and drove on.
I'd recognise her face anywhere.'

Nick was speaking softly, the way he'd learned to do with
Juliana when she was screaming. 'This is my daughter. She's
only seventeen. She wasn't driving two years ago. I think you've
made a mistake.'

The woman stopped as though he'd turned off a switch.
She looked back at Julie, who was still staring, horrified, at
the scene outside. 'Seventeen?'

Nick nodded.

'Fifteen, two years ago?'

'That's right.'

'My Terry was only sixteen. He'd have been eighteen now. A man. He might have had a wife or even a child.'

The car behind Nick hooted. He waved irritably at the driver, indicating there was a problem. The poor woman was hysterical and her eyes were rolling wildly. 'Look, you've had a shock,' he said. 'Let's get you away from here. I'll just park the car and I'll get you a cup of tea.'

The woman shook her head vigorously. 'No. I must go. If it wasn't her, it was someone else. I must look. Not much time.'

Nick watched her run back to her bike, get on to it (extremely agile for someone who had to be in their late fifties) and disappear into the crowd.

'What was all that about?' asked Julie, white-faced, as he got in.

Nick switched off the radio, his mouth dry. 'She mistook you for someone else. Someone she said had run over her son two years ago.'

'But I wasn't driving then.'

'No.'

Neither said anything as Julie moved on and slid into a space at the end of the road. She turned off the engine and began to weep. Nick put his arms round her and breathed in his wife's fragrance, which Julie used every day. 'Put it out of your mind, darling. The poor woman was upset. Your driving was fine, really good today.'

Julie sobbed on to his collar. 'It's not that. I felt so sorry for her, losing a child. And meeting her this week, of all weeks. Two years since Mum, you know . . .'

It was a gaping hole that they were both walking round without saying anything. 'I know. It will be better next month. It always is.'

'Is it?' Julie's eyes filled with fresh tears.

He fumbled in his pocket for a bit of loo paper. 'Look, it's the last day of term today. You can come on a shoot with me tomorrow, if you like.'

'Really?' She blew her nose and checked her mascara in the mirror. It had smudged so she wiped it off.

'Yes, really. And we can take Mutley, if you walk him.'

'That would be cool.' She blew her nose again and tried to smile, just as Juliana had after an upset. 'Pick me up at the usual time so I can practise on the way home?'

He hugged her. Maybe Amber had been right when she'd said that eventually you learned to live with something. Perhaps this time next year the anniversary wouldn't hurt so much.

'See you tonight. Oh, and Julie? Try to have a good day. She'd want that, you know.'

He drove off slowly and waited at the end of the road for the queue in front to clear. It was getting hot again and he wound down the window. A man was sitting in a Volvo, speaking urgently into his mobile. Nick recognised him as Harriet's husband from sports day.

'Bon. Bientôt.'

Nick was almost adjacent to him in the queue and he couldn't help overhearing. Harriet's husband might speak French well but he didn't like the look on his face. It was hard and unforgiving.

'Ce soir. Oui, moi aussi.'

The car ahead moved on and Nick followed, wondering how Harriet was doing. A woman who needed to see a counsellor about her marriage had to be pretty desperate. Sometimes it was easy to forget you weren't the only one who found life painful.

32

'Now for the midday news.'

Evie pulled out of her dad's road, listening intently to the radio in case there was a news item that might, in some way, account for Robin's disappearance, but as usual there was nothing. Her temples throbbing, she drove on miserably to collect Jack from nursery, then headed home.

It was impossible to settle. She had tidied the house and attempted to clear spaces in the girls' bedrooms, but it didn't seem right to be at home during the day when she was normally checking pages or in meetings. Evie couldn't believe how she'd been betrayed, and every time she thought of Janine, her fists clenched.

But none of this compared with the tight panic that was gripping her chest over Robin. Every time the phone rang she sprang at it, hoping it was him. But it never was. Where the hell was he?

Had he really done a bunk? Was it 'just' this awful financial mess he had got himself into? Guiltily Evie thought of all the times she had snapped at her husband. Deep down she knew she had also felt angry because of the insecurity. Men of her father's generation had worked to provide for their families. Why couldn't Robin find a job? Why did she have to be the breadwinner?

Thank God Rachel was coming to get the girls tomorrow. That was why Evie was going into school early this afternoon.

She didn't want Rachel moaning because the girls had left something in the cloakroom. Leonora had come home every day this week without her blazer. When Evie had questioned her about it, the answer was always the same: it was in the cloakroom somewhere. Evie was willing to bet the last twenty quid in her purse that it was in Lost Property but she also knew Leonora wouldn't bother looking. So she'd beat her at her own game and get there first. And if she arrived when they were still in lessons they wouldn't see her.

Evie grabbed her bag and went out to the car. Jack was still asleep in the back – he'd dropped off after she'd picked him up. She hadn't the heart to wake him, poor lamb. This time she'd made sure the car was properly locked.

At least it was easy to park at this time of day. Evie walked smartly towards the school entrance gates. It was an old building in need of modernising, with its stone exterior and draughty windows. The main doors were open and as she went past the glass screen, behind which the school secretary usually sat, she saw that the office was unattended. Never mind. She had a fair idea of where Lost Property was. She'd had to go through it before when Natalie had lost her hockey stick. It hadn't been any old hockey stick, either. Oh, no, it was one of the most expensive you could buy – Robin had insisted on getting it for her as part of her Christmas present. It hadn't turned up in Lost Property so Robin had bought her another.

Robin, Robin, where the hell are you? What was she going to tell the girls if he hadn't turned up by tomorrow? Her father was going to find out as much as he could but, as he'd pointed out, 'Ron' might not mean anything apart from a toddler's garbled invention. If Robin hadn't made contact by the weekend, her father had advised her to inform the police. But she couldn't do that in case he was up to something. Robin had never been the type to be up to anything before, but now Evie wondered exactly what type he was. Was it possible to be married to someone and not know them? And did she have the courage to tell on someone whom – heaven help her – she still trusted?

Here it was. Lost Property. Daft to worry about a school blazer at a time like this but something inside Evie (the desire to make things right?) made her feel that if she could do something practical she could sort out the rest of her life.

Ugh! Gingerly she lifted out a dirty games shirt. No name tape. Then a pair of tracksuits. Several odd socks. A maths book with the owner's name on it. And, success, Leonora's blazer.

Triumphantly, Evie tucked it under her arm and headed up the stairs towards the front door. There was a noise ahead – maybe they were letting the kids out early as it was the end of term. As she crossed the hall, her kitten heels clipping the floor, a group of youths swarmed towards her.

One whistled. 'Posh, eh? What you doing here, lady?'

The spotty one next to him sniggered and grabbed her arm. 'Yeah. We're done with teaching. We don't need you here either.'

'Let go,' said Evie, shocked, shaking herself free. 'How dare you?'

'How dare you?' One giggled, and the others fell about laughing.

Evie could smell something sweet, a distinctive aroma that she recognised from when she had been a student. These kids were smoking cannabis and had maybe taken something else too, judging from the way they were flopping about.

Walk on. Act cool. Just get out.

'Not so fast, lady.'

The spotty one had grabbed her arm again but this time she couldn't shake him off. 'Leave me alone,' she said furiously. 'Ow! That hurts.'

'Then you'd better not struggle.'

She turned to him. He was taller than the others, his face riddled with acne. 'Take her to Room H with the others.'

Evie twisted so that the boy's hand bent. Immediately he slapped her across the face. 'Bitch! Don't do that!'

Stunned, she put up her hand to her cheek, which was burning. 'Let me go,' she said. 'Please. I've left my son in the car outside. He'll be upset.'

As soon as she said it, she knew it was a mistake. 'Your son?' said the spotty one. 'Don't worry, we'll take care of him.'

'Yeah, that's right,' said the boy pulling Evie along the corridor.

'If you touch him, I'll kill you,' yelled Evie.

'You're frightening me,' called the youth.

His laughter rang in Evie's ears as a door opened and she was pushed inside. She stared. On the floor, their hands secured behind their backs with school ties, were a large number of frightened children and a couple of teachers. 'Sit down and shut up,' said the boy, tying her wrists together behind her back.

Evie was too scared to speak. *Don't fight him. Do what the experts said. Pretend to be compliant.* 'Now sit there like the others until we tell you.'

She sat motionless, willing him to go. For a moment, he stood there gloating, and then, to her relief, he went out, slamming the door behind him. He had gone. One of the girls began to cry and Evie felt like doing the same. The whole class was staring at her, as though she was the intruder and not the boy. And one was Leonora.

'Evie,' she said tearfully. 'Evie. Thank God you're here.'

33

'And now for another request from everyone in year ten at Clapham Comprehensive who can't wait for term to be over in precisely ten minutes. Hope you've remembered your teachers, kids. When I was at school, we gave them end-of-year presents!'

Presents! Harriet had been thinking so hard about Pippa, who was, at this very minute, on the operating-table, that she'd forgotten. The children should have taken them to school that morning but, with Charlie coming home, she hadn't been organised enough to get them.

Jess would be distraught if everyone else had given her teacher something and she hadn't. Still, if she pulled in at the newsagent's on the corner, she could buy a box of chocolates and a card.

Great. There were three people in the queue, each paying their paper bill. If they didn't get a move on, she'd be late for school. Harriet glanced at her watch. Five minutes until they came out and the journey would take at least ten. Add another ten for parking and she'd be really late. Jess would wait but Bruce might be climbing the school roof by then or at least the goalpost in the playground.

'Sorry. I'm in a rush.' She slid a five-pound note over the counter and gesticulated to the box of chocolates she had in her hand. 'Keep the change.'

She dashed back to the car – her own car since Charlie had

taken his to the office. It seemed strange to be driving the Fiesta again after the Volvo.

She threw the chocolates on to the passenger seat and realised that Charlie hadn't brought her anything from Dubai. Not that it mattered – she wasn't a materialistic woman. But the lack of a gift seemed significant. Did he care so little? Or would guilt-perfume from Duty Free have made him feel in the wrong?

Stop it, she told herself. Even last night seemed trivial now. So he had felt randy. Hadn't she when he'd been away? And hadn't she indulged in a few fantasies that didn't feature Charlie?

Harriet joined the main road again. The traffic in front was slow: there must be roadworks or an accident ahead. She turned on the radio to see if there was any news.

'Betty from Balham has rung in to say traffic is building up near Acacia Road due to roadworks . . .'

Not again! She could swear the council saved them for school times. Hang on. A blue light was flashing. It was an accident. Cars were slowing down and being diverted into one lane. Harriet looked to her left as she went by. A single motorbike stood upright on the roadside. There was a red helmet on the ground but no rider. No ambulance either. Had it been and gone? Was the rider all right? One thing was certain: she would never let Bruce ride a motorbike.

Finally the traffic was flowing more freely. With luck, she would only be about eight minutes late. Then she'd need to go into the school to gather up the sports kit that Bruce would have left on the floor of the boys' changing room. Jess would have hers neatly folded in her bag. What was happening now? A policeman was standing in the middle of the road, waving people on past the turning to school. Cars weren't being allowed down it. Why not? What had happened?

She wound down her window. 'Excuse me, Officer, I need to get down to the school.'

Under the helmet, his face was impassive. 'I'm sorry, madam, but all cars are being diverted. Please follow the signs.'

'Has something happened?'

'Move along, please.'

Sick with fear, she lurched on. She needed to find a space fast, then rush back. Had a child been run over? Had Bruce done something crazy?

'Betty of Balham has rung in again to say there's some sort of trouble at St Theresa's School, Balham. Not sure what, exactly, but avoid the area if possible as there's severe traffic congestion.'

Oh, my God! If it's on the radio, it's serious! Cars were pulling up on to pavements and worried parents were emerging, talking in huddles and pointing. Harriet squeezed into a space. 'What's going on?' she asked, as she got out.

'I don't know,' said one of the mothers, who was hanging on to a struggling toddler. 'They've told us to stay here. Maybe it's a fire alert.'

'Can't be a practice,' said another. 'Not on the last day of term.'

Harriet began to run towards the do-not-enter sign. On the right she spotted a line of scrappy allotments. She squeezed through the hedge and ducked down out of sight of the policewoman on the other side. With any luck, she might be able to get out further down. Yes, she'd done it. The road ahead, normally crammed with cars, was deserted, apart from four police cars and a large turquoise Discovery. There wasn't a child in sight, but it was well after three thirty.

'Madam, you can't wait here.'

A policeman came up from behind, taking her by surprise.

'But what's happening?' Harriet's throat was so choked she could hardly speak. 'What's going on?'

'There appears to be some disturbance at the senior school.'

My God. Bruce? He wouldn't have done something stupid, would he?

'Can I get my friend's child? She's in the primary school next door.'

A look akin to sympathy crossed the policeman's face. 'We understand that the primary children are in the main building for an end-of-term concert.'

'But why can't they get out?' Harriet was angry now. 'I don't understand.'

'Madam, please go back to the other side of the cordon like everyone else. We will let you know when we have some information.'

'No. *No!* I'm not going back.'

'Harriet!'

It was the man from the counselling centre – Nick. He was on the other side of the orange cordon. 'Harriet, come here.'

'What on earth's happening?'

Nick patted her shoulder. At any other time, she'd have considered the gesture over-familiar but now she was grateful to see a friendly face. 'I don't know. All I've been able to find out is that something's going on in the senior building.'

'I know that.'

'Calm down. I'll call a mate of mine who works for the Press Association. Maybe he can find out what's up. Stay here. I'm going along the road for a better reception.'

Harriet was shaking. What was happening to the children? Where were they? It wasn't just Bruce and Jess, but Lucy and Beth too. Oh, God! Pippa! She couldn't ring her: she'd be coming round from the op right now. But she ought to let Derek know.

'Derek? It's me, Harriet. How's Pippa? Right. Look, don't say anything if she's just come round but something's happened at school . . .'

34

PIPPA

'Where'er you walk, green trees shall fan the breeze . . .'

That song again! Pippa tried to sit up. The room seemed out of focus, rather like it did when she woke up too early in the morning or when she'd had jet-lag in the days when there were nice holidays before children. She had a pain in her back, too, which was odd.

Shaking with apprehension, she touched herself gingerly. Relief washed through her. Thank God! Both her breasts were there, although that didn't mean she was in the clear. Her chest throbbed under the dressing.

'Is it sore?'

How long had he been there?

'Derek?'

'I'm here, love.'

Gratefully she squeezed his hand. 'Am I all right?'

'You're fine.'

He sounded tearful and she knew he was lying. 'The lump. It's malignant, isn't it?'

'Too early to tell. Remember what they told us? They need to analyse it. How do you feel?'

Something wasn't right. She could tell. 'Woozy.'

He dropped a kiss on her forehead. 'Listen, love, will you be all right without me for a bit? I've got to pick up the girls.'

'Harriet's doing that.'

'She's got a problem. I shouldn't be too long.'

'What kind of problem? Charlie again?'

'Something like that.'

Poor Harriet. 'Don't be long. Please. I need you.' She remembered something. 'Weren't you meant to have your appraisal today?'

He nodded. 'Yes, but HR said it could wait in the circumstances. Apparently my department head is really pleased with our performance this year.'

'Good. See? I told you not to worry.'

''Bye.' He gave her another kiss, still on the forehead. Why not on the lips like he usually did? Even in her near-stupor, Pippa could tell something was wrong. Had he found out somehow about Gus?

A nurse popped her head round the screen. 'Everything all right, love? Just ring if you need something.'

She nodded. As she reached out for the plastic cup of water at her side, she saw her mobile. Maybe she'd ring Harriet to find out what was happening. It was hard to lean to one side and pick it up. If it was this difficult, how was she going to manage when she got out?

Awkwardly, she picked up the phone. MESSAGE.

'Hi, Gorgeous. Gd luck for tomorrow. Sorry about today. Love you always. Gus.'

Pippa froze. He must have sent it last night. That was why Derek had been so quiet.

Sorry about today. Love you always.

Pippa retched into the bowl beside her. How could she have been so stupid? Even if her lump was benign, she had a hideous feeling that one part of her life – that comforting security with Derek – had already ended. And she only had herself to blame.

KITTY

'Come here, I want to feel you. Now, let me feel you . . .'

'Turn down that music, you lot. It's not the end of term yet!'

Kitty, who had just had lunch in the canteen, smiled at the sound of another teacher's voice yelling at his class. The end of term had led to great excitement both for the kids and staff who were looking forward to a much-needed rest.

She got on with preparing for the next lesson. They were going to play verb and noun games, which was a sneaky way of improving their grammar. Then she heard the noise. At first it sounded like a crowd of children running along the corridor, which wasn't allowed at St Theresa's so she put her head out of the door, ready to calm them down. She'd just been reading a fascinating book on communicating with pupils that had been recommended in the *Times Educational Supplement*. It included a section on meditation, which Kitty was considering trying out on year eight. It wasn't difficult. All you had to do was close your eyes, focus on an image in your head and shut out all noise round you. As you breathed out, you said, 'One,' in your head. Apparently, some children identified with 'One' better than 'Omm', according to the book. Kitty could see that it might help pupils like Bruce.

'What's going on?' she said, walking to the door.

Three lads from the sixth form raced by, almost knocking her to the ground.

'Be careful,' she shouted angrily.

'Do what you're told and no one will get hurt, Miss,' said one, and stopped.

Kitty's heart began to pound. There was no mistaking those hard black eyes and that very short hair. Or his height, which made him look more like a tough adult than a seventeen-year-old. It was the boy on the bus from yesterday.

'Don't you dare threaten me,' she said. 'Ouch, let go of my arm. Stop it! Help!'

'Shut up, Miss,' said the second boy. 'We don't want to hurt no one. Just get in there and look after the class, will you?'

'What?' gasped Kitty.

She found herself thrown into a room packed with children, some at the tables and others on the floor. Many were crying but they all looked at her expectantly as she picked herself up.

Kitty ran to the door but it wouldn't open. On the other side, she could hear something heavy being moved towards it, as though to bar it. Her head reeled and she went to the window. No one was around but they couldn't get out as they were three storeys up. What on earth was going on?

She turned to find all the children's eyes on her. 'Right, everyone,' she said, trying to sound calm. 'I'm not sure what's happening but let's just try to make the best of the situation, shall we, until someone lets us out? Have you all got your books with you?'

Most of them nodded. Kieran from the bus was there, Kitty noticed, and Bruce, as well as children from other years. 'Good. I think we'll start with something light like some poetry.'

There was a groan. 'Please, Miss,' said a girl. 'I don't feel like doing any work. I'm too scared.'

Kitty went up to her and put her arms round her. To hell with protocol. 'It's OK, Jess,' she whispered. 'I'm a bit scared too, but we're all together so we'll help each other.'

Jess nodded and so did some others.

'Tell you what,' said Kitty, 'why don't we play a game I've been reading about?' She tried to smile. 'I want you to close your eyes and think of something really nice. As you breathe out, say, "One," really softly so that it hums in your ears. When other thoughts come into your head, ignore them. Shall we have a go? Right. Everyone together now. One . . .'

The meditation helped her too, thought Kitty, as she sat in front of the class, legs crossed. She'd been so preoccupied over the last few months with finding Mr Right. Now, in the middle of this nightmare that was scarily like that American school siege, she could see how unimportant it was. All that mattered was common decency towards each other. As a teacher, she could help the children to understand that.

'Miss, I'm scared,' said a year five boy in the front row.

Kitty jumped up and put him on her knee. These kids needed comforting and it was her job – her *vocation* – to do that.

BETTY

> *'Desperate Dan has rung in to say there's some trouble outside St Theresa's School in Balham.'*

How did he get in first? I put my call in ages ago.

'Sorry, madam. Do you mind if I listen through the window to your radio? It might tell us what's going on. No, you're right. They've gone on to music now. Can you call me over if there's more news? Meanwhile, would you like some tea? Or a leaflet? Thank you, madam. Yes, I'm in charge of a safety campaign for parents. Can I tell you more about it?'

I like being useful. Terry's the same. Very good at helping the customers. That's what the deputy manager told me afterwards.

Lucky I've got all these spare Thermoses. Terry and I used to like picnics, especially when he was little. Smell a bit musty now but they still do the job. 'It's hot,' I say, holding out a mug.

Some take it and some don't. 'I know how you feel,' I say to one. 'I lost a child once. Several, actually.'

That makes her cry even more.

I couldn't cry afterwards. Still can't.

'Tea?' I say, to one of the camera crew. Quite a few have arrived now. School sieges are getting popular, after America and Russia. One of the newsmen is saying something about drug-dealing and kids falling out with each other. Wouldn't surprise me. They all take something nowadays. Apart from my Terry, of course.

'Sugar?' I ask one of the men. He looks at me sharply. Thankfully, I recognise him first. It's the man in the car this morning. The one I stopped.

'Move,' hisses Terry.

So I snatch my Thermos and my bag of sugar and disappear into the crowd.

Time to go home. I'll catch up with the news on the radio.

35

NICK

> *'News flash. St Theresa's School in Balham, south London, is being held in a siege by two rival teenage gangs, thought to be involved in an argument over drug-dealing. A number of children and teachers are believed to be held inside.'*

God, he wished he could do more. He felt so hopeless, sitting there. They both did.

'Did you get hold of him?'

'No.' Harriet spoke flatly as she put her mobile back in her pocket. 'His secretary hasn't seen him all day, which is odd as he was meant to be going into the office.'

Nick twisted his wedding ring. 'He couldn't do anything if he was here, anyway.'

'No, but he ought to know.'

Nick felt sorry for her. It wasn't fair that she should have to handle this without her husband. He wondered if he should mention seeing him in the car that day, speaking to someone in French, but decided against it. Best not to interfere in other people's marriages and, besides, she was worried enough about the children. Her pretty face was drawn with the same kind of tension he felt inside.

'Look!' He nudged Harriet. 'See that woman?'

'Where?'

'She's just walked past us. There, in that pink coat – walking fast past that group of parents.'

They both watched the woman scurry across the road into a dark-looking terraced house.

'What about her?'

Nick rubbed his eyes: he was tired and things that should have made sense didn't – and vice versa. 'I think there's something weird about her. I found her outside school talking to a toddler this week. And this morning she tried to stop my daughter in the car.'

'Why?'

Nick wondered if Harriet would understand. 'She was crazy. Said something about Julie running over her kid two years ago. I tried to calm her down by pointing out that Julie wasn't even driving then but she's definitely a bit touched.'

'Two years ago.' Harriet looked pensive. 'Was that the boy from the senior school? I remember that. He was knocked down by a hit-and-run driver. Terrible.'

'What sort of time in the morning?'

'Before the school run had really built up, from what I remember. Yes, that's right. I was caught in the traffic queues. Horrible.'

From what the woman on the bike had said, the child had died just a week or two before Juliana. Towards the end, she had hardly had the energy to get out of bed. Her ribs had stuck out and she'd been listless. Lifeless. So different from the old Juliana who had laughed and moved all the time. If she'd been standing here now, she wouldn't have allowed her daughter to be trapped in school. She'd be doing something about it.

'Just going to chase my newspaper friend,' he said, snapping open his mobile. 'He should have got back to me by now . . . Ross? It's Nick. Got anything? . . . I see. How much? . . . Are the police moving in? . . . Why not? Christ, Ross, that's not on. Julie's in there. So are God knows how many other kids . . . I know. OK . . . Thanks.'

He walked back to Harriet. 'Did you know there was a drugs problem at the main school?'

'No.'

'Me neither but it fits in with that newsflash. One of these druggy gangs has taken a load of younger kids hostage because the other gang owes them money. Now they've phoned the local radio station, demanding cash.'

He watched her eyes fill with tears, again wanting to reach out and comfort her. Would she misread it? Possibly.

'What are the police doing about it?'

He snorted with disgust. 'Apparently, they're reluctant to move in yet in case someone gets hurt. They reckon the teenagers will give in. Look, I want you to wait here. I've got your mobile number. I'll call you when I find something.'

'Where are you going?'

Nick looked round to check that no one was listening. 'Where do you think?'

Then he walked away, ducked under the hedge by the allotments and made his way back to the school, crouching low so that no one could see him.

If the police weren't going to rescue his daughter, he'd just have to do it himself.

EVIE

If only there was a radio or television, she might know what was going on. Instead there was an eerie silence outside, punctuated only by children sniffling and fidgeting. She'd have to do something: she owed it to the kids to take charge.

'Excuse me, but I need the loo.' Evie stared defiantly at the spotty youth, who had come in with a jug of water for the kids. They were passing it round, one or two still whimpering. On the whole, though, they had calmed down. Evie was sitting with one arm round Leonora. 'I need the loo,' she repeated. Look him in the eyes. Firmly. That's what *Just For You* had advised in last month's feature on 'What To Do If You're Threatened'. Be rational. Practical. Appeal to his own values.

'I'm not as young as this lot,' she continued. 'I'm probably your mother's age. I need to go to the lavatory more often.'

One or two children tittered and something gave in the eyes of the boy in front of her. He was so young. So hard. 'I'll take you.'

'No. Just tell me where it is and I'll come straight back. You can't leave the kids anyway.'

He nodded in reluctant recognition of what she was saying.

'Stand at the door and you can see me going down the corridor. I'll come straight back, I promise.'

He hesitated.

'If I was your mum you'd let me go, wouldn't you?' said Evie, gently.

It was working. She could see it in his face.

'Go on, then. But be quick. Turn left and left again. If you don't come back in two minutes, I'm coming in after you.'

Evie didn't need telling twice. Left and left again. The corridor was empty.

God, these lavatories were in a filthy state. The girls had moaned about them but she hadn't realised just how bad they were, with loo paper strewn around the floor and tampons in the washbasins. Half the locks didn't work. Eventually she found one that did. Amazing, really, that the boy hadn't checked her for a phone. Quickly she texted Robin's number, noticing as she did so that she'd missed another call, the second that day from someone who hadn't left a number.

Her fingers flew across the keypad.

Ct in sch siege. Rm H. Jk in car. Help.

It was all she had time for. Would he get it? Where would he be if and when he got it? She'd rather have texted her dad but he didn't have a mobile and she couldn't risk speaking in case that boy had followed her in.

She squatted – anything not to touch that disgusting seat –

and did what she was desperate to do. She hadn't, she thought wryly, lied about her weak bladder. Then, having rinsed her hands (no soap), she ventured back into the corridor. The door was open on the left. She could make a dash for it, but if she did what would happen to the classroom of kids and, most importantly, Leonora? That boy was so irrational he might do anything to them. Besides, despite what he'd said about Jack, common sense told her he was all right. They wouldn't be able to get into the car. She'd locked it. The windows were shatterproof, and if they tried to break them the alarm would go off.

As she walked briskly back to the classroom, she heard voices. A beautiful West Indian girl was standing on the stairs, arguing with a spotty youth, a different one from the kid in Room H. 'Ring someone, Jason. You've got to ring someone.'

'I have, Julie. Calm down. If you make a fuss, it will all go wrong and people will get hurt. Trust me.'

They looked at her and Evie froze. Did they have guns? Would they try to knife her? But the couple on the stairs seemed as scared by her appearance as she was by theirs.

'Quickly,' said the boy, tugging at the girl's arm. 'You can't do anything and I'm not having you getting hurt. Come on. The others will be here to help soon.'

They ran out of sight. The classroom door opened and the spotty youth emerged. 'Get back in,' he ordered. Powerless, she obeyed.

36

NICK AND HARRIET

'Are you reading me? Are you reading me?'

Nick tried to listen to the crackling radio on the policeman's chest as he was marched back from the school gates to the car park. But all he could hear was a network of unclear voices.

'Calm down, sir, or I'll have to take you in.'

'Let go of me.' Nick threw off the policeman's arm as they approached the orange cordon. 'My daughter's in there! What if it was your kid?'

'I understand how you feel, sir, but you're hindering our procedures by trying to get into the building. Everything is under control.'

'Then why the hell aren't you doing something about it?'

The policeman – young under his helmet – appealed to Harriet with his eyes for help.

'Nick, he's right. Just stay here for a bit and let the police do their work. If we all start running in, the kids will get scared and do something daft.' She was shivering.

'Take my coat. Here.' Nick wrapped his Barbour round her. 'Thanks.'

Her teeth were still chattering, he observed. It was the shock. He'd been the same when he found Juliana on the bed, lifeless, her beautiful eyes staring blindly at the ceiling.

'Come on. We'll sit in the car. We can listen to the radio and get you a bit warmer.'

He'd brought the van this afternoon, rather than the Fiesta.

His equipment was in the back with Mutley, who licked Harriet enthusiastically.

She stroked him. 'The children would love a dog but Charlie won't allow it.'

'Why?'

'The mess. Commitment. Usual things.'

'I can't stand people like that,' said Nick.

'Nor me. I mean – well, I didn't mean I can't stand my husband but . . . it's so boring and unimaginative. Oh, God, I'm sorry, I didn't mean to start blubbing.'

'It's OK,' said Nick, and gave her a hug. Had he really just done that? 'Here, have some bog roll.' He handed her some blue lavatory paper from the van's side pocket.

Harriet blew her nose, which was red but not unattractively so. 'It's not just the children.' She sniffed. 'Well, it is, but it's Charlie too. I still don't know where I am. He says the break in Dubai has made him realise he wants to start again, but he doesn't show me any affection. And I'm beginning to wonder if . . . well, if there is anyone else.'

'He says there isn't?'

'Yes. And I believe him. He wouldn't lie to me, I know he wouldn't. None of it makes sense.'

'I'm sorry.' Nick was unscrewing the top of a bulky Thermos flask, the kind that took food too. He didn't trust himself to say anything. Just because he hadn't liked the furtive look on Harriet's husband's face in the car didn't mean he was a liar. 'Want a drink?'

Harriet shook her head. 'No, thanks.'

'It's not coffee. Go on, take a nip.'

She didn't normally drink whisky but it was surprisingly warming.

'It's good.' She smiled. 'A bit like Wibena.'

'Wibena?'

'It's a joke my friend Pippa and I have. It's when you drink wine out of a mug so the kids think you're drinking Ribena because it's only twelve o'clock and too early, theoretically, to drink the real stuff.'

Nick smiled. 'I like that.' He wiped his mouth on his sleeve. Maybe it was the situation that had thrown them together or maybe it was her kind eyes, but he felt able to talk to this woman. 'Two years ago today my wife died.'

Harriet swallowed. 'I'm so sorry.'

'Our daughter thinks she had cancer. But she didn't. She had bulimia to begin with. And later, anorexia topped up with a handful of pills she swallowed when I was out.' He laughed hoarsely. 'I was always trying to get her to eat properly. I just didn't think she'd eat my sleeping tablets.'

'Bulimia? Anorexia?' Harriet's eyes opened. 'You're not talking about Juliana? I knew her.'

Nick stared at her. 'You did?'

'From the PTA. I just hadn't realised you were her husband. She was lovely.'

He nodded.

'Not just because of her looks,' added Harriet. 'She was a really nice person. I joined when the kids were little. She used to talk about getting back into modelling.'

'That was what killed her.' Nick took another swig. 'No one wanted her. She was too old. Not thin enough. I even helped her go on a diet . . .'

'And now you think it's your fault.'

'Wouldn't you?'

'The irrational bit of me would. But it's not true, you know. If someone wants to stop eating, there's not a lot you can do about it.'

'You sound very sure.'

'I am. I went through a stage like that in my teens when my parents split up.'

'I'm sorry. What got you out of it?'

'Realising I wouldn't get to university unless I got better. It gave me a goal.'

Nick glanced at her. 'You're still very slim.'

'I always stop eating when I'm upset. Like now.'

'Are you going to have it out with him? Find out what's really wrong?'

'I've tried. He won't talk.'

Nick laughed shortly. 'Typical man. Go on – you were going to say that, weren't you?'

Harriet smiled. 'Yes. I wrote to you, you know, after Juliana died. You probably don't remember. You must have had loads of letters. But I told you how kind she was to me. I was going through some problems with my son at the time – still am, actually – and she gave me some advice. She said her daughter was strong-willed too.'

'She is. Just like her mother. I've probably been over-protective but I just want her to be all right.' His eyes felt unbearably heavy. 'She's learning to drive, for God's sake! Suppose something happens to her? I couldn't bear it if she went, like Juliana.'

'I can identify with that,' said Harriet quietly. 'I hate the kids crossing the road on their own and I've often thought how hard it's going to be when they're teenagers. But remember when we were that age? We thought we were so grown-up – and although we did some daft things, we survived.'

He felt a ridiculous urge to reach out and hold her hand. 'That's true.'

She leaned back against her seat, eyes closed. 'You've got to keep communication open with teenagers. I fell out with my dad when I was a bit older than your daughter and now I regret it. I hardly ever see him.'

'What a shame.'

She shrugged. 'It was half and half. Bringing up kids isn't easy. Bruce is a real challenge to me. He's so strong-willed – like Charlie, only neither of them recognises it.' She covered her face with her hands. 'Suppose Bruce tries to stand up to those big boys. They'll hurt him . . .' Her voice trailed away.

Somehow Nick found himself pressing her to him, patting her back comfortingly as he'd patted Julie's when she was a baby. To his amazement, he could feel her relaxing into him. Reluctantly, he pulled away. 'I'm sorry.'

'Don't be.' She turned her head away so he couldn't read her face. 'You've really helped me.'

'And you me.'

For a while they sat in silence.

I've been wrapping Julie up in cotton wool, Nick told himself. Harriet was right. If he didn't cut her some slack, she might just go off and do her own thing. He should be more honest about his own needs too. She was nearly eighteen, surely old enough to understand. And maybe Harriet had a point about food phobias: if someone wanted to stop eating, there was little anyone could do about it until the sufferer had learned to change his or her own mind.

'I'd like to learn how to take photographs – properly,' said Harriet, suddenly.

Nick's eyes were focused ahead, straining to see what was happening. 'Then why don't you do a course? There are plenty on offer.'

'I might. Next term. Oh, God, Nick, will there be another term? Are the kids going to be all right?'

He put his arm round her again. The warmth of her body was comforting. Reassuring. Natural. This time he didn't pull away. 'Yes, Harriet. They are. They've got to be.'

37

*'And now it's request time for the canteen staff of City
Hospital. They want us to play "Food Glorious Food"
and they want to know what you patients think of the
meals you're getting.'*

Funny. She hadn't remembered putting her headphones on.
Had someone done it for her?

'Pippa, look what someone's sent you!'

Still sleepy from her nap, she tried to focus on the nurse, who
held the most enormous bouquet of stargazers that Pippa had
ever seen. Lilies were her favourite. 'Smelly flowers', Lucy called
them, when Derek occasionally brought them home as a treat.
How like him to send them when he could have just brought
them in.

'Has my husband been back?'

Something she couldn't read crossed the nurse's face. 'Not
yet. He rang to say he might be a bit delayed.'

'Why?'

'He didn't say.'

Uneasily, Pippa read the card: 'Pippa dearest. Get well soon.
All my love. Gus.' She ripped the card into tiny pieces. 'Take
them away.'

'What?'

'Take the flowers away. I don't bloody want them.'

The nurse gave her a strange look and picked up the bouquet. 'Where shall I put them?'

'I don't care. The bin. The morgue. Someone's bed. Just get them out of here.'

Pippa waited until the nurse had gone, then turned towards the wall, tears running down her face. How could Gus be so tactless? If he wasn't more careful, Derek would find out and her marriage would be over. Providing she hadn't received her death warrant first.

'Newsflash. The siege at St Theresa's School, Balham, is continuing. It is now known that nearly a hundred children are being held hostage, including the two children of Simon and Sally Pargeter, popular presenters of the programme Time For Tea. We'll update you as soon as we get more news.'

MARTINE
Dear Diary,
This news, it is worrying but I am not to blame. I tell Simon and Sally this but they do not hear me. I explain, I arrive to pick up les enfants but I am prohibited from entering the road by the gendarmes.

So I go home.

Sally say it was imperative on me to ring and explain the problems. But she was in the studio, having makeup. I would like makeup like that. Maybe I borrow some before I go. It would look good before my photograph with the paper.

I say to Sally, do not worry. Sam is a difficult child. When the kidnappers at his school see this, they will handle him back. She cry when I say this. I have never seen Sally cry before. It makes me feel bad. But it is not my fault.

When I am a mother, I will not have an au pair. I do it all myself, and my mother, she will help me.

BETTY

> '*Row, row, row, the boat, gently down the stream,*
> *Merrily, merrily, merrily, merrily, Life is but a dream.*'

Do you like that tape, duck? Terry and I used to sing along to it at your age. That's right, darling, eat up. Terry liked soldiers with his boiled egg, too. What am I talking about? You *are* Terry, aren't you, duck? Your hair's longer but we can soon sort that out.

It was so easy to rescue you. Mummy had locked the doors this time, hadn't she? Naughty Mummy. But when I tapped on the window, you opened it for me. Clever boy. All you had to do was put your little finger on the button and down the window came. I pulled you out before the police turned up. Just as well. You'd be cold if you were still out there. Here, you're nice and warm and I can look after you. Don't cry, pet. Mum's here.

EVIE

They were getting hot and tired now. It was almost five o'clock. Time for Simon and Sally on television. Time for normal life again.

'I'm starving,' whispered Leonora. It wasn't like her to be so timid but they were all scared of talking too loudly in case they annoyed their captors.

Evie felt in her pockets. There was some chewing-gum and some chocolate, of which she gave half to Leonora and half to the child next to her, then glanced at the clock on the wall. They'd been here for three hours but it felt far longer. Many of the children were quietly complaining that they were hungry and thirsty, and some had asked to go to the loo, only to be denied permission.

'You'll have to give them something to eat and drink if you're going to keep us here much longer, you know,' she said to the youth.

He glared at her. 'Shut up.'

Evie was silent for a bit. There was no point in inflaming him. Suddenly, she became aware of an arm round her shoulders. 'Jack will be all right,' said Leonora.

'I hope so. How did you know what I was thinking?'

'We often do, just by looking at your face. You don't like us much, do you?'

Evie was indignant. 'Yes, I do.'

'No, you don't. You just want to be with Dad and Jack. You don't like it when Mum dumps us on you.'

At any other time, Evie would have flounced out of the room. 'I wouldn't say that, exactly.'

'We love Dad. And we love Mum, although she can be weird. Jack's great too.' Leonora stopped.

'And me?'

She looked almost shy. 'I like you at times but I never know where I am with you. Sometimes you're nice and sometimes you're really angry.'

'I've had pressure with work.'

'I know. Mum said that.'

'She did?'

'She said it couldn't be easy for you and that we should be nicer.'

'When?'

'Last time we were with her. She's changing. Even Dad thinks so. Chris is good for her, he says.'

Evie began to wonder if she'd been living in the same family. 'Your dad has gone away for a bit,' she said carefully. 'Do you know where he might be?'

Leonora looked worried. 'No. Don't you?'

'Maybe he's gone for some more job interviews.'

'Maybe.' Leonora was silent for a while. 'He needs the money, I know. Nattie kept going on about that skiing trip. Mum said she couldn't afford it and she wasn't asking Chris for any more so Dad said he'd make sure we could still go.'

'Did he?'

'Is that OK?'

'We'll have to see.' Was that why Robin had borrowed money? But a skiing trip wasn't likely to cost thousands of pounds. 'What about Natalie? What does she think of me?'

Leonora shrugged. 'She wants Mum and Dad to get back together. But it isn't going to happen.'

'And you're sure she's in the room next door?'

'I saw her being pushed in.' She sobbed softly. 'I hope she's all right.'

Evie hugged her. 'They've got to let us out soon. They can't keep us here for ever.'

Leonora leaned into her shoulder and Evie felt a pang. She should have done this before – should have cuddled them when they got angry instead of shouting back. How could she have been so worried about her job when the only thing that mattered was your family – and the kids of the person you loved?

'I'm sorry, Leonora,' she whispered.

'Me too.'

Evie felt a wave of happiness despite the cramp in her bottom. She held the girl tight – and smelt her own shampoo, but now wasn't the time to accuse her of pinching things. 'I'll try to be a nicer step-mother. Promise.'

Leonora sniffed. 'And I'll be nicer too, if we ever get out of here.'

Evie still held her close. 'We will. Somehow – don't ask me how – I'll make sure we do.'

38

'Quick. *Now!*'

Jason waited until Curt walked out of Room H, then pushed him into a smaller room next door and locked him in. He and Julie ran to Room H. 'Everyone out, now!' he yelled.

Evie stared. It was the couple she'd seen on the stairs and now they were rescuing them. Was it a trick?

'Quick,' hissed the girl. 'Before they come back. Get out. Just get the kids out!'

Evie helped the children up. 'Go on, Lennie, out.'

'No! I'm helping you find Nattie.'

'There she is – look!'

Another youth was helping more children out of the room next door. Natalie ran towards her sister and hugged her.

'Come on, everyone,' called Evie, to the children who were still in the room. She glanced nervously up the stairs. Someone was shouting at the top. 'Let's get out before they stop us.'

Evie ran out into the street behind the girls. The car was where she'd left it, but it was empty.

'My little boy!' She ran up to one of the waiting policemen. 'My little boy! Where did you take him?'

'Sorry, madam? I don't understand.'

She pointed to the car, almost unable to speak for the fear that had engulfed her. She'd been so certain that he'd still be there or that someone would have rescued him. 'My son, Jack. He's two. I left him in the car. Before all this. Before the siege.'

The policeman looked worried. 'Madam, as far as I know

the car was empty when we arrived. Could a friend have taken him?'

'No!' Evie felt her bowels loosen with fear. 'No. Jack! *Jack, where are you?*'

HARRIET

'*Over and out. Over and out.*'

The policeman turned off his crackling radio. 'Stand back, everyone, please, let the children past.'

Harriet was still standing by the school gates, hugging Bruce and Jess, her face wet with relief. Another policeman walked past, holding a teenager by the collar of his leather jacket. The boy scowled at her as the policeman pushed him into a car, and she shielded the children's faces.

Nick was standing a little away from her and she tried not to catch his eye. She was sure he would feel as embarrassed as she did about what had happened between them in the car. Now he was cuddling Julie, who had finally finished sobbing into his coat. From what Harriet could hear, Julie was refusing to go until Jason had finished talking to the police. There was still some doubt as to whether he would be taken in for questioning even though Julie had assured them he had nothing to do with the gangs who had fallen out over drug-dealing and unpaid debts.

'See that woman over there,' said Bruce. 'She's lost her child. I heard someone say he got taken from her car.'

Harriet was appalled. 'How awful.'

Nick strode up. 'That's Evie Brookes. She's a magazine editor. I do some work for her. She's the mother of that child I told you about. The one I found with that odd woman in the pink coat I pointed out this afternoon.'

'The crazy one who tried to stop me this morning?' asked Julie, wide-eyed.

'Yes.' Nick's brow furrowed. 'I'll just have a quick word with the police.'

'I'm coming too,' said Julie, grabbing his sleeve.

'Why don't you go back to my car, Harriet? The police might not let us go for ages. There's quite a queue up there. You'll find some drinks in the boot – I always keep them there for emergencies.'

She smiled gratefully, understanding the unspoken implication behind his words. It might be reassuring for them – and their kids – to have company until they could leave.

She watched Julie hanging on to her father's arm as they walked up to an officer. She doesn't want to let him out of her sight, poor child, thought Harriet, taking her two back to Nick's car. What a good father he must be.

'Are you sure you're all right?' she asked, opening two small cartons of orange juice, which had been in the boot as Nick said, and handing one each to them. She felt awful now, for originally thinking Bruce might have caused trouble.

'Fine.' Bruce seemed quite excited, although Jess was subdued. 'This big bloke came in and said we had to sit in another class. Then we played word games on the blackboard. It was brilliant. We didn't have to do any work at all.'

Some teachers, thought Harriet admiringly, were truly dedicated. 'I just want to switch on the radio to see if there's any news.'

'We've just heard that the siege at St Theresa's School in south London has ended, seemingly without casualties. Reports suggest that some of the teenagers involved managed to release the children and lock up the gang leaders. More details when we get them.'

'That's us,' said Bruce excitedly. 'Will we be famous?'

Harriet smiled wryly. 'Maybe.'

Jess snuggled up to her. 'Do you think Daddy's heard? Is he coming over too?'

'I'm not sure,' said Harriet. 'Maybe later.'

'Ring him now.'

'All right. Actually, Bruce, can you show me something? How do you work out who you've rung before? I can do the last number but what about the ones before that?'

'Honestly, Mum, don't you know?'

He took the phone from her and she watched admiringly as his fingers flew across the buttons. 'Not so fast, Bruce. Slower. Oh, I see.'

'Why do you want to know?'

Harriet shrugged. 'It might come in useful.'

Eventually Nick came back. 'The police are allowing everyone to move on now.'

'Right. Come on, you two. Let's get going. Dad will probably be at home waiting for us.' She turned to Nick. 'Thanks for the company. I'm not sure how I'd have got through this without it.'

He gave her a meaningful look. 'Nor me. I'll ring some time to see how you're doing.'

Harriet flushed. 'OK. Thanks. Come on, Bruce. No, don't start fiddling with that cordon or the police will come over. Let's go home. You must be exhausted.'

39

EVIE

'Can you give me an update, please? Over and out.'

Evie's mouth was dry with fear as she sat in the back of the police car. The driver was speaking urgently into the microphone on the dashboard and the replies were distorted by crackling. Evie strained to hear but it was difficult to make out what the person at the other end was saying. Something about reinforcements, she thought.

Fancy thinking she'd sorted out her life during all that time in the classroom. Now she really knew what her priorities were. Not Robin. Not her job. Just the kids. In particular Jack. How could she have left him in the car?

'What's going on?' she said, feeling her voice disintegrate into the air. 'I don't understand.'

The policeman in the passenger seat turned round. 'Mrs Brookes, I have to be honest with you, we're not sure. All we know is that one of the other parents saw an older woman waiting outside the school during the siege. He thought it was the same woman who was with your son earlier this week.'

'So you think she's got him,' interrupted Natalie.

'Shut up, Nattie, you're scaring Evie,' said Leonora. 'It doesn't mean that, does it?'

The policeman ignored her question. 'We're waiting for reinforcements and then we're going into the house where the suspect is thought to live.'

'Why can't we go in now?' Evie's voice rose hysterically. 'The longer we wait, the more danger there is of her doing something terrible to him. Oh, my God, Jack! I should never have left him.'

'It's all right, Evie.' Natalie put an arm round her. 'We'll find him. He's so sweet – no one will hurt him.' She burst into loud sobs. 'Will they?'

Evie gripped her hand so tightly that her wedding ring cut into her own fingers. Dear God, please, I'll do anything – anything – if you just let Jack be all right. I will never, ever be awful to the girls again. I'll give up work to be a proper mum to Jack. I'll—

The microphone burst into more frenzied crackling.

'Right,' said the driver. 'We're off. Mrs Brookes, I want you to wait in the car with me, round the corner from the house.'

'Bugger that,' said Natalie. 'We're going in too.'

The policewoman gave Evie the sort of look that wanted to know what kind of a mother she was to allow her daughter to come out with such expletives. At any other time Evie would have put them straight. 'She's right,' she said, looking the woman hard in the eye. 'They're not kids. We want to come too.'

The main road was suspiciously quiet. They must have blocked it off, thought Evie, as the car pulled into a side-street. If there were reinforcements, they'd kept themselves well hidden. All she could see was the lamp-post on the corner with its bouquet of roses.

'We're waiting here,' said the policewoman, firmly. 'The officer who's going in will contact me as soon as he finds anything.'

Evie whimpered. One of the girls stroked her hand. 'I want to be there,' she sobbed. 'I want to be with my little boy.'

She tried the handle of the rear door. It was locked. Childproofed. If she had locked Jack in properly, none of this would have happened. But she had been sure she had.

They waited in almost unbearable suspense.

'Isn't it weird?' whispered Natalie. 'No cars.'

'Shut up,' said Leonora, tersely.

'Why? I'm scared too, you know. Supposing this woman—'

'Shut *up*,' repeated Lennie.

Evie put an arm round each girl and pulled them to her. 'It's all right,' she said quietly. 'Say your prayers.'

'Prayers?' Leonora was incredulous. 'We don't say prayers. That's for kids.'

'Anyway, we're Buddhist like Mum.'

'Well, I'm Jewish and your dad is . . . well, whatever he is. But, frankly, I don't think it matters. Just do it.'

Evie watched the clock on the dashboard. It had to be wrong: it couldn't possibly be only seven and a half minutes since they had parked here. Seven and a half minutes. That small amount of time alone was enough for the woman to do anything to Jack. Was he screaming for her? Tied up in a corner? Slumped, lifeless, on the floor? Already in a shallow grave . . .

'*No*,' she screamed. 'No, I've got to go in!'

She dived towards the front of the car.

'Stop it, Evie!' yelled Natalie.

At the same time, the microphone burst into life.

'Shut up, everyone,' commanded the policewoman. 'I can't bloody well hear.'

They stopped. The voice was urgent and desperate.

'They've got him.' The policewoman was calm.

'Is he all right?'

'I don't know. The reception was terrible. We can go in but I must warn you, Mrs Brookes, I don't know what we're going to find. It's inadvisable, in my opinion, to bring your daughters with you.'

'But—' began Natalie.

'Shush.' Evie's eyes flashed. 'She's right. It *is* inadvisable. But you're still coming. Now.'

Following the policewoman, they ran across the road

towards the shabby end-of-terrace house. Breathless, Evie pushed open the rusty metal gate, which was hanging off its hinges. The front door was open. She stopped. Her little boy was in this place: she could feel it. But that gut instinct inside her – the one that had made her fall for Robin and warned her against Janine – was telling her something she couldn't ignore. This hideous little house, with its peeling brown wallpaper in the hall, stank of stale cabbage and death.

'Mrs Brookes?'

A dishevelled policewoman took her arm. 'He's through here.'

She allowed herself to be led along the dark hall and into the narrow kitchen at the back. She gasped. Plastered on every inch of the wall were newspaper cuttings, many yellowed and curled with age and sunlight. Each one bore a gruesome headline: 'Killed On Killer Road'; 'Third Child In Year To Die On Busy Stretch'.

The sink was overflowing. The kitchen table had five cereal packets on it, all open. Next to them was an array of the free plastic figures that had come with them. At one end there was a high-chair, the old-fashioned type with a wooden tray and plastic seat, and at the other, a wooden chair with a boy's blazer draped round it. In the corner a box of child's building bricks lay next to a bicycle with stabilisers. On the floor was a pile of what looked like school exercise books and a black schoolbag with a child's name written on the tag: Terry Holmes. On the old-fashioned yellow- and black-flecked plastic work surface she saw a large rectangular brown radio with round knobs. It was still on, as though someone had recently been listening to it.

'Where is he?' demanded Evie hoarsely. 'I want to see him.'

She was taken to a small door at the end. Someone opened it and Evie dimly remembered thinking it was like her grandmother's lean-to conservatory. There, on a policewoman's lap, in a rickety old chair, was Jack.

'Mum!' he said delightedly. 'Look! 'Eggo!'

He was holding up a piece of Lego, triumphantly.

Evie let out a howl, dropped to her knees and clasped him to her. 'Jack, Jack,' she crooned, smelling his hair, drinking in the scent of his skin.

'Jack!' said Natalie, crying. 'Are you all right?'

Jack's face was wreathed in smiles over his mother's shoulder. 'Lennie, Lennie,' he said, holding out the piece of Lego.

'See,' said Lennie, sniffling. 'I told you he loved me best, Nattie. I told you.'

Evie wasn't sure how long she stayed there. She didn't want to move. It was so comforting just to hold Jack even though he was wriggling to escape.

'Why?' she said, through his hair. 'Why did she take him?'

The policewoman – the one who had driven them there – knelt down beside her. 'Her son was killed in a road accident two years ago. She's never got over it. See all these newspaper cuttings? The house is full of them. Apparently she's got quite a name as a local campaigner for child safety.'

'That doesn't mean she's entitled to take someone else's child,' said Evie, angrily.

'How old was he, the boy who was killed?' asked Natalie.

'Sixteen,' said the policewoman.

'Only two years older than us,' said Leonora, quietly.

'I'm sorry we couldn't tell you immediately that Jack was all right,' said the policewoman. 'The reception was bad and they couldn't find him at first. She hid him in the conservatory when she heard them coming in. But it looks as though she's been taking care of him.'

She pointed to the kitchen table on which, Evie now noticed, there was an egg cup with the remains of a hard-boiled egg in it. 'Jack hates eggs,' she said shakily.

'Where is she now?' asked Natalie.

'We took her down to the station.'

'Are you going to arrest her?'

'We're waiting for a doctor's report first. We've got to get Jack checked over too, just to make sure.'

Evie held her son tightly. 'Just to make sure of what?'

'That he hasn't been abused in any way.'

Evie gasped, holding Jack tighter. 'But she wouldn't . . . I mean no one would . . . Oh, God, how awful.'

'It's all right, Evie,' said Natalie. 'He's here, isn't he? Besides, there's a girl in my class who's been abused and she's fine about it . . .'

'Shut *up*,' said Leonora. 'For God's sake, don't you know when to stop?'

We ought to take Jack to hospital now,' said the police-woman. 'It won't take long. Then you can go home.'

'Home!' said Jack. 'Dad?'

Evie felt a stab of pain mixed with anger. 'I don't know, sweetheart.' She hugged him again. 'But Mum's here. And Lennie and Nattie. We love you, Jack.'

Jack gave her a slobbery wet kiss on her cheek in return. Why wasn't he crying? Jack had never been one of those clingy two-year-olds who refused to go to other people. Nursery had encouraged him to be sociable. But she couldn't help feeling hurt by his acceptance of the situation.

'And us, Jack,' said Natalie, picking him up and jiggling him in her arms. 'You love us too, don't you?'

In answer, he laid his head on her shoulder and yawned.

'He's tired,' said the policewoman. 'Come on. Let's get this over with.'

BETTY

'Three blind mice, See how they run . . .'

No, please, don't turn that off. He likes it. Terry always liked that one best. I haven't hurt him. Honest. See? I let him watch a video with Terry until I heard a noise and had to hide him in the conservatory. He's had his boiled egg and soldiers, he has, so he won't need no tea tonight. Give us a kiss goodbye, then, love. I wish I could keep him. You'd like that too, Terry, wouldn't you, duck?

FRIDAY P.M.

'Duck down, Sam. And you, Ellie. There are cameras outside. Right. You can come up now – we've gone past them. Are you sure you're all right?'

'Y-yes, Dad. I told them who you and Mum were but they didn't believe me. I s-said you'd name them on t-television but they j-just laughed.'

'I'm starving, Mum. We haven't had anything since lunch and that was disgusting.'

'It's all right, darling. We're going straight home to a nice takeaway.'

'Is Marty getting it?'

'No, Ellie. Martine has left.'

'Good. Can you stay at home and look after us like Hugo's mum?'

'I wish we could, darling, but you know Mummy and Daddy need to work. I've found a very nice French woman to look after you for a while.'

'I h-h-hate the French.'

'Now, don't be racist, Sam. It's good to have French help. It should improve your school work. Damn. The cameras are outside the house. Duck, everyone!'

'Why is Mummy still in hospital?'

'Dad told you, Beth. She's had an operation but she'll be home tomorrow.'

'Were you scared, girls?'

'Not really. Miss Hayling was lovely. She got us to mari-nate.'

'Meditate, stupid.'

'Why did she do that?'

'To help us relax. It's really good. You just think of something really nice and concentrate. I'll tell Mummy about it when she's back. It might help her get better.'

'Sure you're OK?'

'Not really. It was scary, Dad. Really scary. If Jason hadn't locked up Curt and that lot, I don't know what would have happened.'

'Are you sure Jason doesn't take drugs?'

'*Dad*, I *told* you! He's clean. But loads of kids aren't at our school. They even try to sell drugs to the little ones. Don't let's talk about it any more. I just want to get into the bath and close my eyes. OK?'

'Where's Dad?'

'At the office.'

'Doesn't he know what's happened?'

'I don't think so or he would have rung. Are you sure you're all right, Jess? You look awfully pale. Bruce, *please* put your head back in the car.'

'I'm waving at the cameras.'

'Well, don't. We'll be home soon and then we'll have some tea. Are you hungry?'

'Starving.'

'I'm not. I feel sick, Mum.'

'I'll eat hers, then. Can we have it in front of the telly?'

40

FRIDAY NIGHT

NICK

'So relax with Classic FM to soothe you through Friday evening towards the weekend . . .'

Nick turned down the volume and poured himself a large glass of Chablis. He did the same for his daughter. She was grown-up now.

She sat opposite him on the sofa, her face creased with determination just like her mother's had been when she wanted to make a point. 'It wasn't his fault, Dad, I've told you. Jason doesn't do drugs. It was the others. He tried to stop them but it was difficult. They'd have got him if he hadn't pretended to be part of it. Anyway, we're safe, aren't we? No one's hurt.'

Nick was still trying to make sense of what had happened. According to Julie, there were two factions at school who had been selling drugs to younger pupils. Why no one had cottoned on to this earlier, he didn't know. An argument had broken out and one of the gangs had demanded money in return for the kids. But Jason and his mates – including Julie – had got them out.

Thank God his daughter was all right. And Evie had been lucky too. His suspicions about the woman in the pink coat had been right. Harriet had rung to say she'd heard they'd found the little boy, thankfully unharmed. Evie probably didn't know he'd helped but that didn't matter. He hated to think of the poor kid in that woman's clutches. 'I think we ought to have an early night,' he said to Julie.

'I'm sorry, Dad.'

She clung to him and he put his arms round her, breathing in his wife's scent. Correction. Breathing in his daughter's scent. A woman who had a different identity from Juliana and himself; a young woman whom he had to learn to release. 'What for?'

'Everything. Being difficult. And for lying to you, the other night. I was driving without L-plates because Jason didn't have any.'

Nick stiffened. 'It's breaking the law.'

'I know. But I want to drive so much. I want the independence.'

'I understand. But it was stupid and *incredibly* dangerous.'

'And I miss Mum so much.'

He held her tight. 'I know that too. I wish you'd talk to someone about it. It might help. I could talk to school – they have people for this kind of thing.'

'Maybe next term.' She sniffed.

'Wipe your nose on my shoulder.'

She giggled. 'I can't.'

'Yes, you can.'

'OK.'

They both smiled through their tears. 'There's something else, Dad,' she said slowly. 'Well, two, actually.'

Nick's skin crawed with apprehension.

'That woman today,' she began. 'The one who's got that hyperactive kid.'

'She's just a friend,' said Nick.

'I'm not having a go. I liked her. She's got a kind face. And I've been thinking about how I have all the fun and you're just here, working. Maybe I've been unfair. If you want to go out with someone, I suppose that's all right, providing she's like that woman and not like that photographer. She was a tough bitch – you just didn't see it.'

'She was?' Nick was shocked.

'You're so naïve sometimes, you men.' She grinned.

'Thanks. And the second thing?'

Julie twisted her hair nervously, the way her mother used to. 'I've sort of done something you might not approve of . . .'

Nick took a deep breath. 'Go on.'

Julie tossed her head defiantly. 'It's like this.'

And then she told him.

KITTY

'Gosh, you've had quite a day, then.'

Kitty shrugged. 'You could say that.'

The man opposite her at the fashionable restaurant, looked concerned. 'Are you sure you're feeling all right? We could leave now if you want to.'

If she'd been honest, Kitty would have admitted that she would much rather go home and have an early night. But when she'd got out of school and made sure, along with the other teachers, that the children were safe (amazingly, no one had been hurt although some had been in tears and needed comforting), she had made her way home on the bus to find Duncan already at her door. 'Sorry I'm early,' he had said. 'Terrible habit, I know, but I'm still getting used to this part of London and I wanted to make sure I wasn't late.'

She'd explained about the siege – which he'd heard about on the news but hadn't realised it was her school – and he'd insisted on coming back when she'd had a chance to relax. Later, he had whisked her off in a taxi to a smart restaurant where he entertained her with tales about the bank where he worked. It had been just what she needed to take her mind off the gruelling events of the day. But now, after a delicious dinner, she felt exhausted. 'I keep thinking of what might have happened,' she said.

He had nodded understandingly. 'I can see that.'

'I mean, supposing they'd hurt the children . . .'

Duncan reached across the table and took her hand. 'You were so brave. And helping them to meditate was a real inspiration.'

She retrieved her hand. His clammy touch and those too-understanding eyes were getting on her nerves. It wasn't his fault, poor man, she was just irritable and tired and . . . 'Duncan, I'm really sorry but you're right. I'm shattered. Do you mind if I go home now?'

His face was a picture of disappointment. 'Of course not. I understand. Let me just sort out the bill and then I'll get a cab.'

She allowed him to take charge. 'I'm sorry I can't ask you in for coffee,' she said.

He squeezed her hand. 'Another time.'

'Actually,' began Kitty, 'there was something I was going to ask you . . .'

'Fire away.'

She took a deep breath. Could she really do this? Alex's face, Champneys and the Ofsted inspector's moustache flashed through her mind. Yes, she could.

'So relax with Classic FM to soothe you through Friday evening . . .'

Harriet was chopping onions for chilli con carne when she heard Charlie's key in the lock. She turned off the radio, which had been keeping her company.

'Do you know what's happened?' she said, rinsing her hands under the tap.

'What?'

She told him all about the siege. 'Didn't you hear about it on the radio?'

'No, I told you. I was in a meeting.'

Her eyes were watering from the onions and she dabbed at them with a tea-towel. 'Not according to your secretary.'

'I told you about that, too. She's a temp. She should have known where I was but obviously she didn't.'

He had an answer for everything, though Harriet, as she put the dish in the oven. Later that night when they watched the news on television, it was some consolation to see the astonishment on his face when the siege came on, showing pictures of the culprits being led away by the police. 'I hadn't realised it was so bad,' he murmured. For a moment, the horror on his face actually made her feel sorry for him. And there was something else: Charlie, shoulders slumped, looked really unhappy. He didn't want to be here. But his sense of obligation made him stay. Was that what she wanted?

He got up and left the room. Harriet heard him pad upstairs and along the landing to the children's rooms. He'd be kissing them goodnight – too late, as they'd nodded off ages ago. He loves them, she thought. It's me who irritates him.

He was asleep – pretending? – when she went into their bedroom. The wet towels in the children's bathroom indicated he'd showered there. Harriet lay and listened to his even breathing. Was he awake too, wondering what was going to happen to them?

You have a choice.

Monica was right. It wasn't a one-way street. All she had to do was cross the road. Without anyone to hold her hand.

EVIE

'And now for Book at Bedtime.'

'Can't we have Radio One?' complained Leonora.

Evie hesitated. 'We ought to turn it off and go to sleep. I was really waiting for the news but I think we've missed it.'

'Lie down, Mum,' demanded Jack. He was in her king-size

bed instead of his own. Evie needed him close – and the girls, who were also on Evie's bed, felt the same. No one wanted to sleep alone after what they'd been through so the girls were at the bottom and Jack at the top. Later, she'd just slide in beside Jack.

'Can we have some hot chocolate?' asked Natalie. 'Mum always gives it to us if we're pissed off.'

Evie nodded – ignoring the language – went downstairs and returned with a tray of steaming mugs. She hated to admit it but Rachel was right: even in the summer, hot chocolate could be comforting. They sipped it together, and somehow Evie managed not to warn the girls against spilling any.

'Fun! Camping!' said Jack, his eyes gleaming.

'It is,' said Leonora, ruffling his hair.

'How's your leg, Natalie?' asked Evie. She'd bruised it in her eagerness to fly into her sister's arms.

'OK, thanks.'

'Have some more witch hazel.'

Natalie rubbed it in. 'Do you think Dad will call?'

'I don't know. I wish I did. I'm sure he will at some point.' She drew a deep breath. They had a right to know what was going on – or, at least, a censored version.

'As you know, your dad owed some money – I don't know why but there'll be a good reason for it. I think he's gone away to sort it out.'

'But he'll come back?' Leonora's eyes were wide with anxiety.

Evie crossed her fingers mentally. 'Of course.' He'd bloody better, she told herself. It was all very well telling the girls that Robin was 'sorting things out'. That was what she'd thought at first. But suppose something else had happened? Evie had always thought of suicide as the coward's way out and Robin was no coward. But he was a proud man. Redundancy had been a hard pill for him to swallow. She should have been more understanding. She would have been if she'd had more time but she had always been rushing – rushing to get the kids off to school, rushing to work, rushing to a meeting, rushing to get the magazine's figures turned round. And for what? Evie asked herself bitterly. Just so that bloody Janine could take over. Typical, absolutely typical, that she should offer to shorten her maternity leave in order to concentrate on the job. Shit! The car! She should have returned it. Well, it would just have to wait until Monday now.

Gradually, over the next half-hour, the girls and Jack fell asleep. Jack was sucking his thumb and whimpering occasionally. He was bound to be unsettled, Evie thought. She lay on the bed and dozed until the phone rang. Grabbing the receiver, she ran to the top of the stairs so as not to wake the kids.

'Evie? It's me. Sorry to ring so late.'

Her heart plummeted. 'Hi, Dad.'

'Any news?'

'Not yet.'

'I still think you should tell the police. I don't trust those loan people.'

Evie would have laughed if the idea hadn't been so preposterous. 'You think they've taken him away? Come off it, Dad. That sort of thing only happens in films.'

'Well, you thought Bad Ron was involved, didn't you?'

She allowed herself a wry smile. Whoever Bad Ron was, it hadn't rung any bells with her dad's contacts. But it showed what a terrible state she'd allowed herself to get into, if she thought her son's garbled sentences were that important.

'If I haven't heard anything by tomorrow, I will call the police,' she said, 'but I've got this odd feeling that he wouldn't want me to. Besides, you know those missed calls I've been having? I'm sure they're from him.'

She said goodbye and went back to her bedroom. The girls' chests were rising and falling slowly, and Jack was curled up against Natalie's back. Thank God, thought Evie, that the hospital examination had shown he hadn't been abused.

She resigned herself to a sleepless night. The shock had woken every nerve in her body. Being taken hostage was nothing to the terror of discovering Jack had been snatched. If the policewoman hadn't found him in that horrible little house, God knows what might have happened. She should never have left him. She was a bad mother. Softly she began to cry.

'It's all right, Evie,' said a voice.

'Who's that?'

'Nattie.'

'I thought you were asleep.'

'I was. Then I heard you crying.'

'Sorry.'

'It's all right. You must have been awfully scared about Jack.' Evie became aware of a hand holding hers. 'Sorry I've been such a bitch.'

'You haven't. Well, you have, but so have I.'

'Friends?'

Evie squeezed her hand. 'More than that.'

'Thanks. Night, Evie.'

'Night, love.'

SATURDAY

41

'Traffic is building up on the Marylebone bypass and there are reports of . . .'

Time to get up, Harriet thought. No, it wasn't. It was Saturday. There had been no need to set the radio alarm last night. She had forgotten in the aftermath of what had happened that she could sleep in. Now she'd been woken up early. She switched off the radio. Still, no school run for two months. Summer holidays. Charlie home. She turned towards him and he moved away. Her heart sank. This morning, she felt as confused as she had last night. Maybe she needed to do more for herself. The photography idea had come to her out of the blue during the siege. Maybe Nick was right. You *did* think of irrelevant things during crises that were actually quite important.

It was hard to breathe with the window shut, the way Charlie liked it. During his absence she'd kept it open. Since his return, she'd tried to leave a gap but he'd closed it, declaring he got cold in the night. The stale air had induced a headache and she got out of bed to make tea.

While she was waiting for the kettle to boil, she went through Bruce's schoolbag for his report. It was a complete mess, full of hand-outs that he should have stuck into the relevant exercise books plus three notes that he should have handed to her about school trips, long past, and arrangements for yesterday's sports day. The report was at the bottom, heavily stained with an unidentifiable purple substance that might or might not have been fizzy drink.

Harriet sighed as she flicked through it.

Maths: Bruce needs to pay more attention.

Science: Bruce would do better if he could sit still in class.

Geography: Bruce must learn to put up his hand instead of shouting out.

English: Bruce shows terrific imagination and writes wonderful stories. With help, I believe his spelling could improve.

The last paragraph was written by that new teacher, Miss Hayling. Harriet reread it; the first positive comment he'd had since nursery. She put the report into a kitchen drawer. She'd show it to Charlie later, maybe even next week. He would home in on the criticisms, which outweighed the nugget of praise. She thought of Nick, who would, she suspected, react in a more balanced way. He seemed such a natural father. Far more so, she thought, than Charlie.

The rest of Bruce's schoolbag stank of stale crisps and liquorice. It was dry-clean only so she'd have to take it in. That reminded her: a pile of Charlie's suits needed to go too but she ought to clear out the pockets first. Might as well do it now while the house was quiet.

She took out a couple of pens and a flight boarding card. There were some handkerchiefs (he hated tissues) and receipts. He might need those for his expenses.

Harriet put them on the kitchen table and noticed the name of a smart hotel in Knightsbridge. Strange. Charlie hadn't had to stay overnight in central London for months. She examined it more closely. The date was the night that he had left for the airport on his way to Dubai. Yet it had been an afternoon flight and he hadn't needed to stay in London. Harriet looked again. A double room. And what was this? No. Dear God. Breakfast for two persons.

Stop! It might have been a business associate. For a few minutes, she sat at the kitchen table, staring at the receipt with its pink heading. Then she opened her husband's brief-case and took out his mobile.

How had Bruce told her to check recent outgoing calls? That was it. She recognised most of the numbers Charlie had used: home, his mother, the office, and another that didn't ring any bells. A number that, according to the time on the phone, Charlie had called at eleven last night when he would have been in the bathroom.

Call.

It rang four times and someone answered as she was about to switch off the phone.

'*Oui?*'

It took Harriet a few seconds to register that the woman – unmistakably a woman – was French.

'Charlie? *C'est toi?*'

Swiftly, Harriet cut her off. The phone rang in her hand. The number on the screen was the one she had dialled. She switched it off, then walked leadenly up the stairs. Charlie lay in a hump under the duvet, eyes shut, snoring.

'Charlie, wake up. Wake *up*.'

She shook him.

'What is it?' he mumbled.

'This.' She pushed the receipt in front of him. 'Why do you have a receipt for a London hotel on the night you went to Dubai?'

'For God's sake, Harriet, is that what you woke me up for? The flight was delayed. Didn't I tell you?'

She grabbed his wrists violently, wanting to hurt him the way she was hurting inside. 'No, you didn't. And what about the breakfast-for-two bit? Is that something you thought you'd told me about too?'

If he denied that, she'd tell him about the phone. But supposing she was wrong? She didn't want him to think she'd been snooping.

'Harriet,' he said slowly.

No, no. Tell me it isn't true.

She grabbed him by the lapels of his pyjamas. 'Do you love her?' she hissed.

He slumped back on the pillow. 'Harriet,' he said quietly, 'there's something I need to tell you.'

42

'This is your very own hospital radio on a cool Saturday morning. The heatwave looks like it's over, folks, and—'

'Mummy!'

Pippa took off her headphones, held out her arms and hugged the girls to her.

'You're hurting me,' squealed Beth.

Reluctantly she released them. 'I can't believe you didn't tell me before,' she said to Derek. They'd been over the siege when he'd come in earlier, but she was still churned up inside. If she hadn't confiscated Lucy's mobile earlier in the week her daughter might have raised the alarm. It was her fault. Like everything else.

'Don't be cross,' he said. 'The doctors said I shouldn't worry you. Besides, they were fine, weren't you, girls?'

'We were on television,' added Beth. 'The boys weren't as bad as they said. Some were quite nice. But they took everyone's mobile and we still haven't got them back.'

So Pippa was let off that one.

'Then we did number games until they let us out.'

Derek smiled at her over the children's heads. 'I've got another surprise too, a nice one. Guess who's coming to visit this morning?'

Pippa froze. Oh, God, *no*.

'There she is. Over here, Susie!'

A portly, grey-haired woman in a tweed skirt and cardigan waddled in. 'Darling, I came as soon as Derek called me.'

Pippa closed her eyes with relief. 'Aunt Susie, you shouldn't have.'

'Nonsense! You ought to have told me sooner.'

'But it's such a long way.'

'I might be old, dear, but I'm still in one piece. Sorry. What a thoughtless thing to say.'

'It's all right.' Pippa lay back. 'We're still waiting. The doctor hasn't made his rounds yet.'

'I think that's him now,' said Derek quietly.

Pippa's aunt stood up briskly. 'Right, girls, come with me. Let's leave Mummy and Daddy alone for a bit with the doctor, shall we?'

Pippa's mouth was dry. So much had happened. The girls were all right, thank God, but what about her? It was like waiting for exam results, but far worse. If the lump was malignant, it could mean chemo and an uncertain future. But she wasn't as terrified as she had been at the beginning of the week when all the fears had been in her head. Now that it was happening she had the strength to deal with it. Not like poor Derek, who needed her to reassure him. But how long could she go on deceiving him?

The doctor was standing by the screen, clipboard in hand. 'Mrs Hallet? Mr Hallet? I'm Dr Robson. We've got the results.'

KITTY

'And it's Lunchtime Requests from Classic FM . . .'

Honestly, thought Kitty, as she toyed with her crab salad at a smart brasserie off Kensington High Street just after 1 p.m., why couldn't someone take her to a restaurant with *live* music? On the other hand, if she went on any more dates this week, she'd never fit into the pretty primrose suit she'd bought for the christening.

Another thing. Why was it that she kept attracting these financial types? She knew nothing about the stock market or the world debt deficit, or whatever Mark had called it. All she knew was that the Oasis suit had cost her most of last month's wages so it had better be worth it.

Sneaking a look at Mark's crisp, striped Gieves and Hawkes shirt under his navy blazer, she suspected that money wasn't a problem for him. Keeping his promises, however, was not one of his strengths.

'I'm really sorry about cancelling on Monday and Friday,' he said, leaning across the table in what he probably thought was a conciliatory gesture, 'but these meetings came up that I absolutely couldn't miss.'

'No problem,' said Kitty coolly. 'Actually, I didn't realise you were expecting me on Friday. I thought you were going to ring, but in the event I was out anyway.'

Mark's eyes flickered. 'Really? Anywhere nice?'

'Le Poiret,' she said casually.

She could see he was dying to ask whom she had gone with but good manners prevented him. Kitty decided not to put him out of his misery. Nor would she refer to her experience on Friday: he had probably read about it in the paper but, like Duncan, had not made the connection. Kitty wanted to put it out of her mind. During the night she had woken several times in a cold sweat, in her horrible stark bedsit, panicking about what might have happened if they hadn't been released.

'So tell me,' she said artfully, 'how exactly does the stock market work? I've never really understood it.'

She could see from the expression on his face that she had said exactly the right thing. Mark loved explaining things, and while he was doing so, Kitty could sit back and work out her next move.

'Fascinating,' she said, when he had finished and the waiter was hovering.

Mark beamed. 'You make a charming audience.' His large hairy hand crossed the table and settled on hers. 'Actually, I was wondering what you were doing tomorrow.'

Kitty felt her heart flutter. 'I'm going to a christening. I'm rather looking forward to it as I'm the godmother.' She looked at him calculatingly. 'What are you doing?'

Mark looked hopeful. 'Nothing, as it happens.'

Kitty leaned forwards. 'Actually, there was something I was going to ask *you* . . .'

HARRIET

'And now for Home Truths.'

'Hang on, I've just got to turn down the radio. So what was it again?'

'A benign reactive lymph node. Definitely *not* malignant.' Pippa's voice was light with relief down the phone. 'But Derek's fussing around me as though I was actually ill. I've got to have regular checks, though. Apparently there are a few other so-called cysts and nodules they want to watch. Anyway, how's Charlie? Are you getting used to having a man about the house again?'

'We're going to separate.' Harriet's voice was flat. 'Charlie's been seeing someone else for nearly a year. She's French. He says he met her through work but I don't know what to believe any more. In some ways it's a relief because it explains why he's been so cold and distant all these months. I thought it was something I was doing.'

'Bastard.' Pippa sounded refreshingly angry.

'The worst bit is that he loves her. I can't fight that. I want to feel angry but I'm too hurt. All those lies he must have told. All those nights when I thought he was working late.'

'Please don't cry. Not when I can't hug you. How did you find out?'

'A hotel receipt. For a London hotel on the night he was meant to have flown out to Dubai. Probably their little farewell.'

'Does she have children?'

'No. Nor a husband.' Harriet laughed. 'So I'm the only obstacle. I feel like ringing her up and telling her she's destroyed my life.'

'Why don't you?'

'Because I'm scared of her. And it should be her who's scared of me.'

'Bitch.'

'I know, and for some reason I blame her, not Charlie. I almost feel sorry for him. He's stopped being hard and says he's just relieved it's out in the open. It's as though my old Charlie's back but now he's going again.'

'Have you told the children?' Pippa's sympathy made her feel worse. Neither of them could pretend now that it might be 'all right'.

'Yes. Sort of. Sorry, hang on a minute.' Harriet took a deep breath to ease the pressure at the top of her chest. 'We've said Daddy's office is moving so he's going to live away during the week and come to see them at weekends.'

'Is he moving in with her?'

'I suppose so. He says I can stay here until we've got it sorted.'

'Big of him. You need to see a solicitor, Harry, fast. Take the receipt with you.'

'I will. Next week. I need time to get used to it. It's so sudden.'

'Is it?' Pippa sounded kind but persistent. 'Haven't you suspected, deep down? . . . Harry? Are you there?'

'Yes.'

'I don't want to be harsh, darling, but at least you know

where you are now. You've managed without him for two months or more. You can do it, Harry. We'll be here to help you. Shall I come over?'

'No. You've got to rest.'

'Actually, I'd like to. There's something I've got to tell you. I know it's selfish on top of Charlie but there's no one else who'd understand.'

Harriet blew her nose again. 'Tomorrow? About ten? We're going down to Mum's later. We were just going to go for the day but now I've asked if we can stay longer. I haven't told her why.'

'Will she understand?'

'I don't know.' If she didn't end this conversation now, she'd crumble. 'Must go, now. See you tomorrow.'

NICK

'And now, over to Jonathan Ross with . . .'

Juliana pouted at him from the pages of the glossy supplement that came with a Saturday newspaper Nick didn't normally buy. She was crossing her legs, exactly as she used to, in a tasteful red dress. *How do I look, darling? Do you think they'll like me?*

'What do you think?' Julie was hanging over his shoulder, watching his every expression. 'Do you like the pictures?'

Nick was silent, trying to find the right words. It was easier to let the kitchen radio do the talking in the background while he got his head round this.

'Dad, say something.'

'You look fabulous. Just like she did.'

Julie's face broke into a beautiful smile. She'd had her eyebrows plucked, Nick noticed.

'Then you don't mind? The agency wants me to do more. I won't let it interfere with my schoolwork. Promise.'

Nick was still looking at the photographs, remembering the first time he had seen Juliana through a lens. The first time he had kissed her. The first time they had been together. 'What does Jason think?'

'He's all for it. I told you. He's behind me. You've got to change your mind about him, Dad.'

'Sure he's clean?'

'Absolutely.'

He held his daughter close. 'But it can lead to other things. You've got to listen to your old dad sometimes. I only want you to be happy.'

'I know, I know. Well, this is what makes me happy. And it helps.'

Nick swallowed. 'I thought we ought to go through Mum's things today. It's time, don't you think?'

During their sessions, Amber had expressed surprise that he hadn't done this already but he hadn't been able to face Juliana's dresses, each one smelling and dancing of her. 'It might help you and Julie come to terms with what happened,' she had suggested.

'I'd like that,' said Julie, slowly.

'Really?'

'Yeah.' Julie was looking at her pictures again, critically. 'I'm not as thin as Mum was, am I?'

No.

'I'm glad, actually,' she continued, without waiting for an answer. 'She was too thin, don't you think?'

'Yes.' Nick nodded. 'Yes, I do.'

'Is that what killed her? As well as the cancer?'

He could hardly breathe. 'Partly.'

Julie put an arm round him. 'I'm never going to be like that, Dad, don't worry.'

'But you don't get it, Julie. The agency people might influence you like they did her – like we all did. It's a shallow world, modelling.'

'But I'm not going to let them change me.' Julie spoke with clear conviction. 'And if they try, I'm out. I'm nearly eighteen now. You've got to let me grow up. I've said I'm mature enough to accept you seeing other women, haven't I? Well, it works both ways.' She gave him a hug, a real bear-hug like she used to when she was little. Nick's throat swelled. 'You have to trust me. I'll be sensible.'

She was right. And if he didn't tell her the truth now, he never would. He clutched the back of the sofa for support. 'It wasn't just the anorexia and it wasn't cancer,' he muttered.

'*What?*' Her beautiful eyes widened in alarm.

God, what had he started? 'Julie, I'm sorry. She ended it all with pills.'

'Not an overdose?'

He moved towards her. 'I'm sorry. So sorry. And it was all my fault . . .'

43

Ring, Ring.

For a moment Evie thought it was the radio alarm, then realised it was the doorbell. Who could it be at this hour? What was it? Seven. Ridiculous! It wasn't even a school morning.

It rang again and she heard someone open it. The girls must have woken up early.

'Dad! It's Dad!'

She ran downstairs. Robin was standing in the hall, unshaven, hair slicked back, looking at her uncertainly. 'Are you all right? I heard about the school on the news. Is everyone OK?'

'We're fine.' She pulled him to her and he held her tightly. His face rubbed against hers and she could feel the stubble. He spoke into her shoulder, voice muffled: 'Evie, I'm sorry. But it's all right now. I've got a job. In the States. We can get out there today and start again.'

She pushed him away, staring at him. 'You went abroad? Without telling us?'

Robin looked shamefaced. 'You'd have tried to stop me and then I'd have failed again. But I didn't. Not this time.'

His face shone, like Jack's when he was excited. He looked exhausted and the skin below his eyes was puffy.

'I've got a fantastic job, Evie. Someone in Westport who owes me a favour. You'll like it over there. So will the kids. We can have a new start and no one will find us.'

'Why didn't you leave a message?' Evie heard herself

309

sounding cold and calm. 'We were terrified. We thought you'd hurt yourself or someone had hurt you.'

Robin appeared cross now. 'I needed time to sort it out so I could come back and tell you it was settled. And I did try to ring but you didn't pick up.'

She grabbed him by the collar, forcing him to look into her eyes. 'Get real, Robin. You borrow God knows how much money from your old firm to do something that I don't know about—'

'It was to pay for that skiiing holiday for the kids,' he said.

'And the rest?'

'I gave it to Rachel. For the girls again. She said she was skint and didn't want to ask Chris. Then I borrowed a bit more to invest. Someone gave me this tip.' His face fell. 'But it didn't pay off.'

Evie could have shaken him. 'You always know someone who owes you a favour but it never turns out as it should, does it? So then you try to pay the money back by borrowing from a loan shark charging the most ridiculous amount of interest.'

Robin's brow darkened. 'How do you know all this?'

'Because you're not very organised, are you? You'd left all the paperwork in the back of your car.'

He scowled. 'It was the safest place I could think of. Well, since we're having some home truths here, Evie, let me tell you a few.' His eyes glistened with anger. 'You've made me feel totally inadequate. There you are, with your fantastic job, telling me I mustn't spend so much money in the supermarket or that I ought to do this and that with Jack. Then you criticise the girls, and when I try to talk to you about all this, you're always in some bloody meeting. No wonder I needed space.'

'I know.'

'What?'

'You're right. I've worked it all out. But we're both to blame, Robin. It's not just me.'

His face lightened. 'Then you'll give up your job and come to Westport? But I warn you, I'm going to ask Rachel if the girls can come with us for the holidays.'

'No.'

He rubbed his eyes. 'I knew it.'

'Yes to the girls. No to Westport. We're staying here, Robin, and facing the music. I'm not running away from anyone.'

'But the loan company – you don't understand. I borrowed money and then I invested again and lost and then—'

'I do understand. My dad also knew someone who knew someone in that bloody company you borrowed from. They've given us time to pay it back.'

'How?'

'I'm not sure. We need to think about it. But you've got to promise me something, Robin. You can't go shooting off like that again. I know it isn't easy with me working . . . Actually, I'm not any more but that's another story.'

'What do you mean?'

'They fired me. Don't look like that. They've given me money – enough to get by on for a while. Look, just come in and have a wash. We've missed you.'

Robin clung to her, kissing her neck the way he used to. Nuzzling her so she began to melt. 'You mean that?'

'Yes.' She felt weak all over at his touch. God, it was good to have him home.

Robin buried his face in her hair. 'We've done it wrong, Evie, but it's not too late, is it?'

She thought of what might have happened to Jack. She'd tell him, but not yet. It was all too much, too soon. 'No, it's not too late.'

She could almost feel the relief washing through him.

'You're a girl in a million, Evie Brookes,' he said. 'A girl in a million.'

'Girl?' said Natalie, sharply. 'Isn't she a bit old for that?'

They both looked at her.

'Where've you been?'

'Listening behind the door, as any self-respecting teenager would.'

'Oh, God,' said Robin.

'It's OK, Dad. We've got gamblers in our class too. That's what investing is, isn't it? We've had a talk on it at school. I've got a helpline number if you're interested.' She came up to Robin, pushing Evie gently out of the way. 'Welcome home, Dad. I knew you'd come back. Want to see our reports? They're brilliant. Evie said so.'

NICK

And now a very special Love Song, dedicated to Marlene by her husband Jo as a belated birthday present. Marlene, Jo says he loves you very much. In fact, he couldn't live without you.'

Nick kept the radio on while he was searching. He needed the haunting pain of the song – one that had always sent shivers down his spine – to remind him how far he had come. Juliana was dead. But he still needed to live. And not just for their daughter's sake.

'No, Dad,' Julie had said, when he'd told her the truth about her mother's death. 'It wasn't your fault. She had ambition and it killed her. When you're obsessed like that, it takes you over. I'm ambitious too, but not like that. Poor Mum. And poor you.'

They'd had an emotional few hours, saying all the things they should have said years ago. In the afternoon she'd had her driving lesson – which gave Nick time to do what he had put off for too long. He sifted through Juliana's drawers, which still smelt of her signature scent. Every now and then he was distracted by things that brought her back to him with such intensity he could hardly breathe. The black stockings he had given her the Christmas before she was ill. The first Mothering Sunday card Julie had made at school. *'To my mummy,'* it said.

He put it to one side.

Then he found what he'd been looking for. The piece of paper she had left by the pills. At the time he had hidden it, scared in case someone else had found and misinterpreted it. He had pushed it to the bottom of a drawer, hoping never to see it again but also aware that perhaps he should keep it: this last word from the woman he had loved so much. The writing was shaky, indicating how weak she had been, and it was hard to make out the words. 'I should have stopped.'

He had always assumed she was talking about the anorexia but now he wasn't so sure, so he went on searching for clues. He'd exhausted the drawers but maybe there was something in the bookcase, in the files they had kept on housekeeping matters. And then at the bottom, labelled 'Miscellaneous', he finally found what he was looking for.

A garage bill. For a repair to the car. Dated a few days before she'd died. Damage to the front bumper. At the time, it had seemed unimportant. His wife was ill. What did it matter if the car had been dented?

I hit a bollard. Stop fussing, Nick. You've done it.

He could hear her saying it, see her, clear as day. He'd remembered wondering how she'd had the strength to get out of bed that morning.

I needed to get out, Nick. You can't keep me cooped up here. I'm not ill. I'm fat. Gross. And it's all your fault. You got me pregnant and now my body's never going to be the same. I hate you, Nick, hate you. Look at these magazines. Can you see me in them? No. And do you know why? Because everyone else is prettier and thinner. I'm finished, Nick. Finished.

He had tried to comfort her, feeling her ribs poking sharply against him. If he had known then what he knew now he would have understood why she was so hysterical.

She had killed a child. Had she known she'd killed him? Or had she driven off, hoping desperately he was all right?

It's only a dent, Nick. Stop fussing. I hit a bollard, that's all.

How much damage would a child's body inflict? A small dent? A big one? Early, Harriet had said. The accident had been early in the day. Juliana had got up early towards the end. Somehow, despite that terrible lack of energy, she had insisted on driving herself to the newsagent at seven thirty, and return with piles of the glossy magazines that tortured her because she was no longer in them.

Why hadn't she stopped? She would have been terrified. Scared witless. Unable to live with it.

Should he tell someone what he thought? Who? Certainly not Julie. It would destroy her, especially now that she was turning the corner. Instinctively he felt Harriet might understand. But that wouldn't solve anything. He had to put that poor mother's mind at rest, if that was what you could call it. She deserved to know that the driver who killed – might have killed – her son was dead too.

He leafed through the telephone book for the number he needed, then picked up the phone.

MARTINE

'More coffee, love?'

'*Non, merci.*'

I have had enough. I will sit here, writing my diary and waiting in this funny little shop where they play this strange radio station that speaks so fast. My beau comes to pick me up shortly. My cases are sorted. He bought them for me from his trip. They are pigskin. *Rouge.* Very stylish, yes?

Dear Diary,
I am glad to go. But I have some nice things. I am a great
admirer of Sally's clothes. And it is not wise of Simon to abandon
money in his dressing room.

I am glad I will not be here tomorrow when the newspapers come out. Sally will not admire it either. 'Fifty Things You Did Not Know About Simon and Sally'. That is what the reporter is going to title it. I could only think of thirty-two but she can think of more.

I can see mon chéri now coming in through the door. He is smiling but he does not look as I remembered. His hair, he is missing at the front. Goodbye, Simon and Sally. Goodbye, Sam and Ellie. I am going home, at last.

SATURDAY P.M.

'Why has Daddy gone away again? He's only just got back.'

'It was us, wasn't it? I told Bruce not to paint his room. I tried to clear it up before Dad knocked over the tin. But he should have been looking where he was going, shouldn't he? That's what he's always telling us.'

'Maybe he ought to meditate. It might make him feel better. Our new teacher has taught us. Look, you close your eyes like this and go "One". You sing it like a note. Go on, try!'

'You're not going out again, are you, Dad?'

'Nattie's right, Dad. You can't – even if Benjamin does want to see you. Anyway, Mum's coming tomorrow. Didn't Evie tell you? With Chris. We haven't met him before and we've got to be really polite. In your dreams.'

'Feeling better now, Mum? Aunt Susie says we've got to look after you and that she can't go until you're better. But you are, aren't you? When's she going? She keeps hogging Sky and then she tells *us* we watch too much television. She'll get hyper like Bruce if she carries on sitting in front of the box. Can't you tell her? *Please.*'

'My instructor says I can put in for my test now. He says I'm ready. Mum was my age when she passed, wasn't she?'

'I'm g-g-glad Farty Marty's gone. I don't want another French person. Can we have a Croatian n-nanny n-n-next, like Hugo? She lets him skateboard in the kitchen when she's snogging her boyfriend upstairs.'

'Yes, Mandy, I am bringing someone actually. I think you'll like her, although you might be a bit surprised. Yes. A her. You met her ages ago but she's changed. Eleven thirty at St Nicholas's? We'll be there.'

SUNDAY

44

'*And at eleven fifteen, this morning, Sue Lawley will be
presenting a repeat series of* Desert Island Discs . . .'

Harriet made the bed up with fresh sheets, as she always did
on Sundays, listening to the preview for *Desert Island Discs*
(a programme Charlie deplored but which she adored –
especially when guessing the castaway from the introduction).
The pillows smelt of a new brand of conditioner. The realisation that they no longer smelt of her husband both saddened
and relieved her.

Her first night alone – the first proper one, undisguised by
the term 'business trip' – hadn't been as bad as she'd thought.
The receipt had made it easier. It wouldn't have been the same
if they'd tried to start again. She'd heard of couples who had
succeeded but only when one of them, usually the husband,
confessed to making a mistake. Love was a different matter.
When had he started to love this woman, whose name he
refused to divulge? What had Harriet been doing at the time?
Had it been a day when one of the children had been at home
ill? Their first day at school? Sports day – he hadn't made it
last year? All those late nights when he'd been 'working', had
he really been in some seedy car park somewhere or a hotel
room or *her* house? Harriet wanted to know, but at the same
time she didn't.

The children had been upset last night, asking why Daddy
had to go away again on business, but this morning they'd

seemed almost normal when they'd come in to kiss her, then gone down to watch breakfast television.

Harriet tucked in Charlie's side. His old side. Last week there'd been a piece in the *Mail* about predatory women who stalked men at work, not caring if they were married. Had *she* done that? That was what she wanted to ask her husband. That was what she should have asked him, when he was still at home. But now he was gone, leaving her to mop up the mess.

She remembered how she'd felt when her father had left, closing the front door with a quiet click, leaving her mother weeping at the kitchen table. Suddenly *Desert Island Discs* seemed irrelevant.

She turned off the radio and padded downstairs to sort out breakfast. Empty crisps packets and KitKat wrappers were strewn on the sitting-room carpet. 'I've told you before, if you're going to help yourself to breakfast, have some cereal, not snacks. Bruce, listen to me. And you, Jess.'

Both children remained glued to the television – well, at least that was normal behaviour. She got out the vacuum. Since Charlie had left, she'd become almost obsessive about cleaning. She'd once heard someone on the radio who had been the same after a family tragedy and the psychologist had said it was the one area of her life she could control.

That was better.

'Would you like some bacon, you two?'

'Yes.'

'Yes, *please*, Jess.'

She went back into the kitchen and put the bacon under the grill. No, stupid, not eight rashers. Just six.

'Why are you crying, Mum?' asked Jess, coming up behind her.

'It's the onions, darling.'

'You're not cooking any.'

Harriet turned the bacon over. 'Go back into the sitting room and I'll bring it in.'

Eating in front of the television was a strict no-no when Charlie was at home. But he wasn't at home, Harriet told herself, as she took two trays in and instructed them not to drop the ketchup on the carpet. Then she made herself a cup of Earl Grey in her favourite Emma Bridgewater mug. Hopeless trying to eat – her stomach was still churning with the momentous repercussions of the last two days. Only an hour to get ready for Sussex, before Pippa arrived. Only the rest of her life ahead, quite possibly on her own. But others had done it. And so could she. She had to be positive, for the children's sake.

EVIE

'And now for your last record . . .'

Evie had missed the name of the celebrity, which was always annoying. Not that it was important today. Lunch would be burned if her guests didn't get here soon. Twelve, she had said. Early, to fit in with Jack's nap. The beef was perfect and the smell was making her hungry.

I must be mad, thought Evie. It had been her idea to feed Rachel and her lover. Usually Rachel knocked at the door to pick up the girls, flaunting herself with the latest tan. But something had made Evie tell them that when their mother rang to make arrangements for picking up they must invite her to lunch. With Chris.

She should have known they would be late. The joint would be ruined (she must have miscalculated the cooking time) and Rachel would have the satisfaction of reminding the girls of those summer barbecues they used to have when Dad was at home. She'd tell it in such a way that an onlooker would assume Robin had left rather than her. Only Evie would know it was done for effect: Robin would be too busy talking to the girls, prolonging contact.

No, that was unfair. She could understand it now. It must be terrible to have your child taken away from you, not just once but again and again, while the person who had made that child with you decided when – if – you could see them again. When Jack was snatched away she had been in agony. Now she saw that her husband had gone through similar pain for years. No wonder he was slightly crazy.

'They're here! They're here!' Leonora ran to the door and something like jealousy twinged in Evie's chest. Since Friday the girls had been so nice to her. She was almost sorry they were going. If Rachel wasn't around, she might be able to get quite close to them. As it was, she hardly stood a chance. How could a step-mother ever make it work when she had only a weekend here and there to forge a relationship? Still, the last week had helped more than any other time since she had known the girls. Could they have turned the corner?

There was the sound of excited voices. Evie took off her apron and stepped into the hall.

'Hi, Evie, how are you doing? I hear you've had quite a week. Thank God the girls were OK. I hear they let those boys out on bail. Typical!'

Rachel, skin glowing from the sun, airkissed Evie's cheek. 'This is Chris, everyone. Chris, this is Leonora, Nattie, Robin, of course, Jack and Ella—'

'Evie,' corrected Robin.

She always did that, thought Evie, grimly. You had to hand it to her: she knew how to make an entrance – this time more than ever.

Chris had the sunniest, whitest smile she had ever seen. Evie tried, without success, to stop staring. So, too, did the girls and Robin, although Jack was too young to twig. Chris had a better tan than Rachel. She also had a better figure and a kinder smile. And just in case there was any doubt about her role, she was holding Rachel's hand in a very flamboyant manner.

Evie looked at the girls. Their faces were horrorstricken. 'Come on in, both of you. I'm so glad you could make lunch. It will give us time to talk for a change. Nattie and Lennie, do you want to come into the kitchen with me and get some nibbles?'

The girls followed her. 'What is she? A dyke?' hissed Leonora.

Evie held her shoulders. 'Listen, both of you. There are times when parents don't do the kind of things you expect.' She took a deep breath. 'Your mother has had some rough times. She seems happy now, so maybe we should try to be happy for her, even if Chris isn't what we expected. All right? Now, go out there and take the olives and nuts with you. Don't eat too many because lunch is ready.'

Robin came in with glasses for a refill. 'I'd never have thought it,' he said palely. 'Do you think it was because of me?'

Evie laughed. 'I'm the one who's meant to have Jewish guilt. No, I just think Rachel looks happier than she has for years.'

Robin shrugged on his way out with the tray. 'Possibly. But I still find it really weird. Oh, hi Chris.'

'Hi.'

Chris rewarded him with a look of bemusement as he almost collided with her on his way out of the kitchen as she suddenly came in. Evie turned, embarrassed by Robin's faux pas. To be honest, Chris also made her feel confused. She didn't have a deep voice and she seemed perfectly normal. Serena at work, who was definitely that way inclined, had looked very masculine, down to her collection of embroidered waistcoats, which she wore over striped black trousers. But Chris was beautifully dressed – she could swear that was a Stella McCartney outfit – and her face was made up like that of an Yves St Laurent model.

'I hear Robin's in a bit of trouble.'

Evie took in the cloud of perfume. Poison? Chanel? 'Who told you?'

'The girls, when they spoke to Rachel. Can I do anything to help?'

Evie narrowed her eyes. 'Why would you want to do that?'

Chris drained her G and T and sat down at the kitchen bar. 'Look, Evie, my parents were divorced too and I know what it's like to be handed from one parent to another. Robin borrowed that money to spend it on the girls. I know that too. I'm a wealthy woman, Evie. I can afford to bail you out.'

'We wouldn't want that.' They both turned as Robin came in. 'I appreciate it, but it wouldn't be right.'

Chris flashed him a dynamic smile. 'I don't mean for free. You could pay me back. I need a good accountant for a new venture I'm about to set up. I'm in shipping. I expect Rachel told you.'

Robin was frowning. 'Why would you need an accountant? You must have people already.'

'Of course. But I don't want them to know everything about me. No shady stuff, though, for me or you. I want an honest accountant.'

Robin's neck coloured. 'I am. Basically.'

Chris nodded, satisfied. 'Good. Then that's settled. I'm basing it on the other side of the river but we can talk details on Monday.' Her eyes travelled to Evie's chest where they settled, unashamedly.

'In the meantime, let's just get to know each other, shall we? By the way, did you read all that stuff about Simon and Sally Pargeter in the paper?'

'I've been too busy cooking to look at the papers,' said Evie, pointedly.

Chris touched her arm. 'Well, you must read this. It's riveting. Rachel says you do a school run with their au pair. Well, it's her who spilt the beans. You could have got an exclusive with her for your magazine.'

'Maybe.' Evie was strangely unwilling to look at the feature. It was smut, that was all, and after all her years in journalism, it was losing its appeal.

'Evie, Evie!'

'Yes?'

Leonora stood there, panting with importance. 'We've just been watching cartoons with Jack on Nickelodeon. And guess who we saw?'

Evie was frantically trying to baste the beef. 'Who?'

'Bad Ron! He's a new kid in the series – always naughty. Jack is riveted by him. Come and look. He's wicked!'

Chris raised her eyebrows.

'Sometimes,' said Evie, giving up on the beef, 'there's no accounting for children's tastes.'

45

'*And that was the Beatles with . . .*'

Kitty pulled off her headphones, and stared at the driver as the bus pulled up twenty minutes late. 'Good morning! I didn't know you worked Sundays.'

Clive shrugged. 'Only one in four. And I get time and a half so it's worth it. How's the book going?'

'Finished it. It was amazing. If I'd known I was going to bump into you I'd have brought it with me. You won't be seeing me for a bit because it's the holidays.'

'Going away, are you?' Clive's eyes swept over her approvingly. 'I thought you looked all dressed up.'

Kitty flushed. 'Actually, I'm just off to a christening in Richmond.'

'Well, you look very pretty. I hope the baby appreciates it.'

Kitty smiled and sat down on the empty seat almost opposite the cab. There was no one else on the bus, which made a pleasant change from the crush during the school week.

'You're running late,' she said conversationally.

'Yeah. We thought we'd emulate the trains.'

'Very funny.'

He glanced sideways at her. 'Are you the godmother, then?'

'How did you guess?'

'I just thought you might be. You look the type.'

'Is that a compliment?'

He grinned. 'Maybe. You get out of the habit of paying compliments when you drive a bus. That reminds me. That

326

thing you asked me, about coming in and talking to the kids about my job, do you really think they'd be interested?'

'Absolutely.' Kitty sat forward. 'The head's doing a big drive – excuse the pun – on road safety. It would be great if you could tell them about crossing the road and watching out for traffic and that sort of thing.'

'And will you be there?' asked Clive, eyes straight ahead.

'Should be,' said Kitty carefully.

'Good. Then I'll do it.'

'I'm so glad,' said Kitty. 'Shall I ring you?'

'No.'

Her heart plummeted.

'Write down your number and I'll ring you. My mum always said that a man should call a woman and not the other way round.'

'How funny,' said Kitty. 'My mother says exactly the same thing.'

They looked at each other. 'We seem to be on the same wavelength,' said Clive. 'I don't suppose you fancy a drink some time?'

'That would be nice,' said Kitty. Part of her was surprised, while the rest was relieved that at last he had made a move. 'I'd like that.'

PIPPA

Din, din, clack, clack, shout, shout.

'Pippa, come in. Hang on while I make them stop playing those hideous drums. *Bruce? Jess? Quieter.* That's better. Coffee? Let's take it into the sitting room. I'm so fed up with the kitchen.'

Pippa followed her, wondering how Harriet managed to keep her house so tidy. Hers was a tip, just like her life. Unsteadily, she sat down on Harriet's beautiful cream sofa (it had to have been Charlie's choice – so unsuitable for Bruce).

Harriet looked at her. 'You haven't had any bad news from the hospital, have you?'

Pippa leaned forward and clutched her friend's hand. 'Oh, Harriet, I've done something terrible. I've had an affair.'

'An affair?'

The shock on her friend's face confirmed the terrible apprehension she'd had inside about telling her.

Then Harriet's face softened. 'Do you want to tell me about it?'

'Derek might not have read the text message,' said Harriet, when she'd finished. 'And even if he did, he might just think Gus was being friendly.'

Pippa sniffed. 'Maybe. But I still feel so guilty. Now I'll have to tell Derek—'

'No.' Harriet's firm tone startled her. 'You might if you were still seeing Gus but it was a one-afternoon thing. It's Derek you love. The only person you'll help by spilling the beans is yourself. And that will only be for a few seconds of relief at having come clean. After that, you're right, he might leave you.'

'But I'm no better than Charlie.'

Harriet shook her head. 'It's different. You were scared. The lump gave you a kind of mid-week crisis.'

'How am I going to put it behind me?'

'Maybe that's your penance. Derek has been your rock. You owe it to him to start again.'

'But I've changed.'

Harriet smiled ruefully. 'We all have.'

Pippa put down her mug. 'True. I used to think Derek didn't care or that he was simply obtuse. But now I can see it was his way of coping. He told himself everything would be all right because he was too scared of it not being all right.'

'He really loves you, Pippa.'

'And I love him. Not the kind of superficial love I thought I felt for Gus, but a proper love. A deep one that's built on having had the children and shared so much over the years.'

She got up. 'Thanks, Harriet. You're the best friend anyone could have. I don't want to keep you any more if you're going to your mum's. Sure you'll be all right to drive?'

Harriet nodded. 'We'll have lunch here first, I think, and then a leisurely drive down. I'll be back in a week and I'll ring you then. By the way, did you hear about the poor child who was taken out of his mother's car during the siege?'

'No!'

'There's a rumour going round that he was snatched by a woman whose own son was run over two years ago. Remember? The driver didn't stop. She's never got over it, poor soul. Nick – he's one of the dads at school – heard she'd gone a bit ga-ga. The police had to go in and rescue the child from her house but he was all right. The woman's having medical treatment.'

'How awful! Losing a child. It's the worst thing you can think of, isn't it?'

'Exactly. Makes you count your blessings.' She kissed her friend's cheek. 'Just give it time, Pippa.'

'And you. Thanks for everything.'

Pippa walked back to her house to get Sunday lunch ready. It was nice to feel the air on her face but she couldn't help thinking about the child in the car. She'd left hers sometimes but never again.

When she got in, there was a note on the table: 'Taken the girls to the park. Back by one.'

Derek was trying to get life back to normal. Now she had to do the same. Well, she'd start with lunch. The phone rang as she put the potatoes on.

'Hi, Pippa.'

No 'Gorgeous' this time. Just 'Pippa'.

'Hi.'

'How are you?'

'Fine. The lump was what they call "a benign reactive lymph node".'

'I know. Derek told me.'

A cold fear came over her. 'I didn't know you two had spoken.'

'I rang on Friday to see what was happening.' His voice dropped. 'Is he there?'

'No.'

'Right. Look, Pippa, I'm sorry. I should never have . . . Well, you know what I mean.'

She felt the same but it was still galling to know he had regrets too. 'So it was a "pity" lay? You thought I was about to pop my socks and you decided to give me something I'd remember?'

'You know it wasn't like that.' Gus's voice sounded tenderly reproachful. 'I've always loved you, Pippa, but not in that way. I've thought about it a few times – you must have as well – but I didn't want anything to ruin our friendship. Now I'm worried it has.'

She swallowed. 'We could try not to let it.'

'I was hoping you'd say that. There's something else, something I tried to explain before . . . well, before.'

Oh, God. He hadn't given her some awful disease, had he?

'I'm getting married, Pip, to a girl who works for me. Angie's quite a bit younger but I think you'll like her. You don't mind, do you?'

Mind? Of course she did. But at the same time she was relieved. 'I'm really pleased for you, Gus. Honestly. When's the wedding?'

'September. Do you think the girls would like to be bridesmaids?'

She gulped. Feeling regret was one thing. Forgiving Gus for similar regrets was another. But allowing the girls to be bridesmaids and having to take them to fittings while this nubile Angie was there, wreathed in netting and smiles and a thirty-six double C – that was something else.

'Bridesmaids?' she repeated. 'I don't think so, Gus. Thanks for the offer but, somehow, I think that's going a bit too far. Don't you?'

46

'This is Steve Wright with a selection of Sunday morning love songs.'

Dear Diary,
I would like to turn the radio off but it will not stop. It comes
out of the walls, I think, in pipes. It is preventing me
concentrating on the newspaper, which I do not understand.
I did not tell the reporter that thing about Sally and the feather
duster. Perhaps someone else told her. Still, my photograph she
looks quite pretty.
Maurice, he says he is worried that Simon and Sally might take
me to court. But why? If there was such a danger, the paper would
tell me, yes? And it was true. Simon did advance on me but I push
him away.
I like this hotel; it is very comfortable. Maurice said I would
admire his house but his wife admires it too. This bed, he is very
big and there are mirrors on the wall and ceiling. We can do a
lot of admiring and I can ring my mother whenever I want. She
is very keen on my new friend and has invited him to stay.
Maurice says I will like his son Hugo. I do not tell him that
when he comes to play with Sam I think he is full of noise and
rudeness. My father had a son before he married my mother but
he does not see him now.
There is only one problème. I suspect my head, she is itching
again. Maurice, hers is itching too. But there is only enough
shampoo for one so I am going to take my shower now.

And then I am going to get Maurice to make me pregnant. He will be surprised, I think, when he sees how different the baby will be from Hugo.

KITTY

She could hear the organ music from here. Not a hymn yet – thank heavens – but definitely a pre-christening jingle. Kitty ran as fast as her heels would allow towards St Nicholas's. It had taken her a lot longer than she'd anticipated to get to the church by public transport. If she'd taken up Duncan's offer to accompany her, she could have come with him in that smart car he had kept boasting about. And if she'd asked Mark, she would have had a chauffeur.

As it was, she was only just going to make it.

'I thought you weren't coming,' said Mandy, from the door where she'd been hovering on the lookout for her friend. She was every inch the Richmond mother, with her pale pink suit and matching kitten-heeled shoes, thought Kitty. 'Where's your date?'

'Here,' said Kitty, smiling.

'Where?'

'You're looking at her. I've brought myself.'

'Yourself? From your phone call, I thought you were bringing another girl. I was worried you might have gone the other way.'

'That's one I hadn't considered, but I have decided I don't need a man to prove myself any more – at least not just any man. Don't look so pitying. I could have persuaded someone to come along – three people, in fact. But I thought, Blow it. So what if Alex thinks I'm a sad old maid? In fact, I've met someone I really think I might—'

'Kitty?'

She turned and found herself looking up at a pair of bright blue eyes, a sensitive face that was not that dissimilar from Will Young's (she used to tease him about that), and a very expensive suit. 'Alex? Hi, how are you? I hadn't realised you were here. Well, I had but I thought you were with that fiancée of yours.'

'Actually, we broke up last week.'

'I'm sorry.'

'Don't be. I had an attack of last-minute pre-nuptial nerves and please don't tell me that sounds familiar.'

'Sounds familiar,' murmured Kitty.

Mandy nudged her. 'Can we remember why we're here, *please*? The vicar's arrived and the organist is waiting for you two to stop yacking. Come and sit down in the front row.'

'Sorry.' Kitty felt like a rebuked pupil.

'Me too.' Alex grinned. 'We'll just have to catch up after the service. By the way, Kitty, you look gorgeous.'

She flushed furiously. 'Thanks.'

It was during the christening tea that it hit her. Alex was a complete and utter prat! Having told her she was gorgeous before the ceremony, he was now intent on chatting up one of Rod's nieces who was barely past her eighteenth birthday.

'Some men never grow up,' said Mandy, sitting next to her with Tom. 'Now, who's this new chap? You've obviously found someone – that kind of glow doesn't come from a bottle!'

'Well, I did rather fancy the Ofsted inspector last week, but since it's unethical for him to ask school for my number, I've decided to put him out of my mind.'

'I'm serious, Kitty. Who is he?'

Kitty took a swig of expensive bubbly. 'I hope you're not going to interrogate my godson like this when he's older. If you must know, he's – whoops! Tom, how could you? And all over my lovely new Oasis suit! Now no one will ever fancy me, with this gunk all over me.' She winked at Mandy. 'Well, maybe I can think of one. . . .'

47

'See saw, Margery Daw, Johnny shall have a new master
. . .'

Nick heard the mother singing before he spotted the boy on the see-saw in the park. With those amazing curls, he really was a striking child, crying out to be photographed.

'Swing, Mum. I want swing!'

'I'll race you.'

He watched as mother and son ran towards the swings. She lifted him up, put him on the toddler seat, then pushed him.

Nick thought about moving on but she might have seen him and consider him rude. After Friday he felt linked somehow to Evie and all the other parents involved.

He drew nearer to the swings and coughed to get her attention. 'Hi. I'm Nick, remember? From school.' Somehow, the photographic connection seemed less relevant.

She looked at him for a few seconds before registering.

The silence made him feel awkward. 'That was quite a day, wasn't it? Friday, I mean.'

'You've done some work for me, haven't you?' Evie's forehead creased in thought. 'And you've got a child at St Theresa's.'

Nick nodded.

She slapped her forehead. 'God, I'd forgotten. You got Jack back for me when he got out of the car at the beginning of the week.' Remorse flickered across her well-made-up face like a shadow. 'So much has happened since then.'

Nick wasn't going to push. If she didn't want to talk about Jack being taken, he wouldn't either. He knew how she felt. Sometimes he was desperate to talk about Juliana to almost anyone who would listen. And at other times he couldn't.

'I've got a shoot for your magazine tomorrow, actually.'

She laughed bitterly. 'It's not my magazine any more. They got rid of me the day before that trouble at school.'

'I'm sorry. I hadn't heard.'

They stood in silence as she pushed Jack on the swing.

'What will you do?'

'No idea. There aren't many vacancies for a magazine editor approaching forty.'

'But it's experience that counts, surely?'

'You'd think so.'

'Have you heard of that new magazine Empa are about to launch? *Fabulous Forties*, I think it's called.'

Evie shook her head. 'Crap title. Mind you, I haven't had my ear to the ground as much as I should recently. I've had a lot on my mind.'

'Worth checking out.'

She looked brighter. 'Maybe. Although, to be honest, I'd quite like some time with Jack. I've missed out on so much already. But thanks anyway, Nick.'

'Don't mention it.' He looked at his watch. Julie would be back from her driving lesson. 'Come on, Mutley, home.'

'Dog,' cooed Jack.

'He's a natural model,' commented Nick.

'I wouldn't want him to get into that world.'

'Right.' Nick swallowed hard. 'I know what you mean. 'Bye, then. Maybe see you next term.'

'Probably not. We're moving. My husband's got a new job. To be honest, I'm looking forward to a fresh start.'

'Well, good luck.'

'Thanks.' She smiled at him. She ought to do that more often, he thought. It made her seem softer. 'See you around maybe.'

He nodded, whistled to Mutley and walked on. He'd spent most of the morning at the police station, telling the superintendent what he knew and showing him the note Julie had left. He'd also given a statement, which had been scary. On Monday he would phone his solicitor for advice. The superintendent had indicated that the coroner might have to reopen that poor kid's case in the light of new evidence. Nick knew it would be almost impossible to keep Julie ignorant of what might have happened but at least he had done the right thing. If his own daughter were run over, God forbid, he would want to know the full facts.

At least they couldn't put Juliana in prison, he thought grimly. And there was still the outside chance that her ramblings on paper might not be seen as proof – even the garage bill might be innocent.

God, it would be good to talk to someone – and not just anyone. Nick's right hand closed round the mobile in his pocket. Should he? No. What the hell?

'Harriet? It's Nick. From school. Sorry, is this a bad time? . . . Oh, right. Listen, I was just wondering if you were free for coffee next week?'

HARRIET

'It's nearly five o'clock on a warm Sunday afternoon and we're going to wrap up now with some gentle music to ease you into the week ahead.'

Harriet turned off the engine. It had been a long drive to Sussex with those roadworks and the children had fallen asleep on the way, their heads peacefully slumped together. She looked at them tenderly. They'd all been through so much and in just one week.

Stiffly, she got out of the car. Through the cottage window she could see her mother waiting for them. 'Mum!' she said, as her mother came out to the gate. She looked older, Harriet thought, with a pang. I should have come down before.

'Darling, I'm so glad you got here safely. I always worry about you on the motorway.' Harriet's mother glanced into the back of the car. 'What poppets! Do you want to wake them? Otherwise they won't sleep tonight.'

Together, they woke Bruce and Jess and brought them into the kitchen for a drink.

'It's so good to see you,' Harriet said again, allowing herself to be enveloped in her mother's arms.

'You too, sweetheart. Shall we take our tea into the drawing room and let the children get on with theirs?'

Harriet only just managed to get out of the room before the tears started. 'Sorry, Mum, but I can't help it,' she said, and buried her head in her mother's shoulder. 'Something really terrible has happened.'

'You know,' said her mother quietly, 'I never thought you and Charlie were very well suited.'

Harriet blew her nose on the handkerchief her mother had given her. 'You didn't say so.'

'I didn't want to interfere.'

'I'm scared, Mum, of being alone.'

'Scared?' Her mother put an arm round her. 'Look at me, darling. I've done it.'

'Exactly! And you've found it hard.'

'Well, it was at the beginning but, darling, you found it harder than I did when your father left. I was almost relieved because I didn't have to pretend any more.'

Harriet nodded. 'I can understand that.'

'If it makes you feel any better, darling, there's something I've been trying to tell you for ages but it's been difficult on the phone.' She flushed. 'I've met someone else. He's a widower and he moved into the village two years ago. His name is Michael. I hope you'll like him. He's going to come over tomorrow for tea, if that's all right.'

Harriet could hardly believe it. 'You've met someone else? That's wonderful.'

'You're sure you don't mind?'

'Why should I? I just want you to be happy.'

Her mother looked relieved. 'Thank you. And one day, Harriet, you will, too, although it may take time.' She put down her cup and gazed across the lawn. 'Do you see anything of your father?'

'I sometimes ring him but we haven't met for ages,' said Harriet, quietly.

'Well, do so, dear. Sometimes I wonder if I put you against him. You do things like that, during a divorce, and you need to consider that with Charlie. It would be good for you to meet and, besides, the children shouldn't be deprived of a grandfather. Promise?'

'I'll think about it, Mum.'

'Mum. *Mum!*'

Harriet jumped up as Jess appeared in the doorway.

'What?' She hadn't heard anything, had she?

'Bruce has just knocked over the Ribena on to the floor and it's stuck to my feet.' She held up a pretty heart-shaped box. 'And I don't know why you got me this, Mum. I'm too old for Polly Pocket now. Besides, it's really weird inside. There's a plastic space capsule for Polly and some metal circles.'

Harriet didn't know whether to laugh or cry. 'Did you find that in my bag?'

Jess nodded. 'Sorry.'

'If I were you,' said Harriet's mother, gravely, 'I wouldn't go looking in other people's bags or pockets. You don't know what you might find.'

Harriet's skin crawled. 'Mum,' she whispered, when Jess had gone back to the kitchen, 'perhaps I shouldn't have gone through Charlie's suit. If I hadn't found that hotel bill, none of this would have happened.'

'Darling, I didn't think when I said that. No, you did the right thing. Besides, you weren't snooping – you were trying to take it to the dry-cleaner.'

'But would it have been better if I'd pretended not to know?' persisted Harriet.

'If I were you I'd stop thinking about what might have happened and get on with the present. You're young enough to start again – we all are, whether we're thirty-five or sixty-five. The world out there is a lot more exciting and less terrifying than you think. Trust me.'

BETTY

'Well, Gaby, this is what all parents have been waiting for! Your tips on how to keep the kids happy and quiet in the summer holidays.'

I like Sky. It's much better than ordinary television or the radio. And fancy me forgetting it's the summer holidays next week! I don't have to worry about getting Terry ready for school.

Just as well, really. They make you go to bed so early in this place that it's hard to fit it all in. Television, talking to people, the craft class. I hadn't realised I was so good at watercolours or finger painting. I must tell Terry about that when he gets back from Tesco's. He used to be good at art when he was little. I've got all his paintings at home, in a folder marked 'Terry's Art Work'. It's next to 'Terry's School Reports' and 'Terry's Swimming Certificates'.

I could find his birth certificate at the drop of a hat.

That reminds me. Must get his new school uniform for next term. Better check his collar size too. Arthur was a seventeen and a half, you know, and I wouldn't be surprised if Terry was heading that way.

He'll be visiting me any time now. Maybe he'll bring me some more roses. I need a fresh bunch for the lamp-post. Otherwise people will think I've forgotten.

SUNDAY P.M.

'Night, Dad. See you next weekend? . . . Alton Towers? Cool. Do you want to talk to Bruce? He's abseiling off Granny's sofa. I can spell "abseil". Want to test me? . . . Yes, I know it's difficult over the phone but I learned it specially for you.'

'Mum, if Aunt Susie goes tomorrow, I promise I'll be good. Really good. Get rid of her. Please.'

'Dad, I forgot to say. The agency wants me to do something on Thursday. I can, can't I? It's the holidays. It's for a new magazine for teenagers that's going to be really big. You won't believe what they're paying me! I thought I could start saving for a car of my own. Mum would have been proud of that, wouldn't she?'

'Dad? It's Harriet. Yes, I'm fine, thanks. And you? Listen, I wondered if I could bring the children over to see you during the summer holidays. No, no one's ill. There are just a few things I need to talk to you about. Good. See you, then.'

'No, Mum, I said I wanted a Croatian au pair. Not another French one. I bet he can't even play football. Look at his picture – he's a real prat with those sticky-out ears and goofy grin. And turn off that radio. I don't care if you're on *Desert Island Discs* next week. I want to hear *my* music. If you don't do what I say, I'll get my stutter again. You know what the doctor said yesterday. Hugo's caught my stutter now his dad's gone. His mum says it's stress.'

'Yes, that *is* what he does for a living and when you meet him you'll understand. Really? Champneys? Gosh! Good old Rod.'

> *Dear Miss Hayling,*
>
> *My husband and I have separated and, as Bruce's new form teacher next term, I thought you ought to know. Bruce is naturally upset but he will see his father regularly and I am hoping we can get through this difficult time in as civilised a manner as possible. I would be grateful if we could have a meeting early next term to discuss his progress.*
>
> *Yours sincerely,*
> *Harriet Chapman*

'Bonne nuit, chéri.'

next term

'It's a bright autumn morning, and this is Capital Radio bringing you the latest . . .'

'Jess, Bruce? Omigod, getupnow, we'relateforthefirstdayof-school. Is that the phone? Who's got the receiver? Pippa? . . . Oh, *Nick*. Hi. Sorry, can't make tonight – I'm starting that new course . . . Tomorrow? Great! Charlie's having them then. Must dash. It's a bit hectic here at the moment . . .'

'Wake up, Mum. Come on, Dad. It's late. The alarm went off ages ago. Lucy's making breakfast and it's all over the floor. Aren't you going to get us to school? And why are your pyjamas on the floor, Dad? Aren't you cold?'

'Jack, come on, love. First day at your new nursery school. Won't that be fun?'

'I don't like my new school, Chris. Can you ask Mum if I can go to another? What about that one near Dad and Evie?'

'There aren't any flowers on that lamp-post any more, Mum. Why not? Do you think that person loves someone else now, like Dad and Thérèse?'

'And on tomorrow's brand-new breakfast show, Simon and Sally will be asking how we can make our schools safer in the wake of the recent sieges both in Britain and the States. They'll also be calling on the government to

> *tighten up laws on au-pair employment and their*
> *employers' right to privacy.'*

'I'll be fine, Dad. Stop fussing. Everyone drives themselves to school. And I'll wear the P-plates. Promise.'

It's Monday. If Terry were alive, he'd be going to school. But he's not. He's never going to school again. There's another woman here whose son isn't going to school again, either. Sometimes we talk about it and sometimes we don't. Dr Butler says that's fine. She says I'm getting there. But we're in for a long haul.

'Well done, Kitty, about the Ofsted report. Haven't you seen it yet? It's in the staffroom. The inspector was particularly impressed by the pastoral care displayed to year seven. That *was* you, wasn't it? By the way, do I hear well done too, for responding to my plea for more careers speakers? I gather you've found us a banker and stockbroker to talk to the sixth form. And a talk on road safety is always useful. Finally, do I hear congratulations are in order? Fantastic. Nice to see you haven't missed the bus – sorry! Couldn't resist that one . . .'

I am so glad to be back in France! But Maurice, he was not happy. He said he missed his son Hugo too much. I say come back when you have grown up. I am not so sick now, which is good, yes? It is so exciting! I have a new friend, too. He is French and he does not mind about the baby. Frenchmen are so much more understanding. The English, they are very strange. As Maman says, anyone who drives on the left of the road is to be avoided. Maybe when the baby is older, I train as a teacher. Then I look after her in the holidays. I think I would make a good teacher. Maman thinks so too.

'ParcelForce? Brilliant. I've been waiting for this.' *Squeeze.*

Squeeze. Up to the third floor and down, one by one. YES!
'No, Bruce, you can't open it – it's my college stuff – but you can sign for it. Heavens, is that the time? I don't suppose you'd like to drop off the children *en route*, would you? Don't worry. Only joking.'